AMEI

SHORT STORIES

SELECTED AND EDITED

WITH AN INTRODUCTORY ESSAY ON THE SHORT STORY

BY

CHARLES SEARS BALDWIN, A.M., Ph.D.

PROFESSOR OF RHETORIC IN COLUMBIA UNIVERSITY

NEW IMPRESSION

LONGMANS, GREEN AND CO.

FOURTH AVENUE & 30TH STREET, NEW YORK
39 PATERNOSTER ROW, LONDON
BOMBAY, CALCUTTA, AND MADRAS
1921

TO

G. E. B.

In the brief tale, however, the author is enabled to carry out the fulness of his intention, be it what it may. During the hour of perusal the soul of the reader is at the writer's control. There are no external or extrinsic influences resulting from weariness or interruption.

A skilful literary artist has constructed a tale. If wise, he has not fashioned his thoughts to accommodate his incidents; but having conceived, with deliberate care, a certain unique or single effect to be wrought out, he then invents such incidents, he then combines such events as may best aid him in establishing this preconceived effect. If his very initial sentence tend not to the out-bringing of this effect, then he has failed in his first step. In the whole composition there should be no word written of which the tendency, direct or indirect, is not to the one pre-established design. — EDGAR ALLAN POE.

PREFACE

THE object of this volume is not to collect the best American short stories. So delicate a choice may the more readily be left to time, since it must include some authors now living. That dramatic concentration which is the habit of a hundred writers for our magazines to-day was extremely rare before 1835; it was not common before 1870; it has become habitual within the memory of its younger practitioners. This collection, then, seeks to exhibit, and the introductory essay seeks to follow and formulate, a development. The development from inchoate tales into that distinct and self-consistent form which, for lack of a distinctive term, we have tacitly agreed to call the short story is a chapter of American literary history.

Influences from abroad and from the past, though they could not be displayed at large, have been indicated in the aspects that seemed most suggestive for research. The significance in form of Boccaccio's experiments, for example, because it has hardly been defined before, is proposed in

PREFACE

outline to students of comparative literature. But the American development is so far independent that it may be fairly comprehended in one volume. To exhibit this by typical instances, from Irving down, did not preclude variety alike of talents and of scenes. Indeed, that the collection should thus express many tempers — Knickerbocker leisure, Yankee adaptability, Irish fervor; and many localities, from elder New England to the new coast of gold, from the rude Michigan frontier to the gentle colonies of the lower Mississippi — makes it the more American.

It is a pleasure to record my obligation to Walter Austin, Esq., for the rare edition of his grandfather's literary papers, and to the publishers whose courtesy permits me to include some stories valuable in copyright as in art.

C. S. B.

[NOTE. — The story entitled 'The Eve of the Fourth' is printed here (page 305) by permission of Mr. William Heinemann, publisher of 'The Copperhead, and Other Stories, etc.,' by Harold Frederic.]

CONTENTS

INTRODUCTION   Page

I. The Tale in America before 1835 . . . 1

II. Poe's Invention of the Short Story . . . 15

III. A Glance at Derivation: Ancient Tales, Mediæval Tales, The Modern French Short Story 23

PART I. THE TENTATIVE PERIOD

Chapter

I. WASHINGTON IRVING
  Rip Van Winkle . . . . 1820 . . 39

II. WILLIAM AUSTIN
  Peter Rugg, the Missing Man 1824 . . 61

III. JAMES HALL
  The French Village . . . 1829 . . 99

IV. ALBERT PIKE
  The Inroad of the Nabajo . . 1833 . . 115

PART II. THE PERIOD OF THE
NEW FORM

V. NATHANIEL HAWTHORNE
  The White Old Maid . . 1835 . . 131

VI. HENRY WADSWORTH LONGFELLOW
  The Notary of Périgueux . . 1835 . . 145

CONTENTS

Chapter

VII. EDGAR ALLAN POE   Page

The Fall of the House of Usher *1839* . . 155

VIII. NATHANIEL PARKER WILLIS

The Inlet of Peach Blossoms . *1840–5* . 179

IX. CAROLINE MATILDA STANSBURY KIRKLAND

The Bee-Tree . . . . . *1846* . . 195

X. FITZ-JAMES O'BRIEN

✓ *What was It? A Mystery* . *1859* . . 213

XI. FRANCIS BRET HARTE

The Outcasts of Poker Flat . *1869* . . 231

XII. ALBERT FALVEY WEBSTER

Miss Eunice's Glove . . . *1873* . . 247

XIII. BAYARD TAYLOR

♥ *Who was She?* . . . . . *1874* . . 269

XIV. HENRY CUYLER BUNNER

The Love-Letters of Smith . *1890* . . 291

XV. HAROLD FREDERIC

The Eve of the Fourth . . *1897* . . 305

BIBLIOGRAPHICAL NOTE 325

INDEX 327

AMERICAN SHORT STORIES

INTRODUCTION

I. THE TALE IN AMERICA BEFORE 1835

HOW few years comprise the history of American literature is strikingly suggested by the fact that so much of it can be covered by the reminiscence of a single man of letters.[1] A life beginning in the '20's had actual touch in boyhood with Irving, and seized fresh from the press the romances of Cooper. And if the history of American literature be read more exclusively as the history of literary development essentially American, its years are still fewer. " I perceive," says a foreign visitor in Austin's story of *Joseph Natterstrom*, " this is a very young country, but a very old people."[2] Some critics, indeed, have been so irritated by the spreading of the eagle in larger pretensions as to deprecate entirely the phrase " American literature." Our literature, they retort, has shown no national, essential difference from the literature of the other peoples using the same language. How these carpers accommodate to their view Thoreau, for instance, is not clear. But waiving other claims, the case might almost be made out from

[1] Donald G. Mitchell, *American Lands and Letters.*
[2] *Literary Papers of William Austin*, Boston, 1890, page 43.

the indigenous growth of one literary form. Our
short story, at least, is definitely American.

The significance of the short story as a new form
of fiction appears on comparison of the staple product
of tales before 1835 with the staple product thereafter.
1835 is the date of Poe's *Berenice*. Before it lies a
period of experiment, of turning the accepted anecdotes, short romances, historical sketches, toward
something vaguely felt after as more workmanlike.
This is the period of precocious local magazines,[1] and
of that ornament of the marble-topped tables of our
grandmothers, the annual. Various in name and in
color, the annual gift-books are alike, — externally in
profusion of design and gilding, internally in serving
up, as staples of their miscellany, poems and tales.
Keepsakes they were called generically in England,
France, and America; their particular style might be
Garland or *Gem*.[2] The *Atlantic Souvenir*, earliest in
this country, so throve during seven years (1826–1832)
as to buy and unite with itself (1833) its chief rival,
the *Token*. The utterly changed taste which smiles at
these annuals, as at the clothes of their readers, ob-
scures the fact that they were a medium, not only for
the stories of writers forgotten long since, but also
for the earlier work of Hawthorne. By 1835 the *New
England Magazine* had survived its infancy, and the
Southern Literary Messenger was born with promise.
Since then — since the realisation of the definite form

[1] See Prof. William B. Cairns, *On the Development of American Literature from 1815 to 1833, with especial reference to
periodicals;* Bulletin of the University of Wisconsin, Philology and Literature Series, volume i, No. 1.

[2] For a pungent characterisation of the annuals, see Prof.
Henry A. Beers's life of N. P. Willis (American Men of Letters), pages 77 and following.

in Poe's *Berenice* — the short story has been explored and tested to its utmost capacity by almost every American prose-writer of note, and by many without note, as the chief American form of fiction. The great purveyor has been the monthly magazine. Before 1835, then, is a period of experiment with tales; after 1835, a period of the manifold exercise of the short story. The tales of the former have much that is national in matter; the short stories of the latter show nationality also in form.

Nationality, even provinciality, in subject-matter has been too much in demand. The best modern literature knows best that it is heir of all the ages, and that its goal should be, not local peculiarity, but such humanity as passes place and time.[1] Therefore we have heard too much, doubtless, of local color. At any rate, many purveyors of local color in fiction have given us documents rather than stories. Still there was some justice in asking of America the things of America. If the critics who begged us to be American have not always seemed to know clearly what they meant, still they may fairly be interpreted to mean in general something reasonable enough, — namely, that we ought to catch from the breadth and diversity of our new country new inspirations. The world, then, was looking to us, in so far as it looked at all, for the impulse from untrodden and picturesque ways, for a direct transmission of Indians, cataracts, prairies, bayous, and Sierras. Well and good. But, according to our abilities, we were giving the world just that. Years before England decided that our only American writers in this sense were Whitman,

---

[1] Fromentin (*Un Été dans le Sahara*, page 59 ; *Une Année dans le Sahel*, pages 215 and following) lays this down for painting.

Mark Twain, and Bret Harte, — seventy years before
the third of this perversely chosen group complacently
informed the British public [1] that he was a pioneer
only in the sense of making the short story American
in scenes and motives, — American writers were ex-
ploring their country for fiction north and south, east
and west, up and down its history. What we lacked
was, not appreciation of our material, but skill in ex-
pressing it; not inspiration, but art. We had to wait,
not indeed for Bret Harte in the '60's, but for Poe in
the '30's. The material was known and felt, and again
and again attempted. Nothing could expose more
vividly the fallacy that new material makes new literature. We were at school for our short story; but we
had long known what stories we had to tell. In that
sense American fiction has always been American.

For by 1830 the preference of native subjects for
tales, to say nothing of novels, is plainly marked. The
example of Irving in this direction could not fail of
followers. From their beginning the early magazines
and annuals essay in fiction the legends, the history,
and even the local manners of the United States, in
circles widening with the area of the country. Thus
the *Atlantic Souvenir* for 1829, furnishing forth in
its short fictions an historical romance of mediæval
France, a moral tale in oriental setting, a melodrama
of the Pacific Islands, and a lively farce on the
revolution in Peru, presented also, with occasional
attempt at native scenery, the following: *The Methodist's Story*, a moral situation of the anger of father
and son; *Narantsauk*, an historical tale of Baron
Castine; *The Catholic*, weaving into King Philip's
attack on Springfield the hopeless affection of a

[1] Bret Harte, *The Rise of the Short Story*, Cornhill Magazine, July, 1899.

INTRODUCTION

Catholic girl and a Protestant youth — the very field of Hawthorne; and a melodramatic *Emigrant's Daughter*. In the same year, 1829, James Hall, then fairly afloat on his vocation of law and his avocation of letters, compiled, indeed largely composed, the first *Western Souvenir* at Vandalia, Illinois. Its most significant tales are three of his own, set, with more careful locality than most of the seaboard attempts, in the frontier life along the Mississippi. *The Indian Hater* and *Pete Featherton* present backwoodsmen of Illinois and Ohio. *The French Village* is definitely a *genre* study. Loose enough in plot, it has in detail a delicacy and local truth not unworthy the material of Cable. That there was a definite tendency toward native themes is amply confirmed by the annuals of subsequent years before 1835. Besides Hawthorne's earlier pieces in the *Token*, there had appeared by 1831 studies of the Natchez and of the Minnesota Indians, the Maryland Romanists, Shays's Rebellion, the North-River Dutch, and the Quakers. And the same tendency appears in the early magazines. *The Western Monthly Review*, adventurously put forth by Timothy Flint in Cincinnati, had among its few tales before 1831 an Irish-Shawnee farce on the Big Miami, *The Hermit of the Prairies*, a romance of French Louisiana, a rather forcible study of Simon Girty and the attack on Bryant's Station, and two local character sketches entitled *Mike Shuck* and *Colonel Plug*. To extend the period of consideration is to record the strengthening of the tendency established by Irving and Cooper. The books of John Pendleton Kennedy are collections of local sketches. Mrs. Hale, praised for her fidelity to local truth, was supported in the same ambition by Mrs. Gilman. Mrs. Kirkland's

sketches of early Michigan are as convincing as they
are vivacious. Most of these studies emerge, if that
can be said to emerge which is occasionally fished
up by the antiquary, only by force of what we have
been berated for lacking — local inspiration.
What were the forms of this evident endeavor to
interpret American life in brief fictions; and, more
important, what was the form toward which they
were groping? For this inquiry the natural point
of departure is the tales of Irving. Any reapprecia-
tion of Irving would now be officious. We know
that classical serenity, alike of pathos and of humor;
and we have heard often enough that he got his style
of Addison. Indeed no attentive reader of English
literature could well fail to discern either Irving's
schooling with the finest prose of the previous century — with Goldsmith, for instance, as well as Addison — or the essential originality of his own prose.
He is a pupil of the *Spectator*.[1] That is a momentous
fact in the history of American literature. We know
what it means in diction. What does it mean in
form? That our first eminent short fictions were
written by the pupil of a school of essayists vitally
affected their structure. The matter of the *Spectator*
suggested in England a certain type of novel;[2] its
manner was not the manner to suggest in America
the short story, even to an author whose head was
full of the proper material. For though it may be
hard to prove in the face of certain novels that an

[1] See Cairns, as above, page 64. The influence of the Spectator form in France appears strikingly in *L'Hermite de la
Chaussée d'Antin*, ou observations sur les mœurs et les usages
français au commencement du xixme siècle, par M. de Jouy,
Paris (collective volumes), 1813.
[2] Cross, *Development of the English Novel*, pages 24, 25.

essay is one thing and a story another, it is obvious to any craftsman, *a priori*, that the way of the essay will not lead to the short story. And in fact it did not lead to the short story. The tales of Irving need no praise. Composed in the manner typical of the short story, they might have been better or worse; but they are not so composed. It was not at random that Irving called his first collection of them (1819–20) *The Sketch Book*. *The Wife*, for instance, is a short-story plot; it is handled, precisely in the method of the British essay, as an illustrative anecdote. So *The Widow and Her Son;* so *The Pride of the Village*, most evidently in its expository introduction; so, in essence of method, many of the others. And *Rip Van Winkle?* Here, indeed, is a difference, but not, as may at first appear, a significant difference. True, the descriptive beginning is modern rather than Addisonian; romanticism had opened the eyes of the son of the classicals; but how far the typical looseness of romanticism is from the typical compactness of the short story may be seen in Irving's German tale of the *Spectre Bridegroom*, and it may be seen here. True again, the characterisation, though often expository, is deliciously concrete; but it is not more so than the characterisation of Sir Roger de Coverley; nor is Rip's conversation with his dog, for instance, in itself the way of the short story any more than Sir Roger's counting of heads in church. Unity of tone there is, unity clearer than in Irving's models, and therefore doubtless more conscious. But Irving did not go so far as to show his successors that the surer way to unity of tone is unity of narrative form. Still less did he display the value of unity of form for itself. His stories do not culminate. As there is little emphasis on any given incident, so there is no direction of incidents toward a single goal of action. Think of the Catskill legend done *à la mode*. Almost any clever writer for to-morrow's magazines would begin with Rip's awakening, keep the action within one day by letting the previous twenty years transpire through Rip's own narrative at the new tavern, and culminate on the main disclosure. That he might easily thus spoil *Rip Van Winkle* is not in point. The point is that he would thus make a typical short story, and that the *Sketch Book* did not tend in that direction. Nor as a whole do the *Tales of a Traveller*. Not only is *Buckthorne and His Friends* avowedly a sketch for a novel, but the involved and somewhat laborious machinery of the whole collection will not serve to move any of its separable parts in the short-story manner. Even the *German Student*, which is potentially much nearer to narrative singleness, has an explanatory introduction and a blurred climax. Such few of the Italian bandit stories as show compression of time remain otherwise, like the rest, essentially the same in form as other romantic tales of the period. In narrative adjustment Irving did not choose to make experiments.[1]

It is not surprising, therefore, that Irving's influence, so far at it is discernible in subsequent short fictions, seems rather to have retarded than to have furthered the development toward distinct form. Our native sense of form appears in that the short story emerged fifteen years after the *Sketch Book*; but where we feel Irving we feel a current from another source moving in another direction. The

[1] For Irving's own view of his tales, see a quotation from his letters at page xix of Professor Brander Matthews's edition of the *Tales of a Traveller*.

short descriptive sketches composing John Pendleton
Kennedy's *Swallow Barn* (1832) have so slight a
sequence,[1] and sometimes so clear a capacity for self-
consistent form, that it is easy to imagine them as
separate short stories of local manners; but, whether
through Irving, or directly through the literary tradition of Virginia, they keep the way of the *Spectator.*
James Hall, who had been still nearer to the short
story of local manners in his *French Village* (1829),
was poaching on Irving's manor in his *Village Musician* (1831) with evident disintegration. In Hawthorne, who, of course, was nearest of all before
Poe's genius for form seized and fixed the short
story, it is difficult to be sure of the influence of
Irving. True, Hawthorne's earlier historical tales,
though they have far greater imaginative realisation, are not essentially different in method from
Irving's *Philip of Pokanoket;* but it was quite as
likely Hawthorne's natural bent toward the descriptive essay that made his earlier development in fiction
tentative and vacillating, as any counsel from the
happy, leisurely form of the elder master. Be that
as it may, Irving's influence in general, if not deter-
rent, seems at least not to have counted positively
in the development of the short story.

Rather Irving left the writers for the annuals and
abortive early magazines to feel after a form. What
were the modes already accepted; and what were
their several capacities for this shaping? The moral
tale, of course, is obvious to any one who has glanced
over the literary diversions of his forbears; and this,
equally of course, had often its unity of purpose.

---

[1] "A rivulet of story meandering through a broad meadow of
episode — a book of episodes with occasional digressions into
the plot." Kennedy's preface to *Swallow Barn.*

But since the message, instead of permeating the tale by suggestion, was commonly formulated in expository introduction or hortatory conclusion, it did not suffice to keep the whole in unity of form. Indeed, the moral tale was hardly a form. It might be mere applied anecdote; it might be the bare skeleton of a story, as likely material for a novel as for a short story; it was often shapeless romance.[1] But two tendencies are fairly distinct. Negatively there was a general avoidance, before Hawthorne, of allegory or symbolism. For a moral tale allegory seems an obvious method; but it is a method of suggestion, and these tales, with a few exceptions, such as Austin's *Peter Rugg*, hardly rise above the method of formal propounding. Positively there was a natural use of oriental manner and setting, as in Austin's *Joseph Natterstrom* and Paulding's *Ben Hadar*.[2]

Another typical ingredient of the annual salad is the yarn or hoax-story. The significance of this as American has been often urged; and indeed it spread with little seeding, and, as orally spontaneous, has made a favorite diversion of the frontier. Its significance in form is that it absolutely demands an arrangement of incidents for suspense. The superiority of form, however, was associated, unfortunately for any influence, with triviality of matter. Again, the annuals are full of short historical sketches. Sometimes these are mere summary of facts or mere anecdote, to serve as explanatory text for the steel

[1] This is the character of the tales of Mme. de Genlis, of which a volume was published in New York, 1825: *New Moral Tales, selected and translated from the French of Mme. de Genlis, by an American.*

[2] Nodier adopts the same setting for the same purpose (cf. *Les Quatre Talismans*, 1838); but the habit is at least as old as Voltaire.

engravings then fashionable as "embellishments";
sometimes they are humorous renderings of recent
events; [1] more commonly they are painstaking studies,
— Delia Bacon's, for instance, or Charlotte Sedgwick's, in the setting of American Colonial and Revolutionary history; most commonly of all, whether
native or foreign, modern or mediæval, they are
thorough-going romances, running often into swash-
buckling and almost always into melodrama.[2] The
tendency to melodramatic variety, with the typical
looseness of romanticism, then everywhere dominant
in letters, held the historical sketches back from
compactness, or even definiteness, of form.[3] So
clever a writer as Hall leaves many of his historical
pieces with the ends loose, as mere sketches for
novels. The theoretical difference between a novelette and a short story[4] is thus practically evident
throughout this phase of the annuals in lack of
focus.

Still the studies of historical environment were
more promising in themselves and also confirmed
that attempt to realise the locality, as it were, of the
present or the immediate past which emerges as
genre or local color. The intention of Miss Sedgwick's *Reminiscence of Federalism* (1835) is the same
as that of Miss Wilkins's stories of the same environment. Her *Mary Dyre* comes as near in form as

---

[1] So Godfrey Wallace's *Esmeralda*, Atlantic Souvenir for
1829.

[2] Miss Sedgwick's *Chivalric Sailor* (1835) is essentially like
our current historical romances. A typical instance is Dana's
Paul Felton (1822).

[3] This tendency was confirmed, of course, by the predomi-
nance of Scott.

[4] Brander Matthews, *The Philosophy of the Short-Story*,
page 15.

Hawthorne's *Gentle Boy* to extracting the essence of Quakerdom. Where her studies fail is in that vital intensity which depends most of all on compression of place and time. Now an easier way toward this was open through the more descriptive sketch of local manners. To realise the genius of a place is a single aim; to keep the tale on the one spot is almost a necessity; to keep it within a brief time by focusing on one significant situation is a further counsel of unity which, though it had not occurred to American writers often, could not be long delayed. Thus, before 1835, Albert Pike had so far focused his picturesque incidents of New Mexico as to burn an impression of that colored frontier life; and James Hall, in spite of the bungling, unnecessary time-lapse, had so turned his *French Village* (1829) as to give a single picture of French colonial manners.

Hawthorne, indeed, had gone further. His affecting *Wives of the Dead* (1832) is brought within the compass of a single night. If the significance of this experiment was clear to Hawthorne, then he must have abandoned deliberately what Poe seized as vital; for he recurred to the method but now and then. The trend of his work is quite different. But there is room to believe that the significance of the form escaped him; for as to literary method, as to form, Hawthorne seems not to see much farther than the forgotten writers whose tales stand beside his in the annuals. An obvious defect of these short fictions is in measure. The writers do not distinguish between what will make a good thirty-page story and what will make a good three-hundred-page story. They cannot gauge their material. Austin's *Peter Rugg* is too long for its best effect; it is definitely a short-story plot. Many of

the others are far too short for any clear effect; they
are definitely not short-story plots, but novel plots;
they demand development of character or revolution
of incidents. Aristotle's distinction between simple
and complex plots [1] underlies the difference between
the two modern forms. Now even Hawthorne seems
not quite aware of this difference. The conception
of *Roger Malvin's Burial* (1832) demands more development of character than is possible within its twenty-
eight pages. The sense of artistic unity appears in
the expiation at the scene of guilt; but the deficiency
of form also appears in the long time-lapse. *Alice
Doane's Appeal* (1835) is the hint of a tragedy, a
conception not far below that of the *Scarlet Letter.*
For lack of scope the tragic import is obscured by
trivial description; it cannot emerge from the awkward mechanism of a tale within a tale; it remains
partial, not entire. Like *Alice Doane, Ethan Brand*
is conceived as the culmination of a novel. To say
that either might have taken form as a short story is
not to belittle Hawthorne's art, but to indicate his
preference of method. *Ethan Brand* achieves a pic-
turesqueness more vivid than is usual in Hawthorne's
shorter pieces. The action begins, as in Hawthorne
it does not often begin, at once. The narrative skill
appears in the delicate and thoroughly characteristic
device of the little boy; but imagine the increase of
purely narrative interest if Hawthorne had focused
this tale as he focused *The White Old Maid;* and then
imagine *The White Old Maid* itself composed without
the superfluous lapse of time, like *The Wives of the
Dead.* That Hawthorne seems not to have realised
distinctly the proper scope of the short story, and
further that he did not follow its typical mode when

[1] *Poetics*, chapter x.

that mode seems most apt, — both these inferences are supported by the whole trend of his habit.

For Hawthorne's genius was not bent in the direction of narrative form. Much of his characteristic work is rather descriptive, — *Sunday at Home, Sights from a Steeple, Main Street, The Village Uncle,* — to turn over the leaves of his collections is to be reminded how many of his short pieces are like these.[1] Again, his habitual symbolism is handled quite unevenly, without narrative sureness. At its best it has a fine, permeating suggestiveness, as in *The Ambitious Guest;* at its worst, as in *Fancy's Show Box,* it is moral allegory hardly above the children's page of the religious weekly journal. Lying between these two extremes, a great bulk of his short fictions shows imperfect command of narrative adjustments. The delicate symbolism of *David Swan* is introduced, like fifty pieces in the annuals, whose authors were incapable of Hawthorne's fancy, by formal exposition of the meaning. The poetry of the *Snow Image* is crudely embodied, and has also to be expounded after the tale is done. The lovely morality of the *Great Stone Face* has a form almost as for a sermon. The point for consideration is not the ultimate merit of Hawthorne's tales, but simply the tendency of their habit of form. For this view it is important to remember also his bent toward essay. Description and essay, separately and together, sum up the character of much of his work that was evidently most spontaneous. Perhaps nothing that Hawthorne wrote is finer or more masterly than the introduction to the *Scarlet Letter.* For this one masterpiece who would

---

[1] Poe's review of Hawthorne's tales (1842) begins by remarking that they are not all tales (Stedman and Woodberry edition of Poe, vol. vii, page 28).

not give volumes of formally perfect short stories?
Yet if it is characteristic of his genius, — and few
would deny that it is, — it suggests strongly why the
development of a new form of narrative was not for
him. This habit of mind explains why the *Marble
Faun*, for all the beauty of its parts, fails to hold the
impulse of its highly imaginative conception in singleness of artistic form. In his other long pieces Hawthorne did not so fail. The form of the novel he felt;
and it gave him room for that discursiveness which is
equally natural to him and delightful to his readers.
But the form of the short story, though he achieved
it now and again — as often in his early work as in his
later — he seems not to have felt distinctly. And,
whether he felt it or not, his bent and preference were
not to carry it forward.

II. POE'S INVENTION OF THE
SHORT STORY

FOR the realisation and development of the short-
story form lying there *in posse*, the man of the hour
was Poe. Poe could write trenchant essays; he
turned sometimes to longer fictions; but he is above
all, in his prose, a writer of short stories. For this
work was he born. His artistic bent unconsciously,
his artistic skill consciously, moved in this direction.
In theory and in practice he displayed for America
and for the world [1] a substantially new literary form.
What is there in the form, then, of Poe's tales which,
marking them off from the past, marks them as models

---

[1] Poe's tales were translated into French, German, Italian,
and Spanish. He was reviewed in the *Revue des Deux
Mondes*, Oct. 15, 1846 (new series, vol. xvi, page 341).

for the future?   Primarily Poe, as a literary artist, was preoccupied with problems of construction.   More than any American before him he felt narrative as structure; — not as interpretation of life, for he lived within the walls of his own brain; not as presentation of character or of locality, for there is not in all his tales one man, one woman, and the stage is " out of space, out of time "; but as structure.   His chief concern was how to reach an emotional effect by placing and building.   When he talked of literary art, he talked habitually in terms of construction.   When he worked, at least he planned an ingeniously suspended solution of incidents; for he was always pleased with mere solutions, and he was master of the detective story.   At best he planned a rising edifice of emotional impressions, a work of creative, structural imagination.

This habit of mind, this artistic point of view, manifests itself most obviously in harmonisation.   Every detail of setting and style is selected for its architectural fitness.   The Poe scenery is remarkable not more for its original, phantasmal beauty or horror than for the strictness of its keeping.   Like the landscape gardening of the Japanese, it is in each case very part of its castle of dreams.   Its contrivance to further the mood may be seen in the use of a single physical detail as a recurring dominant, — most crudely in the dreadful teeth of Berenice, more surely in the horse of Metzengerstein and the sound of Morella's name, most subtly in the wondrous eyes of Ligeia.   These recurrences in his prose are like the refrain of which he was so fond in his verse.   And the scheme of harmonisation includes every smallest detail of style.   Poe's vocabulary has not the amplitude of Hawthorne's; but in color and in cadence, in suggestion alike of meaning and of sound, its smaller compass is made to yield fuller answer in declaring and sustaining and intensifying the required mood. Even in 1835, the first year of his conscious prose form, the harmonising of scene and of diction had reached this degree : —

"But one autumnal evening, when the winds lay still in heaven, Morella called me to her bedside. There was a dim mist over all the earth, and a warm glow upon the waters ; and, amid the rich October leaves of the forest, a rainbow from the firmament had surely fallen.

"'It is a day of days,' she said, as I approached ; 'a day of all days either to live or die. It is a fair day for the sons of earth and life — ah, more fair for the daughters of heaven and death ! '

"I kissed her forehead, and she continued :

"'I am dying; yet shall I live.'

"'Morella ! '

"'The days have never been when thou couldst love me — but her whom in life thou didst abhor, in death thou shalt adore.'

"'Morella ! '

"'I repeat that I am dying. But within me is a pledge of that affection — ah, how little ! — which thou didst feel for me, Morella. And when my spirit departs shall the child live — thy child and mine, Morella's.'"

It is almost the last word of adaptation.

Yet in all this Poe simply did better what his predecessors had done already. His harmonising of scene, of style, was no new thing. The narrative form itself needed more artistic adjustment. To begin with what now seems to us the commonest and most obvious defect, the narrative mood and the narrative progress must not be disturbed by introductory exposition. Not only the ruck of writers for the

annuals, but even Irving, but even sometimes Hawthorne, seem unable to begin a story forthwith. They
seem fatally constrained to lay down first a bit of
essay. Whether it be an adjuration to the patient
reader to mind the import, or a morsel of philosophy
for a text, or a bridge from the general to the particular, or an historical summary, or a humorous intimation, it is like the juggler's piece of carpet; it must
be laid down first. Poe's intolerance of anything extraneous demanded that this be cut off. And though
since his time many worthy tales have managed to
rise in spite of this inarticulate member, the best art
of the short story, thanks to his surgery, has gained
greatly in impulse. One can almost see Poe experimenting from tale to tale. In *Berenice* he charged the
introduction with mysterious suggestion; that is, he
used it like an overture; he made it integral. In
Morella, the point of departure being similar, the
theme is struck more swiftly and surely, and the action
begins more promptly. In *King Pest*, working evidently for more rapid movement, he began with lively
description. *Metzengerstein* recurs to the method of
Berenice; but *Ligeia* and *Usher*, the summit of his
achievement, have no introduction, nor have more
than two or three of the typical tales that follow.

"True! nervous — very, very dreadfully nervous, I had
been and am ; but why will you say that I am mad? The
disease had sharpened my senses — not destroyed — not
dulled them. Above all was the sense of hearing acute. I
heard all things in the heaven and in the earth. I heard
many things in hell. How, then, am I mad? Hearken !
and observe how healthily — how calmly I can tell you the
whole story."   *The Tell-Tale Heart* (1843).

Every one feels the force for this tale of this method
of beginning; and to many story-readers of to-day it

may seem obvious; but it was Poe, more than any
one else, who taught us to begin so.

The idea of this innovation was negatively to reject
what is from the point of view of narrative form
extraneous; positively it was to make the narrative
progress more direct. And the evident care to
simplify the narrative mechanism for directness of
effect is the clue to Poe's advance in form, and his
most instructive contribution to technic. This principle explains more fully his method of setting the
scene. The harmonisation is secured mainly by suppression. The tale is stripped of every least incongruity. In real life emotion is disturbed, confused,
perhaps thwarted; in art it cannot be interpreted
without arbitrary simplification; in Poe's art the
simplification brooks no intrusive fact. We are kept
in a dreamland that knows no disturbing sound.
The emotion has no more friction to overcome than
a body in a vacuum. For Poe's directness is not the
directness of spontaneity; it has nothing conversational or "natural"; it is the directness of calculation.
So he had little occasion to improve his skill in dialogue. Dialogue is the artistic imitation of real life.
He had little use for it. His best tales are typically
conducted by monologue in the first person. What
he desired, what he achieved, what his example
taught, was reduction to a straight, predetermined
course. Everything that might hinder this consistency were best away. So, as he reduced his scene
to proper symbols, he reduced it also, in his typical
tales, to one place. Change of place, lapse of time,
are either excluded as by the law of the classical
unities,[1] or, if they are admitted, are never evident

[1] See Aristotle's *Poetics*, chapters vii and viii. The "classical" French drama deduced from Aristotle's general principle

enough to be remarked. What this meant as a lesson in form can be appreciated only by inspecting the heavy machinery that sank many good tales before him. What it means in ultimate import is the peculiar value and the peculiar limitation of the short story — in a word, its capacity as a literary form. The simplification that he set forth is the way to intensity; but perhaps Hawthorne saw that it might be the way to artificiality.

The history, then, of the short story — the feeling after the form, the final achievement, will yield the definition of the form. The practical process of defining by experiment compiles most surely the theoretical definition. And to complete this definition it is safe to scrutinise the art of Poe in still other aspects. His structure, appearing as harmonisation and as simplification, appears also as gradation. That the incidents of a tale should be arranged as progressive to a climax is an elementary narrative principle not so axiomatic in the practice, at least, of Poe's time as to bind without the force of his example. Even his detective stories, in their ingenious suspense and their swift and steady mounting to climax, were a lesson in narrative. But this is the least of his skill. The emotional and spiritual effects that he sought as his artistic birthright could be achieved only by adjustments far more subtle. The progressive heightening of the style corresponds to a nice order of small details more and more significant up to the final intensity of revelation. Little suggestion is laid to suggestion until the great hypnotist has us in the mood to hear and feel what he will. It is a minute process, and it is unhurried;

of unity of action a strict system of practice. Of Poe's adherence to this system a good instance is *The Cask of Amontillado*.

but it is not too slow to be accomplished within what before him would have seemed incredible brevity. The grading of everything to scale and perspective, that the little whole may be as complete, as satisfying, as any larger whole — nay, that any larger treatment may seem, for the time of comparison, too broad and coarse, — this is Poe's finer architecture. But for him we should hardly have guessed what might be done in fifteen pages; but for him we should not know so clearly that the art of fifteen pages is not the art of a hundred and fifty.

Berenice casts a shadow first from the fatal library, chamber of doubtful lore, of death, of birth, of prenatal recollection " like a shadow — vague, variable, indefinite, unsteady; and like a shadow, too, in the impossibility of my getting rid of it while the sunlight of my reason shall exist." The last words deepen the shadow. Then the " boyhood in books " turns vision into reality, reality into vision. Berenice flashes across the darkened stage, and pines, and falls into trances, "disturbing even the identity of her person." While the light from her is thus turning to darkness, the visionary's morbid attentiveness is warped toward a monomania of brooding over trivial single objects. For the sake of the past and visionary Berenice betrothed with horror to the decaying real Berenice, he is riveted in brooding upon her person — her emaciation — her face — her lips — her teeth. The teeth are his final curse. The rest is madness, realised too horribly, but with what final swiftness of force ! No catalogue of details can convey the effect of this gradation of eight pages. Yet *Berenice* is Poe's first and crudest elaboration. The same static art in the same year moves *Morella* more

swiftly through finer and surer degrees to a perfectly modulated close in five pages. His next study,
still of the same year, is in the grotesque. The freer
and more active movement of *King Pest* shows his
command of the kinetic short story of incident as
well as of the static short story of intensifying emotion. By the next year he had contrived to unite
in *Metzengerstein* the two processes, culminating intensity of feeling and culminating swiftness of action
for a direct stroke of terror and retribution. By
1836 Poe knew his art; he had only to refine it.
Continuing to apply his method of gradation in
both modes, he gained his own peculiar triumphs in
the static, — in a situation developed by exquisite
gradation of such infinitesimal incidents as compose
Berenice to an intense climax of emotional suggestion, rather than in a situation developed by gradation of events to a climax of action. But in both
he disclosed the fine art of the short story in drawing down everything to a point.

For all this was comprehended in Poe's conception
of unity. All these points of technical skill are derived from what he showed to be the vital principle
of the short story, its defining mark, — unity of impression through strict unity of form. "Totality of
interest," an idea caught from Schlegel, he laid down
first as the principle of the short poem,[1] and then as
the principle of the tale.[2] And what this theory of
narrative should imply in practice is seen best in Poe.

[1] In a review of Mrs. Sigourney, Southern Literary Messenger, volume ii, page 113 (January, 1836); quoted in Woodberry's Life of Poe, page 94.

[2] In a review of Hawthorne, Graham's Magazine, May, 1842;
Stedman and Woodberry's edition of Poe, volume vii, page
30; quoted in the appendix to Brander Matthews's *Philosophy
of the Short-Story.*

For Hawthorne, though he too achieves totality of
interest, is not so surely a master of it precisely because he is not so sure of the technic. His symbolism is often unified, as it were, by logical summary;
for Poe's symbolism summary would be an impertinence. Poe's harmonisation, not otherwise, perhaps,
superior to Hawthorne's, is more instructive as being
more strictly the accord of every word with one constantly dominant impression. His simplification of
narrative mechanism went in sheer technical skill beyond the skill of any previous writer in opening a
direct course to a single revealing climax. His gradation, too, was a progressive heightening and a nice
drawing to scale. All this means that he divined,
realised, formulated the short story as a distinct form
of art. Before him was the tale, which, though by
chance it might attain self-consistency, was usually
and typically incomplete, either a part or an outline
sketch; from his brain was born the short story as a
complete, finished, and self-sufficing whole.

III. A GLANCE AT DERIVATION

ANCIENT TALES, MEDIÆVAL TALES, THE MODERN FRENCH SHORT STORY

THE nice questions of literary derivation cannot be
finally answered for the tale, any more than for
other literary forms, without large citation   Milesian
and analysis in particular. But, pending   Tales.
fuller discussion, a general survey of the typical late
Greek, late Latin, and mediæval forms is full of suggestion. Stories being primarily for pleasure and
the pleasures of decadent Greece being largely car-
nal, it can give no long amazement to find that the

tales popular along the Mediterranean of the Seleu-
cids and the Ptolemies were erotic and often frankly
obscene. Known as Milesian[1] tales, doubtless from
the bad eminence of some collection in the Ionian
city of pleasure, they set a fashion for those Roman
studies in the naturally and the unnaturally sexual of
which the *Satyricon*[2] of Petronius may stand as a
type. The famous tale of the Matron of Ephesus,
which has more consistency than most of this collection, reveals at once how far such pieces went in
narrative form. Clearly a capital plot for a short
story, it is just as clearly not a short story, but only
a plot. It is as it were a narrative sketch or study,
like the scenario for a play. And in this it is like
many other tales of its class. The rest, the majority,
are simply anecdote.[3]   They are such stories as men
of free life and free speech have in all ages told
after dinner. That is their character of subject;
that is their capacity of form. Speaking broadly,
then, the short tales of antiquity are never short
stories in our modern sense. They are either anecdote or scenario.

Of the longer tale of antiquity a convenient type is
the *Daphnis and Chloe* ascribed to Longus. A plot
no less ancient than that of the foundling reared in
simple life and ultimately reclaimed by noble parents receives from the Greek author the form of a

---

[1] A collection ascribed to Antonius Diogenes, compiled by
Aristides of Miletus, was translated into Latin by Cornelius
Sisenna (119-67 B.C.).   The translation is lost.

[2] The *Cena* of Petronius has more consistency, is in form
more like the longer tales of antiquity.

[3] The object of Lucian is always satire. This, not any purely
narrative end, determines his method.   But it is worth observing that *The Ass* is picaresque.   For the rest, no single adventure of the string is more than anecdote.

pastoral[1] romance, with episodes, complications, and a fairy-tale ending. Its form, then, is essentially the same as the form of *Aucassin and Nicolette*, *Florus and Jehane*, *Amis and Amile*, and other typical short romances of the middle age. Between such short romances and the modern short story there is the same difference of form as between Chaucer's tale of the Man of Law, which is one of the former, and his tale of the Pardoner, which foreshadows how such material may be handled in the way of the latter. For Chaucer, as in his *Troilus and Criseyde* he anticipates the modern novel, so in his Pardoner anticipates the modern short story. The middle age and the Renaissance, even antiquity,[2] show isolated, sporadic instances of short story, whether in prose or in verse; but these are apart from the drift of the time. Aside from such sporadic cases, the longer mediæval tale or short romance, though often in length within the limits of short story, is typically loose as to time and place, and as to incident accumulative of marvels. It is to the long mediæval romance what the modern tale — not the modern short story — is to the modern novel. And it is a constant form from Greece — even from India and Egypt,[3] down to the present. In form the Alexandrian *Daphnis and Chloe*, the mediæval *Aucassin and Nicolette*, and the whole herd of modern tales,

(marginal note:) Daphnis and Chloe, Aucassin and Nicolette.

---

[1] The Greek title is ποιμενικά.

[2] *E. g.*, the fifteenth idyl of Theocritus, and the opening of the seventh oration of Dio Chrysostom. The latter, though brought in as anecdote, has extraordinary ingenuity and finish of form.

[3] See the introduction by Joseph Jacobs to *Old French Romances done into English by William Morris.*

such as Miss Edgeworth's, are essentially alike. The modern time has differentiated two forms: first, the novel, in which character is progressively developed, incidents progressively complicated and resolved; second, the short story, in which character and action are so compressed as to suggest by a single situation without development. The former is as it were an expansion of the tale; the latter, a compression. In both cases the modern art of fiction seems to have learned from the drama. Meantime the original, naïve tale has endured, and doubtless will endure. To employ the figure of speech by which M. Brunetière is enabled to speak of literature in terms of evolution, the tale is the original jackal. From it have been developed two distinct species; but their parent stock persists. Indeed, for aught we can see from the past, posterity may behold a reversion to type.

The significance of a division of ancient and early mediæval tales into anecdote and scenario or summary romance becomes at once clearer by reference to the greatest mediæval collection, the *Decameron* (1353) of Boccaccio. More than half the tales of the *Decameron* may readily be grouped as anecdote — all of the sixth day, for instance, most of the first and eighth, half of the ninth. Of these some approach consistency of form. Having long introductions, unnecessary lapse of time, or other looseness of structure, they still work out a main situation in one day or one night; they sometimes show dramatic ingenuity of incident; less frequently they reach distinct climax. Where the climax, as in the majority of cases, is merely an ingenious escape or a triumphant retort, of course the tale remains simple anecdote; but in some few the climax is the result of the action, is more nearly a culmination. This is the character of the seventh day. Another class in the *Decameron* rapidly summarises a large plot, the action ranging widely in time and place. A narrative sketch, usually of a romance, it corresponds essentially to the *Aucassin and Nicolette* type,[1] and includes nearly one half. Here was an open mine for the romantic drama of later centuries. The *Decameron*, then, is almost all either anecdote or scenario.

But not quite all. Besides those tales which seem to show a working for consistency, there are a few that definitely achieve it. The fourth of the first day (The Monk, the Woman, and the Abbot) is compact within one place and a few hours. All it lacks for short story is definite climax. Very like in compactness is the first of the second day (The Three Florentines and the Body of the New Saint). Firmer still is the eighth of the eighth day (Two Husbands and Two Wives). Here the climax is not only definite, but is a solution, and includes all four characters. If it is not convincing, that is because the *Decameron* is hardly concerned with characterisation. The action covers two days. It might almost as easily have been kept within one. Finally there are two tales that cannot, without hair-splitting, be distinguished from modern short story. The second tale of the second day (Rinaldo, for his prayer to St. Julian, well lodged in spite of mishap) is compressed within a single afternoon and night and a few miles of a single road. The climax is definitely a solution. The movement is largely by dialogue. In a word, the tale is a self-

---

[1] This, perhaps, is typically the *novella;* but Boccaccio will not fix the term : "intendo di raccontare cento *novelle, o favole o parabole o istorie, che dire le vogliamo* . . . nelle quali *novelle* . ." — *Preface to Decameron.*

consistent whole. Equally self-consistent, and quite
similar in method, is that farce comedy of errors, the
sixth tale of the ninth day (Two Travellers in a
Room of Three Beds), which Chaucer has among his
Canterbury Tales. Both these are short stories. If the
other three be counted with them, we have five out of
a hundred.[1]

The middle age, then, had the short story, but
did not recognise, or did not value, that opportunity.
Les Cent   Not only does Boccaccio employ the form
Nouvelles, seldom and, as it were, quite casually, but
Bandello,   subsequent writers do not carry it forward.
The Hep·   In fact, they practically ignore it. *Les
tameron.   cent nouvelles nouvelles* (1450-1460), most
famous of French collections, shows no discernment
of Boccaccio's nicer art. In form, as in subject, there
is no essential change from the habit of antiquity.
True, here and there among the everlasting *histoires
grivoises* is a piece of greater consistency and artistic
promise. That delicious story (the sixth *nouvelle*)
of the drunken man who insisted on making his con-

[1] For reference in more detailed study of mediaeval forms,
this tentative classification of the *Decameron* may be tabulated
as follows : —

anecdote 55
   (a) *simple anecdote* 34
      I, all but nov. 4; III, nov. 4; V, nov. 4; VI, entire;
      VIII, all but nov. 7 & 8; IX, nov. 1 & 7-10.
   (b) *anecdote more artistically elaborated* 21
      III, nov. 1, 2, 3, 5, 6; V, nov. 10; VII, entire;
      VIII, nov. 7 ; IX, nov. 2-5.
scenario or summary romance 40
      II, nov. 3-10; III, nov. 7-10; IV, entire; V, all
      but nov. 4 & 10 ; X, entire.
approaching short story 3
      I, nov. 4; II, nov. 1 ; VIII, nov. 8.
short story 2
      II, nov. 2 ; IX, nov. 6.
                              100

fession on the highway to a priest unfortunately passing, who had absolution at the point of the knife, and
then resolved to die before he lapsed from the state
of grace, is not only a short-story plot; it goes so far
toward short-story form as to focus upon a few hours.
Yet even this hints the short story to us because we
look back from the achieved form. After all it remains anecdote; and it has few peers in all the huge
collection. Bandello (1480-1562), in this regard,
shows even a retrogression from Boccaccio. His
brief romances are looser, often indeed utterly extravagant of time and space. His anecdotes, though they
often have a stir of action, show less sense of bringing
people together on the stage. So the *Heptameron*
(1558-1559) of the Queen of Navarre fails — so in
general subsequent tale-mongers fail — to appreciate
the distinctive value of the terser form. Up to the
nineteenth century the short story was merely sporadic. It was achieved now and again by writers of too
much artistic sense to be quite unaware of its value;
but it never took its place as an accepted form.

Thus the modern development of the short story
in France has both its own artistic interest and the
further historical interest of background.
When Charles Nodier (1783-1844), in the   Nodier.
time of our own Irving, harked back from the novel
to the tale, he but followed consciously what others
had followed unconsciously, a tradition of his race.[1]
Some of Nodier's legends are as mediæval in form as
in subject. But when he wrote *La combe à l'homme
mort* he made of the same material something which,
emerging here and there in the middle age, waited
for definite acceptance till Nodier's own time — a

---

[1] E. Gilbert, *Le roman en France pendant le xixe siècle*,
page 65; A. France, *La vie littéraire, Ire série*, page 47.

short story. The hypothesis that Nodier was a master to Hawthorne is not supported by any close likeness. Yet there are resemblances. Both loved to write tales for children; both lapse toward the overt moral and fall easily into essay; both use the more compact short-story form as it were by the way and not from preference. *Smarra* (66 pages, 1821), acknowledging a suggestion from Apuleius, is an essentially original fantasy, creating the effect of a waking dream. The nearest English parallel is, not Hawthorne, but De Quincey, or, in more elaborate and restrained eloquence, Landor. *Smarra*, as Nodier says in his preface, is an exercise in style to produce a certain phantasmagorical impression. The clue to the effect he sought is given by the frequent quotations from the *Tempest*. It is " such stuff as dreams are made on." *Jean François-les-bas-bleus* (1836) and *Lidivine*, on the other hand, are almost documentary studies of character. *La filleule du Seigneur* (1806), legendary anecdote like Irving's, shows where Nodier's art began. He carried his art much further; but his pieces of compactness, like *La combe à l'homme mort*, are so rare that one may doubt their direct influence on the modern development of form.

For the bulk of Nodier's work is not *conte*, but *nouvelle*. These two terms have never been sharply differentiated in French use. *Les cent nouvelles nouvelles* are not only shorter, in average, than the *novelle* of Boccaccio; they are substantially like the *Contes de la Reine de Navarre*. Some of the *nouvelles* of Nodier, Mérimée, and Gautier are indistinguishable in form from the *contes* of Flaubert, Daudet, and Maupassant. But though even to-day a collection of French tales might bear either name, the short story as it grew in distinctness and popularity seems

to have taken more peculiarly to itself the name
conte.[1] Correspondingly *nouvelle* is a convenient
name for those more extended tales, written sometimes in chapters, which in English are occasionally
called novelettes, and which have their type in *Aucassin and Nicolette*. In this sense Nodier's writing is
mainly, and from preference, *nouvelle*. Taking as his
type for modern adaptation the longer mediæval tale,
he did not work in the direction of short story.

Nor, oddly enough, did Mérimée. People who
assign to him the rôle of pioneer in the short story,
on account of his extraordinary narrative
conciseness, appear to forget that his typi- Mérimée.
cal tales — *Carmen*, *Colomba*,[2] *Arsène Guillot*, are
too long for the form; and that many of his shorter
pieces — *L'enlèvement de la redoute*, *Tamango*, *La
vision de Charles XI.*, are deliberately composed
as descriptive anecdotes. Mérimée's compactness
consists rather in reducing to a *nouvelle* what most
writers would have made a *roman* than in focusing
on a single situation in a *conte*. *Carmen*, though
compact in its main structure, has a long prelude.
Beyond question the method is well adapted; but
it shows no tendency to short story. And the habit
is equally marked in *Le vase étrusque*, with its superfluous characters. Evidently his artistic bent, like
Hawthorne's, like Nodier's, was not in that direction.
All the more striking, therefore, is his single experiment. *La Vénus d'Ille* (1837) is definitely and perfectly a short story. Giving the antecedent action
and the key in skilful opening dialogue, it proceeds
by a series of increasingly stronger premonitions to

---

[1] Brander Matthews, *The Philosophy of the Short-Story*,
page 65.
[2] *Colomba* has one hundred and fifty pages.

a seizing climax. Like Poe, Mérimée intensifies a
mood till it can receive whatever he chooses, but not
at all in Poe's way. Instead, the mystery and horror
are accentuated by a tone of worldly-wise skepticism.
Less compressed, too, than Poe, he can be more
" natural." Withal he keeps the same perfection of
grading. Strange that a man who did this once should
never have done it again. But the single achievement was marked enough to compel imitation.

That the propagation of the short story in France
owes much to Balzac might readily be presumed from
the enormous influence of Balzac's work
Balzac. in general, but can hardly be held after
scrutiny of his short pieces in particular. Of these,
two will serve to recall the limitations of the great
observer. *El Verdugo* (1829), though it is reduced
to two days and substantially one scene, hardly real-
ises the gain from such compression. Instead of intensifying progressively, Balzac has at last to append
his conclusion, and for lack of gradation to leave his
tale barely credible. *Les Proscrits* (1831), more unified in imaginative conception, and again limited
in time-lapse, again fails of that progressive intensity
which is the very essence of Poe's force and Mérimée's. It is not even held steady, but lapses into
intrusive erudition and falls into three quite separate
scenes. Others of Balzac's short pieces, *La messe de
l'athée* (1836), for example, and *Z. Marcas* (1840),
are obviously in form, like many of Hawthorne's,
essays woven on anecdote or character. Some of his
tales may, indeed, have suggested the opportunity of
different handling. Some of them, at any rate, seem
from our point of view almost to call for that. But
his own handling does not seem, as Poe's does, di-
rective. And in general, much as Balzac had to

teach his successors, had he much to teach them of form?

The tales of Musset, which are but incidental in his development, and are confined, most of them, within the years 1837–1838, show no grasp of form. Gautier, even more evidently than Mérimée, preferred the *nouvelle*, partly from indolent fluency, partly from a slight sense of narrative conclusion. Few even of his most compact *contes*, such as *Le nid de rossignols*, compress the time. He was garrulous; he had read Sterne [1]; above all, he was bent, like Sterne, on description. But Gautier too shows a striking exception. *La morte amoureuse*, though it has not Poe's mechanism of compression, is otherwise so startlingly like Poe that one turns involuntarily to the dates. *La morte amoureuse* appeared in 1836; *Berenice*, in 1835. The *Southern Literary Messenger* could not have reached the boulevards in a year. Indeed, the debt of either country to the other can hardly be proved. Remarkable as is the coincident appearance in Paris and in Richmond of a new literary form, it remains a coincidence. And whereas by 1837 Poe was in full career on his hobby, Gautier and Mérimée did not repeat the excursion.

The history of the tale in England, however important otherwise, is hardly distinct enough as a development of form to demand separate discussion here. For England, apparently trying the short-story form later than France and the United States, apparently also learned it from them. Perhaps the foremost short-story

Gautier.

France and America.

---

[1] See an essay on *The Literary Influence of Sterne in France*, Publications of the Modern Language Association of America, volume xvii, pages 221–236.

writers of our time in English — though that must
still be a moot point — are Kipling and Stevenson.
But Stevenson's short story looks to France; and Kipling probably owes much to the American magazine.
Without venturing on the more complicated question
of the relations of Germany, Russia,[1] and Scandinavia
to France, it is safe to put forward as a working hypothesis that the new form was invented by France
and America, and by each independently for itself.
Our priority, if it be substantiated, can be but of
a year or two. The important fact is that after due
incubation the new form, in each country, has germi-
nated and spread with extraordinary vigor. Daudet,
Richepin, Maupassant — to make a list of French
short-story writers in the time just past, is to include
almost all writers of eminence in fiction. What is
true of France is even more obviously true of the
United States. Our most familiar names in recent
fiction were made familiar largely through distinction
in the short story. The native American yarn, still
thriving in spontaneous oral vigour, has been turned
to various art in *The Jumping Frog* and *Marjorie Daw*
and *The Wreck of the Thomas Hyke*. The capacity
of the short story for focusing interest dramatically
on a strictly limited scene and a few hours, no less
than its capacity for fixing local color, is exhibited
most strikingly in the human significance of *Posson
Jone*. Mr. James, though his preoccupation with
scientific analysis demands typically, as it demanded
of Mérimée, a somewhat larger scope, vindicates his
skill more obviously in such intense pieces of compression as *The Great Good Place*. To instance further
would but lead into catalogue. In a word, the two

---

[1] It would be interesting, for instance, to determine whether
Mérimée learned anything in form from Poushkin.

nations that have in our time shown keenest consciousness of form in fiction have most fostered the short story. For ourselves, we may find in this development of a literary form one warrant for asserting that we have a literary history.

PART I

THE TENTATIVE PERIOD

WASHINGTON IRVING
1783 – 1859

FOR a discussion of Irving in general, and of *Rip Van Winkle* in particular, see pages 6–9 of the Introduction. The pseudo-documentary notes before and after the tale show incidentally the strong contemporary influence of Scott. The text is that of the first edition (1819).

(The following tale was found among the papers of the late Diedrich Knickerbocker, an old gentleman of New York, who was very curious in the Dutch history of the province, and the manners of the descendants from its primitive settlers. His historical researches, however, did not lie so much among books as among men; for the former are lamentably scanty on his favourite topics; whereas he found the old burghers, and still more their wives, rich in that legendary lore so invaluable to true history. Whenever, therefore, he happened upon a genuine Dutch family, snugly shut up in its low-roofed farmhouse, under a spreading sycamore, he looked upon it as a little clasped volume of black-letter, and studied it with the zeal of a book-worm.

The result of all these researches was a history of the province during the reign of the Dutch governors, which he published some years since. There have been various opinions as to the literary character of his work, and, to tell the truth, it is not a whit better than it should be. Its chief merit is its scrupulous accuracy, which indeed was a little questioned on its first appearance, but has since been completely established; and it is now admitted into all historical collections as a book of unquestionable authority.

The old gentleman died shortly after the publication of his work, and now, that he is dead and gone, it cannot do much harm to his memory, to say, that his time might have been much better employed in weightier labours. He, however, was apt to ride his hobby in his own way; and though it did now and then kick up the dust a little in the eyes of his neighbours, and grieve the spirit of some friends, for whom he felt the truest deference and affection; yet his errors and follies are remembered "more in sorrow than in anger,[1]" and it begins to be suspected that he never intended to injure or offend. But however his memory may be appreciated by critics, it is still held dear among many folk, whose good opinion is well worth having; particularly by certain biscuit bakers, who have gone so far as to imprint his likeness on their New Year cakes, and have thus given him a chance for immortality, almost equal to the being stamped on a Waterloo medal, or a Queen Anne's farthing.)

[1] Vide the excellent discourse of G. C. Verplanck, Esq., before the New York Historical Society.

RIP VAN WINKLE

A POSTHUMOUS WRITING OF DIEDRICH KNICKERBOCKER

[*From the " Sketch Book," 1819-1820*]

By Woden, God of Saxons,
From whence comes Wensday, that is Wodensday,
Truth is a thing that ever I will keep
Unto thylke day in which I creep into
My sepulchre ——— CARTWRIGHT.

WHOEVER has made a voyage up the Hudson, must remember the Kaatskill mountains. They are a dismembered branch of the great Appalachian family, and are seen away to the west of the river, swelling up to a noble height, and lording it over the surrounding country. Every change of season, every change of weather, indeed, every hour of the day, produces some change in the magical hues and shapes of these mountains, and they are regarded by all the good wives, far and near, as perfect barometers. When the weather is fair and settled, they are clothed in blue and purple, and print their bold outlines on the clear evening sky; but sometimes, when the rest of the landscape is cloudless, they will gather a hood of gray vapours about their summits, which, in the last rays of the setting sun, will glow and light up like a crown of glory.

At the foot of these fairy mountains, the voyager may have descried the light smoke curling up from a village, whose shingle roofs gleam among the trees, just where the blue tints of the upland melt away into the fresh green of the nearer landscape. It is a little village of great antiquity, having been founded by some of the Dutch colonists, in the early times of the province, just about the beginning of the government of the good Peter Stuyvesant (may he rest in peace !), and there were some of the houses of the original settlers standing within a few years with lattice windows, gable fronts surmounted with weathercocks, and built of small yellow bricks brought from Holland.

In that same village, and in one of these very houses, (which, to tell the precise truth, was sadly timeworn and weatherbeaten,) there lived many years since, while the country was yet a province of Great Britain, a simple goodnatured fellow, of the name of Rip Van Winkle. He was a descendant of the Van Winkles who figured so gallantly in the chivalrous days of Peter Stuyvesant, and accompanied him to the siege of Fort Christina. He inherited, however, but little of the martial character of his ancestors. I have observed that he was a simple goodnatured man; he was moreover a kind neighbour, and an obedient, henpecked husband. Indeed, to the latter circumstance might be owing that meekness of spirit which gained him such universal popularity; for those men are most apt to be obsequious and conciliating abroad, who are under the discipline of shrews at home. Their tempers, doubtless, are rendered pliant and malleable in the fiery furnace of domestic tribulation, and a curtain lecture is worth all the sermons in the world for teaching the virtues of patience and long suffering. A termagant wife may, therefore, in some respects, be considered a tolerable blessing; and if so, Rip Van Winkle was thrice blessed.

Certain it is, that he was a great favourite among all the good wives of the village, who, as usual with the amiable sex, took his part in all family squabbles, and never failed, whenever they talked those matters over in their evening gossippings, to lay all the blame on Dame Van Winkle. The children of the village, too, would shout with joy whenever he approached. He assisted at their sports, made their playthings, taught them to fly kites and shoot marbles, and told them long stories of ghosts, witches, and Indians. Whenever he went dodging about the village, he was surrounded by a troop of them, hanging on his skirts, clambering on his back, and playing a thousand tricks on him with impunity; and not a dog would bark at him throughout the neighbourhood.

The great error in Rip's composition was an insuperable aversion to all kinds of profitable labour. It could not be from the want of assiduity or perseverance; for he would sit on a wet rock, with a rod as long and heavy as a Tartar's lance, and fish all day without a murmur, even though he should not be encouraged by a single nibble. He would carry a fowling-piece on his shoulder, for hours together, trudging through woods and swamps, and up hill and down dale, to shoot a few squirrels or wild pigeons. He would never even refuse to assist a neighbour in the roughest toil, and was a foremost man at all country frolicks for husking Indian corn, or building stone fences. The women of the village, too, used to employ him to run their errands, and to do such little odd jobs as their less obliging husbands would not do for them; — in a word, Rip was ready to attend to anybody's business but his own; but as to doing family duty, and keeping his farm in order, it was impossible.

In fact, he declared it was of no use to work on his farm; it was the most pestilent little piece of ground in the whole country; everything about it went wrong, and would go wrong, in spite of him. His fences were continually falling to pieces; his cow would either go astray, or get among the cabbages; weeds were sure to grow quicker in his fields than anywhere else; the rain always made a point of setting in just as he had some out-door work to do; so that though his patrimonial estate had dwindled away under his management, acre by acre, until there was little more left than a mere patch of Indian corn and potatoes, yet it was the worst conditioned farm in the neighbourhood.

His children, too, were as ragged and wild as if they

belonged to nobody. His son Rip, an urchin begotten in his own likeness, promised to inherit the habits, with the old clothes of his father. He was generally seen trooping like a colt at his mother's heels, equipped in a pair of his father's cast-off galligaskins, which he had much ado to hold up with one hand, as a fine lady does her train in bad weather.

Rip Van Winkle, however, was one of those happy mortals, of foolish, well-oiled dispositions, who take the world easy, eat white bread or brown, whichever can be got with least thought or trouble, and would rather starve on a penny than work for a pound. If left to himself, he would have whistled life away, in perfect contentment; but his wife kept continually dinning in his ears about his idleness, his carelessness, and the ruin he was bringing on his family. Morning, noon, and night, her tongue was incessantly going, and everything he said or did was sure to produce a torrent of household eloquence. Rip had but one way of replying to all lectures of the kind, and that, by frequent use, had grown into a habit. He shrugged his shoulders, shook his head, cast up his eyes, but said nothing. This, however, always provoked a fresh volley from his wife, so that he was fain to draw off his forces, and take to the outside of the house — the only side which, in truth, belongs to a henpecked husband.

Rip's sole domestic adherent was his dog Wolf, who was as much henpecked as his master; for Dame Van Winkle regarded them as companions in idleness, and even looked upon Wolf with an evil eye, as the cause of his master's so often going astray. True it is, in all points of spirit befitting an honourable dog, he was as courageous an animal as ever scoured the woods — but what courage can withstand the ever-during and all-besetting terrors of a woman's tongue? The moment Wolf entered the house, his crest fell, his tail drooped to the ground, or curled between his legs, he sneaked about with a gallows air, casting many a sidelong glance at Dame Van Winkle, and at the least flourish of a broomstick or ladle, would fly to the door with yelping precipitation.

Times grew worse and worse with Rip Van Winkle as years of matrimony rolled on ; a tart temper never mellows with age, and a sharp tongue is the only edged tool that grows keener by constant use. For a long while he used to console himself, when driven from home, by frequenting a kind of perpetual club of the sages, philosophers, and other idle personages of the village, which held its sessions on a bench before a small inn, designated by a rubicund portrait of his majesty George the Third. Here they used to sit in the shade, of a long lazy summer's day, talk-ing listlessly over village gossip, or telling endless sleepy stories about nothing. But it would have been worth any statesman's money to have heard the profound discussions which sometimes took place, when by chance an old news-paper fell into their hands, from some passing traveller. How solemnly they would listen to the contents, as drawled out by Derrick Van Bummel, the schoolmaster, a dapper learned little man, who was not to be daunted by the most gigantic word in the dictionary ; and how sagely they would deliberate upon public events some months after they had taken place.

The opinions of this junto were completely controlled by Nicholas Vedder, a patriarch of the village, and landlord of the inn, at the door of which he took his seat from morn-ing till night, just moving sufficiently to avoid the sun, and keep in the shade of a large tree ; so that the neighbours could tell the hour by his movements as accurately as by a sun dial. It is true, he was rarely heard to speak, but smoked his pipe incessantly. His adherents, however, (for every great man has his adherents,) perfectly understood him, and knew how to gather his opinions. When any-thing that was read or related displeased him, he was observed to smoke his pipe vehemently, and send forth short, frequent, and angry puffs ; but when pleased, he would inhale the smoke slowly and tranquilly, and emit it in light and placid clouds, and sometimes taking the pipe from his mouth, and letting the fragrant vapour curl about his nose, would gravely nod his head in token of perfect approbation.

From even this stronghold the unlucky Rip was at length routed by his termagant wife, who would ᵤuddenly break in upon the tranquillity of the assemblage, and call the members all to nought ; nor was that august personage, Nicholas Vedder himself, sacred from the daring tongue of this terrible virago, who charged him outright with encouraging her husband in habits of idleness.

Poor Rip was at last reduced almost to despair ; and his only alternative to· escape from the labour of the farm and clamour of his wife, was to take gun in hand, and stroll away into the woods.   Here he would sometimes seat himself at the foot of a tree, and share the contents of his wallet with Wolf, with whom he sympathized as a fellow sufferer in persecution.   "Poor Wolf," he would say, "thy mistress leads thee a dog's life of it ; but never mind, my lad, while I live thou shalt never want a friend to stand by thee !" Wolf would wag his tail, look wistfully in his master's face, and if dogs can feel pity, I verily believe he reciprocated the sentiment with all his heart.

In a long ramble of the kind on a fine autumnal day, Rip had unconsciously scrambled to one of the highest parts of the Kaatskill mountains.   He was after his favourite sport of squirrel shooting, and the still solitudes had echoed and re-echoed with the reports of his gun.   Panting and fatigued, he threw himself, late in the afternoon, on a green knoll, covered with mountain herbage, that crowned the brow of a precipice.   From an opening between the trees, he could overlook all the lower country for many a mile of rich woodland.   He saw at a distance the lordly Hudson, far, far below him, moving on its silent but majestic course, the reflection of a purple cloud, or the sail of a lagging bark, here and there sleeping on its glassy bosom, and at last losing itself in the blue highlands.

On the other side he looked down into a deep mountain glen, wild, lonely, and shagged, the bottom filled with fragments from the impending cliffs, and scarcely lighted by the reflected rays of the setting sun. For some time Rip lay musing on this scene; evening was gradually advancing, the mountains began to throw their long, blue shadows over the valleys, he saw that it would be dark long before he could reach the village, and he heaved a heavy sigh when he thought of encountering the terrors of Dame Van Winkle.

As he was about to descend, he heard a voice from a distance, hallooing, " Rip Van Winkle ! Rip Van Winkle ! " He looked around, but could see nothing but a crow winging its solitary flight across the mountain. He thought his fancy must have deceived him, and turned again to descend, when he heard the same cry ring through the still evening air; " Rip Van Winkle ! Rip Van Winkle ! " — at the same time Wolf bristled up his back, and giving a low growl, skulked to his master's side, looking fearfully down into the glen. Rip now felt a vague apprehension stealing over him; he looked anxiously in the same direction, and perceived a strange figure slowly toiling up the rocks, and bending under the weight of something he carried on his back. He was surprised to see any human being in this lonely and unfrequented place, but supposing it to be some one of the neighbourhood in need of his assistance, he hastened down to yield it.

On nearer approach, he was still more surprised at the singularity of the stranger's appearance. He was a short square built old fellow, with thick bushy hair, and a grizzled beard. His dress was of the antique Dutch fashion — a cloth jerkin strapped round the waist — several pair of breeches, the outer one of ample volume, decorated with rows of buttons down the sides, and bunches at the knees. He bore on his shoulders a stout keg, that seemed full of liquor, and made signs for Rip to approach and assist him with the load. Though rather shy and distrustful of this new acquaintance, Rip complied with his usual alacrity, and mutually relieving one another, they clambered up a narrow gully, apparently the dry bed of a mountain torrent. As they ascended, Rip every now and then heard long rolling peals, like distant thunder, that seemed to issue out of a deep ravine, or rather cleft between lofty rocks, toward which their rugged path conducted. He paused for an instant, but supposing it to be the muttering of one of those transient thunder showers which often take place in mountain heights, he proceeded. Passing through the ravine, they came to a hollow, like a small amphitheatre, surrounded by perpendicular precipices, over the brinks of which impending trees shot their branches, so that you only caught glimpses of the azure sky, and the bright evening cloud. During the whole time, Rip and his companion had laboured on in silence; for though the former marvelled greatly what could be the object of carrying a keg of liquor up this wild mountain, yet there was something strange and incomprehensible about the unknown, that inspired awe, and checked familiarity.

On entering the amphitheatre, new objects of wonder presented themselves. On a level spot in the centre was a company of odd-looking personages playing at nine-pins. They were dressed in a quaint, outlandish fashion : some wore short doublets, others jerkins, with long knives in their belts, and most had enormous breeches, of similar style with that of the guide's. Their visages, too, were peculiar : one had a large head, broad face, and small piggish eyes ; the face of another seemed to consist entirely of nose, and was surmounted by a white sugar-loaf hat, set off with a little red cock's tail. They all had beards, of various shapes and colours. There was one who seemed to be the commander. He was a stout old gentleman, with a weather-beaten countenance ; he wore a laced doublet, broad belt and hanger, high crowned hat and feather, red stockings, and high heeled shoes, with roses in them. The whole group reminded Rip of the figures in an old Flemish painting, in the parlour of Dominie Van Schaick, the village parson, and which had been brought over from Holland at the time of the settlement.

What seemed particularly odd to Rip, was that though these folks were evidently amusing themselves, yet they maintained the gravest faces, the most mysterious silence, and were, withal, the most melancholy party of pleasure he had ever witnessed. Nothing interrupted the stillness of the scene, but the noise of the balls, which, whenever they were rolled, echoed along the mountains like rumbling peals of thunder.

As Rip and his companion approached them, they suddenly desisted from their play, and stared at him with such fixed statue-like gaze, and such strange, uncouth, lacklustre countenances, that his heart turned within him, and his knees smote together. His companion now emptied the contents of the keg into large flagons, and made signs to him to wait upon the company. He obeyed with fear and trembling; they quaffed the liquor in profound silence, and then returned to their game.

By degrees, Rip's awe and apprehension subsided. He even ventured, when no eye was fixed upon him, to taste the beverage, which he found had much of the flavour of excellent Hollands. He was naturally a thirsty soul, and was soon tempted to repeat the draught. One taste provoked another, and he reiterated his visits to the flagon so often, that at length his senses were overpowered, his eyes swam in his head, his head gradually declined, and he fell into a deep sleep.

On awaking, he found himself on the green knoll from whence he had first seen the old man of the glen. He rubbed his eyes — it was a bright sunny morning. The birds were hopping and twittering among the bushes, and the eagle was wheeling aloft, and breasting the pure mountain breeze. " Surely," thought Rip, " I have not slept here all night." He recalled the occurrences before he fell asleep. The strange man with a keg of liquor — the mountain ravine — the wild retreat among the rocks — the woe-begone party at nine-pins — the flagon — "Oh! that flagon! that wicked flagon!" thought Rip — "what excuse shall I make to Dame Van Winkle?"

He looked round for his gun, but in place of the clean well-oiled fowling-piece, he found an old firelock lying by him, the barrel encrusted with rust, the lock falling off, and the stock worm-eaten. He now suspected that the grave roysters of the mountain had put a trick upon him, and having dosed him with liquor, had robbed him of his gun. Wolf, too, had disappeared, but he might have strayed away after a squirrel or partridge. He whistled after him, shouted his name, but all in vain; the echoes repeated his whistle and shout, but no dog was to be seen.

He determined to revisit the scene of the last evening's gambol, and if he met with any of the party, to demand his dog and gun. As he rose to walk, he found himself stiff in the joints, and wanting in his usual activity. "These mountain beds do not agree with me," thought Rip, "and if this frolic should lay me up with a fit of the rheumatism, I shall have a blessed time with Dame Van Winkle." With some difficulty he got down into the glen; he found the gully up which he and his companion had ascended the preceding evening; but to his astonishment a mountain stream was now foaming down it, leaping from rock to rock, and filling the glen with babbling murmurs. He, however, made shift to scramble up its sides, working his toilsome way through thickets of birch, sassafras, and witch hazle, and sometimes tripped up or entangled by the wild grape vines that twisted their coils and tendrils from tree to tree, and spread a kind of network in his path.

At length he reached to where the ravine had opened through the cliffs, to the amphitheatre; but no traces of such opening remained. The rocks presented a high impenetrable wall, over which the torrent came tumbling in a sheet of feathery foam, and fell into a broad deep basin, black from the shadows of the surrounding forest. Here, then, poor Rip was brought to a stand. He again called and whistled after his dog; he was only answered by the cawing of a flock of idle crows, sporting high in air about a dry tree that overhung a sunny precipice; and who, secure in their elevation, seemed to look down and scoff at the poor man's perplexities. What was to be done? the morning was passing away, and Rip felt famished for want of his breakfast. He grieved to give up his dog and gun; he dreaded to meet his wife; but it would not do to starve among the mountains. He shook his head, shouldered the rusty firelock, and, with a heart full of trouble and anxiety, turned his steps homeward.

As he approached the village, he met a number of people, but none whom he knew, which somewhat surprised him, for he had thought himself acquainted with every one in the country round. Their dress, too, was of a different fashion from that to which he was accustomed. They all stared at him with equal marks of surprise, and whenever they cast their eyes upon him, invariably stroked their chins. The constant recurrence of this gesture induced Rip, involuntarily, to do the same, when, to his astonishment, he found his beard had grown a foot long!

He had now entered the skirts of the village. A troop of strange children ran at his heels, hooting after him, and pointing at his gray beard. The dogs, too, none of which he recognized for his old acquaintances, barked at him as he passed. The very village was altered: it was larger and more populous. There were rows of houses which he had never seen before, and those which had been his familiar haunts had disappeared. Strange names were over the doors — strange faces at the windows — everything was strange. His mind now began to misgive him; he doubted whether both he and the world around him were not bewitched. Surely this was his native village, which he had left but the day before. There stood the Kaatskill mountains — there ran the silver Hudson at a distance — there was every hill and dale precisely as it had always been — Rip was sorely perplexed — "That flagon last night," thought he, "has addled my poor head sadly!"

It was with some difficulty he found the way to his own house, which he approached with silent awe, expecting every moment to hear the shrill voice of Dame Van Winkle. He found the house gone to decay — the roof fallen in, the windows shattered, and the doors off the hinges. A half-starved dog, that looked like Wolf, was skulking about it. Rip called him by name, but the cur snarled, showed his teeth, and passed on. This was an unkind cut indeed — "My very dog," sighed poor Rip, "has forgotten me!"

He entered the house, which, to tell the truth, Dame Van Winkle had always kept in neat order. It was empty, forlorn, and apparently abandoned. This desolateness overcame all his connubial fears — he called loudly for his wife and children — the lonely chambers rung for a moment with his voice, and then all again was silence.

He now hurried forth, and hastened to his old resort, the little village inn — but it too was gone. A large ricketty wooden building stood in its place, with great gaping windows, some of them broken, and mended with old hats and petticoats, and over the door was painted, "The Union Hotel, by Jonathan Doolittle." Instead of the great tree which used to shelter the quiet little Dutch inn of yore, there now was reared a tall naked pole, with something on the top that looked like a red nightcap, and from it was fluttering a flag, on which was a singular assemblage of stars and stripes — all this was strange and incomprehensible. He recognised on the sign, however, the ruby face of King George, under which he had smoked so many a peaceful pipe, but even this was singularly metamorphosed. The red coat was changed for one of blue and buff, a sword was stuck in the hand instead of a sceptre, the head was decorated with a cocked hat, and underneath was painted in large characters, GENERAL WASHINGTON.

There was, as usual, a crowd of folk about the door, but none whom Rip recollected. The very character of the people seemed changed. There was a busy, bustling, disputatious tone about it, instead of the accustomed phlegm and drowsy tranquillity. He looked in vain for the sage Nicholas Vedder, with his broad face, double chin, and fair long pipe, uttering clouds of tobacco smoke instead of idle speeches; or Van Bummel, the schoolmaster, doling forth the contents of an ancient newspaper. In place of these, a lean bilious looking fellow, with his pockets full of hand-bills, was haranguing vehemently about rights of citizens — election — members of Congress — liberty — Bunker's Hill — heroes of '76 — and other words, that were a perfect Babylonish jargon to the bewildered Van Winkle.

The appearance of Rip, with his long grizzled beard, his rusty fowling piece, his uncouth dress, and the army of women and children that had gathered at his heels, soon attracted the attention of the tavern politicians. They crowded around him, eying him from head to foot, with great curiosity. The orator bustled up to him, and drawing him partly aside, inquired " on which side he voted ? " Rip stared in vacant stupidity. Another short but busy little fellow pulled him by the arm, and raising on tiptoe, inquired in his ear, " whether he was Federal or Democrat." Rip was equally at a loss to comprehend the question; when a knowing, self-important old gentleman, in a sharp cocked hat, made his way through the crowd, putting them to the right and left with his elbows as he passed, and planting himself before Van Winkle, with one arm akimbo, the other resting on his cane, his keen eyes and sharp hat penetrating, as it were, into his very soul, demanded, in an austere tone, " what brought him to the election with a gun on his shoulder, and a mob at his heels, and whether he meant to breed a riot in the village ? " " Alas ! gentlemen," cried Rip, somewhat dismayed, " I am a poor quiet man, a native of the place, and a loyal subject of the King, God bless him ! "

Here a general shout burst from the bystanders — " A tory ! a tory ! a spy ! a refugee ! hustle him ! away with

him ! " It was with great difficulty that the self-important man in the cocked hat restored order; and having
assumed a tenfold austerity of brow, demanded again of
the unknown culprit, what he came there for, and whom
he was seeking. The poor man humbly assured him that
he meant no harm ; but merely came there in search of
some of his neighbours, who used to keep about the tavern.

"Well — who are they? — name them."

Rip bethought himself a moment, and inquired, " where 's
Nicholas Vedder? "

There was a silence for a little while, when an old man
replied, in a thin piping voice, " Nicholas Vedder? why
he is dead and gone these eighteen years ! There was a
wooden tombstone in the churchyard that used to tell all
about him, but that's rotted and gone too."

"Where 's Brom Dutcher? "

" Oh, he went off to the army in the beginning of the
war; some say he was killed at the battle of Stoney-Point
— others say he was drowned in a squall, at the foot of
Antony's Nose. I don't know — he never came back
again."

"Where's Van Bummel, the schoolmaster? "

" He went off to the wars too, was a great militia general, and is now in Congress."

Rip's heart died away, at hearing of these sad changes in
his home and friends, and finding himself thus alone in the
world. Every answer puzzled him, too, by treating of such
enormous lapses of time, and of matters which he could
not understand : war — Congress — Stoney Point ! — he
had no courage to ask after any more friends, but cried out
in despair, " Does nobody here know Rip Van Winkle? "

" Oh, Rip Van Winkle ! " exclaimed two or three, " Oh,
to be sure ! that 's Rip Van Winkle yonder, leaning against
the tree."

Rip looked, and beheld a precise counterpart of himself,
as he went up the mountain : apparently as lazy, and certainly as ragged. The poor fellow was now completely con-

founded. He doubted his own identity, and whether he was himself or another man. In the midst of his bewilderment, the man in the cocked hat demanded who he was, and what was his name?

"God knows," exclaimed he, at his wit's end ; "I'm not myself — I'm somebody else — that's me yonder — no — that's somebody else, got into my shoes — I was myself last night, but I fell asleep on the mountain, and they've changed my gun, and everything's changed, and I'm changed, and I can't tell what's my name, or who I am!"

The bystanders began now to look at each other, nod, wink significantly, and tap their fingers against their foreheads. There was a whisper, also, about securing the gun, and keeping the old fellow from doing mischief; at the very suggestion of which, the self-important man in the cocked hat retired with some precipitation. At this critical moment a fresh likely woman pressed through the throng to get a peep at the graybearded man. She had a chubby child in her arms, which, frightened at his looks, began to cry. "Hush, Rip," cried she, "hush, you little fool, the old man won't hurt you." The name of the child, the air of the mother, the tone of her voice, all awakened a train of recollections in his mind. "What is your name, my good woman?" asked he.

"Judith Gardenier."

"And your father's name?"

"Ah, poor man, his name was Rip Van Winkle ; it's twenty years since he went away from home with his gun, and never has been heard of since — his dog came home without him ; but whether he shot himself, or was carried away by the Indians, nobody can tell. I was then but a little girl."

Rip had but one question more to ask ; but he put it with a faltering voice :

"Where's your mother?"

"Oh, she too had died but a short time since ; she broke a blood vessel in a fit of passion at a New-England peddler."

There was a drop of comfort, at least, in this intelligence. The honest man could contain himself no longer. — He caught his daughter and her child in his arms. — " I am your father ! " cried he — " Young Rip Van Winkle once — old Rip Van Winkle now ! — Does nobody know poor Rip Van Winkle ! "

All stood amazed, until an old woman, tottering out from among the crowd, put her hand to her brow, and peering under it in his face for a moment, exclaimed, " Sure enough ! it is Rip Van Winkle — it is himself. Welcome home again, old neighbour. — Why, where have you been these twenty long years? "

Rip's story was soon told, for the whole twenty years had been to him but as one night. The neighbours stared when they heard it; some were seen to wink at each other, and put their tongues in their cheeks; and the self-important man in the cocked hat, who, when the alarm was over, had returned to the field, screwed down the corners of his mouth, and shook his head — upon which there was a general shaking of the head throughout the assemblage.

It was determined, however, to take the opinion of old Peter Vanderdonk, who was seen slowly advancing up the road. He was a descendant of the historian of that name, who wrote one of the earliest accounts of the province. Peter was the most ancient inhabitant of the village, and well versed in all the wonderful events and traditions of the neighbourhood. He recollected Rip at once, and corroborated his story in the most satisfactory manner. He assured the company that it was a fact, handed down from his ancestor the historian, that the Kaatskill mountains had always been haunted by strange beings. That it was affirmed that the great Hendrick Hudson, the first discoverer of the river and country, kept a kind of vigil there every twenty years, with his crew of the Half-moon, being permitted in this way to revisit the scenes of his enterprize, and keep a guardian eye upon the river, and the great city called by his name. That his father had once seen them in their old

Dutch dresses playing at ninepins in a hollow of the mountain; and that he himself had heard, one summer afternoon, the sound of their balls, like long peals of thunder.

To make a long story short, the company broke up, and returned to the more important concerns of the election. Rip's daughter took him home to live with her; she had a snug, well-furnished house, and a stout cheery farmer for a husband, whom Rip recollected for one of the urchins that used to climb upon his back. As to Rip's son and heir, who was the ditto of himself, seen leaning against the tree, he was employed to work on the farm; but evinced an hereditary disposition to attend to anything else but his business.

Rip now resumed his old walks and habits; he soon found many of his former cronies, though all rather the worse for the wear and tear of time; and preferred making friends among the rising generation, with whom he soon grew into great favour.

Having nothing to do at home, and being arrived at that happy age when a man can do nothing with impunity, he took his place once more on the bench, at the inn door, and was reverenced as one of the patriarchs of the village, and a chronicle of the old times "before the war." It was some time before he could get into the regular track of gossip, or could be made to comprehend the strange events that had taken place during his torpor. How that there had been a revolutionary war — that the country had thrown off the yoke of old England — and that, instead of being a subject of his Majesty, George III., he was now a free citizen of the United States. Rip, in fact, was no politician; the changes of states and empires made but little impression on him; but there was one species of despotism under which he had long groaned, and that was — petticoat government; happily, that was at an end; he had got his neck out of the yoke of matrimony, and could go in and out whenever he pleased, without dreading the tyranny of Dame Van Winkle. Whenever her name was mentioned, however, he shook his head, shrugged his shoulders, and cast up his eyes; which might pass either for an expression of resignation to his fate, or joy at his deliverance. He used to tell his story to every stranger that arrived at Mr. Doolittle's hotel. He was observed, at first, to vary on some points every time he told it, which was, doubtless, owing to his having so recently awaked. It at last settled down precisely to the tale I have related, and not a man, woman, or child in the neighbourhood but knew it by heart. Some always pretended to doubt the reality of it, and insisted that Rip had been out of his head, and that this was one point on which he always remained flighty. The old Dutch inhabitants, however, almost universally gave it full credit. Even to this day they never hear a thunder storm of a summer afternoon, about the Kaatskill, but they say Hendrick Hudson and his crew are at their game of nine-pins; and it is a common wish of all henpecked husbands in the neighbourhood, when life hangs heavy on their hands, that they might have a quieting draught out of Rip Van Winkle's flagon.

NOTE

THE foregoing tale, one would suspect, had been suggested to Mr. Knickerbocker by a little German superstition about the Emperor Frederick and the Kypphauser mountain; the subjoined note, however, which he had appended to the tale, shows that it is an absolute fact, narrated with his usual fidelity.

"The story of Rip Van Winkle may seem incredible to many, but nevertheless I give it my full belief, for I know the vicinity of our old Dutch settlements to have been very subject to marvellous events and appearances. Indeed, I have heard many stranger stories than this, in the villages along the Hudson; all of which were too well authenticated to admit of a doubt. I have even talked with Rip Van Winkle myself, who, when last I saw him, was a very venerable old man, and so perfectly rational and consistent on every other point, that I think no conscientious person could refuse to take this into the bargain; nay, I have seen a certificate on the subject taken before a country justice and signed with a cross, in the justice's own handwriting. The story, therefore, is beyond the possibility of a doubt.

" D. K."

POSTSCRIPT [1]

THE following are travelling notes from a memorandum book of Mr. Knickerbocker:

The Kaatsberg, or Catskill Mountains, have always been a region full of fable. The Indians considered them the abode of spirits, who influenced the weather, spreading sunshine or clouds over the landscape, and sending good or bad hunting seasons. They were ruled by an old squaw spirit, said to be their mother. She dwelt on the highest peak of the Catskills, and had charge of the doors of day and night to open and shut them at the proper hour. She hung up the new moon in the skies, and cut up the old ones into stars. In times of drought, if properly propitiated, she would spin light summer clouds out of cobwebs and morning dew, and send them off from the crest of the mountain, flake after flake, like flakes of carded cotton, to float in the air; until, dissolved by the heat of the sun, they would fall in gentle showers, causing the grass to spring, the fruits to ripen, and the corn to grow an inch an hour. If displeased, however, she would brew up clouds black as ink, sitting in the midst of them like a bottle-bellied spider in the midst of its web; and when these clouds broke, woe betide the valleys!

In old times, say the Indian traditions, there was a kind of Manitou or Spirit, who kept about the wildest recesses of the Catskill Mountains, and took a mischievous pleasure in wreaking all kinds of evils and vexations upon the red men. Sometimes he would assume the form of a bear, a panther, or a deer, lead the bewildered hunter a weary chase through tangled forests and among ragged rocks; and then spring off with a loud ho! ho! leaving him aghast on the brink of a beetling precipice or raging torrent.

The favorite abode of this Manitou is still shown. It is a great rock or cliff on the loneliest part of the mountains, and, from the flowering vines which clamber about it, and the wild flowers which abound in its neighborhood, is known by the name of the Garden Rock. Near the foot of it is a small lake,

---

[1] Not in the first edition.

the haunt of the solitary bittern, with water-snakes basking in the sun on the leaves of the pond-lilies which lie on the surface. This place was held in great awe by the Indians, insomuch that the boldest hunter would not pursue his game within its precincts.   Once upon a time, however, a hunter who had lost his way, penetrated to the Garden Rock, where he beheld a number of gourds placed in the crotches of trees.   One of these he seized and made off with it, but in the hurry of his retreat he let it fall among the rocks, when a great stream gushed forth, which washed him away and swept him down precipices, where he was dashed to pieces, and the stream made its way to the Hudson, and continues to flow to the present day; being the identical stream known by the name of the Kaaterskill.

WILLIAM AUSTIN

1778 – 1841

WILLIAM AUSTIN was a Boston lawyer of literary tastes. He saw something of the world in his cruises (1799–1800) on the " Constitution " as chaplain, and of society during his eighteen months at Lincoln's Inn. An account of his life and works is prefixed to the collective edition, now out of print, edited by his son, John Walker Austin (*The Literary Papers of William Austin*, Boston, 1890). This also reprints a large part of Col. T. W. Higginson's " A Precursor of Hawthorne " (*Independent*, 29th March, 1888. A reference will also be found at pages 64 and 68 of Col. Higginson's *Longfellow*). Of his few tales only *Peter Rugg* has had any currency. Indeed, the significance of Austin's narrative art is mainly negative. Even *Peter Rugg* shows wherein what might have been a short story failed of its form. For all its undoubted quality, it is a short story *manqué;* and in this it is quite typical of its time. If artistic sense is apparent in the cumulation of foreshadowings, crudity of mechanism is equally apparent in the management of each through a different interlocutor. It is artistically right that Rugg should at last be brought home ; it is artistically wrong that the conclusion should be so like a moralising summary. A conception much like Hawthorne's is developed as it were by mere accumulation instead of being focused in a unified progression. (See also pages 10 and 12 of the Introduction.)

PETER RUGG, THE MISSING MAN

[*First part printed in Buckingham's " New England Galaxy,"
10th September, 1824 ; several times reprinted entire, e. g., in the
" Boston Book " for 1841 ; reprinted here from the standard collection noted above*]

From JONATHAN DUNWELL *of* NEW YORK *to* MR. HERMAN KRAUFF

SIR, — Agreeably to my promise, I now relate to you
all the particulars of the lost man and child which
I have been able to collect. It is entirely owing to the
humane interest you seemed to take in the report, that I
have pursued the inquiry to the following result.

You may remember that business called me to Boston in
the summer of 1820. I sailed in the packet to Providence,
and when I arrived there I learned that every seat in the
stage was engaged. I was thus obliged either to wait a few
hours or accept a seat with the driver, who civilly offered
me that accommodation. Accordingly, I took my seat by
his side, and soon found him intelligent and communica-
tive. When we had travelled about ten miles, the horses
suddenly threw their ears on their necks, as flat as a hare's.
Said the driver, " Have you a surtout with you? "

"No," said I ; " why do you ask? "

" You will want one soon," said he. " Do you observe
the ears of all the horses? "

" Yes ; and was just about to ask the reason."

" They see the storm-breeder, and we shall see him
soon."

At this moment there was not a cloud visible in the firmament. Soon after, a small speck appeared in the road.

"There," said my companion, "comes the storm-breeder. He always leaves a Scotch mist behind him. By many a wet jacket do I remember him. I suppose the poor fellow suffers much himself, — much more than is known to the world."

Presently a man with a child beside him, with a large black horse, and a weather-beaten chair, once built for a chaise-body, passed in great haste, apparently at the rate of twelve miles an hour. He seemed to grasp the reins of his horse with firmness, and appeared to anticipate his speed. He seemed dejected, and looked anxiously at the passengers, particularly at the stage-driver and myself. In a moment after he passed us, the horses' ears were up, and bent themselves forward so that they nearly met.

"Who is that man?" said I; "he seems in great trouble."

"Nobody knows who he is, but his person and the child are familiar to me. I have met him more than a hundred times, and have been so often asked the way to Boston by that man, even when he was travelling directly from that town, that of late I have refused any communication with him; and that is the reason he gave me such a fixed look."

"But does he never stop anywhere?"

"I have never known him to stop anywhere longer than to inquire the way to Boston; and let him be where he may, he will tell you he cannot stay a moment, for he must reach Boston that night."

We were now ascending a high hill in Walpole; and as we had a fair view of the heavens, I was rather disposed to jeer the driver for thinking of his surtout, as not a cloud as big as a marble could be discerned.

"Do you look," said he, "in the direction whence the man came; that is the place to look. The storm never meets him; it follows him."

We presently approached another hill; and when at the height, the driver pointed out in an eastern direction a little black speck about as big as a hat. "There," said he, "is the seed-storm. We may possibly reach Polley's before it reaches us, but the wanderer and his child will go to Providence through rain, thunder, and lightning."

And now the horses, as though taught by instinct, hastened with increased speed. The little black cloud came on rolling over the turnpike, and doubled and trebled itself in all directions. The appearance of this cloud attracted the notice of all the passengers, for after it had spread itself to a great bulk it suddenly became more limited in circumference, grew more compact, dark, and consolidated. And now the successive flashes of chain lightning caused the whole cloud to appear like a sort of irregular net-work, and displayed a thousand fantastic images. The driver bespoke my attention to a remarkable configuration in the cloud. He said every flash of lightning near its centre discovered to him, distinctly, the form of a man sitting in an open carriage drawn by a black horse. But in truth I saw no such thing; the man's fancy was doubtless at fault. It is a very common thing for the imagination to paint for the senses, both in the visible and invisible world.

In the mean time the distant thunder gave notice of a shower at hand; and just as we reached Polley's tavern the rain poured down in torrents. It was soon over, the cloud passing in the direction of the turnpike toward Providence. In a few moments after, a respectable-looking man in a chaise stopped at the door. The man and child in the chair having excited some little sympathy among the passengers, the gentleman was asked if he had observed them. He said he had met them; that the man seemed bewildered, and inquired the way to Boston; that he was driving at great speed, as though he expected to outstrip the tempest; that the moment he had passed him, a thunder-clap broke directly over the man's head, and seemed to envelop both man and child, horse and carriage.

"I stopped," said the gentleman, "supposing the lightning had struck him, but the horse only seemed to loom up and increase his speed; and as well as I could judge, he travelled just as fast as the thunder-cloud."

While this man was speaking, a pedler with a cart of tin merchandise came up, all dripping; and on being questioned, he said he had met that man and carriage, within a fortnight, in four different States; that at each time he had inquired the way to Boston; and that a thunder-shower like the present had each time deluged his wagon and his wares, setting his tin pots, etc. afloat, so that he had determined to get a marine insurance for the future. But that which excited his surprise most was the strange conduct of his horse, for long before he could distinguish the man in the chair, his own horse stood still in the road, and flung back his ears. "In short," said the pedler, "I wish never to see that man and horse again; they do not look to me as though they belonged to this world."

This was all I could learn at that time; and the occurrence soon after would have become with me, "like one of those things which had never happened," had I not, as I stood recently on the door-step of Bennett's hotel in Hartford, heard a man say, "There goes Peter Rugg and his child! he looks wet and weary, and farther from Boston than ever." I was satisfied it was the same man I had seen more than three years before; for whoever has once seen Peter Rugg can never after be deceived as to his identity.

"Peter Rugg!" said I; "and who is Peter Rugg?"

"That," said the stranger, "is more than any one can tell exactly. He is a famous traveller, held in light esteem by all innholders, for he never stops to eat, drink, or sleep. I wonder why the government does not employ him to carry the mail."

"Ay," said a by-stander, "that is a thought bright only on one side; how long would it take in that case to send a letter to Boston, for Peter has already, to my knowledge, been more than twenty years travelling to that place."

"But," said I, "does the man never stop anywhere; does he never converse with any one? I saw the same man more than three years since, near Providence, and I heard a strange story about him. Pray, sir, give me some account of this man."

"Sir," said the stranger, "those who know the most respecting that man, say the least. I have heard it asserted that Heaven sometimes sets a mark on a man, either for judgment or a trial. Under which Peter Rugg now labors, I cannot say; therefore I am rather inclined to pity than to judge."

"You speak like a humane man," said I; "and if you have known him so long, I pray you will give me some account of him. Has his appearance much altered in that time?"

"Why, yes. He looks as though he never ate, drank, or slept; and his child looks older than himself, and he looks like time broken off from eternity, and anxious to gain a resting-place."

"And how does his horse look?" said I.

"As for his horse, he looks fatter and gayer, and shows more animation and courage than he did twenty years ago. The last time Rugg spoke to me he inquired how far it was to Boston. I told him just one hundred miles."

"'Why,' said he, 'how can you deceive me so? It is cruel to mislead a traveller. I have lost my way; pray direct me the nearest way to Boston.'

"I repeated, it was one hundred miles.

"'How can you say so?' said he; 'I was told last evening it was but fifty, and I have travelled all night.'

"'But,' said I, 'you are now travelling from Boston. You must turn back.'

"'Alas,' said he, 'it is all turn back! Boston shifts with the wind, and plays all around the compass. One man tells me it is to the east, another to the west; and the guide-posts too, they all point the wrong way.'

"'But will you not stop and rest?' said I; 'you seem wet and weary.'

" ' Yes,' said he, ' it has been foul weather since I left home.'

" ' Stop, then, and refresh yourself.'

" ' I must not stop ; I must reach home to-night, if possible : though I think you must be mistaken in the distance to Boston.'

" He then gave the reins to his horse, which he restrained with difficulty, and disappeared in a moment. A few days afterward I met the man a little this side of Claremont,[1] winding around the hills in Unity, at the rate, I believe, of twelve miles an hour."

" Is Peter Rugg his real name, or has he accidentally gained that name ? "

" I know not, but presume he will not deny his name ; you can ask him, — for see, he has turned his horse, and is passing this way."

In a moment a dark-colored, high-spirited horse approached, and would have passed without stopping, but I had resolved to speak to Peter Rugg, or whoever the man might be. Accordingly I stepped into the street ; and as the horse approached, I made a feint of stopping him. The man immediately reined in his horse. " Sir," said I, " may I be so bold as to inquire if you are not Mr. Rugg ? for I think I have seen you before."

" My name is Peter Rugg," said he. " I have unfortunately lost my way ; I am wet and weary, and will take it kindly of you to direct me to Boston."

" You live in Boston, do you ; and in what street ? "

" In Middle Street."

" When did you leave Boston ? "

" I cannot tell precisely ; it seems a considerable time."

" But how did you and your child become so wet ? It has not rained here to-day."

" It has just rained a heavy shower up the river. But I shall not reach Boston to-night if I tarry. Would you advise me to take the old road or the turnpike ? "

---

[1] In New Hampshire.

"Why, the old road is one hundred and seventeen miles, and the turnpike is ninety-seven."

"How can you say so? You impose on me; it is wrong to trifle with a traveller; you know it is but forty miles from Newburyport to Boston."

"But this is not Newburyport; this is Hartford."

"Do not deceive me, sir. Is not this town Newburyport, and the river that I have been following the Merrimack?"

"No, sir; this is Hartford, and the river the Connecticut."

He wrung his hands and looked incredulous. "Have the rivers, too, changed their courses, as the cities have changed places? But see! the clouds are gathering in the south, and we shall have a rainy night. Ah, that fatal oath!"

He would tarry no longer; his impatient horse leaped off, his hind flanks rising like wings; he seemed to devour all before him, and to scorn all behind.

I had now, as I thought, discovered a clew to the history of Peter Rugg; and I determined, the next time my business called me to Boston, to make a further inquiry. Soon after, I was enabled to collect the following particulars from Mrs. Croft, an aged lady in Middle Street, who has resided in Boston during the last twenty years. Her narration is this:

Just at twilight last summer a person stopped at the door of the late Mrs. Rugg. Mrs. Croft on coming to the door perceived a stranger, with a child by his side, in an old weather-beaten carriage, with a black horse. The stranger asked for Mrs. Rugg, and was informed that Mrs. Rugg had died at a good old age, more than twenty years before that time.

The stranger replied, "How can you deceive me so? Do ask Mrs. Rugg to step to the door."

"Sir, I assure you Mrs. Rugg has not lived here these twenty years; no one lives here but myself, and my name is Betsy Croft."

The stranger paused, looked up and down the street, and

said, " Though the paint is rather faded, this looks like my house."

" Yes," said the child, " that is the stone before the door that I used to sit on to eat my bread and milk."

" But," said the stranger, " it seems to be on the wrong side of the street. Indeed, everything here seems to be misplaced. The streets are all changed, the people are all changed, the town seems changed, and what is strangest of all, Catherine Rugg has deserted her husband and child. Pray," continued the stranger, " has John Foy come home from sea ? He went a long voyage ; he is my kinsman. If I could see him, he could give me some account of Mrs. Rugg."

" Sir," said Mrs. Croft, " I never heard of John Foy. Where did he live ? "

" Just above here, in Orange-tree Lane."

" There is no such place in this neighborhood."

" What do you tell me ! Are the streets gone ? Orange-tree Lane is at the head of Hanover Street, near Pemberton's Hill."

" There is no such lane now."

" Madam, you cannot be serious ! But you doubtless know my brother, William Rugg. He lives in Royal Exchange Lane, near King Street."

" I know of no such lane ; and I am sure there is no such street as King Street in this town."

" No such street as King Street ! Why, woman, you mock me ! You may as well tell me there is no King George. However, madam, you see I am wet and weary, I must find a resting-place. I will go to Hart's tavern, near the market."

" Which market, sir ? for you seem perplexed ; we have several markets."

" You know there is but one market near the town dock."

" Oh, the old market ; but no such person has kept there these twenty years."

Here the stranger seemed disconcerted, and uttered to himself quite audibly: "Strange mistake; how much this looks like the town of Boston! It certainly has a great resemblance to it; but I perceive my mistake now. Some other Mrs. Rugg, some other Middle Street. — Then," said he, "madam, can you direct me to Boston?"

"Why, this is Boston, the city of Boston; I know of no other Boston."

"City of Boston it may be; but it is not the Boston where I live. I recollect now, I came over a bridge instead of a ferry. Pray, what bridge is that I just came over?"

"It is Charles River bridge."

"I perceive my mistake : there is a ferry between Boston and Charlestown; there is no bridge. Ah, I perceive my mistake. If I were in Boston my horse would carry me directly to my own door. But my horse shows by his impatience that he is in a strange place. Absurd, that I should have mistaken this place for the old town of Boston! It is a much finer city than the town of Boston. It has been built long since Boston. I fancy Boston must lie at a distance from this city, as the good woman seems ignorant of it."

At these words his horse began to chafe, and strike the pavement with his forefeet. The stranger seemed a little bewildered, and said, "No home to-night;" and giving the reins to his horse, passed up the street, and I saw no more of him.

It was evident that the generation to which Peter Rugg belonged had passed away.

This was all the account of Peter Rugg I could obtain from Mrs. Croft; but she directed me to an elderly man, Mr. James Felt, who lived near her, and who had kept a record of the principal occurrences for the last fifty years. At my request she sent for him; and after I had related to him the object of my inquiry, Mr. Felt told me he had known Rugg in his youth, and that his disappearance had caused some surprise; but as it sometimes happens that men run away, — sometimes to be rid of others, and sometimes to be rid of themselves, — and Rugg took his child with him, and his own horse and chair, and as it did not appear that any creditors made a stir, the occurrence soon mingled itself in the stream of oblivion; and Rugg and his child, horse, and chair were soon forgotten.

"It is true," said Mr. Felt, "sundry stories grew out of Rugg's affair, whether true or false I cannot tell; but stranger things have happened in my day, without even a newspaper notice."

"Sir," said I, "Peter Rugg is now living. I have lately seen Peter Rugg and his child, horse, and chair; therefore I pray you to relate to me all you know or ever heard of him."

"Why, my friend," said James Felt, "that Peter Rugg is now a living man, I will not deny; but that you have seen Peter Rugg and his child, is impossible, if you mean a small child; for Jenny Rugg, if living, must be at least — let me see — Boston massacre, 1770 — Jenny Rugg was about ten years old. Why, sir, Jenny Rugg, if living, must be more than sixty years of age. That Peter Rugg is living, is highly probable, as he was only ten years older than myself, and I was only eighty last March; and I am as likely to live twenty years longer as any man."

Here I perceived that Mr. Felt was in his dotage, and I despaired of gaining any intelligence from him on which I could depend.

I took my leave of Mrs. Croft, and proceeded to my lodgings at the Marlborough Hotel.

"If Peter Rugg," thought I, "has been travelling since the Boston massacre, there is no reason why he should not travel to the end of time. If the present generation know little of him, the next will know less, and Peter and his child will have no hold on this world."

In the course of the evening, I related my adventure in Middle Street.

"Ha!" said one of the company, smiling, "do you really think you have seen Peter Rugg? I have heard my grandfather speak of him, as though he seriously believed his own story."

"Sir," said I, "pray let us compare your grandfather's story of Mr. Rugg with my own."

"Peter Rugg, sir, — if my grandfather was worthy of credit, — once lived in Middle Street, in this city. He was a man in comfortable circumstances, had a wife and one daughter, and was generally esteemed for his sober life and manners. But unhappily, his temper, at times, was altogether ungovernable, and then his language was terrible. In these fits of passion, if a door stood in his way, he would never do less than kick a panel through. He would sometimes throw his heels over his head, and come down on his feet, uttering oaths in a circle ; and thus in a rage, he was the first who performed a somerset, and did what others have since learned to do for merriment and money. Once Rugg was seen to bite a tenpenny nail in halves. In those days everybody, both men and boys, wore wigs; and Peter, at these moments of violent passion, would become so profane that his wig would rise up from his head. Some said it was on account of his terrible language ; others accounted for it in a more philosophical way, and said it was caused by the expansion of his scalp, as violent passion, we know, will swell the veins and expand the head. While these fits were on him, Rugg had no respect for heaven or earth. Except this infirmity, all agreed that Rugg was a good sort of a man ; for when his fits were over, nobody was so ready to commend a placid temper as Peter.

"One morning, late in autumn, Rugg, in his own chair, with a fine large bay horse, took his daughter and proceeded to Concord. On his return a violent storm overtook him. At dark he stopped in Menotomy, now West Cambridge, at the door of a Mr. Cutter, a friend of his, who urged him to tarry the night. On Rugg's declining to stop, Mr. Cutter urged him vehemently. 'Why, Mr. Rugg,' said Cutter, 'the storm is overwhelming you. The night is exceedingly dark. Your little daughter will perish. You are in an open chair, and the tempest is increasing.' ' *Let the storm increase*,' said Rugg, with a fearful oath, ' *I will see home to-night, in spite of the last tempest, or may I never see home !*' At these words he gave his whip to his high-spirited horse and disappeared in a moment. But Peter Rugg did not reach home that night, nor the next ; nor, when he became a missing man, could he ever be traced beyond Mr. Cutter's, in Menotomy.

"For a long time after, on every dark and stormy night the wife of Peter Rugg would fancy she heard the crack of a whip, and the fleet tread of a horse, and the rattling of a carriage passing her door. The neighbors, too, heard the same noises, and some said they knew it was Rugg's horse ; the tread on the pavement was perfectly familiar to them. This occurred so repeatedly that at length the neighbors watched with lanterns, and saw the real Peter Rugg, with his own horse and chair and the child sitting beside him, pass directly before his own door, his head turned toward his house, and himself making every effort to stop his horse, but in vain.

"The next day the friends of Mrs. Rugg exerted themselves to find her husband and child. They inquired at every public house and stable in town ; but it did not appear that Rugg made any stay in Boston. No one, after Rugg had passed his own door, could give any account of him, though it was asserted by some that the clatter of Rugg's horse and carriage over the pavements shook the houses on both sides of the streets. And this is credible, if indeed Rugg's horse and carriage did pass on that night ; for at this day, in many of the streets, a loaded truck or team in passing will shake the houses like an earthquake. However, Rugg's neighbors never afterward watched. Some of them treated it all as a delusion, and thought no more of it. Others of a different opinion shook their heads and said nothing.

"Thus Rugg and his child, horse, and chair were soon

forgotten; and probably many in the neighborhood never heard a word on the subject.

"There was indeed a rumor that Rugg was seen afterward in Connecticut, between Suffield and Hartford, passing through the country at headlong speed. This gave occasion to Rugg's friends to make further inquiry; but the more they inquired, the more they were baffled. If they heard of Rugg one day in Connecticut, the next they heard of him winding round the hills in New Hampshire; and soon after a man in a chair, with a small child, exactly answering the description of Peter Rugg, would be seen in Rhode Island inquiring the way to Boston.

" But that which chiefly gave a color of mystery to the story of Peter Rugg was the affair at Charleston bridge. The toll-gatherer asserted that sometimes, on the darkest and most stormy nights, when no object could be discerned, about the time Rugg was missing, a horse and wheel-carriage, with a noise equal to a troop, would at midnight, in utter contempt of the rates of toll, pass over the bridge. This occurred so frequently that the toll-gatherer resolved to attempt a discovery. Soon after, at the usual time, apparently the same horse and carriage approached the bridge from Charlestown square. The toll-gatherer, prepared, took his stand as near the middle of the bridge as he dared, with a large three-legged stool in his hand; as the appearance passed, he threw the stool at the horse, but heard nothing except the noise of the stool skipping across the bridge. The toll-gatherer on the next day asserted that the stool went directly through the body of the horse, and he persisted in that belief ever after. Whether Rugg, or whoever the person was, ever passed the bridge again, the toll-gatherer would never tell; and when questioned, seemed anxious to waive the subject. And thus Peter Rugg and his child, horse, and carriage, remain a mystery to this day."

This, sir, is all that I could learn of Peter Rugg in Boston.

FURTHER ACCOUNT OF PETER RUGG

By JONATHAN DUNWELL

IN the autumn of 1825 I attended the races at Richmond in Virginia. As two new horses of great promise were run, the race-ground was never better attended, nor was expectation ever more deeply excited. The partisans of Dart and Lightning, the two race-horses, were equally anxious and equally dubious of the result. To an indifferent spectator, it was impossible to perceive any difference. They were equally beautiful to behold, alike in color and height, and as they stood side by side they measured from heel to forefeet within half an inch of each other. The eyes of each were full, prominent, and resolute; and when at times they regarded each other, they assumed a lofty demeanor, seemed to shorten their necks, project their eyes, and rest their bodies equally on their four hoofs. They certainly showed signs of intelligence, and displayed a courtesy to each other unusual even with statesmen.

It was now nearly twelve o'clock, the hour of expectation, doubt, and anxiety. The riders mounted their horses; and so trim, light, and airy they sat on the animals as to seem a part of them. The spectators, many deep in a solid column, had taken their places, and as many thousand breathing statues were there as spectators. All eyes were turned to Dart and Lightning and their two fairy riders. There was nothing to disturb this calm except a busy woodpecker on a neighboring tree. The signal was given, and Dart and Lightning answered it with ready intelligence. At first they proceed at a slow trot, then they quicken to a canter, and then a gallop; presently they sweep the plain. Both horses lay themselves flat on the ground, their riders bending forward and resting their chins between their horses' ears. Had not the ground been perfectly level, had there been any undulation, the least rise and fall, the spectator would now and then have lost sight of both horses and riders.

While these horses, side by side, thus appeared, flying without wings, flat as a hare, and neither gaining on the other, all eyes were diverted to a new spectacle. Directly in the rear of Dart and Lightning, a majestic black horse of unusual size, drawing an old weather-beaten chair, strode over the plain; and although he appeared to make no effort, for he maintained a steady trot, before Dart and Lightning approached the goal the black horse and chair had overtaken the racers, who, on perceiving this new competitor pass them, threw back their ears, and suddenly stopped in their course. Thus neither Dart nor Lightning carried away the purse.

The spectators now were exceedingly curious to learn whence came the black horse and chair. With many it was the opinion that nobody was in the vehicle. Indeed, this began to be the prevalent opinion; for those at a short distance, so fleet was the black horse, could not easily discern who, if anybody, was in the carriage. But both the riders, very near to whom the black horse passed, agreed in this particular, — that a sad-looking man and a little girl were in the chair. When they stated this I was satisfied that the man was Peter Rugg. But what caused no little surprise, John Spring, one of the riders (he who rode Lightning) asserted that no earthly horse without breaking his trot could, in a carriage, outstrip his race-horse; and he persisted, with some passion, that it was not a horse, — or, he was sure it was not a horse, but a large black ox. "What a great black ox can do," said John, "I cannot pretend to say; but no race-horse, not even flying Childers, could out-trot Lightning in a fair race."

This opinion of John Spring excited no little merriment, for it was obvious to every one that it was a powerful black horse that interrupted the race; but John Spring, jealous of Lightning's reputation as a horse, would rather have it thought that any other beast, even an ox, had been the victor. However, the "horse-laugh" at John Spring's expense was soon suppressed; for as soon as Dart and Lightning began to breathe more freely, it was observed that both of them walked deliberately to the track of the raceground, and putting their heads to the earth, suddenly raised them again and began to snort. They repeated this till John Spring said, — "These horses have discovered something strange; they suspect foul play. Let me go and talk with Lightning."

He went up to Lightning and took hold of his mane; and Lightning put his nose toward the ground and smelt of the earth without touching it, then reared his head very high, and snorted so loudly that the sound echoed from the next hill. Dart did the same. John Spring stooped down to examine the spot where Lightning had smelled. In a moment he raised himself up, and the countenance of the man was changed. His strength failed him, and he sidled against Lightning.

At length John Spring recovered from his stupor and exclaimed, "It was an ox! I told you it was an ox. No real horse ever yet beat Lightning."

And now, on a close inspection of the black horse's tracks in the path, it was evident to every one that the forefeet of the black horse were cloven. Notwithstanding these appearances, to me it was evident that the strange horse was in reality a horse. Yet when the people left the raceground, I presume one half of all those present would have testified that a large black ox had distanced two of the fleetest coursers that ever trod the Virginia turf. So uncertain are all things called historical facts.

While I was proceeding to my lodgings, pondering on the events of the day, a stranger rode up to me, and accosted me thus, — "I think your name is Dunwell, sir."

"Yes, sir," I replied.

"Did I not see you a year or two since in Boston, at the Marlborough Hotel?"

"Very likely, sir, for I was there."

"And you heard a story about one Peter Rugg?"

"I recollect it all," said I.

"The account you heard in Boston must be true, for here he was to-day. The man has found his way to Virginia, and for aught that appears, has been to Cape Horn. I have seen him before to-day, but never saw him travel with such fearful velocity. Pray, sir, where does Peter Rugg spend his winters, for I have seen him only in summer, and always in foul weather, except this time?"

I replied, "No one knows where Peter Rugg spends his winters; where or when he eats, drinks, sleeps, or lodges. He seems to have an indistinct idea of day and night, time and space, storm and sunshine. His only object is Boston. It appears to me that Rugg's horse has some control of the chair; and that Rugg himself is, in some sort, under the control of his horse."

I then inquired of the stranger where he first saw the man and horse.

"Why, sir," said he, "in the summer of 1824, I travelled to the North for my health; and soon after I saw you at the Marlborough Hotel I returned homeward to Virginia, and, if my memory is correct, I saw this man and horse in every State between here and Massachusetts. Sometimes he would meet me, but oftener overtake me. He never spoke but once, and that once was in Delaware. On his approach he checked his horse with some difficulty. A more beautiful horse I never saw; his hide was as fair and rotund and glossy as the skin of a Congo beauty. When Rugg's horse approached mine he reined in his neck, bent his ears forward until they met, and looked my horse full in the face. My horse immediately withered into half a horse, his hide curling up like a piece of burnt leather; spell-bound, he was fixed to the earth as though a nail had been driven through each hoof.

"'Sir,' said Rugg, 'perhaps you are travelling to Boston; and if so, I should be happy to accompany you, for I have lost my way, and I must reach home to-night. See how sleepy this little girl looks ; poor thing, she is a picture of patience.'

"'Sir,' said I, 'it is impossible for you to reach home to-night, for you are in Concord, in the county of Sussex, in the State of Delaware.'

"'What do you mean,' said he, 'by State of Delaware? If I were in Concord, that is only twenty miles from Boston, and my horse Lightfoot could carry me to Charlestown ferry in less than two hours. You mistake, sir ; you are a stranger here ; this town is nothing like Concord. I am well acquainted with Concord. I went to Concord when I left Boston.'

"But,' said I, 'you are in Concord, in the State of Delaware.'

"'What do you mean by State?' said Rugg.

"'Why, one of the United States.'

"'States!' said he, in a low voice ; 'the man is a wag, and would persuade me I am in Holland.' Then, raising his voice, he said, 'You seem, sir, to be a gentleman, and I entreat you to mislead me not : tell me, quickly, for pity's sake, the right road to Boston, for you see my horse will swallow his bits ; he has eaten nothing since I left Concord.'

"'Sir,' said I, 'this town is Concord, — Concord in Delaware, not Concord in Massachusetts ; and you are now five hundred miles from Boston.'

"Rugg looked at me for a moment, more in sorrow than resentment, and then repeated, 'Five hundred miles ! Unhappy man, who would have thought him deranged ; but nothing in this world is so deceitful as appearances. Five hundred miles ! This beats Connecticut River.'

"What he meant by Connecticut River, I know not ; his horse broke away, and Rugg disappeared in a moment."

I explained to the stranger the meaning of Rugg's expression, "Connecticut River," and the incident respecting him that occurred at Hartford, as I stood on the doorstone of Mr. Bennett's excellent hotel. We both agreed that the man we had seen that day was the true Peter Rugg.

Soon after, I saw Rugg again, at the toll-gate on the turnpike between Alexandria and Middleburgh. While I was paying the toll, I observed to the toll-gatherer that the drought was more severe in his vicinity than farther south.

" Yes," said he, " the drought is excessive ; but if I had not heard yesterday, by a traveller, that the man with the black horse was seen in Kentucky a day or two since, I should be sure of a shower in a few minutes."

I looked all around the horizon, and could not discern a cloud that could hold a pint of water.

" Look, sir," said the toll-gatherer, " you perceive to the eastward, just above that hill, a small black cloud not bigger than a blackberry, and while I am speaking it is doubling and trebling itself, and rolling up the turnpike steadily, as if its sole design was to deluge some object."

" True," said I, " I do perceive it ; but what connection is there between a thunder-cloud and a man and horse? "

" More than you imagine, or I can tell you ; but stop a moment, sir, I may need your assistance. I know that cloud ; I have seen it several times before, and can testify to its identity. You will soon see a man and black horse under it."

While he was speaking, true enough, we began to hear the distant thunder, and soon the chain-lightning performed all the figures of a country-dance. About a mile distant we saw the man and black horse under the cloud ; but before he arrived at the toll-gate, the thunder-cloud had spent itself, and not even a sprinkle fell near us.

As the man, whom I instantly knew to be Rugg, attempted to pass, the toll-gatherer swung the gate across the road, seized Rugg's horse by the reins, and demanded two dollars.

Feeling some little regard for Rugg, I interfered, and began to question the toll-gatherer, and requested him not to be wroth with the man. The toll-gatherer replied that he had just cause, for the man had run his toll ten times, and moreover that the horse had discharged a cannon-ball at him, to the great danger of his life ; that the man had always before approached so rapidly that he was too quick for the rusty hinges of the toll-gate ; " but now I will have full satisfaction."

Rugg looked wistfully at me, and said, " I entreat you, sir, to delay me not ; I have found at length the direct road to Boston, and shall not reach home before night if you detain me. You see I am dripping wet, and ought to change my clothes."

The toll-gatherer then demanded why he had run his toll so many times.

"Toll ! Why," said Rugg, " do you demand toll ? There is no toll to pay on the king's highway."

" King's highway ! Do you not perceive this is a turnpike ? "

" Turnpike ! there are no turnpikes in Massachusetts."

" That may be, but we have several in Virginia."

" Virginia ! Do you pretend I am in Virginia ? "

Rugg then, appealing to me, asked how far it was to Boston.

Said I, " Mr. Rugg, I perceive you are bewildered, and am sorry to see you so far from home ; you are, indeed, in Virginia."

" You know me, then, sir, it seems ; and you say I am in Virginia. Give me leave to tell you, sir, you are the most impudent man alive ; for I was never forty miles from Boston, and I never saw a Virginian in my life. This beats Delaware ! "

" Your toll, sir, your toll ! "

" I will not pay you a penny," said Rugg ; " you are both of you highway robbers. There are no turnpikes in this country. Take toll on the king's highway ! Robbers take toll on the king's highway ! " Then in a low tone, he said, " Here is evidently a conspiracy against me ; alas, I shall never see Boston ! The highways refuse me a passage, the rivers change their courses, and there is no faith in the compass."

But Rugg's horse had no idea of stopping more than one minute ; for in the midst of this altercation, the horse, whose nose was resting on the upper bar of the turnpike-gate, seized it between his teeth, lifted it gently off its staples, and trotted off with it. The toll-gatherer, confounded, strained his eyes after his gate.

"Let him go," said I, "the horse will soon drop your gate, and you will get it again."

I then questioned the toll-gatherer respecting his knowledge of this man ; and he related the following particulars :—

"The first time," said he, "that man ever passed this toll-gate was in the year 1806, at the moment of the great eclipse. I thought the horse was frightened at the sudden darkness, and concluded he had run away with the man. But within a few days after, the same man and horse repassed with equal speed, without the least respect to the toll-gate or to me, except by a vacant stare. Some few years afterward, during the late war, I saw the same man approaching again, and I resolved to check his career. Accordingly I stepped into the middle of the road, and stretched wide both my arms, and cried, ' Stop, sir, on your peril ! ' At this the man said, ' Now, Lightfoot, confound the robber ! ' at the same time he gave the whip liberally to the flank of his horse, which bounded off with such force that it appeared to me two such horses, give them a place to stand, would overcome any check man could devise. An ammunition wagon which had just passed on to Baltimore had dropped an eighteen pounder in the road ; this unlucky ball lay in the way of the horse's heels, and the beast, with the sagacity of a demon, clinched it with one of his heels and hurled it behind him. I feel dizzy in relating the fact, but so nearly did the ball pass my head, that the wind thereof blew off my hat ; and the ball

6

embedded itself in that gate-post, as you may see if you
will cast your eye on the post. I have permitted it to remain there in memory of the occurrence, — as the people
of Boston, I am told, preserve the eighteen-pounder which
is now to be seen half imbedded in Brattle Street church."

I then took leave of the toll-gatherer, and promised him
if I saw or heard of his gate I would send him notice.

A strong inclination had possessed me to arrest Rugg
and search his pockets, thinking great discoveries might be
made in the examination; but what I saw and heard that
day convinced me that no human force could detain Peter
Rugg against his consent. I therefore determined if I
ever saw Rugg again to treat him in the gentlest manner.

In pursuing my way to New York, I entered on the
turnpike in Trenton; and when I arrived at New Bruns-
wick, I perceived the road was newly macadamized. The
small stones had just been laid thereon. As I passed this
piece of road, I observed that, at regular distances of about
eight feet, the stones were entirely displaced from spots
as large as the circumference of a half-bushel measure.
This singular appearance induced me to inquire the cause
of it at the turnpike-gate.

" Sir," said the toll-gatherer, " I wonder not at the question, but I am unable to give you a satisfactory answer.
Indeed, sir, I believe I am bewitched, and that the turnpike is under a spell of enchantment; for what appeared
to me last night cannot be a real transaction, otherwise a
turnpike-gate is a useless thing."

" I do not believe in witchcraft or enchantment," said I;
" and if you will relate circumstantially what happened last
night, I will endeavor to account for it by natural means."

" You may recollect the night was uncommonly dark.
Well, sir, just after I had closed the gate for the night,
down the turnpike, as far as my eye could reach, I beheld
what at first appeared to be two armies engaged. The
report of the musketry, and the flashes of their firelocks,
were incessant and continuous. As this strange spectacle

approached me with the fury of a tornado, the noise increased; and the appearance rolled on in one compact body over the surface of the ground. The most splendid fireworks rose out of the earth and encircled this moving spectacle. The divers tints of the rainbow, the most brilliant dyes that the sun lays in the lap of spring, added to the whole family of gems, could not display a more beautiful, radiant, and dazzling spectacle than accompanied the black horse. You would have thought all the stars of heaven had met in merriment on the turnpike. In the midst of this luminous configuration sat a man, distinctly to be seen, in a miserable-looking chair, drawn by a black horse. The turnpike-gate ought, by the laws of Nature and the laws of the State, to have made a wreck of the whole, and have dissolved the enchantment; but no, the horse without an effort passed over the gate, and drew the man and chair horizontally after him without touching the bar. This was what I call enchantment. What think you, sir?"

"My friend," said I, "you have grossly magnified a natural occurrence. The man was Peter Rugg, on his way to Boston. It is true, his horse travelled with unequalled speed, but as he reared high his forefeet, he could not help displacing the thousand small stones on which he trod, which flying in all directions struck one another, and resounded and scintillated. The top bar of your gate is not more than two feet from the ground, and Rugg's horse at every vault could easily lift the carriage over that gate."

This satisfied Mr. McDoubt, and I was pleased at that occurrence; for otherwise Mr. McDoubt, who is a worthy man, late from the Highlands, might have added to his calendar of superstitions. Having thus disenchanted the macadamized road and the turnpike-gate, and also Mr. McDoubt, I pursued my journey homeward to New York.

Little did I expect to see or hear anything further of Mr. Rugg, for he was now more than twelve hours in advance

of me. I could hear nothing of him on my way to Eliza-
bethtown, and therefore concluded that during the past
night he had turned off from the turnpike and pursued a
westerly direction; but just before I arrived at Powles's
Hook, I observed a considerable collection of passengers in
the ferry-boat, all standing motionless, and steadily looking
at the same object. One of the ferry-men, Mr. Hardy, who
knew me well, observing my approach delayed a minute, in
order to afford me a passage, and coming up, said, "Mr.
Dunwell, we have a curiosity on board that would puzzle
Dr. Mitchell."

"Some strange fish, I suppose, has found its way into
the Hudson."

"No," said he, "it is a man who looks as if he had lain
hidden in the ark, and had just now ventured out. He has
a little girl with him, the counterpart of himself, and the
finest horse you ever saw, harnessed to the queerest-looking
carriage that ever was made."

"Ah, Mr. Hardy," said I, "you have, indeed, hooked a
prize; no one before you could ever detain Peter Rugg
long enough to examine him."

"Do you know the man?" said Mr. Hardy.

"No, nobody knows him, but everybody has seen him.
Detain him as long as possible; delay the boat under any
pretence, cut the gear of the horse, do anything to detain
him."

As I entered the ferry-boat, I was struck at the spectacle
before me. There, indeed, sat Peter Rugg and Jenny Rugg
in the chair, and there stood the black horse, all as quiet
as lambs, surrounded by more than fifty men and women,
who seemed to have lost all their senses but one. Not a
motion, not a breath, not a rustle. They were all eye.
Rugg appeared to them to be a man not of this world;
and they appeared to Rugg a strange generation of men.
Rugg spoke not, and they spoke not; nor was I disposed
to disturb the calm, satisfied to reconnoitre Rugg in a state
of rest. Presently, Rugg observed in a low voice, addressed

to nobody, "A new contrivance, horses instead of oars;
Boston folks are full of notions."

It was plain that Rugg was of Dutch extraction. He had
on three pairs of small clothes, called in former days of
simplicity breeches, not much the worse for wear; but
time had proved the fabric, and shrunk one more than
another, so that they showed at the knees their different
qualities and colors. His several waistcoats, the flaps of
which rested on his knees, made him appear rather corpulent. His capacious drab coat would supply the stuff for
half a dozen modern ones; the sleeves were like meal bags,
in the cuffs of which you might nurse a child to sleep. His
hat, probably once black, now of a tan color, was neither
round nor crooked, but in shape much like the one President Monroe wore on his late tour. This dress gave the
rotund face of Rugg an antiquated dignity. The man,
though deeply sunburned, did not appear to be more than
thirty years of age. He had lost his sad and anxious look,
was quite composed, and seemed happy. The chair in
which Rugg sat was very capacious, evidently made for
service, and calculated to last for ages; the timber would
supply material for three modern carriages. This chair,
like a Nantucket coach, would answer for everything that
ever went on wheels. The horse, too, was an object of
curiosity; his majestic height, his natural mane and tail,
gave him a commanding appearance, and his large open nostrils indicated inexhaustible wind. It was apparent that the
hoofs of his forefeet had been split, probably on some newly
macadamized road, and were now growing together again;
so that John Spring was not altogether in the wrong.

How long this dumb scene would otherwise have continued I cannot tell. Rugg discovered no sign of impatience.
But Rugg's horse having been quiet more than five minutes,
had no idea of standing idle; he began to whinny, and in
a moment after, with his right forefoot he started a plank.
Said Rugg, "My horse is impatient, he sees the North
End. You must be quick, or he will be ungovernable."

At these words, the horse raised his left forefoot; and when he laid it down every inch of the ferry-boat trembled. Two men immediately seized Rugg's horse by the nostrils. The horse nodded, and both of them were in the Hudson. While we were fishing up the men, the horse was perfectly quiet.

"Fret not the horse," said Rugg, "and he will do no harm. He is only anxious, like myself, to arrive at yonder beautiful shore; he sees the North Church, and smells his own stable."

"Sir," said I to Rugg, practising a little deception, "pray tell me, for I am a stranger here, what river is this, and what city is that opposite, for you seem to be an inhabitant of it?"

"This river, sir, is called Mystic River, and this is Winnisimmet ferry, — we have retained the Indian names, — and that town is Boston. You must, indeed, be a stranger in these parts, not to know that yonder is Boston, the capital of the New England provinces."

"Pray, sir, how long have you been absent from Boston?"

"Why, that I cannot exactly tell. I lately went with this little girl of mine to Concord, to see my friends; and I am ashamed to tell you, in returning lost the way, and have been travelling ever since. No one would direct me right. It is cruel to mislead a traveller. My horse, Lightfoot, has boxed the compass; and it seems to me he has boxed it back again. But, sir, you perceive my horse is uneasy; Lightfoot, as yet, has only given a hint and a nod. I cannot be answerable for his heels."

At these words Lightfoot reared his long tail, and snapped it as you would a whiplash. The Hudson reverberated with the sound. Instantly the six horses began to move the boat. The Hudson was a sea of glass, smooth as oil, not a ripple. The horses, from a smart trot, soon pressed into a gallop; water now ran over the gunwale; the ferry-boat was soon buried in an ocean of foam, and the noise of the spray was like the roaring of many waters. When we arrived at New York, you might see the beautiful white wake of the ferry-boat across the Hudson.

Though Rugg refused to pay toll at turnpikes, when Mr. Hardy reached his hand for the ferriage, Rugg readily put his hand into one of his many pockets, took out a piece of silver, and handed it to Hardy.

"What is this?" said Mr. Hardy.

"It is thirty shillings," said Rugg.

"It might once have been thirty shillings, old tenor," said Mr. Hardy, "but it is not at present."

"The money is good English coin," said Rugg; "my grandfather brought a bag of them from England, and had them hot from the mint."

Hearing this, I approached near to Rugg, and asked permission to see the coin. It was a half-crown, coined by the English Parliament, dated in the year 1649. On one side, "The Commonwealth of England," and St. George's cross encircled with a wreath of laurel. On the other, "God with us," and a harp and St. George's cross united. I winked at Mr. Hardy, and pronounced it good current money; and said loudly, "I will not permit the gentleman to be imposed on, for I will exchange the money myself."

On this, Rugg spoke, — "Please to give me your name, sir."

"My name is Dunwell, sir," I replied.

"Mr. Dunwell," said Rugg, "you are the only honest man I have seen since I left Boston. As you are a stranger here, my house is your home; Dame Rugg will be happy to see her husband's friend. Step into my chair, sir, there is room enough; move a little, Jenny, for the gentleman, and we will be in Middle Street in a minute."

Accordingly I took a seat by Peter Rugg.

"Were you never in Boston before?" said Rugg.

"No," said I.

"Well, you will now see the queen of New England, a town second only to Philadelphia, in all North America."

"You forget New York," said I.

"Poh, New York is nothing; though I never was there. I am told you might put all New York in our mill-pond. No, sir, New York, I assure you, is but a sorry affair; no more to be compared with Boston than a wigwam with a palace."

As Rugg's horse turned into Pearl Street, I looked Rugg as fully in the face as good manners would allow, and said, "Sir, if this is Boston, I acknowledge New York is not worthy to be one of its suburbs."

Before we had proceeded far in Pearl Street, Rugg's countenance changed: his nerves began to twitch; his eyes trembled in their sockets; he was evidently bewildered. "What is the matter, Mr. Rugg; you seem disturbed."

"This surpasses all human comprehension; if you know, sir, where we are, I beseech you to tell me."

"If this place," I replied, "is not Boston, it must be New York."

"No, sir, it is not Boston; nor can it be New York. How could I be in New York, which is nearly two hundred miles from Boston?"

By this time we had passed into Broadway, and then Rugg, in truth, discovered a chaotic mind. "There is no such place as this in North America. This is all the effect of enchantment; this is a grand delusion, nothing real. Here is seemingly a great city, magnificent houses, shops and goods, men and women innumerable, and as busy as in real life, all sprung up in one night from the wilderness; or what is more probable, some tremendous convulsion of Nature has thrown London or Amsterdam on the shores of New England. Or, possibly, I may be dreaming, though the night seems rather long; but before now I have sailed in one night to Amsterdam, bought goods of Vandogger, and returned to Boston before morning."

At this moment a hue-and-cry was heard, "Stop the madmen, they will endanger the lives of thousands!" In vain hundreds attempted to stop Rugg's horse. Lightfoot interfered with nothing; his course was straight as a shooting-star. But on my part, fearful that before night I should find myself behind the Alleghanies, I addressed Mr. Rugg in a tone of entreaty, and requested him to restrain the horse and permit me to alight.

"My friend," said he, "we shall be in Boston before dark, and Dame Rugg will be most exceeding glad to see us."

"Mr. Rugg," said I, "you must excuse me. Pray look to the west; see that thunder-cloud swelling with rage, as if in pursuit of us."

"Ah!" said Rugg, "it is in vain to attempt to escape. I know that cloud; it is collecting new wrath to spend on my head." Then checking his horse, he permitted me to descend, saying, "Farewell, Mr. Dunwell, I shall be happy to see you in Boston; I live in Middle Street."

It is uncertain in what direction Mr. Rugg pursued his course, after he disappeared in Broadway; but one thing is sufficiently known to everybody, — that in the course of two months after he was seen in New York, he found his way most opportunely to Boston.

It seems the estate of Peter Rugg had recently fallen to the Commonwealth of Massachusetts for want of heirs; and the Legislature had ordered the solicitor-general to advertise and sell it at public auction. Happening to be in Boston at the time, and observing his advertisement, which described a considerable extent of land, I felt a kindly curiosity to see the spot where Rugg once lived. Taking the advertisement in my hand, I wandered a little way down Middle Street, and without asking a question of any one, when I came to a certain spot I said to myself, "This is Rugg's estate; I will proceed no farther. This must be the spot; it is a counterpart of Peter Rugg." The premises, indeed, looked as if they had fulfilled a sad prophecy. Fronting on Middle Street, they extended in the rear to Ann Street, and embraced about half an acre of land. It was not uncommon in former times to have half

an acre for a house-lot; for an acre of land then, in many
parts of Boston, was not more valuable than a foot in some
places at present. The old mansion-house had become
a powder-post, and been blown away. One other building,
uninhabited, stood ominous, courting dilapidation. The
street had been so much raised that the bed-chamber had
descended to the kitchen and was level with the street.
The house seemed conscious of its fate; and as though
tired of standing there, the front was fast retreating from
the rear, and waiting the next south wind to project itself
into the street. If the most wary animals had sought a
place of refuge, here they would have rendezvoused.
Here, under the ridge-pole, the crow would have perched
in security; and in the recesses below, you might have
caught the fox and the weasel asleep. " The hand of
destiny," said I, " has pressed heavy on this spot; still
heavier on the former owners. Strange that so large a lot
of land as this should want an heir! Yet Peter Rugg, at
this day, might pass by his own door-stone, and ask, ' Who
once lived here? ' "

The auctioneer, appointed by the solicitor to sell this
estate, was a man of eloquence, as many of the auctioneers
of Boston are. The occasion seemed to warrant, and his
duty urged, him to make a display. He addressed his
audience as follows, —

" The estate, gentlemen, which we offer you this day,
was once the property of a family now extinct. For that
reason it has escheated to the Commonwealth. Lest any
one of you should be deterred from bidding on so large
an estate as this for fear of a disputed title, I am authorized by the solicitor-general to proclaim that the purchaser
shall have the best of all titles, — a warranty-deed from the
Commonwealth. I state this, gentlemen, because I know
there is an idle rumor in this vicinity, that one Peter
Rugg, the original owner of this estate, is still living.
This rumor, gentlemen, has no foundation, and can have
no foundation in the nature of things. It originated about

two years since, from the incredible story of one Jonathan
Dunwell, of New York. Mrs. Croft, indeed, whose husband I see present, and whose mouth waters for this estate,
has countenanced this fiction. But, gentlemen, was it ever
known that any estate, especially an estate of this value,
lay unclaimed for nearly half a century, if any heir, ever so
remote, were existing? For, gentlemen, all agree that old
Peter Rugg, if living, would be at least one hundred years
of age. It is said that he and his daughter, with a horse
and chaise, were missed more than half a century ago ; and
because they never returned home, forsooth, they must be
now living, and will some day come and claim this great
estate. Such logic, gentlemen, never led to a good invest-
ment. Let not this idle story cross the noble purpose of
consigning these ruins to the genius of architecture. If
such a contingency could check the spirit of enterprise,
farewell to all mercantile excitement. Your surplus money,
instead of refreshing your sleep with the golden dreams of
new sources of speculation, would turn to the nightmare.
A man's money, if not employed, serves only to disturb
his rest. Look, then, to the prospect before you. Here is
half an acre of land, — more than twenty thousand square
feet, — a corner lot, with wonderful capabilities ; none of
your contracted lots of forty feet by fifty, where, in dog-
days, you can breathe only through your scuttles. On
. the contrary, an architect cannot contemplate this lot of
land without rapture, for here is room enough for his
genius to shame the temple of Solomon. Then the prospect — how commanding ! To the east, so near to the
Atlantic that Neptune, freighted with the select treasures
of the whole earth, can knock at your door with his tri-
dent. From the west, the produce of the river of Paradise — the Connecticut — will soon, by the blessings of
steam, railways, and canals pass under your windows ; and
thus, on this spot, Neptune shall marry Ceres, and Pomona
from Roxbury, and Flora from Cambridge, shall dance at
the wedding.

"Gentlemen of science, men of taste, ye of the literary emporium, — for I perceive many of you present, — to you this is holy ground. If the spot on which in times past a hero left only the print of a footstep is now sacred, of what price is the birthplace of one who all the world knows was born in Middle Street, directly opposite to this lot ; and who, if his birthplace were not well known, would now be claimed by more than seven cities. To you, then, the value of these premises must be inestimable. For ere long there will arise in full view of the edifice to be erected here, a monument, the wonder and veneration of the world. A column shall spring to the clouds ; and on that column will be engraven one word which will convey all that is wise in intellect, useful in science, good in morals, prudent in counsel, and benevolent in principle, — a name of one who, when living, was the patron of the poor, the delight of the cottage, and the admiration of kings ; now dead, worth the whole seven wise men of Greece. Need I tell you his name ? He fixed the thunder and guided the lightning.

"Men of the North End ! Need I appeal to your patriotism, in order to enhance the value of this lot ? The earth affords no such scenery as this ; there, around that corner, lived James Otis ; here, Samuel Adams ; there, Joseph Warren ; and around that other corner, Josiah Quincy. Here was the birthplace of Freedom ; here Liberty was born, and nursed, and grew to manhood. Here man was newly created. Here is the nursery of American Independence — I am too modest — here began the emancipation of the world ; a thousand generations hence millions of men will cross the Atlantic just to look at the north end of Boston. Your fathers — what do I say — yourselves, — yes, this moment, I behold several attending this auction who lent a hand to rock the cradle of Independence.

"Men of speculation, — ye who are deaf to everything except the sound of money, — you, I know, will give me both of your ears when I tell you the city of Boston must

have a piece of this estate in order to widen Ann Street.
Do you hear me, — do you all hear me? I say the city
must have a large piece of this land in order to widen Ann
Street. What a chance! The city scorns to take a man's
land for nothing. If it seizes your property, it is generous
beyond the dreams of avarice. The only oppression is, you
are in danger of being smothered under a load of wealth.
Witness the old lady who lately died of a broken heart
when the mayor paid her for a piece of her kitchen-garden.
All the faculty agreed that the sight of the treasure, which
the mayor incautiously paid her in dazzling dollars, warm
from the mint, sped joyfully all the blood of her body into
her heart, and rent it with raptures. Therefore, let him
who purchases this estate fear his good fortune, and not
Peter Rugg. Bid, then, liberally, and do not let the name
of Rugg damp your ardor. How much will you give per
foot for this estate?"

Thus spoke the auctioneer, and gracefully waved his
ivory hammer. From fifty to seventy-five cents per foot
were offered in a few moments. The bidding labored from
seventy-five to ninety. At length one dollar was offered.
The auctioneer seemed satisfied; and looking at his watch,
said he would knock off the estate in five minutes, if no
one offered more.

There was a deep silence during this short period.
While the hammer was suspended, a strange rumbling
noise was heard, which arrested the attention of every one.
Presently, it was like the sound of many shipwrights driving home the bolts of a seventy-four. As the sound approached nearer, some exclaimed, "The buildings in the
new market are falling in promiscuous ruins." Others
said, "No, it is an earthquake; we perceive the earth,
tremble." Others said, "Not so; the sound proceeds from
Hanover Street, and approaches nearer;" and this proved
true, for presently Peter Rugg was in the midst of us.

"Alas, Jenny," said Peter, "I am ruined; our house
has been burned, and here are all our neighbors around

the ruins. Heaven grant your mother, Dame Rugg, is safe."

"They don't look like our neighbors," said Jenny; "but sure enough our house is burned, and nothing left but the door-stone and an old cedar post. Do ask where mother is."

In the mean time more than a thousand men had surrounded Rugg and his horse and chair. Yet neither Rugg personally, nor his horse and carriage, attracted more attention than the auctioneer. The confident look and searching eyes of Rugg carried more conviction to every one present that the estate was his, than could any parchment or paper with signature and seal. The impression which the auctioneer had just made on the company was effaced in a moment; and although the latter words of the auctioneer were, "Fear not Peter Rugg," the moment the auctioneer met the eye of Rugg his occupation was gone; his arm fell down to his hips, his late lively hammer hung heavy in his hand, and the auction was forgotten. The black horse, too, gave his evidence. He knew his journey was ended; for he stretched himself into a horse and a half, rested his head over the cedar post, and whinnied thrice, causing his harness to tremble from headstall to crupper.

Rugg then stood upright in his chair, and asked with some authority, "Who has demolished my house in my absence, for I see no signs of a conflagration? I demand by what accident this has happened, and wherefore this collection of strange people has assembled before my door-step. I thought I knew every man in Boston, but you appear to me a new generation of men. Yet I am familiar with many of the countenances here present, and I can call some of you by name; but in truth I do not recollect that before this moment I ever saw any one of you. There, I am certain, is a Winslow, and here a Sargent; there stands a Sewall, and next to him a Dudley. Will none of you speak to me, — or is this all a delusion? I see, indeed, many forms of men, and no want of eyes, but of motion.

speech, and hearing, you seem to be destitute. Strange! Will no one inform me who has demolished my house?"

Then spake a voice from the crowd, but whence it came I could not discern : "There is nothing strange here but yourself, Mr. Rugg. Time, which destroys and renews all things, has dilapidated your house, and placed us here. You have suffered many years under an illusion. The tempest which you profanely defied at Menotomy has at length subsided ; but you will never see home, for your house and wife and neighbors have all disappeared. Your estate, indeed, remains, but no home. You were cut off from the last age, and you can never be fitted to the present. Your home is gone, and you can never have another home in this world."

JAMES HALL
1793 – 1868

JUDGE HALL gained eminence in the early Middle West at both law and letters. His law studies in Philadelphia, where he was born, were interrupted by the war of 1812. After soldiering along the Niagara he went sailoring with Decatur in the Mediterranean (1815). Then completing his studies at Pittsburgh, he emigrated to Shawneetown, where he became public prosecutor. The office of state treasurer bringing him to Vandalia, he edited there, with Robert Blackwell, the *Illinois Intelligencer*. The *Western Souvenir*, projected, edited, and largely written by him, was published at Cincinnati in 1829; the *Illinois Magazine*, at Vandalia, 1829–1831, then successively at Cincinnati, St. Louis, and again at Cincinnati. Following himself its last remove, Hall continued it there, 1833–1835, as the *Western Monthly Magazine*. *Letters from the West*, which appeared first, 1821–1824, in the *Portfolio*, were printed collectively in London, 1828. His scattered observations were brought into more consistent form : *Sketches of the West*, Philadelphia, 1835; *Notes on the Western States*, Philadelphia, 1838. A collection of his tales, entitled *The Wilderness and the War Path*, appeared in Wiley and Putnam's " Library of American Books," 1846. A uniform edition of his works was published in four volumes, 1853–1856 (a list is given in the American Cyclopedia). Some details of his life not compiled in the cyclopedias were published by Hiram W. Beckwith of Danville, in the fifth of the papers entitled " The Land of the Illini," Chicago *Tribune*, 8th September, 1895.

A writer of tolerable verse and historically valuable descriptive sketches of the frontier, Hall gave much of his leisure also to embodying the history, legend, and local color of the Mississippi valley and the prairies beyond in tales. These are often removed from our present taste by the magniloquence then considered literary ; but they keep the interest of close observation and have their flashes of enduring human import. The local truth of Hall's tales is commended in the *Western Monthly Review* for November, 1828 (volume ii, page 367). Unless the reference be to some of the early *Letters from the West*, the tale printed below may have appeared earlier than the date of its incorporation in the *Western Souvenir*. (See also pages 5, 9 and 12 of the Introduction.)

7

THE FRENCH VILLAGE

[*From the "Western Souvenir," 1829*]

[A long introduction and a concluding summary of the effects
of American development have been omitted as not essential to
the narrative; and certain obvious corrections have been made
in the text.]

. . . .

THIS little colony was composed partly of emigrants
from France, and partly of natives — not Indians,
but *bona fide* French, born in America, but preserving
their language, their manners, and their agility in dancing,
although several generations had passed away since their
first settlement. Here they lived perfectly happy, and well
they might, for they enjoyed to the full extent those three
blessings on which our declaration of independence has
laid so much stress — life, liberty, and the pursuit of happiness. Their lives, it is true, were sometimes threatened
by the miasm aforesaid; but this was soon ascertained
to be an imaginary danger. For whether it was owing to
their temperance or their cheerfulness, their activity or
their being acclimated, or to the want of attraction between
French people and fever, or to all these together, certain
it is that they were blessed with a degree of health enjoyed
only by the most favoured nations. As to liberty, the wild
Indian scarcely possessed more; for although the " grand
monarque " had not more loyal subjects in his wide do-
mains, he had never condescended to honor them with a
single act of oppression, unless the occasional visits of the
Commandant could be so called. He sometimes, when
levying supplies, called upon the village for its portion,

which they always contributed with many protestations of gratitude for the honor conferred on them. And as for happiness, they pursued nothing else. Inverting the usual order, to enjoy life was their daily business, to provide for its wants an occasional labor, sweetened by its brief continuance, and its abundant fruit. A large tract of land around the village was called the " common field." Most of this was allowed to remain in open pasturage; but spots of it were cultivated by any who chose to enclose them; and such enclosure gave a firm title to the individual so long as the occupancy lasted, but no longer. They were *not* an agricultural people, further than the rearing of a few esculents for the table made them such; relying chiefly on their large herds, and on the produce of the chase for support. With the Indians they drove an amicable, though not extensive, trade, for furs and peltry; giving them in exchange, merchandize and trinkets, which they procured from their countrymen at St. Louis. To the latter place they annually carried their skins, bringing back a fresh supply of goods for barter, together with such articles as their own wants required; not forgetting a large portion of finery for the ladies, a plentiful supply of rosin and catgut for the fiddler, and liberal presents for his reverence, the priest.

If this village had no other recommendation, it is endeared to my recollection as the birth-place and residence of Monsieur Baptiste Menou, who was one of its principal inhabitants when I first visited it. He was a bachelor of forty, a tall, lank, hard featured personage, as straight as a ramrod, and almost as thin, with stiff, black hair, sunken cheeks, and a complexion a tinge darker than that of the aborigines. His person was remarkably erect, his countenance grave, his gait deliberate; and when to all this is added an enormous pair of sable whiskers, it will be admitted that Mons. Baptiste was no insignificant person. He had many estimable qualities of mind and person which endeared him to his friends, whose respect was increased by the fact of his having been a soldier and a traveller. In his youth he had followed the French Commandant in two campaigns; and not a comrade in the ranks was better dressed, or cleaner shaved on parade than Baptiste, who fought besides with the characteristic bravery of the nation to which he owed his lineage. He acknowledged, however, that war was not as pleasant a business as is generally supposed. Accustomed to a life totally free from constraint, he complained of being obliged to eat and drink and sleep at the call of the drum. Burnishing a gun, and brushing a coat, and polishing shoes, were duties beneath a gentleman; and after all, Baptiste saw but little honor in tracking the wily Indians through endless swamps. Besides he began to have some scruples as to the propriety of cutting the throats of the respectable gentry whom he had been in the habit of considering as the original and lawful possessors of the soil. He therefore proposed to resign, and was surprised when his commander informed him that he was enlisted for a term, which was not yet expired. He bowed, shrugged his shoulders, and submitted to his fate. He had too much honor to desert, and was too loyal, and too polite, to murmur; but he forthwith made a solemn vow to his patron saint never again to get into a scrape from which he could not retreat whenever it suited his convenience. It was thought that he owed his celibacy in some measure to this vow. He had since accompanied the friendly Indians on several hunting expeditions towards the sources of the Mississippi, and had made a trading voyage to New Orleans. Thus accomplished, he had been more than once called upon by the Commandant to act as a guide, or an interpreter; honors which failed not to elicit suitable marks of respect from his fellow villagers, but which had not inflated the honest heart of Baptiste with any unbecoming pride. On the contrary there was not a more modest man in the village.

In his habits he was the most regular of men. He might be seen at any hour of the day, either sauntering through the village, or seated in front of his own door, smoking a

large pipe formed of a piece of buckhorn, curiously hol-
lowed out, and lined with tin; to which was affixed a short
stem of cane from the neighboring swamp. This pipe was
his inseparable companion; and he evinced towards it a
constancy which would have immortalized his name, had it
been displayed in a better cause. When he walked abroad,
it was to stroll leisurely from door to door, chatting familiarly with his neighbours, patting the white-haired children
on the head, and continuing his lounge, until he had pere-
grinated the village. His gravity was not a "mysterious
carriage of the body to conceal the defects of the mind,"
but a constitutional seriousness of aspect, which covered as
happy and as humane a spirit as ever existed. It was
simply a want of sympathy between his muscles and his
brains; the former utterly refusing to express any agreeable
sensation which might happily titillate the organs of the
latter. Honest Baptiste loved a joke, and uttered many,
and good ones; but his rigid features refused to smile even
at his own wit — a circumstance which I am the more particular in mentioning, as it is not common. He had an
orphan niece whom he had reared from childhood to
maturity, — a lovely girl, of whose beautiful complexion
a poet might say that its roses were cushioned upon
ermine. A sweeter flower bloomed not upon the prairie
than Gabrielle Menou. But as she was never afflicted with
weak nerves, dyspepsia or consumption, and had but one
avowed lover, whom she treated with uniform kindness, and
married with the consent of all parties, she has no claim to
be considered as the heroine of this history. That station
will be awarded by every sensible reader to the important
personage who will be presently introduced.

Across the street, immediately opposite to Mons. Baptiste, lived Mademoiselle Jeannette Duval, a lady who resembled him in some respects, but in many others was his
very antipode. Like him, she was cheerful and happy, and
single; but unlike him, she was brisk, and fat, and plump.
Monsieur was the very pink of gravity; and Mademoiselle

was blessed with a goodly portion thereof, — but hers was specific gravity. Her hair was dark, but her heart was light, and her eyes, though black, were as brilliant a pair of orbs as ever beamed upon the dreary solitude of a bachelor's heart. Jeannette's heels were as light as her heart, and her tongue as active as her heels, so that notwithstanding her rotundity, she was as brisk a Frenchwoman as ever frisked through the mazes of a cotillion. To sum her perfections, her complexion was of a darker olive than the genial sun of France confers on her brunettes, and her skin was as smooth and shining as polished mahogany. Her whole household consisted of herself and a female negro servant. A spacious garden, which surrounded her house, a pony, and a herd of cattle, constituted, in addition to her personal charms, all the wealth of this amiable spinster. But with these she was rich, as they supplied her table without adding much to her cares. Her quadrupeds, according to the example set by their superiors, pursued their own happiness without let or molestation, wherever they could find it — waxing fat or lean, as nature was more or less bountiful in supplying their wants ; and when they strayed too far, or when her agricultural labours became too arduous for the feminine strength of herself and her sable assistant, every monsieur of the village was proud of an occasion to serve Mam'selle. And well they might be, for she was the most noticeable lady in the village, the life of every party, the soul of every frolic. She participated in every festive meeting, and every sad solemnity. Not a neighbor could get up a dance, or get down a dose of bark, without her assistance. If the ball grew dull, Mam'selle bounced on the floor, and infused new spirit into the weary dancers. If the conversation flagged, Jeannette, who occupied a kind of neutral ground between the young and the old, the married and the single, chatted with all, and loosened all tongues. If the girls wished to stroll in the woods, or romp on the prairie, Mam'selle was taken along to keep off the wolves and the rude young men; and in respect to the latter, she faithfully performed her office by attracting them around her own person. Then she was the best neighbour and the kindest soul! She made the richest soup, the clearest coffee, and the neatest pastry in the village ; and in virtue of her confectionery was the prime favourite of all the children. Her hospitality was not confined to her own domicile, but found its way in the shape of sundry savoury viands, to every table in the vicinity. In the sick chamber she was the most assiduous nurse, her step was the lightest, and her voice the most cheerful — so that the priest must inevitably have become jealous of her skill, had it not been for divers plates of rich soup, and bottles of cordial, with which she conciliated his favour, and purchased absolution for these and other offences.

Baptiste and Jeannette were the best of neighbours. He always rose at the dawn, and after lighting his pipe, sallied forth into the open air, where Jeannette usually made her appearance at the same time ; for there was an emulation of long standing between them, which should be the earlier riser.

"Bon jour! Mam'selle Jeannette," was his daily salutation.

"Ah! bon jour! Mons. Menou," was her daily reply.

Then as he gradually approximated the little paling which surrounded her door, he hoped Mam'selle was well this morning, and she reiterated the kind inquiry, but with increased emphasis. Then Monsieur enquired after Mam'selle's pony and Mam'selle's cow, and her garden, and everything appertaining to her, real, personal and mixed ; and she displayed a corresponding interest in all concerns of her kind neighbour. These discussions were mutually beneficial. If Mam'selle's cattle ailed, or if her pony was guilty of an impropriety, who was so able to advise her as Mons. Baptiste? And if his plants drooped, or his poultry died, who so skilful in such matters as Mam'selle Jeanette? Sometimes Baptiste forgot his pipe in the superior interest of the "tête à tête," and must needs step in to light it at Jeannette's fire, which caused the gossips of the village to say that he purposely let his pipe go out, in order that he might himself go in. But he denied this, and, indeed, before offering to enter the dwelling of Mam'selle on such occasions, he usually solicited permission to light his pipe at Jeannette's sparkling eyes, a compliment at which, although it had been repeated some scores of times, Mam'selle never failed to laugh and curtesy, with great good humour and good breeding.

It cannot be supposed that a bachelor of so much discernment could long remain insensible to the galaxy of charms which centered in the person of Mam'selle Jeannette ; and accordingly it was currently reported that a courtship of some ten years standing had been slyly conducted on his part, and as cunningly eluded on hers. It was not averred that Baptiste had actually gone the fearful length of offering his hand ; or that Jeannette had been so imprudent as to discourage, far less reject, a lover of such respectable pretensions. But there was thought to exist a strong hankering on the part of the gentleman, which the lady had managed so skilfully as to keep his mind in a kind of equilibrium, like that of the patient animal between the two bundles of hay — so that he would sometimes halt in the street, midway between the two cottages, and cast furtive glances, first at the one, and then at the other, as if weighing the balance of comfort, while the increased volumes of smoke which issued from his mouth seemed to argue that the fire of his love had other fuel than tobacco, and was literally consuming the inward man. The wary spinster was always on the alert on such occasions, manœuvering like a skilful general according to circumstances. If honest Baptiste, after such a consultation, turned on his heel and retired to his former cautious position at his own door, Mam'selle rallied all her attractions, and by a sudden demonstration drew him again into the field ; but if he marched with an embarrassed air towards her gate, she retired into her castle, or kept shy, and by able evolutions avoided everything which might bring matters to an issue. Thus the courtship continued longer than the siege of Troy, and Jeannette maintained her freedom, while Baptiste with a magnanimity superior to that of Agamemnon, kept his temper, and smoked his pipe in good humour with Jeannette and all the world.

Such was the situation of affairs when I first visited this village, about the time of the cession of Louisiana to the United States. The news of that event had just reached this sequestered spot, and was but indifferently relished. Independently of the national attachment, which all men feel, and the French so justly, the inhabitants of this region had reason to prefer to all others the government which had afforded them protection without constraining their freedom, or subjecting them to any burthens; and with the kindest feelings towards the Americans, they would willingly have dispensed with any nearer connexion than that which already existed. They, however, said little on the subject; and that little was expressive of their cheerful acquiescence in the honor done them by the American people, in buying the country which the Emperor had done them the honor to sell.

It was on the first day of the Carnival that I arrived in the village, about sunset, seeking shelter only for the night, and intending to proceed on my journey in the morning. The notes of the violin and the groups of gaily attired people who thronged the street attracted my attention, and induced me to inquire the occasion of this merriment. My host informed me that a " King Ball " was to be given at the house of a neighbour, adding the agreeable intimation that strangers were always expected to attend without invitation. Young and ardent, I required little persuasion to change my dress, and hasten to the scene of festivity. The moment I entered the room, I felt that I was welcome. Not a single look of surprise, not a glance of more than ordinary attention, denoted me as a stranger, or an unexpected guest. The gentlemen nearest the door,

bowed as they opened a passage for me through the crowd,
in which for a time I mingled, apparently unnoticed. At
length a young gentleman adorned with a large nosegay
approached me, invited me to join the dancers, and after
inquiring my name, introduced me to several females,
among whom I had no difficulty in selecting a graceful
partner. I was passionately fond of dancing, so that
readily imbibing the joyous spirit of those around me, I
advanced rapidly in their estimation. The native ease
and elegance of the females, reared in the wilderness,
and unhackneyed in the forms of society, surprised and
delighted me, as much as the amiable frankness of all
classes. By and by the dancing ceased, and four young
ladies of exquisite beauty, who had appeared during the
evening to assume more consequence than the others,
stood alone on the floor. For a moment their arch glances
wandered over the company who stood silently around,
when one of them advancing to a young gentleman led
him into the circle, and taking a large bouquet from her
own bosom, pinned it upon the left breast of his coat, and
pronounced him "KING!" The gentleman kissed his
fair elector, and led her to a seat. Two others were
selected almost at the same moment. The fourth lady
hesitated for an instant, then advancing to the spot where
I stood, presented me her hand, led me forward and
placed the symbol on my breast, before I could recover
from the surprise into which the incident had thrown
me. I regained my presence of mind, however, in time
to salute my lovely consort; and never did king enjoy
with more delight the first fruits of his elevation; for
the beautiful Gabrielle, with whom I had just danced,
and who had so unexpectedly raised me, as it were, to
the purple, was the freshest and fairest flower in this
assemblage.

The ceremony was soon explained to me. On the first
day of the Carnival, four self-appointed kings, having
selected their queens, give a ball, at their own proper

costs, to the whole village. In the course of that evening
the queens select, in the manner described, the kings for
the ensuing day, who choose their queens, in turn, by presenting the nosegay and the kiss. This is repeated every
evening in the week, the kings for the time being giving
the ball at their own expense, and all the inhabitants
attending without invitation. On the morning after each
ball, the kings of the preceding evening make small presents to their late queens, and their temporary alliance is
dissolved. Thus commenced my acquaintance with Gabrielle Menou, who, if she cost me a few sleepless nights,
amply repaid me in the many happy hours for which I was
indebted to her friendship.

I remained several weeks at this hospitable village. Few
evenings passed without a dance, at which all were assembled, young and old; the mothers vying in agility with
their daughters, and the old men setting examples of gal-
lantry to the young. I accompanied their young men to
the Indian towns, and was hospitably entertained. I followed them to the chase, and witnessed the fall of many
a noble buck. In their light canoes I glided over the
turbid waters of the Mississippi, or through the labyrinths
of the morass, in pursuit of water fowl. I visited the
mounds where the bones of thousands of warriors were
mouldering, overgrown with prairie violets and thousands
of nameless flowers. I saw the moccasin snake basking
in the sun, the elk feeding on the prairie ; and returned
to mingle in the amusements of a circle, where, if there
was not Parisian elegance, there was more than Parisian
cordiality.

Several years passed away before I again visited this
country. The jurisdiction of the American government
was now extended over this immense region, and its beneficial effects were beginning to be widely disseminated.
The roads were crowded with the teams, and herds, and
families of emigrants, hastening to the land of promise.
Steamboats navigated every stream, the axe was heard in

every forest, and the plough broke the sod whose verdure had covered the prairie for ages.

It was sunset when I reached the margin of the prairie on which the village is situated. My horse, wearied with a long day's travel, sprang forward with new vigour, when his hoof struck the smooth, firm road which led across the plain. It was a narrow path, winding among the tall grass, now tinged with the mellow hues of autumn. I gazed with delight over the beautiful surface. The mounds, and the solitary trees, were there, just as I had left them ; and they were familiar to my eye as the objects of yesterday. It was eight miles across the prairie, and I had not passed half the distance when night set in. I strained my eyes to catch a glimpse of the village ; but two large mounds and a clump of trees, which intervened, defeated my purpose. I thought of Gabrielle, and Jeannette, and Baptiste, and the priest — the fiddles, dances, and French ponies; and fancied every minute an hour, and every foot a mile, which separated me from scenes and persons so deeply impressed on my imagination.

At length I passed the mounds, and beheld the lights twinkling in the village, now about two miles off, like a brilliant constellation in the horizon. The lights seemed very numerous — I thought they moved ; and at last discovered that they were rapidly passing about. "What can be going on in the village?" thought I — then a strain of music met my ear — "they are going to dance," said I, striking my spurs into my jaded nag, "and I shall see all my friends together." But as I drew near, a volume of sounds burst upon me such as defied all conjecture. Fiddles, flutes and tambourines, drums, cow-horns, tin trumpets, and kettles mingled their discordant notes with a strange accompaniment of laughter, shouts and singing. This singular concert proceeded from a mob of men and boys, who paraded through the streets, preceded by one who blew an immense tin horn, and ever and anon shouted, "Cha-ri-va-ry ! Charivary !" to which the mob responded "Charivary !" I now recollected having heard of a custom which prevails among the American French of serenading at the marriage of a widow or widower, with such a concert as I now witnessed ; and I rode towards the crowd, who had halted before a well known door, to ascertain who were the happy parties.

"Charivary!" shouted the leader.

"Pour qui?" said another voice.

"Pour Mons. Baptiste Menou. Il s'est marié!"

"Avec qui?"

"Avec Mam'selle Jeannette Duval — Charivary!"

"Charivary!" shouted the whole company, and a torrent of music poured from the full band — tin kettles, cow-horns and all.

The door of the little cabin, whose hospitable threshold I had so often crossed, now opened, and Baptiste made his appearance, — the identical, lank, sallow, erect personage with whom I had parted several years before, with the same pipe in his mouth. His visage was as long and as melancholy as ever, except that there was a slight tinge of triumph in its expression, and a bashful casting down of the eye, reminding one of a conqueror, proud but modest in his glory. He gazed with an embarrassed air at the serenaders, bowed repeatedly, as if conscious that he was the hero of the night, and then exclaimed,

"For what make you this charivary?"

"Charivary!" shouted the mob; and the tin trumpets gave an exquisite flourish.

"Gentlemen!" expostulated the bridegroom, "for why you make this charivary for me? I have never been marry before — and Mam'selle Jeannette has never been marry before!"

Roll went the drum! — cow-horns, kettles, tin trumpets and fiddles poured forth volumes of sound, and the mob shouted in unison.

"Gentlemen! pardonnez moi —" supplicated the distressed Baptiste. "If I understan dis custom, which have

long prevail vid us, it is vat I say — ven a gentilman, who
has been marry before, shall marry de second time — or
ven a lady have de misfortune to lose her husban, and be
so happy to marry some odder gentilman, den we make
de charivary — but 't is not so wid Mam'selle Duval and
me. Upon my honor we have never been marry before dis
time !"

"Why, Baptiste," said one, "you certainly have been
married and have a daughter grown."

"Oh, excuse me sir ! Madame Ste. Marie is my niece.
I have never been so happy to be marry, until Mam'selle
Duval have do me dis honneur."

"Well, well ! it 's all one. If you have not been married, you ought to have been, long ago — and might have
been, if you had said the word."

"Ah, gentilmen, you mistake."

"No, no ! there 's no mistake about it. Mam'selle
Jeanette would have had you ten years ago, if you had
asked her."

"You flatter-too much," said Baptiste, shrugging his
shoulders ; and finding that there was no means of avoid-
ing the charivary, he with great good humour accepted
the serenade, and according to custom invited the whole
party into his house.

I retired to my former quarters, at the house of an old
settler — a little shrivelled, facetious Frenchman, whom
I found in his red flannel nightcap, smoking his pipe,
and seated like Jupiter in the midst of clouds of his own
creating.

"Merry doings in the village !" said I, after we had
shaken hands.

"Eh, bien ! Mons. Baptiste is marry to Mam'selle
Jeannette."

"I see the boys are making merry on the occasion."

"Ah Sacré ! de dem boy ! they have play hell to-
night."

"Indeed ! how so ? "

"For make dis charivary — dat is how so, my friend. Dis come for have d' Americain government to rule de countrie. Parbleu! they make charivary for de old maid, and de old bachelor!"

.   .   .   .

ALBERT PIKE

1809 – 1891

ALBERT PIKE was a pioneer and a free lance. From school-teaching in old Newburyport he broke away in 1831 to the new Southwest. Successively explorer, editor, and lawyer in New Mexico and Arkansas for some fifteen years, he found time also to gratify a strong literary impulse. On his journey out he sent to the *American Monthly Magazine* (1831) both prose and verse, and to the same journal five years later his *Letters from Arkansas*. Meantime (1834) he had published in Boston the thin volume from which is taken the following tale. *Hymns to the Gods* appeared in Blackwood for June, 1839 (volume xlv, page 819 ; see also volume xlvii, page 354), with a letter dated at Little Rock, August 15, 1838. (The American Cyclopedia puts the original publication of these at Boston, 1831.) After serving against Mexico and in the Confederacy, he gave himself mainly to the practice of the law. But he edited the *Memphis Appeal*, 1867–1868, published volumes of his verse in 1854, 1873, and 1882, and wrote extensively, as an adept, on freemasonry.

Though Pike has more narrative directness than Hall, he is usually loose in narrative structure. Plot seems of smaller concern to him than setting. The abundance of vivid detail and some nervous force in the phrase make his sketches permanently convincing as description.

THE INROAD OF THE NABAJO

[*From " Prose Sketches and Poems written in the Western Country," Boston, 1834. The preface is dated Arkansas Territory, May, 1833*]

IT was a keen, cold morning in the latter part of November, when I wound out of the narrow, rocky cañon or valley, in which I had for some time been travelling, and came in sight of the village of San Fernandez, in the valley of Taos. Above, below, and around me, lay the sheeted snow, till, as the eye glanced upward, it was lost among the dark pines which covered the upper part of the mountains, although at the very summit, where the pines were thinnest, it gleamed from among them like a white banner spread between them and heaven. Below me on the left, half open, half frozen, ran the little clear stream, which gave water to the inhabitants of the valley, and along the margin of which I had been traveling. On the right and left the ridges which formed the dark and precipitous sides of the cañon, sweeping apart, formed a spacious amphitheatre. Along their sides extended a belt of deep, dull blue mist, above and below which was to be seen the white snow, and the deep darkness of the pines. On the right, these mountains swelled to a greater and more precipitous height, till their tops gleamed in unsullied whiteness over the plain below. Still farther to the right was a broad opening, where the mountains seemed to sink into the plain ; and afar off in front were the tall and stupendous mountains between me and the city of Santa Fé. Directly in front of me, with the dull color of its mud buildings contrasting with the dazzling whiteness of the snow, lay the little village, resembling an oriental town, with its low, square, mud-roofed houses and its two square church towers, also of mud. On the path to the village were a few Mexicans, wrapped in their striped blankets, and driving their jackasses heavily laden with wood towards the village. Such was the aspect of the place at a distance. On entering it, you found only a few dirty, irregular lanes, and a quantity of mud houses.

To an American the first sight of these New Mexican villages is novel and singular. He seems taken into a different world. Everything is new, strange, and quaint: the men with their pantalones of cloth, gaily ornamented with lace, split up on the outside of the leg to the knee, and covered at the bottom with a broad strip of morocco; the jacket of calico; the botas of stamped and embroidered leather; the zarape or blanket of striped red and white; the broad-brimmed hat, with a black silk handkerchief tied round it in a roll; or in the lower class, the simple attire of breeches of leather reaching only to the knees, a shirt and a zarape; the bonnetless women, with a silken scarf or a red shawl over their heads; and, added to all, the continual chatter of Spanish about him — all remind him that he is in a strange land.

On the evening after my arrival in the village I went to a fandango. I saw the men and women dancing waltzes and drinking whiskey together; and in another room I saw the monti-bank open. It is a strange sight, a Spanish fandango. Well dressed women — they call them ladies — priests, thieves, half-breed Indians — all spinning round together in a waltz. Here a filthy, ragged fellow with half a shirt, a pair of leather breeches, long, dirty woollen stockings, and Apache moccasins, was whirling round with the pretty wife of Pedro Vigil. I was soon disgusted; but among the graceless shapes and more graceless dresses at the fandango I saw one young woman who appeared to me exceedingly pretty. She was under the middle size, slightly formed; and, besides the delicate foot and ancle and the keen black eye common to all the women in that country, she possessed a clear and beautiful complexion, and a modest, downcast look not often to be met with among the New Mexican females.

I was informed to my surprise that she had been married several years before, and was now a widow. There was an air of gentle and deep melancholy in her face which drew my attention to her; but when one week afterward I left Taos, and went down to Santa Fé, the pretty widow was forgotten.

Among my acquaintances in Santa Fé was one American in particular by the name of L———. He had been in the country several years, had much influence there among the people, and was altogether a very talented man. Of his faults, whatever they were, I have nothing to say. It was from him, some time after my arrival, and when the widow had ceased almost to be a thing of memory, that I learned the following particulars respecting her former fortunes. I give them in L's own words as nearly as I can, and can only say that for the truth of them he is my authority. True or not, such as I received them do I present them to my readers.

"You know," said he, "that I have been in this country several years. Six or eight years ago I was at Taos, upon business, and was lodging in the house of an old acquaintance, Dick Taylor. Early the next morning I was suddenly awakened by Dick, who, shaking me roughly by the shoulder, exclaimed, 'Get up, man — get up — if you wish to see sport, and dress yourself.' Half awake and half asleep, I heard an immense clamor in the street. Cries, yells, oaths, and whoops resounded in every direction. I knew it would be useless to ask an explanation of the matter from the sententious Dick; and I therefore quietly finished dressing and, taking my rifle, followed him into the street. For a time I was at a loss to understand what was the matter. Men were running wildly about, some armed with fusees, with locks as big as a gunbrig, some with bows and arrows, and some with spears. Women were scudding hither and thither, with their black hair flying, and their naked feet shaming the ground by their superior filth. Indian girls were to be seen here and there, with suppressed smiles, and looks of triumph. Men, women, and children, however, seemed to trust less in their armor than in the arm of the Lord and of the saints. They were accordingly earnest in calling upon *Tata Dios!* *Dios bendito! Virgen purisima!* and all the saints of the calendar, and above all, upon *Nuestra Señora de Guadalupe,* to aid, protect, and assist them. One cry, at last, explained the whole matter, — '*Los malditos y picaros que son los Nabajos.*' The Nabajos had been robbing them. They had entered the valley below, and were sweeping it of all the flocks and herds; and this produced the consternation. You have never seen any of these Nabajos. They approach much nearer in character to the Indians in the south of the Mexican Republic than any others in this province. They are whiter; they raise corn; they have vast flocks of sheep and large herds of horses; they make blankets, too, and sell them to the Spaniards. Their great men have a number of servants under them; and in fact their government is apparently patriarchal. Sometimes they choose a captain over the nation; but even then they obey him or not, just as they please. They live about three days' journey west of this, and have about ten thousand souls in the tribe. Like most other Indians, they have their medicine men, who intercede for them with the Great Spirit by strange rites and ceremonies.

"Through the tumult we proceeded towards the outer edge of the town, whither all the armed men seemed to be hastening. On arriving in the street which goes out towards the cañon of the river, we found ourselves in the place of action. Nothing was yet to be seen out in the plain, which extends to the foot of the hills and to the cañon. Some fifty Mexicans had gathered there, mostly armed, and were pressing forward towards the extremity of the street. Behind them were a dozen Americans with their rifles, all as cool as might be; for the men that came through the prairie then were all braves. Sundry women were scudding about, exhorting their husbands to fight well, and praising '*Los Señores Americanos.*' We had waited perhaps half an hour when the foe came in sight, sweeping in from the west, and bearing towards the cañon, driving before them numerous herds and flocks, and consisting apparently of about one hundred men. When they were within about half a mile of us, they separated. One portion of them remained with the booty, and the other, all mounted, came sweeping down upon us. The effect was instantaneous and almost magical. In a moment not a woman was to be seen far or near; and the heroes who had been chattering and boasting in front of the Americans, shrunk behind them, and left them to bear the brunt of the battle. We immediately extended ourselves across the street, and waited the charge. The Indians made a beautiful appearance as they came down upon us with their fine looking horses, and their shields ornamented with feathers and fur, and their dresses of unstained deer-skin. At that time they knew nothing about the Americans. They supposed that their good allies, the Spaniards, would run as they commonly do, that they should have the pleasure of frightening the village and shouting in it and going off safely. As they neared us, each of us raised his gun when he judged it proper, and fired. A dozen cracks of the rifle told them the difference. Five or six tumbled out of their saddles, and were immediately picked up by their comrades, who then turned their backs and retreated as swiftly as they had come. The Americans, who were, like myself, not very eager to fight the battles of the New Mexicans, loaded their guns with immense coolness; and we stood gazing at them as they again gathered their booty and prepared to move towards the cañon. The Mexicans tried to induce us to mount and follow; but we, or at least I, was perfectly contented. In fact, I did not care much which whipped. The Nabajos seemed thus in a very good way of going off with their booty unhindered, when suddenly the scene was altered. A considerable body, perhaps sixty, of the Pueblo of Taos, civilized Indians who are Catholics, and citizens of the Republic, appeared suddenly under the mountains, dashing at full speed towards the mouth of the cañon. They were all fine looking men, well mounted, large, and exceedingly brave.

[Here is omitted a digression upon the Pueblos, which, though very interesting historically, is irrelevant to the story.]

"Upon seeing the Pueblo of Taos between them and the mouth of the cañon, the Nabajos uttered a shrill yell of defiance, and moved to meet them. Leaving a few men to guard the cattle, the remainder, diverging like the opening sticks of a fan, rushed to the attack. Each man shot his arrow as he approached, till he was within thirty or forty yards, and then wheeling, retreated, shooting as he went. They were steadily received by the Pueblo with a general discharge of fire-arms and arrows at every charge, and were frustrated in every attempt at routing them. Several were seen to fall at every charge; but they were always taken up and borne to those who were guarding the cattle. During the contest several Mexicans mounted and went out from the village to join the Pueblos, but only two or three ventured to do so; the others kept at a very respectful distance. At length, finding the matter grow desperate, more men were joined to those who guarded the cattle, and they then moved steadily towards the cañon. The others, again diverging, rushed on till they came within fifty yards, and then converging again, charged boldly upon one point; and as the Pueblo were unprepared for this manœuvre, they broke through and again charged back. Drawing them together in this way to oppose, they drove nearly two thirds of the cattle through the line, goaded by arrows and frightened by shouts. Many of the Nabajos, however, fell in the mêlée by the long spears and quick arrows of the Pueblo. In the mean time I had mounted, and approached within two hundred yards of the scene of contest. I observed one tall and good-looking Spaniard, of middle age, who was particularly active in the contest. He had slightly wounded a large, athletic Nabajo with his spear; and I observed that he was continually followed by him. When this large chief had concluded that the cattle were near enough to the mouth of the cañon to be out of danger, he gave a shrill cry; and his men, who were now reduced to about sixty, besides those with the cattle, gathered simultaneously between the Pueblo and the cañon. Only the chief remained behind; and rushing towards the Spaniard who had wounded him, he grasped him with one hand and raised him from the saddle as if he had been a boy. Taken by surprise, the man made no resistance for a moment or two, and that moment or two sufficed for the horse of the Nabajo — a slightly made, Arabian-looking animal — to place him, with two or three bounds, among his own men. Then his knife glittered in the air, and I saw the Spaniard's limbs contract and then collapse. A moment more sufficed for him to tear the scalp from the head. He was then tumbled to the ground; and with a general yell the whole body rushed forward, closely pursued by the Pueblo. In hurrying to the cañon, the Nabajo lost several men and more of the cattle; but when they had once entered its rocky jaws, and the Pueblo turned back, still more than half the plunder remained with the robbers. Fifteen Nabajos only were left dead; and the remainder were borne off before their comrades. The Pueblos lost nearly one third of their number.

"It was this fight, sir, this inroad of the Nabajos, which brought me acquainted with the young widow of whom we have spoken before. She was then an unmarried girl of fourteen; and a very pretty girl too was La Señorita Ana Maria Ortega. I need not trouble you with descriptions of her; for she has saved me the trouble by appearing to your eyes in that sublime place, a fandango — when you first saw the charms of New Mexican beauty, and had your eyes ravished with the melody and harmony of a Spanish waltz — I beg Spain's pardon — a New Mexican waltz."

"Which waltz," said I, "I heard the next morning played over a coffin at a funeral; and in the afternoon, in the procession of the Host."

"Oh! that is common. Melody, harmony, fiddle, banjo, and all — all is common to all occasions. They have but little music, and they are right in being economical with it; and the presence of the priest sanctifies anything. You know the people of Taos?"

"Yes. The people were afraid to get drunk on my first fandango night. I was astonished to find them so sober. The priest was there; and they feared to get drunk until he had done so. That event took place about eleven at night, and then *aguadiente* was in demand."

"Yes, I dare say. That same priest once asked me if England was a province or a state. I told him it was a province. He reads Voltaire's Philosophical Dictionary, and takes the old infidel to be an excellent christian. Ana Maria was his god-daughter, I think, or some such matter; and I became acquainted with her in that way. He wanted me to marry her. She knew nothing of it, though; but I backed out. I did not mind the marrying so much as the baptism and the citizenship. I don't exchange my country for Mexico, or the name American for that of Mexican. Ana was in truth not a girl to be slighted. She was pretty and rich and sensible. Her room was the best furnished mud apartment in Taos. Her zarapes were of the best texture, some of them even from Chihuahua; and they were piled showily around the room. The roses skewered upon the wall were of red silk; and the santos and other images had been brought from Mexico. There were some half dozen of looking-glasses, too, all out of reach, and various other adornments common to great apartments. The medal which she wore round her neck, with a cross-looking San Pablo upon it, was of beaten gold, or some other kind of gold. She had various dresses of calico and silk, all bought at high prices of the new comers; and her little fairy feet were always adorned with shoes. That was a great extrava-

gance in those days. Ana Maria had no mother when I
first saw her; and she had transferred all her affection to
her father. When the knife of the Nabajo made her an
orphan, I suppose she felt as if her last hold upon life were
gone. She appeared to, at least.

"Victorino Alasi had been her lover, and her favored one.
He had never thought of any other than Ana Maria as his
bride, and he had talked of his love to her a hundred times.
But there came in a young trapper who gave him cause to
tremble lest he should lose his treasure. Henry or, as he
was most commonly called, Hentz Wilson, was a formidable
rival. Ana knew not, herself, which to prefer. The long
friendship and love of Victorino were almost balanced by
the different style of beauty, the odd manners, and the
name American, which recommended Hentz. Her vanity
was flattered by the homage of an American, and Victorino
was in danger of losing his bride. The bold, open bearing
of Hentz, and his bravery, as well as his knowledge, which,
though slight at home, was wondrous to the simple New
Mexicans, had recommended him, likewise, to the father,
whose death suspended, for a time, all operations. They
had each of them made application by letter (the common
custom) for the hand of Ana Maria. In the course of a
fortnight after the inroad of the Nabajo, each of the lovers
received, as answer, that she had determined to give her
hand to either of them who should kill the murderer of her
father. And with this they both were obliged to content
themselves for the present.

"Directly after the inroad, I came down to Santa Fé.
The Lieutenant Colonel of the Province, Viscara, was raising a body of men to go out against the Nabajo, and repay
them for this and other depredations lately committed upon
the people, and he was urgent for me to accompany him —
so much so that I was obliged to comply with his requests,
and promised to go. Troops were sent for from below;
and in the course of four months, the expedition was
ready, and we set out upon the Nabajo campaign. We

were a motley set. First there was a body of regular
troops, all armed with British muskets and with lances.
Here was a grey coat and leathern pantaloons; there, no
coat and short breeches. But you have seen the ragged,
ununiformed troops here in the city, and I need not describe them to you. Next there was a parcel of militia,
all mounted, some with lances, some with old fusees; and
last, a body of Indians of the different Pueblos, with bows
and shields — infinitely the best troops we had, as well as
the bravest men. Among the militia of Taos I observed
the young Victorino. Hentz had likewise volunteered to
accompany the expedition, and lived with me in the General's tent.

"It was in the driest part of the summer that we left
Santa Fé, and marched towards the country of the Nabajo.
We went out by the way of Xemes, and then, crossing the
Rio Puerco, went into the mountains of the Nabajo. We
came up with them, fought them, and they fled before us,
driving their cattle and sheep with them into a wide sand
desert; and we, being now out of provisions, were obliged
to overtake them or starve. We were two days without a
drop of water, and nearly all the animals gave out in consequence. On the third day Viscara, fifteen soldiers, and
myself went ahead of the army (which, I forgot to say, was
thirteen hundred strong). Viscara and his men were
mounted. I was on foot, with no clothing except a cloth
round my middle, with a lance in one hand, and a rifle in
the other. That day I think I ran seventy-five miles, bare-
footed, and through the burning sand."

"Viscara tells me that you ran thirty leagues."

"Viscara is mistaken, and overrates it. Just before night
we came up with a large body of Nabajos, and attacked
them. We took about two thousand sheep from them, and
three hundred cattle, and drove them back that night to
the army. The Nabajos supposed, when we rushed on
them, that the whole of our force was at hand, and they
were afraid to pursue us. But it is the battle in which you

are most concerned. When we attacked the Nabajo, they
were drawn up, partly on foot, and partly on horseback, in
the bed of a little creek which was dry. It was the common way of fighting — charge, fire and retreat; and if you
have seen one fight on horseback, you have seen all. I
observed particularly one Nabajo, upon whom three Pueblos
charged, all on foot. He shot two of them down before
they reached him. Another arrow struck the remaining
one in the belly. He still came on with only a tomahawk,
and another arrow struck him in the forehead. Yet still he
braved his foe and they were found lying dead together. I
could have shot the Nabajo with great ease, at the time;
for the whole of this took place within seventy yards of me.

"In the midst of the battle I observed Victorino and
Hentz standing together in the front rank, seeming rather
to be spectators than men interested in the fight. They
were both handsome men, but entirely different in appearance. Victorino was a dark-eyed, slender, agile young
Spaniard, with a tread like a tiger-cat, and with all his
nerves indurate with toil. His face was oval, thin, and of
a rich olive, through which the blood seemed ready to
break; and you could hardly have chosen a better figure
for a statuary as he stood, now and then discharging his
fusee, but commonly glancing his eyes uneasily about from
one part of the enemy to the other. Hentz, on the contrary, was a tall and well-proportioned young fellow, of
immense strength and activity, but with little of the cat-
like quickness of his rival. His skin was fair even to effemi-
nacy, and his blue eyes were shaded by a profusion of
chestnut hair. He, too, seemed expecting some one to
appear amid the enemy; for though he now and then fired
and reloaded, it was but seldom, and he spent more time
in leaning on his long rifle, and gazing about among the
Nabajos.

"On a sudden, a sharp yell was heard, and a party of
Nabajos came dashing down the bank of the creek, all
mounted, and headed by the big chief who had killed the

father of Ana Maria. Then the apathy of the two rivals was at once thrown aside. Hentz quickly threw his gun into the hollow of his arm, examined the priming, and again stood quietly watching the motions of the chief; and Victorino did the same. Wheeling round several times, and discharging a flight of arrows continually upon us, this new body of Nabajo at length bore down directly toward Hentz and Victorino. As the chief came on, Victorino raised his gun, took a steady, long aim, and fired. Another moment, and the Nabajo were upon them, and then retreated again like a wave tossing back from the shore. The chief still sat on his horse as before ; another yell, and they came down again. When they were within about a hundred yards, Hentz raised his rifle, took a steady, quick aim, and fired. Still they came on ; the chief bent down over the saddle-bow, and his horse, seemingly frightened by the strange pressure of the rider, bore down directly towards Hentz, who sprang to meet him, and caught the bridle ; the horse sprang to one side, and the wounded chief lost his balance, and fell upon the ground. The horse dashed away through friend and foe, and was out of sight in a moment. The Nabajo rallied to save the body of their chief, and Viscara himself rushed in with me to the rescue of Hentz. But the long barrel of Hentz's rifle, which he swayed with a giant's strength, the sword of Viscara, and the keen knife of Victorino, who generously sprang in the aid of his rival, would all have failed in saving the body, had not a band of the gallant Pueblo attacked them in the rear and routed them. Hentz immediately dispatched the chief, who was by this time half hidden by a dozen Nabajos, and immediately deprived his head of the hair, which is more valuable to an Indian than life.

"The Nabajos sued for peace, and we returned to Santa Fé. Poor Victorino, I observed, rode generally alone, and had not a word to say to any one. Although formerly he had been the most merry and humorous, now he seemed entirely buried in sorrow. He kept listlessly along, looking neither to the right hand nor to the left, with his bridle lying on the neck of his mule. I tried to comfort him; but he answered me gloomily, 'Why should I cheer up? What have I to live for? Had I lost her by any fault of my own, I would not have thought so hardly of it; but by this cursed old fusee, and because another man can shoot better than I — Oh! sir, leave me to myself, I pray you, and make me no offers which do me no good. I think I shall be happy again, but it will be in my grave, and *Dios me perdone!* I care not how soon I am there.'

"As I fell back towards the rear, where I generally marched, Hentz rode up by me and inquired what the young Spaniard had said. I repeated it to him. 'Do you think he is really that troubled?' inquired he. 'Yes,' said I, 'the poor fellow seems to feel all he says.' Without a word, Hentz rode towards him, and reining up by him, tapped him on the shoulder. Victorino looked fiercely up, and seemed inclined to resent it; but Hentz, without regarding the glance, proceeded with a mass of immensely bad Spanish, which I know not how the poor fellow ever understood. 'Here,' said he, 'you love Ana better than I do, I know — you have known her longer, and will feel her loss more; and after all, you would have killed the chief if you could have done it — and you did help me save the body. Take this bunch of stuff,' holding out the hair, 'and give me your hand.' Victorino did so, and shook the offered hand heartily. Then taking the scalp, he deposited it in his shot-pouch, and dashing the tears from his eyes, rode off towards his comrades like a madman. So much for the inroad of the Nabajos."

"But what became of Victorino?" inquired I.

"He married Ana Maria after she had laid aside the luto (mourning); and two years ago he died of the small-pox, in the Snake country. Poor fellow — he was almost an American."

PART II

THE PERIOD OF THE NEW FORM

NATHANIEL HAWTHORNE

1804 – 1864

For an estimate of Hawthorne as a writer of short stories see pages 12–15 of the Introduction.

THE WHITE OLD MAID

[From " Twice-Told Tales." The story was first published in " The New England Magazine" for July, 1835]

THE moonbeams came through two deep and narrow windows, and showed a spacious chamber richly furnished in an antique fashion. From one lattice the shadow of the diamond panes was thrown upon the floor ; the ghostly light through the other slept upon the bed, falling between the heavy silken curtains and illuminating the face of a young man. But how quietly the slumberer lay ! how pale his features ! And how like a shroud the sheet was wound about his frame ! Yes, it was a corpse in its burial-clothes.

Suddenly the fixed features seemed to move with dark emotion. Strange fantasy ! It was but the shadow of the fringed curtain waving betwixt the dead face and the moonlight as the door of the chamber opened and a girl stole softly to the bedside. Was there delusion in the moonbeams, or did her gesture and her eye betray a gleam of triumph as she bent over the pale corpse, pale as itself, and pressed her living lips to the cold ones of the dead ? As she drew back from that long kiss her features writhed as if a proud heart were fighting with its anguish. Again it seemed that the features of the corpse had moved responsive to her own. Still an illusion. The silken curtains had waved a second time betwixt the dead face and the moonlight as another fair young girl unclosed the door and glided ghostlike to the bedside. There the two maidens stood, both beautiful, with the pale beauty of the dead between

131

them. But she who had first entered was proud and stately, and the other a soft and fragile thing.

"Away!" cried the lofty one. "Thou hadst him living; the dead is mine."

"Thine!" returned the other, shuddering. "Well hast thou spoken. The dead is thine."

The proud girl started, and stared into her face with a ghastly look. But a wild and mournful expression passed across the features of the gentle one, and, weak and helpless, she sank down on the bed, her head pillowed beside that of the corpse and her hair mingling with his dark locks. A creature of hope and joy, the first draught of sorrow had bewildered her.

"Edith!"[1] cried her rival.

Edith groaned as with a sudden compression of the heart; and removing her cheek from the dead youth's pillow, she stood upright, fearfully encountering the eyes of the lofty girl.

"Wilt thou betray me?" said the latter, calmly.

"Till the dead bid me speak I will be silent," answered Edith. "Leave us alone together. Go and live many years, and then return and tell me of thy life. He too will be here. Then, if thou tellest of sufferings more than death, we will both forgive thee."

"And what shall be the token?" asked the proud girl, as if her heart acknowledged a meaning in these wild words.

"This lock of hair," said Edith, lifting one of the dark, clustering curls that lay heavily on the dead man's brow.

The two maidens joined their hands over the bosom of the corpse, and appointed a day and hour far, far in time to come for their next meeting in that chamber. The statelier girl gave one deep look at the motionless countenance and departed — yet turned again and trembled ere she closed the door, almost believing that her dead lover frowned upon her. And Edith, too! Was not her white

[1] In the original publication the name is Patience.

form fading into the moonlight? Scorning her own weakness, she went forth and perceived that a negro slave was waiting in the passage with a wax-light, which he held between her face and his own, and regarded her, as she thought, with an ugly expression of merriment. Lifting his torch on high, the slave lighted her down the staircase and undid the portal of the mansion. The young clergyman of the town had just ascended the steps, and, bowing to the lady, passed in without a word.

Years, many years, rolled on. The world seemed new again, so much older was it grown since the night when those pale girls had clasped their hands across the bosom of the corpse. In the interval a lonely woman had passed from youth to extreme age, and was known by all the town as the " Old Maid in the Winding-Sheet." A taint of insanity had affected her whole life, but so quiet, sad and gentle, so utterly free from violence, that she was suffered to pursue her harmless fantasies unmolested by the world, with whose business or pleasures she had naught to do. She dwelt alone, and never came into the daylight, except to follow funerals. Whenever a corpse was borne along the street, in sunshine, rain or snow, whether a pompous train of the rich and proud thronged after it or few and humble were the mourners, behind them came the lonely woman in a long white garment which the people called her shroud. She took no place among the kindred or the friends, but stood at the door to hear the funeral prayer, and walked in the rear of the procession as one whose earthly charge it was to haunt the house of mourning, and be the shadow of affliction, and see that the dead were duly buried. So long had this been her custom that the inhabitants of the town deemed her a part of every funeral, as much as the coffin-pall or the very corpse itself, and augured ill of the sinner's destiny unless the Old Maid in the Winding-Sheet came gliding like a ghost behind. Once, it is said, she affrighted a bridal party with her pale presence, appearing suddenly in the illuminated hall just as the priest was uniting a false maid to a wealthy man before her lover had been dead a year. Evil was the omen to that marriage! Sometimes she stole forth by moonlight and visited the graves of venerable integrity, and wedded love, and virgin innocence, and every spot where the ashes of a kind and faithful heart were mou'dering. Over the hillocks of those favored dead would she stretch out her arms with a gesture as if she were scattering seeds, and many believed that she brought them from the garden of Paradise; for the graves which she had visited were green beneath the snow and covered with sweet flowers from April to November. Her blessing was better than a holy verse upon the tombstone. Thus wore away her long, sad, peaceful and fantastic life till few were so old as she, and the people of later generations wondered how the dead had ever been buried, or mourners had endured their grief, without the Old Maid in the Winding-Sheet.

Still years went on, and still she followed funerals and was not yet summoned to her own festival of death. One afternoon the great street of the town was all alive with business and bustle, though the sun now gilded only the upper half of the church-spire, having left the house-tops and loftiest trees in shadow. The scene was cheerful and animated in spite of the somber shade between the high brick buildings. Here were pompous merchants in white wigs and laced velvet, the bronzed faces of sea-captains, the foreign garb and air of Spanish creoles, and the disdainful port of natives of Old England, all contrasted with the rough aspect of one or two back-settlers negociating sales of timber from forests where axe had never sounded. Sometimes a lady passed, swelling roundly forth in an embroidered petticoat, balancing her steps in high-heeled shoes, and courtesying with lofty grace to the punctilious obeisances of the gentlemen. The life of the town seemed to have its very centre not far from an old mansion that stood somewhat back from the pavement, surrounded by neglected grass, with a strange air of loneli-

ness, rather deepened than dispelled by the throng so near
it. Its site would have been suitably occupied by a magnificent Exchange or a brick block lettered all over with
various signs; or the large house itself might have made
a noble tavern with the "King's Arms" swinging before
it, and guests in every chamber, instead of the present
solitude. But, owing to some dispute about the right of
inheritance, the mansion had been long without a tenant,
decaying from year to year and throwing the stately gloom
of its shadow over the busiest part of the town. Such was
the scene, and such the time, when a figure unlike any that
have been described was observed at a distance down the
street.

"I espy a strange sail yonder," remarked a Liverpool
captain; "that woman in the long white garment."

The sailor seemed much struck by the object, as were
several others who at the same moment caught a glimpse
of the figure that had attracted his notice. Almost immediately the various topics of conversation gave place to
speculations in an undertone on this unwonted occurrence.

"Can there be a funeral so late this afternoon?" inquired some.

They looked for the signs of death at every door — the
sexton, the hearse, the assemblage of black-clad relatives —
all that makes up the woeful pomp of funerals. They raised
their eyes, also, to the sun-gilt spire of the church, and
wondered that no clang proceeded from its bell, which had
always tolled till now when this figure appeared in the light
of day. But none had heard that a corpse was to be borne
to its home that afternoon, nor was there any token of
a funeral except the apparition of the Old Maid in the
Winding-Sheet.

"What may this portend?" asked each man of his
neighbor.

All smiled as they put the question, yet with a certain
trouble in their eyes, as if pestilence, or some other wide
calamity, were prognosticated by the untimely intrusion

among the living of one whose presence had always been associated with death and woe. What a comet is to the earth was that sad woman to the town. Still she moved on, while the hum of surprise was hushed at her approach, and the proud and the humble stood aside that her white garment might not wave against them. It was a long, loose robe of spotless purity. Its wearer appeared very old, pale, emaciated and feeble, yet glided onward without the unsteady pace of extreme age. At one point of her course a little rosy boy burst forth from a door and ran with open arms towards the ghostly woman, seeming to expect a kiss from her bloodless lips. She made a slight pause, fixing her eye upon him with an expression of no earthly sweetness, so that the child shivered and stood awe-struck rather than affrighted while the Old Maid passed on. Perhaps her garment might have been polluted even by an infant's touch; perhaps her kiss would have been death to the sweet boy within the year.

"She is but a shadow," whispered the superstitious. "The child put forth his arms and could not grasp her robe."

The wonder was increased when the Old Maid passed beneath the porch of the deserted mansion, ascended the moss-covered steps, lifted the iron knocker and gave three raps. The people could only conjecture that some old remembrance, troubling her bewildered brain, had impelled the poor woman hither to visit the friends of her youth; all gone from their home long since and forever, unless their ghosts still haunted it — fit company for the Old Maid in the Winding-Sheet. An elderly man approached the steps and, reverently uncovering his gray locks, essayed to explain the matter.

"None, madam," said he, "have dwelt in this house these fifteen years agone — no, not since the death of old Colonel Fenwicke, whose funeral you may remember to have followed. His heirs, being ill-agreed among themselves, have let the mansion-house go to ruin."

The Old Maid looked slowly round with a slight gesture of one hand and a finger of the other upon her lip, appearing more shadow-like than ever in the obscurity of the porch. But again she lifted the hammer, and gave, this time, a single rap. Could it be that a footstep was now heard coming down the staircase of the old mansion which all conceived to have been so long untenanted? Slowly, feebly, yet heavily, like the pace of an aged and infirm person, the step approached, more distinct on every downward stair, till it reached the portal. The bar fell on the inside; the door was opened. One upward glance toward the church-spire, whence the sunshine had just faded, was the last that the people saw of the " Old Maid in the Winding-Sheet."

" Who undid the door? " asked many.

This question, owing to the depth of shadow beneath the porch, no one could satisfactorily answer. Two or three aged men, while protesting against an inference which might be drawn, affirmed that the person within was a negro, and bore a singular resemblance to old Cæsar, formerly a slave in the house, but freed by death some thirty years before.

" Her summons has waked up a servant of the old family," said one, half seriously.

" Let us wait here," replied another. " More guests will knock at the door anon. But the gate of the grave-yard should be thrown open."

Twilight had overspread the town before the crowd began to separate, or the comments on this incident were exhausted. One after another was wending his way homeward, when a coach — no common spectacle in those days — drove slowly into the street. It was an old-fashioned equipage, hanging close to the ground, with arms on the pannels, a footman behind, and a grave, corpulent coachman seated high in front — the whole giving an idea of solemn state and dignity. There was something awful in the heavy rumbling of the wheels. The coach rolled down the street, till, coming to the gateway of the deserted mansion, it drew up, and the footman sprang to the ground.

"Whose grand coach is this?" asked a very inquisitive body.

The footman made no reply, but ascended the steps of the old house, gave three taps with the iron hammer, and returned to open the coach door. An old man possessed of the heraldic lore so common in that day examined the shield of arms on the pannel.

"Azure, a lion's head erased, between three flower de luces," said he; then whispered the name of the family to whom these bearings belonged. The last inheritor of its honors was recently dead, after a long residence amid the splendor of the British court, where his birth and wealth had given him no mean station. "He left no child," continued the herald, "and these arms, being in a lozenge, betoken that the coach appertains to his widow."

Further disclosures, perhaps, might have been made, had not the speaker been suddenly struck dumb by the stern eye of an ancient lady who thrust forth her head from the coach, preparing to descend. As she emerged the people saw that her dress was magnificent, and her figure dignified in spite of age and infirmity — a stately ruin, but with a look at once of pride and wretchedness. Her strong and rigid features had an awe about them unlike that of the White Old Maid, but as of something evil. She passed up the steps, leaning on a gold-headed cane. The door swung open as she ascended — and the light of a torch glittered on the embroidery of her dress and gleamed on the pillars of the porch. After a momentary pause — a glance backwards — and then a desperate effort — she went in. The decypherer of the coat of arms had ventured up the lowest step, and, shrinking back immediately, pale and tremulous, affirmed that the torch was held by the very image of old Cæsar.

"But such a hideous grin," added he, "was never seen

on the face of mortal man, black or white ! It will haunt me till my dying day."

Meantime the coach had wheeled round, with a prodigious clatter on the pavement, and rumbled up the street, disappearing in the twilight, while the ear still tracked its course. Scarcely was it gone when the people began to question whether the coach and attendants, the ancient lady, the spectre of old Cæsar and the Old Maid herself, were not all a strangely combined delusion with some dark purport in its mystery. The whole town was astir, so that, instead of dispersing, the crowd continually increased, and stood gazing up at the windows of the mansion, now silvered by the brightening moon. The elders, glad to indulge the narrative propensity of age, told of the long-faded splendor of the family, the entertainments they had given and the guests, the greatest of the land, and even titled and noble ones from abroad, who had passed beneath that portal. These graphic reminiscences seemed to call up the ghosts of those to whom they referred. So strong was the impression on some of the more imaginative hearers that two or three were seized with trembling fits at one and the same moment, protesting that they had distinctly heard three other raps of the iron knocker.

"Impossible !" exclaimed others. "See ! The moon shines beneath the porch, and shows every part of it, except in the narrow shade of that pillar. There is no one there."

"Did not the door open?" whispered one of these fanciful persons.

"Didst thou see it too?" said his companion, in a startled tone.

But the general sentiment was opposed to the idea that a third visitant had made application at the door of the deserted house. A few, however, adhered to this new marvel, and even declared that a red gleam like that of a torch had shone through the great front window, as if the negro were lighting a guest up the staircase. This, too, was pronounced a mere fantasy. But at once the whole multitude started, and each man beheld his own terror painted in the faces of all the rest.

"What an awful thing is this!" cried they.

A shriek, too fearfully distinct for doubt, had been heard within the mansion, breaking forth sudd-nly and succeeded by a deep stillness, as if a heart had burst in giving it utterance. The people knew not whether to fly from the very sight of the house, or to rush trembling in and search out the strange mystery. Amid their confusion and affright, they were somewhat reassured by the appearance of their clergyman, a venerable patriarch, and equally a saint, who had taught them and their fathers the way to heaven for more than the space of an ordinary life-time. He was a reverend figure with long white hair upon his shoulders, a white beard upon his breast, and a back so bent over his staff that he seemed to be looking downward continually, as if to choose a proper grave for his weary frame. It was some time before the good old man, being deaf and of impaired intellect, could be made to comprehend such portions of the affair as were comprehensible at all. But, when possessed of the facts, his energies assumed unexpected vigor.

"Verily," said the old gentleman, "it will be fitting that I enter the mansion-house of the worthy Colonel Fenwicke, lest any harm should have befallen that true Christian woman whom ye call the 'Old Maid in the Winding-Sheet.'"

Behold, then, the venerable clergyman ascending the steps of the mansion with a torch-bearer behind him. It was the elderly man who had spoken to the Old Maid, and the same who had afterward explained the shield of arms and recognized the features of the negro. Like their predecessors, they gave three raps with the iron hammer.

"Old Cæsar cometh not," observed the priest. "Well, I wot he no longer doth service in this mansion."

"Assuredly, then, it was something worse in old Cæsar's likeness!" said the other adventurer.

"Be it as God wills," answered the clergyman. "See! my strength, though it be much decayed, hath sufficed to open this heavy door. Let us enter and pass up the staircase."

Here occurred a singular exemplification of the dreamy state of a very old man's mind. As they ascended the wide flight of stairs, the aged clergyman appeared to move with caution, occasionally standing aside, and oftener bending his head, as it were in salutation, thus practicing all the gestures of one who makes his way through a throng. Reaching the head of the staircase, he looked around with sad and solemn benignity, laid aside his staff, bared his hoary locks, and was evidently on the point of commencing a prayer.

"Reverend Sir," said his attendant, who conceived this a very suitable prelude to their further search, "would it not be well that the people join with us in prayer?"

"Well-a-day!" cried the old clergyman, staring strangely around him. "Art thou here with me, and none other? Verily, past times were present to me, and I deemed that I was to make a funeral prayer, as many a time heretofore, from the head of this staircase. Of a truth, I saw the shades of many that are gone. Yea, I have prayed at their burials, one after another, and the Old Maid in the Winding-Sheet hath seen them to their graves!"

Being now more thoroughly awake to their present purpose, he took his staff and struck forcibly on the floor, till there came an echo from each deserted chamber, but no menial to answer their summons. They therefore walked along the passage, and again paused, opposite to the great front window, through which was seen the crowd in the shadow and partial moonlight of the street beneath. On their right hand was the open door of a chamber, and a closed one on their left. The clergyman pointed his cane to the carved oak pannel of the latter.

"Within that chamber," observed he, "a whole life-time since, did I sit by the death-bed of a goodly young man who, being now at the last gasp —— "

Apparently, there was some powerful excitement in the ideas which had now flashed across his mind. He snatched the torch from his companion's hand, and threw open the door with such sudden violence that the flame was extinguished, leaving them no other light than the moonbeams, which fell through two windows into the spacious chamber. It was sufficient to discover all that could be known. In a high-backed oaken arm-chair, upright, with her hands clasped across her breast, and her head thrown back, sat the "Old Maid in the Winding-Sheet." The stately dame had fallen on her knees with her forehead on the holy knees of the Old Maid, one hand upon the floor and the other pressed convulsively against her heart. It clutched a lock of hair, once sable, now discolored with a greenish mould. As the priest and layman advanced into the chamber, the Old Maid's features assumed such a semblance of shifting expression that they trusted to hear the whole mystery explained by a single word. But it was only the shadow of a tattered curtain waving betwixt the dead face and the moonlight.

"Both dead!" said the venerable man. "Then who shall divulge the secret? Methinks it glimmers to and fro in my mind like the light and shadow across the Old Maid's face. And now 't is gone!"

HENRY WADSWORTH LONGFELLOW

1807 – 1882

THE very large proportion of narrative poetry throughout Longfellow's work suggests a native bent toward story. *Outre-Mer* (begun in parts, 1833; published entire, 1835) at once reminded his reviewers of Irving's *Tales of a Traveller*. The parallel is obvious; but *The Notary of Périgueux*, slight as is its substance, is superior to Irving's typical form in narrative compactness.

•

THE NOTARY OF PÉRIGUEUX

[*From " Outre-Mer," 1835*]

Do not trust thy body with a physician. He'll make thy foolish
bones go without flesh in a fortnight, and thy soul walk without a
body in a se'nnight after. SHIRLEY.

YOU must know, gentlemen, that there lived some years
ago, in the city of Périgueux, an honest notary public,
the descendant of a very ancient and broken-down family,
and the occupant of one of those old weather-beaten
tenements which remind you of the times of your great-
grandfather. He was a man of an unoffending, quiet disposition ; the father of a family, though not the head of it
— for in that family " the hen overcrowed the cock," and
the neighbors, when they spake of the notary, shrugged
their shoulders, and exclaimed, " Poor fellow! his spurs
want sharpening." In fine — you understand me, gentlemen — he was hen-pecked.

Well, finding no peace at home, he sought it elsewhere,
as was very natural for him to do ; and at length discovered
a place of rest far beyond the cares and clamors of domestic life. This was a little *café estaminet* a short way out of
the city, whither he repaired every evening to smoke his
pipe, drink sugar-water, and play his favorite game of domino. There he met the boon companions he most loved,
heard all the floating chitchat of the day, laughed when he
' ars in merry mood, found consolation when he was sad,
anu at all times gave vent to his opinions without fear of
being snubbed short by a flat contradiction.

Now the notary's bosom friend was a dealer in claret and
cognac, who lived about a league from the city, and always

10 145

passed his evenings at the *estaminet*. He was a gross, corpulent fellow, raised from a full-blooded Gascon breed, and sired by a comic actor of some reputation in his way. He was remarkable for nothing but his good-humor, his love of cards, and a strong propensity to test the quality of his own liquors by comparing them with those sold at other places.

As evil communications corrupt good manners, the bad practices of the wine-dealer won insensibly upon the worthy notary; and before he was aware of it, he found himself weaned from domino and sugar-water, and addicted to piquet and spiced wine. Indeed, it not infrequently happened that, after a long session at the *estaminet*, the two friends grew so urbane that they would waste a full half-hour at the door in friendly dispute which should conduct the other home.

Though this course of life agreed well enough with the sluggish, phlegmatic temperament of the wine-dealer, it soon began to play the very deuce with the more sensitive organization of the notary, and finally put his nervous system completely out of tune. He lost his appetite, became gaunt and haggard, and could get no sleep. Legions of blue-devils haunted him by day; and by night strange faces peeped through his bed-curtains, and the nightmare snorted in his ear. The worse he grew, the more he smoked and tippled; and the more he smoked and tippled — why, as a matter of course, the worse he grew. His wife alternately stormed, remonstrated, entreated; but all in vain. She made the house too hot for him — he retreated to the tavern; she broke his long-stemmed pipes upon the andirons — he substituted a short-stemmed one, which, for safe keeping, he carried in his waistcoat-pocket.

Thus the unhappy notary ran gradually down . . the . . . What with his bad habits and his domestic grievances, he became completely hipped. He imagined that he was going to die, and suffered in quick succession all the diseases that ever beset mortal man. Every shooting pain was an alarming symptom — every uneasy feeling after dinner a sure prognostic of some mortal disease. In vain did his friends endeavor to reason, and then to laugh him out of his strange whims; for when did ever jest or reason cure a sick imagination? His only answer was, "Do let me alone; I know better than you what ails me."

Well, gentlemen, things were in this state when, one afternoon. in December, as he sat moping in his office, wrapped in an overcoat, with a cap on his head and his feet thrust into a pair of furred slippers, a cabriolet stopped at the door, and a loud knocking without aroused him from his gloomy revery. It was a message from his friend the wine-dealer, who had been suddenly attacked with a violent fever, and, growing worse and worse, had now sent in the greatest haste for the notary to draw up his last will and testament. The case was urgent, and admitted neither excuse nor delay; and the notary, tying a handkerchief round his face, and buttoning up to the chin, jumped into the cabriolet, and suffered himself, though not without some dismal presentiments and misgivings of heart, to be driven to the wine-dealer's house.

When he arrived he found everything in the greatest confusion. On entering the house he ran against the apothecary, who was coming down stairs, with a face as long as your arm; and a few steps farther he met the housekeeper — for the wine-dealer was an old bachelor — running up and down, and wringing her hands, for fear that the good man should die without making his will. He soon reached the chamber of his sick friend, and found him tossing about in a paroxysm of fever and calling aloud for a draught of cold water. The notary shook his head. He thought this a fatal symptom. For ten years back the wine-dealer had been suffering under a species of hydrophobia, which seemed suddenly to have left him.

When the sick man saw who stood by his bedside, he stretched out his hand and exclaimed :

"Ah! my dear friend! have you come at last? You see it is all over with me. You have arrived just in time to draw up that — that passport of mine. Ah, *grand diable!* how hot it is here! Water — water — water! Will nobody give me a drop of cold water?"

As the case was an urgent one, the notary made no delay in getting his papers in readiness; and in a short time the last will and testament of the wine-dealer was drawn up in due form, the notary guiding the sick man's hand as he scrawled his signature at the bottom.

As the evening wore away, the wine-dealer grew worse and worse, and at length became delirious, mingling in his incoherent ravings the phrases of the Credo and Paternoster with the shibboleth of the dram-shop and the card-table.

"Take care! take care! There, now — *Credo in* — pop! ting-a-ling-ling! give me some of that. Cent-é-dize! Why, you old publican, this wine is poisoned — I know your tricks! — *Sanctam ecclesiam Catholicam* — Well, well, we shall see. Imbecile! to have a tierce-major and a seven of hearts, and discard the seven! By St. Anthony, capot! You are lurched — ha! ha! I told you so. I knew very well — there — there — don't interrupt me — *Carnis resurrectionem et vitam eternam!*"

With these words upon his lips the poor wine-dealer expired. Meanwhile the notary sat cowering over the fire, aghast at the fearful scene that was passing before him, and now and then striving to keep up his courage by a glass of cognac. Already his fears were on the alert, and the idea of contagion flitted to and fro through his mind. In order to quiet these thoughts of evil import, he lighted his pipe, and began to prepare for returning home. At that moment the apothecary turned round to him and said:

"Dreadful sickly time, this! The disorder seems to be spreading."

"What disorder?" exclaimed the notary, with a movement of surprise.

"Two died yesterday, and three to-day," continued the apothecary, without answering the question. "Very sickly time, sir — very."

"But what disorder is it? What disease has carried off my friend here so suddenly?"

"What disease? Why, scarlet fever, to be sure."

"And is it contagious?"

"Certainly."

"Then I am a dead man!" ex'.... ... the notary, putting his pipe into his waistcoat-pocket, and beginning to walk up and down the room in despair. "I am a dead man! Now don't deceive me — don't, will you? What — what are the symptoms?"

"A sharp burning pain in the right side," said the apothecary.

"Oh, what a fool I was to come here!"

In vain did the housekeeper and the apothecary strive to pacify him. He was not a man to be reasoned with. He answered that he knew his own constitution better than they did, and insisted upon going home without delay. Unfortunately, the vehicle he came in had returned to the city; and the whole neighbourhood was abed and asleep. What was to be done? Nothing in the world but to take the apothecary's horse, which stood hitched at the door, patiently waiting his master's will.

Well, gentlemen, as there was no remedy, our notary mounted this raw-boned steed, and set forth upon his homeward journey. The night was cold and gusty, and the wind set right in his teeth. Overhead the leaden clouds were beating to and fro, and through them the newly-risen moon seemed to be tossing and drifting along like a cock-boat in the surf; now swallowed up in a huge billow of cloud, and now lifted upon its bosom and dashed with silvery spray. The trees by the roadside groaned with a sound of evil omen, and before him lay three mortal miles, beset with a thousand imaginary perils. Obedient to the whip and spur, the steed leaped forward by fits and starts, now dashing away in a tremendous gallop, and now relaxing into a long, hard trot; while the rider, filled with symptoms of disease and dire presentiments of death, urged him on, as if he were fleeing before the pestilence.

In this way, by dint of whistling and shouting, and beating right and left, one mile of the fatal three was safely passed. The apprehensions of the notary had so far subsided that he even suffered the poor horse to walk up-hill; but these apprehensions were suddenly revived again with tenfold violence by a sharp pain in the right side, which seemed to pierce him like a needle.

" It is upon me at last ! " groaned the fear-stricken man. " Heaven be merciful to me, the greatest of sinners !   And must I die in a ditch, after all ?   He ! get up ! get up ! "

And away went horse and rider at full speed — hurry-scurry — up-hill and down — panting and blowing like a whirlwind.   At every leap the pain in the rider's side seemed to increase.   At first it was a little point like the prick of a needle — then it spread to the size of a half-franc piece — then covered a piece as large as the palm of your hand.   It gained upon him fast.   The poor man groaned aloud in agony ; faster and faster sped the horse over the frozen ground — farther and farther spread the pain over his side.   To complete the dismal picture, the storm commenced — snow mingled with rain.   But snow, and rain, and cold were naught to him ; for, though his arms and legs were frozen to icicles, he felt it not.   The fatal symptom was upon him ; he was doomed to die — not of cold, but of scarlet fever !

At length, he knew not how, more dead than alive, he reached the gate of the city.   A band of ill-bred dogs, that were serenading at a corner of the street, seeing the notary dash by, joined in the hue and cry, and ran barking and yelping at his heels.   It was now late at night, and only here and there a solitary lamp twinkled from an upper story.   But on went the notary, down this street and up that, till at last he reached his own door.   There was a light in his wife's bed chamber. The good woman came to the window, alarmed at such a knocking and howling and clattering at her door so late at night.

"Let me in! let me in! Quick! quick!" he exclaimed, almost breathless from terror and fatigue.

"Who are you, that come to disturb a lone woman at this hour of the night?" cried a sharp voice from above. "Begone about your business, and let quiet people sleep."

"Oh, *diable, diable!* Come down and let me in! I am your husband. Don't you know my voice? Quick, I beseech you; for I am dying here in the street!"

After a few moments of delay and a few more words of parley, the door was opened, and the notary stalked into his domicil, pale and haggard in aspect, and as stiff and straight as a ghost. Cased from head to heel in an armor of ice, as the glare of the lamp fell upon him he looked like a knight-errant mailed in steel. But in one place his armor was broken. On his right side was a circular spot as large as the crown of your hat, and about as black!

"My dear wife!" he exclaimed, with more tenderness than he had exhibited for many years, "reach me a chair. My hours are numbered. I am a dead man!"

Alarmed at these exclamations, his wife stripped off his overcoat. Something fell from beneath it, and was dashed to pieces on the hearth. It was the notary's pipe! He placed his hand upon his side, and, lo! it was bare to the skin! Coat, waistcoat, and linen were burnt through and through, and there was a blister on his side as large over as your head!

The mystery was soon explained, symptom and all. The notary had put his pipe into his pocket without knocking out the ashes! And so my story ends.

EDGAR ALLAN POE

1809 – 1849

For an appreciation of Poe as a short-story writer see pages
15–23 of the Introduction.

THE FALL OF THE HOUSE
OF USHER

[First published in Burton's " Gentleman's Magazine and American Monthly Review," September, 1839]

Son cœur est un luth suspendu ;
Sitôt qu'on le touche il résonne.

DE BÉRANGER.

DURING the whole of a dull, dark, and soundless day in the autumn of the year, when the clouds hung oppressively low in the heavens, I had been passing alone, on horseback, through a singularly dreary tract of country ; and at length found myself, as the shades of the evening drew on, within view of the melancholy House of Usher. I know not how it was ; but, with the first glimpse of the building, a sense of insufferable gloom pervaded my spirit. I say insufferable ; for the feeling was unrelieved by any of that half-pleasurable, because poetic, sentiment, with which the mind usually receives even the sternest natural images of the desolate or terrible. I looked upon the scene before me — upon the mere house, and the simple land-scape features of the domain — upon the bleak walls — upon the vacant eye-like windows — upon a few rank sedges — and upon a few white trunks of decayed trees — with an utter depression of soul which I can compare to no earthly sensation more properly than to the after-dream of the reveller upon opium — the bitter lapse into every-day life — the hideous dropping off of the veil. There was an iciness, a sinking, a sickening of the heart — an unredeemed dreariness of thought which no goading of the imagination

could torture into aught of the sublime. What was it —
I paused to think — what was it that so unnerved me in
the contemplation of the House of Usher? It was a mystery all insoluble; nor could I grapple with the shadowy
fancies that crowded upon me as I pondered. I was
forced to fall back upon the unsatisfactory conclusion that
while, beyond doubt, there *are* combinations of very simple
natural objects which have the power of thus affecting us,
still the analysis of this power lies among considerations
beyond our depth. It was possible, I reflected, that a
mere different arrangement of the particulars of the scene,
of the details of the picture, would be sufficient to modify,
or perhaps to annihilate its capacity for sorrowful impression; and, acting upon this idea, I reined my horse to
the precipitous brink of a black and lurid tarn that lay
in unruffled lustre by the dwelling, and gazed down — but
with a shudder even more thrilling than before — upon
the remodelled and inverted images of the gray sedge,
and the ghastly tree-stems, and the vacant and eye-like
windows.

Nevertheless, in this mansion of gloom I now proposed
to myself a sojourn of some weeks. Its proprietor, Roderick Usher, had been one of my boon companions in boyhood; but many years had elapsed since our last meeting.
A letter, however, had lately reached me in a distant part
of the country — a letter from him — which, in its wildly
importunate nature, had admitted of no other than a personal reply. The MS. gave evidence of nervous agitation.
The writer spoke of acute bodily illness, of a mental disorder which oppressed him, and of an earnest desire to see
me, as his best, and indeed his only personal friend, with
a view of attempting, by the cheerfulness of my society,
some alleviation of his malady. It was the manner in
which all this, and much more, was said — it was the apparent *heart* that went with his request — which allowed me
no room for hesitation; and I accordingly obeyed forthwith what I still considered a very singular summons.

Although, as boys, we had been even intimate associates, yet I really knew little of my friend. His reserve had been always excessive and habitual. I was aware, however, that his very ancient family had been noted, time out of mind, for a peculiar sensibility of temperament, displaying itself, through long ages, in many works of exalted art, and manifested, of late, in repeated deeds of munificent, yet unobtrusive charity, as well as in a passionate devotion to the intricacies, perhaps even more than to the orthodox and easily recognizable beauties, of musical science. I had learned, too, the very remarkable fact that the stem of the Usher race, all time-honored as it was, had put forth, at no period, any enduring branch ; in other words, that the entire family lay in the direct line of descent, and had always, with very trifling and very temporary variation, so lain. It was this deficiency, I considered, while running over in thought the perfect keeping of the character of the premises with the accredited character of the people, and while speculating upon the possible influence which the one, in the long lapse of centuries, might have exercised upon the other — it was this deficiency, perhaps, of collateral issue, and the consequent undeviating transmission, from sire to son, of the patrimony with the name, which had, at length, so identified the two as to merge the original title of the estate in the quaint and equivocal appellation of the " House of Usher " — an appellation which seemed to include, in the minds of the peasantry who used it, both the family and the family mansion.

I have said that the sole effect of my somewhat childish experiment of looking down within the tarn had been to deepen the first singular impression. There can be no doubt that the consciousness of the rapid increase of my superstition — for why should I not so term it? — served mainly to accelerate the increase itself. Such, I have long known, is the paradoxical law of all sentiments having terror as a basis. And it might have been for this reason only, that, when I again uplifted my eyes to the house itself, from its image in the pool, there grew in my mind a strange fancy — a fancy so ridiculous, indeed, that I but mention it to show the vivid force of the sensations which oppressed me. I had so worked upon my imagination as really to believe that about the whole mansion and domain there hung an atmosphere peculiar to themselves and their immediate vicinity — an atmosphere which had no affinity with the air of heaven, but which had reeked up from the decayed trees, and the gray wall, and the silent tarn — a pestilent and mystic vapor, dull, sluggish, faintly discernible, and leaden-hued.

Shaking off from my spirit what *must* have been a dream, I scanned more narrowly the real aspect of the building. Its principal feature seemed to be that of an excessive antiquity. The discoloration of ages had been great. Minute fungi overspread the whole exterior, hanging in a fine, tangled web-work from the eaves. Yet all this was apart from any extraordinary dilapidation. No portion of the masonry had fallen ; and there appeared to be a wild inconsistency between its still perfect adaptation of parts, and the crumbling condition of the individual stones. In this there was much that reminded me of the specious totality of old wood-work which has rotted for years in some neglected vault, with no disturbance from the breath of the external air. Beyond this indication of extensive decay, however, the fabric gave little token of instability. Perhaps the eye of a scrutinizing observer might have discovered a barely perceptible fissure, which, extending from the roof of the building in front, made its way down the wall in a zigzag direction, until it became lost in the sullen waters of the tarn.

Noticing these things, I rode over a short causeway to the house. A servant in waiting took my horse, and I entered the Gothic archway of the hall. A valet, of stealthy step, thence conducted me, in silence, through many dark and intricate passages in my progress to the *studio* of his master. Much that I encountered on the way contributed, I know not how, to heighten the vague sentiments of which I have

already spoken. While the objects around me - while the
carvings of the ceilings, the sombre tapestries of the walls,
the ebon blackness of the floors, and the phantasmagoric
armorial trophies which rattled as I strode, were but matters
to which, or to such as which, I had been accustomed from
my infancy — while I hesitated not to acknowledge how
familiar was all this — I still wondered to find how unfamil-
iar were the fancies which ordinary images were stirring up.
On one of the staircases, I met the physician of the family.
His countenance, I thought, wore a mingled expression of
low cunning and perplexity. He accosted me with trepida-
tion and passed on. The valet now threw open a door and
ushered me into the presence of his master.

The room in which I found myself was very large and lofty.
The windows were long, narrow, and pointed, and at so vast
a distance from the black oaken floor as to be altogether
inaccessible from within. Feeble gleams of encrimsoned
light made their way through the trelliced panes, and served
to render sufficiently distinct the more prominent objects
around ; the eye, however, struggled in vain to reach
the remoter angles of the chamber, or the recesses of the
vaulted and fretted ceiling. Dark draperies hung upon the
walls. The general furniture was profuse, comfortless,
antique, and tattered. Many books and musical instruments lay scattered about, but failed to give any vitality to
the scene. I felt that I breathed an atmosphere of sorrow.
An air of stern, deep, and irredeemable gloom hung over
and pervaded all.

Upon my entrance, Usher arose from a sofa on which he
had been lying at full length, and greeted me with a vivacious warmth which had much in it, I at first thought, of an
overdone cordiality — of the constrained effort of the *ennuyé*
man of the world. A glance, however, at his countenance
convinced me of his perfect sincerity. We sat down ; and
for some moments, while he spoke not, I gazed upon him
with a feeling half of pity, half of awe. Surely, man had
never before so terribly altered, in so brief a period, as had

Roderick Usher! It was with difficulty that I could bring myself to admit the identity of the wan being before me with the companion of my early boyhood. Yet the character of his face had been at all times remarkable. A cadaverousness of complexion; an eye large, liquid, and luminous beyond comparison; lips somewhat thin and very pallid, but of a surpassingly beautiful curve; a nose of a delicate Hebrew model, but with a breadth of nostril unusual in similar formations; a finely moulded chin, speaking, in its want of prominence, of a want of moral energy; hair of a more than web-like softness and tenuity; these features, with an inordinate expansion above the regions of the temple, made up altogether a countenance not easily to be forgotten. And now in the mere exaggeration of the prevailing character of these features, and of the expression they were wont to convey, lay so much of change that I doubted to whom I spoke. The now ghastly pallor of the skin, and the now miraculous lustre of the eye, above all things startled and even awed me. The silken hair, too, had been suffered to grow all unheeded, and as, in its wild gossamer texture, it floated rather than fell about the face, I could not, even with effort, connect its arabesque expression with any idea of simple humanity.

In the manner of my friend I was at once struck with an incoherence — an inconsistency; and I soon found this to arise from a series of feeble and futile struggles to overcome an habitual trepidancy, an excessive nervous agitation. For something of this nature I had indeed been prepared, no less by his letter than by reminiscences of certain boyish traits, and by conclusions deduced from his peculiar physical conformation and temperament. His action was alternately vivacious and sullen. His voice varied rapidly from a tremulous indecision (when the animal spirits seemed utterly in abeyance) to that species of energetic concision — that abrupt, weighty, unhurried, and hollow-sounding enunciation — that leaden, self-balanced and perfectly modulated guttural utterance, which may be observed in the lost drunk-

ard, or the irreclaimable eater of opium, during the periods
of his most intense excitement.

It was thus that he spoke of the object of my visit, of
his earnest desire to see me, and of the solace he expected
me to afford him.   He entered, at some length, into what
he conceived to be the nature of his malady.   It was, he
said, a constitutional and a family evil, and one for which
he despaired to find a remedy — a mere nervous affection,
he immediately added, which would undoubtedly soon pass
off.   It displayed itself in a host of unnatural sensations.
Some of these, as he detailed them, interested and bewildered me; although, perhaps, the terms and the general
manner of the narration had their weight.   He suffered
much from a morbid acuteness of the senses.   The most
insipid food was alone endurable ; he could wear only gar-
ments of certain texture; the odors of all flowers were
oppressive ; his eyes were tortured by even a faint light ;
and there were but peculiar sounds, and these from stringed
instruments, which did not inspire him with horror.

To an anomalous species of terror I found him a bounden
slave.   " I shall perish," said he, " I *must* perish in this
deplorable folly.   Thus, thus, and not otherwise, shall I be
lost.   I dread the events of the future, not in themselves,
but in their results.   I shudder at the thought of any, even
the most trivial, incident, which may operate upon this intolerable agitation of soul.   I have, indeed, no abhorrence
of danger, except in its absolute effect — in terror.   In this
unnerved — in this pitiable condition — I feel that the
period will sooner or later arrive when I must abandon life
and reason together, in some struggle with the grim phantasm, FEAR."

I learned, moreover, at intervals, and through broken and
equivocal hints, another singular feature of his mental condition.   He was enchained by certain superstitious impressions in regard to the dwelling which he tenanted, and
whence, for many years, he had never ventured forth —
in regard to an influence whose supposititious force was

conveyed in terms too shadowy here to be restated — an influence which some peculiarities in the mere form and substance of his family mansion, had, by dint of long sufferance, he said, obtained over his spirit — an effect which the *physique* of the gray walls and turrets, and of the dim tarn into which they all looked down, had, at length, brought about upon the *morale* of his existence.

He admitted, however, although with hesitation, that much of the peculiar gloom which thus afflicted him could be traced to a more natural and far more palpable origin — to the severe and long-continued illness — indeed to the evidently approaching dissolution — of a tenderly beloved sister, his sole companion for long years, his last and only relative on earth. " Her decease," he said, with a bitterness which I can never forget, "would leave him (him the hopeless and the frail) the last of the ancient race of the Ushers." While he spoke, the lady Madeline (for so was she called) passed slowly through a remote portion of the apartment, and, without having noticed my presence, disappeared. I regarded her with an utter astonishment not unmingled with dread ; [1] and yet I found it impossible to account for such feelings. A sensation of stupor oppressed me, as my eyes followed her retreating steps. When a door, at length, closed upon her, my glance sought instinctively and eagerly the countenance of the brother ; but he had buried his face in his hands, and I could only perceive that a far more than ordinary wanness had overspread the emaciated fingers through which trickled many passionate tears.

The disease of the lady Madeline had long baffled the skill of her physicians. A settled apathy, a gradual wasting away of the person, and frequent although transient affections of a partially cataleptical character, were the unusual

[1 " In place of this clause the first edition has : " Her figure, her air, her features, — all, in their very minutest development were those — were identically (I can use no other sufficient term) were identically those of the Roderick Usher who sat beside me. A feeling of stupor," etc.]

diagnosis. Hitherto she had steadily borne up against the pressure of her malady, and had not betaken herself finally to bed ; but, on the closing in of the evening of my arrival at the house, she succumbed (as her brother told me at night with inexpressible agitation) to the prostrating power of the destroyer ; and I learned that the glimpse I had obtained of her person would thus probably be the last I should obtain — that the lady, at least while living, would be seen by me no more.

For several days ensuing her name was unmentioned by either Usher or myself ; and during this period I was busied in earnest endeavors to alleviate the melancholy of my friend. We painted and read together ; or I listened, as if in a dream, to the wild improvisations of his speaking guitar. And thus, as a closer and still closer intimacy admitted me more unreservedly into the recesses of his spirit, the more bitterly did I perceive the futility of all attempt at cheering a mind from which darkness, as if an inherent positive quality, poured forth upon all objects of the moral and physical universe, in one unceasing radiation of gloom.

'I shall ever bear about me a memory of the many solemn hours I thus spent alone with the master of the House of Usher. Yet I should fail in any attempt to convey an idea of the exact character of the studies, or of the occupations in which he involved me, or led me the way. An excited and highly distempered ideality threw a sulphurous lustre over all. His long improvised dirges will ring forever in my ears. Among other things, I hold painfully in mind a certain singular perversion and amplification of the wild air of the last waltz of Von Weber. From the paintings over which his elaborate fancy brooded, and which grew, touch by touch, into vaguenesses at which I shuddered the more thrillingly because I shuddered knowing not why ; — from these paintings (vivid as their images now are before me) I would in vain endeavor to educe more than a small portion which should lie within the compass of merely written words. By the utter simplicity, by the nakedness of his designs, he arrested and overawed attention. If ever mortal painted an idea, that mortal was Roderick Usher. For me at least, in the circumstances then surrounding me, there arose out of the pure abstractions which the hypochondriac contrived to throw upon his canvas, an intensity of intolerable awe, no shadow of which felt I eve. yet in the contemplation of the certainly glowing yet too concrete reveries of Fuseli.

One of the phantasmagoric conceptions of my friend, partaking not so rigidly of the spirit of abstraction, may be shadowed forth, although feebly, in words. A small picture presented the interior of an immensely long and rectangular vault or tunnel, with low walls, smooth, white, and without interruption or device. Certain accessory points of the design served well to convey the idea that this excavation lay at an exceeding depth below the surface of the earth. No outlet was observed in any portion of its vast extent, and no torch, or other artificial source of light was discernible; yet a flood of intense rays rolled throughout, and bathed the whole in a ghastly and inappropriate splendor.

I have just spoken of that morbid condition of the auditory nerve which rendered all music intolerable to the sufferer, with the exception of certain effects of stringed instruments. It was, perhaps, the narrow limits to which he thus confined himself upon the guitar, which gave birth, in great measure, to the fantastic character of his performances. But the fervid *facility* of his *inpromptus* could not be so accounted for. They must have been, and were, in the notes, as well as in the words of his wild fantasias (for he not unfrequently accompanied himself with rhymed verbal improvisations), the result of that intense mental collectedness and concentration to which I have previously alluded as observable only in particular moments of the highest artificial excitement. The words of one of these rhapsodies I have easily remembered. I was, perhaps, the more forcibly impressed with it, as he gave it, because, in the under or mystic current of its meaning, I fancied that I perceived, and for the first time, a full consciousness on the part of Usher, of the tottering of his lofty reason upon her throne. The verses, which were entitled " The Haunted Palace," ran very nearly, if not accurately, thus :

I.

In the greenest of our valleys,
    By good angels tenanted,
Once a fair and stately palace —
    Radiant palace — reared its head.
In the monarch Thought's dominion —
    It stood there !
Never seraph spread a pinion
    Over fabric half so fair.

II.

Banners yellow, glorious, golden,
    On its roof did float and flow ;
(This — all this — was in the olden
    Time long ago)
And every gentle air that dallied,
    In that sweet day,
Along the ramparts plumed and pallid,
    A winged odor went away.

III.

Wanderers in that happy valley
    Through two luminous windows saw
Spirits moving musically
    To a lute's well-tunèd law,
Round about a throne, where sitting
    (Porphyrogene !)
In state his glory well befitting,
    The ruler of the realm was seen.

IV.

And all with pearl and ruby glowing
    Was the fair palace door,
Through which came flowing, flowing, flowing,
    And sparkling evermore,
A troop of Echoes whose sweet duty
    Was but to sing,
In voices of surpassing beauty,
    The wit and wisdom of their king.

V.

But evil things, in robes of sorrow,
  Assailed the monarch's high estate
(Ah, let us mourn, for never morrow
  Shall dawn upon him, desolate !);
And, round about his home, the glory
  That blushed and bloomed
Is but a dim-remembered story
  Of the old time entombed.

VI.

And travellers now within that valley,
  Through the red-litten windows, see
Vast forms that move fantastically
  To a discordant melody;
While, like a rapid ghastly river,
  Through the pale door,
A hideous throng rush out forever,
  And laugh — but smile no more.

I well remember that suggestions arising from this ballad led us into a train of thought wherein there became manifest an opinion of Usher's which I mention not so much on account of its novelty (for other men [1] have thought thus) as on account of the pertinacity with which he maintained it. This opinion, in its general form, was that of the sentience of all vegetable things. But, in his disordered fancy, the idea had assumed a more daring character, and trespassed, under certain conditions, upon the kingdom of inorganization. I lack words to express the full extent or the earnest *abandon* of his persuasion. The belief, however, was connected (as I have previously hinted) with the gray stones of the home of his forefathers. The conditions of the sentience had been here, he imagined, fulfilled in the method of collocation of these stones — in the order of their arrangement, as well as in that of the many *fungi* which overspread them, and of the decayed trees which stood around — above all, in the long undisturbed endur-

[1] Watson, Dr. Percival, Spallanzani, and especially the Bishop of Llandaff.   See Chemical Essays, vol. v.

ance of this arrangement, and in its reduplication in the still waters of the tarn. Its evidence — the evidence of the sentience — was to be seen, he said, (and I here started as he spoke), in the gradual yet certain condensation of an atmosphere of their own about the waters and the walls. The result was discoverable, he added, in that silent, yet importunate and terrible influence which for centuries had moulded the destinies of his family, and which made *him* what I now saw him — what he was. Such opinions need no comment, and I will make none.

Our books — the books, which, for years, had formed no small portion of the mental existence of the invalid — were, as might be supposed, in strict keeping with this character of phantasm. We pored together over such works as the *Ververt et Chartreuse* of Gresset; the *Belphegor* of Machiavelli; the *Heaven and Hell* of Swedenborg; the *Subterranean Voyage of Nicholas Klimm* by Holberg; the *Chiromancy* of Robert Flud, of Jean D'Indaginé, and of De la Chambre; the *Journey into the Blue Distance* of Tieck; and the *City of the Sun* of Campanella. One favorite volume was a small octavo edition of the *Directorium Inquisitorium*, by the Dominican Eymeric de Gironne; and there were passages in Pomponius Mela, about the old African Satyrs and Œgipans, over which Usher would sit dreaming for hours. His chief delight, however, was found in the perusal of an exceedingly rare and curious book in quarto Gothic — the manual of a forgotten church — the *Vigiliæ Mortuorum secundum Chorum Ecclesiæ Maguntinæ*.

I could not help thinking of the wild ritual of this work, and of its probable influence upon the hypochondriac, when, one evening, having informed me abruptly that the lady Madeline was no more, he stated his intention of preserving her corpse for a fortnight (previously to its final interment) in one of the numerous vaults within the main walls of the building. The worldly reason, however, assigned for this singular proceeding was one which I did not feel at liberty to dispute. The brother had been led to his resolution, so

he told me, by consideration of the unusual character of
the malady of the deceased, of certain obtrusive and eager
inquiries on the part of her medical men, and of the remote
and exposed situation of the burial-ground of the family. I
will not deny that when I called to mind the sinister countenance of the person whom I met upon the staircase, on the
day of my arrival at the house, I had no desire to oppose
what I regarded as at best but a harmless, and by no means
an unnatural, precaution.

At the request of Usher, I personally aided him in the
arrangements for the temporary entombment. The body
having been encoffined, we two alone bore it to its rest.
The vault in which we placed it (and which had been so
long unopened that our torches, half smothered in its oppressive atmosphere, gave us little opportunity for investi-
gation) was small, damp, and entirely without means of
admission for light; lying, at great depth, immediately beneath that portion of the building in which was my own
sleeping apartment. It had been used, apparently, in remote
feudal times, for the worst purposes of a donjon-keep, and,
in later days, as a place of deposit for powder, or some other
highly combustible substance, as a portion of its floor, and
the whole interior of a long archway through which we
reached it, were carefully sheathed with copper. The door,
of massive iron, had been, also, similarly protected. Its
immense weight caused an unusually sharp grating sound,
as it moved upon its hinges.

Having deposited our mournful burden upon tressels
within this region of horror, we partially turned aside the
yet unscrewed lid of the coffin, and looked upon the face of
the tenant. A striking similitude between the brother and
sister now first arrested my attention; and Usher, divining,
perhaps, my thoughts, murmured out some few words from
which I learned that the deceased and himself had been
twins, and that sympathies of a scarcely intelligible nature
had always existed between them. Our glances, however,
rested not long upon the dead — for we could not regard her

unawed. The disease which had thus entombed the lady in
the maturity of youth, had left, as usual in all maladies of a
strictly cataleptical character, the mockery of a faint blush
upon the bosom and the face, and that suspiciously linger-
ing smile upon the lip which is so terrible in death. We
replaced and screwed down the lid, and, having secured the
door of iron, made our way, with toil, into the scarcely less
gloomy apartments of the upper portion of the house.

And now, some days of bitter grief having elapsed, an
observable change came over the features of the mental
disorder of my friend. His ordinary manner had vanished.
His ordinary occupations were neglected or forgotten. He
roamed from chamber to chamber with hurried, unequal, and
objectless step. The pallor of his countenance had assumed,
if possible, a more ghastly hue — but the luminousness of his
eye had utterly gone out. The once occasional huskiness of
his tone was heard no more.; and a tremulous quaver, as if
of extreme terror, habitually characterized his utterance.
There were times, indeed, when I thought his unceasingly
agitated mind was laboring with some oppressive secret, to
divulge which he struggled for the necessary courage. At
times, again, I was obliged to resolve all into the mere inexplicable vagaries of madness ; for I beheld him gazing upon
vacancy for long hours, in an attitude of the profoundest
attention, as if listening to some imaginary sound. It was
no wonder that his condition terrified — that it infected me.
I felt creeping upon me, by slow yet certain degrees, the
wild influence of his own fantastic yet impressive superstitions.

It was, especially, upon retiring to bed late in the night of
the seventh or eighth day after the placing of the lady Madeline within the donjon, that I experienced the full power of
such feelings. Sleep came not near my couch, while the
hours waned and waned away. I struggled to reason off the
nervousness which had dominion over me. I endeavored
to believe that much, if not all of what I felt, was due to the
bewildering influence of the gloomy furniture of the room —

of the dark and tattered draperies, which, tortured into motion by the breath of a rising tempest, swayed fitfully to and fro upon the walls, and rustled uneasily about the decorations of the bed. But my efforts were fruitless. An irrepressible tremor gradually pervaded my frame; and, at length, there sat upon my very heart an incubus of utterly causeless alarm. Shaking this off with a gasp and a struggle, I uplifted myself upon the pillows, and, peering earnestly within the intense darkness of the chamber, harkened — I know not why, except that an instinctive spirit prompted me — to certain low and indefinite sounds which came, through the pauses of the storm, at long intervals, I knew not whence. Overpowered by an intense sentiment of horror, unaccountable yet unendurable, I threw on my clothes with haste (for I felt that I should sleep no more during the night), and endeavored to arouse myself from the pitiable condition into which I had fallen, by pacing rapidly to and fro through the apartment.

I had taken but few turns in this manner, when a light step on an adjoining staircase arrested my attention. I presently recognized it as that of Usher. In an instant afterward he rapped, with a gentle touch, at my door, and entered, bearing a lamp. His countenance was, as usual, cadaverously wan — but, moreover, there was a species of mad hilarity in his eyes — and evidently restrained hysteria in his whole demeanor. His air appalled me — but anything was preferable to the solitude which I had so long endured, and I even welcomed his presence as a relief.

"And you have not seen it?" he said abruptly, after having stared about him for some moments in silence — "you have not then seen it? — but stay! you shall." Thus speaking, and having carefully shaded his lamp, he hurried to one of the casements, and threw it freely open to the storm.

The impetuous fury of the entering gust nearly lifted us from our feet. It was, indeed, a tempestuous yet sternly beautiful night, and one wildly singular in its terror and its

beauty. A whirlwind had apparently collected its force in
our vicinity ; for there were frequent and violent alterations
in the direction of the wind ; and the exceeding density of
the clouds (which hung so low as to press upon the turrets
of the house) did not prevent our perceiving the life-like
velocity with which they flew careering from all points
against each other, without passing away into the distance.
I say that even their exceeding density did not prevent our
perceiving this — yet we had no glimpse of the moon or
stars — nor was there any flashing forth of the lightning. But
the under surfaces of the huge masses of agitated vapor, as
well as all terrestrial objects immediately around us, were
glowing in the unnatural light of a faintly luminous and distinctly visible gaseous exhalation which hung about and
enshrouded the mansion.

"You must not — you shall not behold this ! " said I,
shudderingly, to Usher, as I led him, with a gentle violence,
from the window to a seat. "These appearances, which
bewilder you, are merely electrical phenomena not uncommon — or it may be that they have their ghastly origin in
the rank miasma of the tarn. Let us close this casement —
the air is chilling and dangerous to your frame. Here is
one of your favorite romances. I will read, and you shall
listen ; — and so we will pass away this terrible night
together."

The antique volume which I had taken up was the *Mad
Trist* of Sir Launcelot Canning ; but I had called it a favorite of Usher's more in sad jest than in earnest ; for, in truth,
there is little in its uncouth and unimaginative prolixity
which could have had interest for the lofty and spiritual
ideality of my friend. It was, however, the only book
immediately at hand ; and I indulged a vague hope that
the excitement which now agitated the hypochondriac,
might find relief (for the history of mental disorder is full
of similar anomalies) even in the extremeness of the folly
which I should read. Could I have judged, indeed, by the
wild, overstrained air of vivacity with which he harkened, or

apparently harkened, to the words of the tale, I might well have congratulated myself upon the success of my design.

I had arrived at that well-known portion of the story where Ethelred, the hero of the *Trist*, having sought in vain for peaceable admission into the dwelling of the hermit, proceeds to make good an entrance by force. Here, it will be remembered, the words of the narrative run thus :

" And Ethelred, who was by nature of a doughty heart, and who was now mighty withal, on account of the powerfulness of the wine which he had drunken, waited no longer to hold parley with the hermit, who, in sooth, was of an obstinate and maliceful turn ; but, feeling the rain upon his shoulders, and fearing the rising of the tempest, uplifted his mace outright, and, with blows, made quickly room in the plankings of the door for his gauntleted hand ; and now pulling therewith sturdily, he so cracked, and ripped, and tore all asunder, that the noise of the dry and hollow-sounding wood alarummed and reverberated throughout the forest.''

At the termination of this sentence I started, and for a moment paused ; for it appeared to me (although I at once concluded that my excited fancy had deceived me) — it appeared to me that, from some very remote portion of the mansion, there came, indistinctly, to my ears what might have been, in its exact similarity of character, the echo (but a stifled and dull one certainly) of the very cracking and ripping sound which Sir Launcelot had so particularly described.   It was, beyond doubt, the coincidence alone which had arrested my attention ; for, amid the rattling of the sashes of the casements, and the ordinary commingled noises of the still increasing storm, the sound, in itself, had nothing, surely, which should have interested or disturbed me.   I continued the story :

" But the good champion Ethelred, now entering within the door, was sore enraged and amazed to perceive no signal of the maliceful hermit ; but, in the stead thereof, a dragon of a scaly and prodigious demeanor, and of a fiery tongue, which sate in guard before a palace of gold, with a floor of silver; and upon the wall there hung a shield of shining brass with this legend enwritten —

> Who entereth herein, a conqueror hath bin;
> Who slayeth the dragon, the shield he shall win;

And Ethelred uplifted his mace, and struck upon the head of the dragon, which fell before him, and gave up his pesty breath, with a shriek so horrid and harsh, and withal so piercing, that Ethelred had fain to close his ears with his hands against the dreadful noise of it, the like whereof was never before heard."

Here again I paused abruptly, and now with a feeling of wild amazement — for there could be no doubt whatever that, in this instance, I did actually hear (although from what direction it proceeded I found it impossible to say) a low and apparently distant, but harsh, protracted, and most unusual screaming or grating sound — the exact counterpart of what my fancy had already conjured up for the dragon's unnatural shriek as described by the romancer.

Oppressed, as I certainly was, upon the occurrence of this second and most extraordinary coincidence, by a thousand conflicting sensations, in which wonder and extreme terror were predominant, I still retained sufficient presence of mind to avoid exciting, by any observation, the sensitive nervousness of my companion. I was by no means certain that he had noticed the sounds in question; although, assuredly, a strange alteration had, during the last few minutes, taken place in his demeanor. From a position fronting my own, he had gradually brought round his chair, so as to sit with his face to the door of the chamber; and thus I could but partially perceive his features, although I saw that his lips trembled as if he were murmuring inaudibly. His head had dropped upon his breast — yet I knew that he was not asleep, from the wide and rigid opening of the eye as I caught a glance of it in profile. The motion of his body, too, was at variance with this idea — for he rocked from side to side with a gentle yet constant and uniform sway. Having rapidly taken notice of all this, I resumed the narrative of Sir Launcelot, which thus proceeded :

"And now the champion, having escaped from the terrible fury of the dragon, bethinking himself of the brazen shield, and of the breaking up of the enchantment which was upon it, removed the carcass from out of the way before him, and approached valorously over the silver pavement of the castle to where the shield was upon the wall ; which in sooth tarried not for his full coming, but fell down at his feet upon the silver floor, with a mighty great and terrible ringing sound."

No sooner had these syllables passed my lips, than — as if a shield of brass had indeed, at the moment, fallen heavily upon a floor of silver — I became aware of a distinct, hollow, metallic and clangorous, yet apparently muffled reverberation. Completely unnerved, I leaped to my feet ; but the measured rocking movement of Usher was undisturbed. I rushed to the chair in which he sat. His eyes were bent fixedly before him, and throughout his whole countenance there reigned a stony rigidity. But, as I placed my hand upon his shoulder, there came a strong shudder over his whole person ; a sickly smile quivered about his lips ; and I saw that he spoke in a low, hurried, and gibbering murmur, as if unconscious of my presence. Bending closely over him, I at length drank in the hideous import of his words.

"Not hear it? — yes, I hear it, and *have* heard it. Long — long — long — many minutes, many hours, many days have I heard it — yet I dared not — oh pity me, miserable wretch that I am ! — I dared not — I *dared* not speak ! *We have put her living in the tomb !* Said I not that my senses were acute ? I *now* tell you that I heard her first feeble movements in the hollow coffin. I heard them — many, many days ago — yet I dared not — *I dared not speak !* And now — to-night — Ethelred — ha ! ha ! — the breaking of the hermit's door, and the death-cry of

the dragon, and the clangor of the shield ! — say, rather,
the rending of her coffin, and the grating of the iron
hinges of her prison, and her struggles within the cop-
pered archway of the vault !   Oh whither shall I fly?   Will
she not be here anon?   Is she not hurrying to upbraid me
for my haste?   Have I not heard her footstep on the stair?
Do I not distinguish that heavy and horrible beating of her
heart?   Madman ! " — here he sprang furiously to his feet,
and shrieked out his syllables, as if in the effort he were
giving up his soul — "*Madman !   I tell you that she now
stands without the door !*"

As if in the superhuman energy of his utterance there
had been found the potency of a spell — the huge antique
pannels to which the speaker pointed threw slowly back,
upon the instant, their ponderous and ebony jaws.   It was
the work of the rushing gust — but then without those
doors there *did* stand the lofty and enshrouded figure of
the lady Madeline of Usher.   There was blood upon her
white robes, and the evidence of some bitter struggle upon
every portion of her emaciated frame.   For a moment she
remained trembling and reeling to and fro upon the threshold — then, with a low, moaning cry, fell heavily inward
upon the person of her brother, and in her violent and now
final death-agonies, bore him to the floor a corpse, and a
victim to the terrors he had anticipated.

From that chamber, and from that mansion, I fled
aghast.   The storm was still abroad in all its wrath as I
found myself crossing the old causeway.   Suddenly there
shot along the path a wild light, and I turned to see
whence a gleam so unusual could have issued ; for the
vast house and its shadows were alone behind me.   The
radiance was that of the full, setting, and blood-red moon,
which now shone vividly through that once barely-discerni-
ble fissure, of which I have before spoken as extending
from the roof of the building, in a zigzag direction, to the
base.   While I gazed, this fissure rapidly widened — there
came a fierce breath of the whirlwind — the entire orb of

the satellite burst at once upon my sight — my brain reeled as I saw the mighty walls rushing asunder — there was a long tumultuous shouting sound like the voice of a thousand waters — and the deep and dank tarn at my feet closed sullenly and silently over the fragments of the *" House of Usher."*

NATHANIEL PARKER WILLIS
1806 – 1867

Town talk sums up much of Willis, both what he was and
what he wrote. He lived in the public eye; he wrote of the
hour, for the hour. Naturally, therefore, his work was dying
while he was yet alive. Now he is hardly more than a name.
Of Andover and Yale what little impress he received was soon
rubbed away by a life in which the daily cultivation of eminent
society was industriously made to yield the daily crop of journalism. Indeed, a man so quick to take every new impression
was hardly the man to bear the marks of many old ones. And
of course the happy fluency that gave him even in youth a current popularity could dispense with that other and more deliberate merit of form. Form, since he had no native sense of it,
and could get on swimmingly without it, he never seriously
pursued. Few story-writers have spoiled so many good plots.
Not only is he chatty, digressive, episodic, but he rarely has any
clear solution and he never culminates. Such merit as *The
Inlet of Peach Blossoms* has in this aspect is quite exceptional.
Piquant, even vivid sometimes, in sketchy description, he has
no composition. This, doubtless, is why of the hundred tales
that pleased his public not one is read by ours.
Pencillings by the Way were supplied from Paris and London
in the early '30's to the New York *Mirror*, and in collective
form entertained both Britons and Americans. The characteristic title would serve as well for his subsequent collections. A
list is appended to the biography in the American Men of Letters series by Professor Beers, who has also edited a volume of
selections. A New York editor for many years, Willis touched
at so many points the literary life of his time that this biography has been made admirably significant of its main social
aspects. In fact, the life of Willis has more enduring interest
than his works.

THE INLET OF PEACH BLOSSOMS

[*From "Dashes at Life with a Free Pencil," 1845. The story was first published between 1840 and 1845, probably in the " New Mirror' of New York]*

THE Emperor Yuentsoong, of the dynasty Chow, was the most magnificent of the long-descended succession of Chinese sovereigns. On his first accession to the throne, his character was so little understood, that a conspiracy was set on foot among the yellow-caps, or eunuchs, to put out his eyes, and place upon the throne the rebel Szema, in whose warlike hands, they asserted, the empire would more properly maintain its ancient glory. The gravity and reserve which these myrmidons of the palace had construed into stupidity and fear, soon assumed another complexion, however. The eunuchs silently disappeared; the mandarins and princes whom they had seduced from their allegiance were made loyal subjects by a generous pardon; and, in a few days after the period fixed upon for the consummation of the plot, Yuentsoong set forth in complete armor at the head of his troops to give battle to the rebel in the mountains.

In Chinese annals this first enterprise of the youthful Yuentsoong is recorded with great pomp and particularity. Szema was a Tartar prince of uncommon ability, young, like the emperor, and, during the few last imbecile years of the old sovereign, he had gathered strength in his rebellion, till now he was at the head of ninety thousand men, all soldiers of repute and tried valor. The historian has, unfortunately, dimmed the emperor's fame to European eyes by attributing his wonderful achievements in this expedition to his superiority in arts of magic. As this account of his exploits is only prefatory to our tale, we will simply give the reader an idea of the style of the historian by translating literally a passage or two of his description of the battle : —

"Szema now took refuge within a cleft of the mountain, and Yuentsoong, upon his swift steed, outstripping the body-guard in his ardor, dashed amid the paralyzed troops with poised spear, his eyes fixed only on the rebel. There was a silence of an instant, broken only by the rattling hoofs of the intruder ; and then, with dishevelled hair and waving sword, Szema uttered a fearful imprecation. In a moment the wind rushed, the air blackened, and, with the suddenness of a fallen rock, a large cloud enveloped the rebel, and innumerable men and horses issued out of it. Wings flapped against the eyes of the emperor's horse, hellish noises screamed in his ears, and, completely beyond control, the animal turned and fled back through the narrow pass, bearing his imperial master safe into the heart of his army.

"Yuentsoong, that night, commanded some of his most expert soldiers to scale the beetling heights of the ravine, bearing upon their backs the blood of swine, sheep, and dogs, with other impure things, and these they were ordered to shower upon the combatants at the sound of the imperial clarion. On the following morning, Szema came forth again to offer battle, with flags displayed, drums beating, and shouts of triumph and defiance. As on the day previous, the bold emperor divided, in his impatience, rank after rank of his own soldiery, and, followed closely by his body-guard, drove the rebel army once more into their fastness. Szema sat upon his war-horse as before, intrenched amid his officers and ranks of the tallest Tartar spearmen ; and, as the emperor contended hand to hand with one of the opposing rebels, the magic imprecation was again uttered, the air again filled with cloudy horsemen and chariots, and the mountain shaken with discordant thunder. Backing his willing steed, the emperor blew a long sharp note upon his silver clarion, and, in an instant, the sun broke through the darkness, and the air seemed filled with paper men, horses of straw, and phantoms dissolving into smoke. Yuentsoong and Szema now stood face to face, with only mortal aid and weapons."

The historian goes on to record that the two armies suspended hostilities at the command of their leaders, and that, the emperor and his rebel subject having engaged in single combat, Yuentsoong was victorious, and returned to his capital with the formidable enemy whose life he had spared, riding beside him like a brother. The conqueror's career, for several years after this, seems to have been a series of exploits of personal valor ; and the Tartar prince shared in all his dangers and pleasures, his inseparable friend. It was during this period of romantic friendship that the events occurred which have made Yuentsoong one of the idols of Chinese poetry.

By the side of a lake in a distant province of the empire, stood one of the imperial palaces of pleasure, seldom visited, and almost in ruins. Hither, in one of his moody periods of repose from war, came the conqueror Yuentsoong, for the first time in years separated from his faithful Szema. In disguise, and with only one or two attendants, he established himself in the long silent halls of his ancestor Tsinchemong, and with his boat upon the lake, and his spear in the forest, seemed to find all the amusement of which his melancholy was susceptible. On a certain day in the latter part of April, the emperor had set his sail to a fragrant south wind, and, reclining on the cushions of his bark, watched the shore as it softly and silently glided past, and, the lake being entirely encircled by the imperial forest, he felt immersed in what he believed to be the solitude of a deserted paradise. After skirting the fringed sheet of water in this manner for several hours, he suddenly observed that he had shot through a streak of peach-blossoms floating from the shore, and at the same moment he became conscious that his boat was slightly headed off by a current setting outward. Putting up his helm, he returned to the spot, and beneath the droop-

ing branches of some luxuriant willows, thus early in leaf,
he discovered the mouth of an inlet, which, but for the
floating blossoms it brought to the lake, would have escaped
the notice of the closest observer. The emperor now low-
ered his sail, unshipped the slender mast, and betook him to
the oars ; and, as the current was gentle, and the inlet wider
within the mouth, he sped rapidly on through what appeared
to be but a lovely and luxuriant vale of the forest. Still,
those blushing betrayers of some flowering spot beyond extended like a rosy clew before him ; and with impulse of
muscles swelled and indurated in warlike exercise, the swift
keel divided the besprent mirror winding temptingly onward,
and, for a long hour, the royal oarsman untiringly threaded
this sweet vein of the wilderness.

Resting a moment on his oars while the slender bark still
kept her way, he turned his head toward what seemed to be
an opening in the forest on the left, and in the same instant
the boat ran head on, to the shore, the inlet at this point
almost doubling on its course. Beyond, by the humming of
bees and the singing of birds, there should be a spot more
open than the tangled wilderness he had passed ; and, disen-
gaging his prow from the alders, he shoved the boat again
into the stream, and pulled round a high rock, by which the
inlet seemed to have been compelled to curve its channel.
The edge of a bright green meadow now stole into the
perspective, and, still widening with his approach, disclosed
a slightly rising terrace clustered with shrubs, and studded
here and there with vases ; and farther on, upon the same
side of the stream, a skirting edge of peach-trees loaded
with the gay blossoms which had guided him thither.

Astonished at these signs of habitation in what was well
understood to be a privileged wilderness, Yuentsoong kept
his boat in mid-stream, and with his eyes vigilantly on the
alert, slowly made headway against the current. A few
strokes with his oars, however, traced another curve of the
inlet, and brought into view a grove of ancient trees scattered over a gently ascending lawn, beyond which, hidden

from the river till now by the projecting shoulder of a mound, lay a small pavilion with gilded pillars glittering like fairy work in the sun. The emperor fastened his boat to a tree leaning over the water, and with his short spear in his hand, bounded upon the shore, and took his way toward the shining structure, his heart beating with a feeling of wonder and interest altogether new. On a nearer approach, the bases of the pillars seemed decayed by time, and the gilding weather-stained and tarnished; but the trellised porticoes on the southern aspect were laden with flowering shrubs in vases of porcelain, and caged birds sang between the pointed arches, and there were manifest signs of luxurious taste, elegance, and care.

A moment with an indefinable timidity the emperor paused before stepping from the greensward upon the marble floor of the pavilion, and in that moment a curtain was withdrawn from the door, and a female, with step suddenly arrested by the sight of the stranger, stood motionless before him. Ravished with her extraordinary beauty, and awe-struck with the suddenness of the apparition and the novelty of the adventure, the emperor's tongue cleaved to his mouth, and ere he could summon resolution, even for a gesture of courtesy, the fair creature had fled within, and the curtain closed the entrance as before.

Wishing to recover his composure, so strangely troubled, and taking it for granted that some other inmate of the house would soon appear, Yuentsoong turned his steps aside to the grove; and with his head bowed, and his spear in the hollow of his arm, tried to recall more vividly the features of the vision he had seen. He had walked but a few paces when there came toward him from the upper skirt of the grove, a man of unusual stature and erectness, with white hair unbraided on his shoulders, and every sign of age except infirmity of step and mien. The emperor's habitual dignity had now rallied, and on his first salutation the countenance of the old man softened, and he quickened his pace to meet and give him welcome.

"You are noble?" he said with confident inquiry.

Yuentsoong colored slightly.

"I am," he replied, "Lew-melin, a prince of the empire."

"And by what accident here?"

Yuentsoong explained the clew of the peach-blossoms, and represented himself as exiled for a time to the deserted palace upon the lakes.

"I have a daughter," said the old man abruptly, "who has never looked on human face save mine."

"Pardon me," replied his visitor, "I have thoughtlessly intruded on her sight, and a face more heavenly fair" —

The emperor hesitated, but the old man smiled encouragingly.

"It is time," he said, "that I should provide a younger defender for my bright Teh-leen, and Heaven has sent you in the season of peach-blossoms with provident kindness.[1] You have frankly revealed to me your name and rank. Before I offer you the hospitality of my roof, I must tell you mine. I am Choo-tseen, the outlaw, once of your own rank, and the general of the Celestial army."

The emperor started, remembering that this celebrated rebel was the terror of his father's throne.

"You have heard my history," the old man continued. "I had been, before my rebellion, in charge of the imperial palace on the lake. Anticipating an evil day, I secretly prepared this retreat for my family; and when my soldiers deserted me at the battle of Ke-chow, and a price was set upon my head, hither I fled with my women and children; and the last alive is my beautiful Teh-leen. With this brief outline of my life, you are at liberty to leave me as you came, or to enter my house on the condition that you become the protector of my child."

The emperor eagerly turned toward the pavilion, and, with a step as light as his own, the erect and stately outlaw hastened to lift the curtain before him. Leaving his guest for

[1] The season of peach-blossoms was the only season of marriage in ancient China.

a moment in the outer apartment, he entered to an inner chamber in search of his daughter, whom he brought, panting with fear, and blushing with surprise and delight, to her future lover and protector. A portion of an historical tale so delicate as the description of the heroine is not work for imitators, however, and we must copy strictly the portrait of the matchless Teh-leen, as drawn by Le-pih, the Anacreon of Chinese poetry and the contemporary and favorite of Yuentsoong.

"Teh-leen was born while the morning star shone upon the bosom of her mother. Her eye was like the unblemished blue lily, and its light like the white gem unfractured. The plum-blossom is most fragrant when the cold has penetrated its stem, and the mother of Teh-leen had known sorrow. The head of her child drooped in thought, like a violet over-laden with dew. Bewildering was Teh-leen. Her mouth's corners were dimpled, yet pensive. The arch of her brows was like the vein in the tulip's heart, and the lashes shaded the blushes on her cheek. With the delicacy of a pale rose, her complexion put to shame the floating light of day. Her waist, like a thread in fineness, seemed ready to break, yet was it straight and erect, and feared not the fanning breeze; and her shadowy grace was as difficult to delineate as the form of the white bird rising from the ground by moonlight. The natural gloss of her hair resembled the uncertain sheen of calm water, yet without the false aid of unguents. The native intelligence of her mind seemed to have gained strength by retirement; and he who beheld her thought not of her as human. Of rare beauty, of rarer intellect, was Teh-leen, and her heart responded to the poet's lute."

We have not space, nor could we, without copying directly from the admired Le-pih, venture to describe the bringing of Teh-leen to court, and her surprise at finding herself the favorite of the emperor. It is a romantic circumstance, besides, which has had its parallels in other countries. But the sad sequel to the loves of poor Teh-leen is but recorded in the cold page of history; and if the poet, who wound up the climax of her perfections with her susceptibility to his lute, embalmed her sorrows in verse, he was probably too politic to bring it ever to light. Pass we to these neglected and unadorned passages of her history.

Yuentsoong's nature was passionately devoted and confiding ; and, like two brothers with one favorite sister, lived together Teh-leen, Szema, and the emperor. The Tartar prince, if his heart knew a mistress before the arrival of Teh-leen at the palace, owned afterward no other than her ; and, fearless of check or suspicion from the noble confidence and generous friendship of Yuentsoong, he seemed to live but for her service, and to have neither energies nor ambition except for the winning of her smiles. Szema was of great personal beauty, frank when it did not serve him to be wily, bold in his pleasures, and of manners almost femininely soft and voluptuous. He was renowned as a soldier, and, for Teh-leen, he became a poet and master of the lute ; and, like all men formed for ensnaring the heart of women, he seemed to forget himself in the absorbing devotion of his idolatry. His friend the emperor was of another mould. Yuentsoong's heart had three chambers, — love, friendship, and glory. Teh-leen was but a third in his existence, yet he loved her, — the sequel will show how well. In person, he was less beautiful than majestic, of large stature, and with a brow and lip naturally stern and lofty. He seldom smiled, even upon Teh-leen, whom he would watch for hours in pensive and absorbed delight ; but his smile, when it did awake, broke over his sad countenance like morning. All men loved and honored Yuentsoong ; and all men, except only the emperor, looked on Szema with antipathy. To such natures as the former, women give all honor and approbation ; but, for such as the latter, they reserve their weakness !

Wrapt up in his friend and mistress, and reserved in his intercourse with his counsellors, Yuentsoong knew not that, throughout the imperial city, Szema was called "the *kieu*," or robber-bird, and his fair Teh-leen openly charged with dishonor. Going out alone to hunt, as was his custom, and having left his signet with Szema, to pass and repass through the private apartments at his pleasure, his horse fell with him unaccountably in the open field. Somewhat superstitious, and remembering that good spirits sometimes "knit the grass" when other obstacles fail to bar our way into danger, the emperor drew rein, and returned to his palace. It was an hour after noon, and, having dismissed his attendants at the city gate, he entered by a postern to the imperial garden, and bethought himself of the concealed couch in a cool grot by a fountain (a favorite retreat, sacred to himself and Teh-leen), where he fancied it would be refreshing to sleep away the sultriness of the remaining hours till evening. Sitting down by the side of the murmuring fount, he bathed his feet, and left his slippers on the lip of the basin to be unencumbered in his repose within, and so, with unechoing step, entered the resounding grotto. Alas! there slumbered the faithless friend with the guilty Teh-leen upon his bosom!

Grief struck through the noble heart of the emperor like a sword in cold blood. With a word he could consign to torture and death the robber of his honor, but there was agony in his bosom deeper than revenge. He turned silently away, recalling his horse and huntsmen, and, outstripping all, plunged on through the forest till night gathered around him.

Yuentsoong had been absent many days from his capital, and his subjects were murmuring their fears for his safety, when a messenger arrived to the counsellors informing them of the appointment of the captive Tartar prince to the government of the province of Szechuen, the second honor of the Celestial empire. A private order accompanied the announcement, commanding the immediate departure of Szema for the scene of his new authority. Inexplicable as was this riddle to the multitude, there were those who read it truly by their knowledge of the magnanimous soul of the emperor; and among these was the crafty object of his generosity. Losing no time, he set forward with great pomp for Szechuen, and in their joy to see him no more in the palace, the slighted princes of the empire forgave his unmerited advancement. Yuentsoong returned to his capital; but to the terror of his counsellors and people, his hair was blanched white as the head of an old man! He was pale as well, but he was cheerful and kind beyond his wont, and to Teh-leen untiring in pensive and humble attentions. He pleaded only impaired health and restless slumbers as an apology for nights of solitude. Once Teh-leen penetrated to his lonely chamber, but by the dim night lamp she saw that the scroll over the window [1] was changed, and instead of the stimulus to glory which formerly hung in golden letters before his eyes, there was a sentence written tremblingly in black : —

"The close wing of love covers the death-throb of honor."

Six months from this period the capital was thrown into a tumult with the intelligence that the province of Szechuen was in rebellion, and Szema at the head of a numerous army on his way to seize the throne of Yuentsoong. This last sting betrayed the serpent even to the forgiving emperor, and tearing the reptile at last from his heart, he entered with the spirit of other times into the warlike preparations. The imperial army was in a few days on its march, and at Keoyang the opposing forces met and prepared for encounter. With a dread of the popular feeling toward Teh-leen, Yuentsoong had commanded for her a close litter, and she was borne after the imperial standard in the centre of the army. On the eve before the battle, ere the watch-fires were lit, the emperor came to her tent, set apart from his own, and with the delicate care and kind gentleness from

---

[1] The most common decorations of rooms, halls, and temples, in China, are ornamental scrolls or labels of colored paper or wood, painted and gilded, and hung over doors or windows, and inscribed with a line or couplet conveying some allusion to the circumstances of the inhabitant, or some pious or philosophical axiom. For instance, a poetical one recorded by Dr. Morrison :—

" From the pine forest the azure dragon ascends to the milky way," — typical of the prosperous man arising to wealth and honors.

which he never varied, inquired how her wants were supplied, and bade her thus early farewell for the night; his
own custom of passing among his soldiers on the evening
previous to an engagement, promising to interfere with what
was usually his last duty before retiring to his couch. Teh-
leen on this occasion seemed moved by some irrepressible
emotion, and as he rose to depart, she fell forward upon her
face, and bathed his feet with her tears. Attributing it to
one of those excesses of feeling to which all, but especially
hearts ill at ease, are liable, the noble monarch gently raised
her, and with repeated efforts at re-assurance, committed
her to the hands of her women. His own heart beat far
from tranquilly, for, in the excess of his pity for her grief he
had unguardedly called her by one of the sweet names of
their early days of love, — strange word now upon his lip, —
and it brought back, spite of memory and truth, happiness
that would not be forgotten !

It was past midnight, and the moon was riding high in
heaven, when the emperor, returning between the lengthen-
ing watch-fires, sought the small lamp which, suspended like
a star above his own tent, guided him back from the irregular mazes of the camp. Paled by the intense radiance of
the moonlight, the small globe of alabaster at length became
apparent to his weary eye, and with one glance at the peaceful beauty of the heavens, he parted the curtained door beneath it, and stood within. The Chinese historian asserts
that a bird, from whose wing Teh-leen had once plucked an
arrow, restoring it to liberty and life, in grateful attachment
to her destiny, removed the lamp from the imperial tent,
and suspended it over hers. The emperor stood beside
her couch. Startled at his inadvertent error, he turned to
retire ; but the lifted curtain let in a flood of moonlight
upon the sleeping features of Teh-leen, and like dewdrops
the undried tears glistened in her silken lashes. A lamp
burned faintly in the inner apartment of the tent, and her
attendants slept soundly. His soft heart gave way. Taking
up the lamp, he held it over his beautiful mistress, and once

more gazed passionately and unrestrainedly on her unparalleled beauty. The past — the early past — was alone before him. He forgave her, — there, as she slept, unconscious of the throbbing of his injured but noble heart so close beside her, — he forgave her in the long silent abysses of his soul! Unwilling to wake her from her tranquil slumber, but promising to himself, from that hour, such sweets of confiding love as had well-nigh been lost to him forever, he imprinted one kiss upon the parted lips of Teh-leen, and sought his couch for slumber.

Ere daybreak the emperor was aroused by one of his attendants with news too important for delay. Szema, the rebel, had been arrested in the imperial camp, disguised, and on his way back to his own forces; and like wildfire the information had spread among the soldiery, who, in a state of mutinous excitement, were with difficulty restrained from rushing upon the tent of Teh-leen. At the door of his tent, Yuentsoong found messengers from the alarmed princes and officers of the different commands, imploring immediate aid and the imperial presence to allay the excitement; and while the emperor prepared to mount his horse, the guard arrived with the Tartar prince, ignominiously tied, and bearing marks of rough usage from his indignant captors.

"Loose him!" cried the emperor, in a voice of thunder.

The cords were severed, and with a glance whose ferocity expressed no thanks, Szema reared himself up to his fullest height, and looked scornfully around him. Daylight had now broke, and as the group stood upon an eminence in sight of the whole army, shouts began to ascend, and the armed multitude, breaking through all restraint, rolled in toward the centre. Attracted by the commotion, Yuentsoong turned to give some orders to those near him, when Szema suddenly sprang upon an officer of the guard, wrenched his drawn sword from his grasp, and in an instant was lost to sight in the tent of Teh-leen. A sharp scream, a second of thought, and forth again rushed the desperate murderer, with his sword flinging drops of blood, and ere a foot stirred in the paralyzed group, the avenging cimeter of Yuentsoong had cleft him to the chin.

A hush, as if the whole army was struck dumb by a bolt from heaven, followed this rapid tragedy. Dropping the polluted sword from his hand, the emperor, with uncertain step, and the pallor of death upon his countenance, entered the fatal tent.

He came no more forth that day. The army was marshalled by the princes, and the rebels were routed with great slaughter; but Yuentsoong never more wielded sword. " He pined to death," says the historian, " with the wane of the same moon that shone upon the forgiveness of Teh-leen."

CAROLINE MATILDA STANSBURY KIRKLAND

1801 – 1864

MRS. KIRKLAND was recognised as one of the New York literary set during the flourishing of Willis. Her marriage to Professor William Kirkland (1827) took her to Central New York, and in 1839 to the Michigan frontier. The emigration produced immediately *A New Home — Who 'll Follow* (New York, 1839). " Miss Mitford's charming sketches of village life," she says in her preface, " suggested the form." It is the best of her books, not only in its distinct historical value as a document of frontier life, but also in its vivacity and keen intelligence of style. Of structure there is very little, a mere series of descriptions, with an occasional sketch in narrative. Returning to New York in 1842, she opened a school for girls, wrote for the magazines, and published, as a sequel to her first book, *Forest Life* (New York and Boston, 1842). Her tales, collected under the title *Western Clearings* (New York, 1846), show the same qualities as her descriptions — racy dialect, dashes of penetrative characterisation, quick suggestion of manners ; but their narrative consistency is not usually strong enough to hold interest. She returned to her first form in *Holidays Abroad* (1849). After that the titles of her books suggest hack-work. Meantime Mr. Kirkland had won his place as an editor. Poe included them both, the husband perfunctorily, the wife cordially, among his *Literati*.

THE BEE-TREE

[From "Western Clearings," 1846, a collection composed both of contributions to magazines and annuals and of new matter. The reprint below omits an explanatory introduction and an episodic love-story which, besides being feeble, is rendered quite superfluous by the dénouement.]

IT was on one of the lovely mornings of our ever lovely autumn, so early that the sun had scarcely touched the tops of the still verdant forest, that Silas Ashburn and his eldest son sallied forth for a day's chopping on the newly-purchased land of a rich settler, who had been but a few months among us. The tall form of the father, lean and gaunt as the very image of Famine, derived little grace from the rags which streamed from the elbows of his almost sleeveless coat, or flapped round the tops of his heavy boots, as he strode across the long causeway that formed the communication from his house to the dry land. Poor Joe's costume showed, if possible, a still greater need of the aid of that useful implement, the needle. His mother is one who thinks little of the ancient proverb that commends the stitch in time; and the clothing under her care sometimes falls in pieces, seam by seam. For want of this occasional aid is rendered more especially necessary by the slightness of the original sewing; so that the brisk breeze of the morning gave the poor boy no faint resemblance to a tall young aspen,

"With all its leaves fast fluttering, all at once."

The little conversation which passed between the father and son was such as necessarily makes up much of the talk of the poor.

195

"If we had n't had sich bad luck this summer," said Mr. Ashburn, "losing that heifer, and the pony, and them three hogs, — all in that plaguy spring-hole, too, — I thought to have bought that timbered forty of Dean. It would have squared out my farm jist about right."

"The pony did n't die in the spring-hole, father," said Joe.

"No, he did not, but he got his death there, for all. He never stopped shiverin' from the time he fell in. *You* thought he had the agur, but I know'd well enough what ailed him; but I was n't agoin' to let Dean know, because he 'd ha' thought himself so blam'd cunning, after all he 'd said to me about that spring-hole. If the agur could kill, Joe, we 'd all ha' been dead long ago."

Joe sighed, — a sigh of assent. They walked on musingly.

"This is going to be a good job of Keene's," continued Mr. Ashburn, turning to a brighter theme, as they crossed the road and struck into the "timbered land," on their way to the scene of the day's operations. "He has bought three eighties, all lying close together, and he 'll want as much as one forty cleared right off; and I 've a good notion to take the fencin' of it as well as the choppin'. He 's got plenty of money, and they say he don't shave quite so close as some. But I tell you, Joe, if I do take the job, you must turn to like a catamount, for I ain't a-going to make a nigger o' myself, and let my children do nothing but eat."

"Well, father," responded Joe, whose pale face gave token of any thing but high living, "I 'll do what I can; but you know I never work two days at choppin' but what I have the agur like sixty, — and a feller can't work when he 's got the agur."

"Not while the fit 's on, to be sure," said the father, "but I 've worked many an afternoon after my fit was over, when my head felt as big as a half-bushel, and my hands would ha' sizzed if I had put 'em in water. Poor folks has got to work — but Joe! if there is n't bees, by golley! I

wonder if anybody 's been a baitin' for 'em? Stop! hush!
watch which way they go!"

And with breathless interest — forgetful of all troubles,
past, present, and future — they paused to observe the
capricious wheelings and flittings of the little cluster, as
they tried every flower on which the sun shone, or returned
again and again to such as suited best their discriminating
taste. At length, after a weary while, one suddenly rose
into the air with a loud whizz, and after balancing a
moment on a level with the tree-tops, darted off, like a
well-sent arrow, toward the east, followed instantly by the
whole busy company, till not a loiterer remained.

"Well! if this is n't luck!" exclaimed Ashburn, exult-
ingly; "they make right for Keene's land! We 'll have
'em! go ahead, Joe, and keep your eye on 'em!"

Joe obeyed so well in both points that he not only out-
ran his father, but very soon turned a summerset over a
gnarled root or *grub* which lay in his path. This *faux pas*
nearly demolished one side of his face, and what remained
of his jacket sleeve, while his father, not quite so heedless,
escaped falling, but tore his boot almost off with what he
called "a contwisted stub of the toe."

But these were trifling inconveniences, and only taught
them to use a little more caution in their eagerness.
They followed on, unweariedly; crossed several fences, and
threaded much of Mr. Keene's tract of forest-land, scan-
ning with practised eye every decayed tree, whether standing or prostrate, until at length, in the side of a gigantic
but leafless oak, they espied, some forty feet from the
ground, the "sweet home" of the immense swarm whose
scouts had betrayed their hiding-place.

"The Indians have been here;" said Ashburn; "you
see they 've felled this saplin' agin the bee-tree, so as they
could climb up to the hole; but the red devils have been
disturbed afore they had time to dig it out. If they 'd had
axes to cut down the big tree, they would n't have left a
smitchin o' honey, they 're such tarnal thieves!"

Mr. Ashburn's ideas of morality were much shocked at the thought of the dishonesty of the Indians, who, as is well known, have no rights of any kind; but considering himself as first finder, the lawful proprietor of this much-coveted treasure, gained too without the trouble of a protracted search, or the usual amount of baiting, and burning of honeycombs, he lost no time in taking possession after the established mode.

To cut his initials with his axe on the trunk of the bee-tree, and to make *blazes* on several of the trees he had passed, detained him but a few minutes; and with many a cautious noting of the surrounding localities, and many a charge to Joe "not to say nothing to no-body," Silas turned his steps homeward, musing on the important fact that he had had good luck for once, and planning important business quite foreign to the day's chopping.

Now it so happened that Mr. Keene, who is a restless old gentleman, and, moreover, quite green in the dignity of a land-holder, thought proper to turn his horse's head, for this particular morning ride, directly towards these same "three eighties," on which he had engaged Ashburn and his son to commence the important work of clearing. Mr. Keene is low of stature, rather globular in contour, and exceedingly parrot-nosed; wearing, moreover, a face red enough to lead one to suppose he had made his money as a dealer in claret; but, in truth, one of the kindest of men, in spite of a little quickness of temper. He is profoundly versed in the art and mystery of store-keeping, and as profoundly ignorant of all that must sooner or later be learned by every resident land-owner of the western country.

Thus much being premised, we shall hardly wonder that our good old friend felt exceedingly aggrieved at meeting Silas Ashburn and the "lang-legged chiel" Joe, (who has grown longer with every shake of ague,) on the way *from* his tract, instead of *to* it.

"What in the world's the matter now!" began Mr. Keene, rather testily. "Are you never going to begin that work?"

"I don't know but I shall;" was the cool reply of Ashburn; "I can't begin it to-day, though."

"And why not, pray, when I've been so long waiting?"

"Because, I've got something else that must be done first. You don't think your work is all the work there is in the world, do you?"

Mr. Keene was almost too angry to reply, but he made an effort to say, "When am I to expect you, then?"

"Why, I guess we'll come on in a day or two, and then I'll bring both the boys."

So saying, and not dreaming of having been guilty of an incivility, Mr. Ashburn passed on, intent only on his beetree.

Mr. Keene could not help looking after the ragged pair for a moment, and he muttered angrily as he turned away, "Aye! pride and beggary go together in this confounded new country! You feel very independent, no doubt, but I'll try if I can't find somebody that wants money."

And Mr. Keene's pony, as if sympathizing with his master's vexation, started off at a sharp, passionate trot, which he has learned, no doubt, under the habitual influence of the spicy temper of his rider.

To find labourers who wanted money, or who would own that they wanted it, was at that time no easy task. Our poorer neighbours have been so little accustomed to value household comforts, that the opportunity to obtain them presents but feeble incitement to continuous industry. However, it happened in this case that Mr. Keene's star was in the ascendant, and the woods resounded, ere long, under the sturdy strokes of several choppers.

The Ashburns, in the mean time, set themselves busily at work to make due preparations for the expedition which they had planned for the following night. They felt, as does every one who finds a bee-tree in this region, that the prize was their own — that nobody else had the slightest claim to its rich stores; yet the gathering in of the spoils was to be performed, according to the invariable custom where the country is much settled, in the silence of night, and with every precaution of secrecy. This seems inconsistent, yet such is the fact.

The remainder of the "lucky" day and the whole of the succeeding one passed in scooping troughs for the reception of the honey, — tedious work at best, but unusually so in this instance, because several of the family were prostrate with the ague. Ashburn's anxiety lest some of his customary bad luck should intervene between discovery and possession, made him more impatient and harsh than usual; and the interior of that comfortless cabin would have presented to a chance visitor, who knew not of the golden hopes which cheered its inmates, an aspect of unmitigated wretchedness. Mrs. Ashburn sat almost in the fire, with a tattered hood on her head and the relics of a bed-quilt wrapped about her person; while the emaciated limbs of the baby on her lap, — two years old, yet unweaned, — seemed almost to reach the floor, so preternaturally were they lengthened by the stretches of a four months' ague. Two of the boys lay in the trundle-bed, which was drawn as near to the fire as possible; and every spare article of clothing that the house afforded was thrown over them, in the vain attempt to warm their shivering frames. "Stop your whimperin', can't ye!" said Ashburn, as he hewed away with hatchet and jack-knife, "you 'll be hot enough before long." And when the fever came his words were more than verified.

Two nights had passed before the preparations were completed. Ashburn and such of his boys as could work had laboured indefatigably at the troughs; and Mrs. Ashburn had thrown away the milk, and the few other stores which cumbered her small supply of household utensils, to free as many as possible for the grand occasion. This third day

had been "well day" to most of the invalids, and after
the moon had risen to light them through the dense wood,
the family set off, in high spirits, on their long, dewy walk.
They had passed the causeway and were turning from the
highway into the skirts of the forest, when they were
accosted by a stranger, a young man in a hunter's dress,
evidently a traveller, and one who knew nothing of the
place or its inhabitants, as Mr. Ashburn ascertained, to his
entire satisfaction, by the usual number of queries. The
stranger, a handsome youth of one or two and twenty, had
that frank, joyous air which takes so well with us Wol-
verines; and after he had fully satisfied our bee-hunter's
curiosity, he seemed disposed to ask some questions in his
turn. One of the first of these related to the moving cause
of the procession and their voluminous display of *containers.*

"Why, we're goin' straight to a bee-tree that I lit upon
two or three days ago, and if you've a mind to, you may
go 'long, and welcome. It's a real peeler, I tell ye!
There's a hundred and fifty weight of honey in it, if there's
a pound."

The young traveller waited no second invitation. His
light knapsack being but small incumbrance, he took upon
himself the weight of several troughs that seemed too
heavy for the weaker members of the expedition. They
walked on at a rapid and steady pace for a good half
hour, over paths that were none of the smoothest, and
only here and there lighted by the moonbeams. The
mother and children were but ill fitted for the exertion,
but Aladdin, on his midnight way to the wondrous vault
of treasure, would as soon have thought of complaining
of fatigue.

Who then shall describe the astonishment, the almost
breathless rage of Silas Ashburn, — the bitter disappointment of the rest, — when they found, instead of the bee-
tree, a great gap in the dense forest, and the bright moon
shining on the shattered fragments of the immense oak that
had contained their prize? The poor children, fainting

with toil now that the stimulus was gone, threw themselves on the ground; and Mrs. Ashburn, seating her wasted form on a huge branch, burst into tears.

"It's all one!" exclaimed Ashburn, when at length he could find words; "it's all alike! this is just my luck! It ain't none of my neighbour's work, though! They know better than to be so mean! It's the rich! Them that begrudges the poor man the breath of life!" And he cursed bitterly and with clenched teeth, whoever had robbed him of his right.

"Don't cry, Betsey," he continued; "let's go home. I'll find out who has done this, and I'll let 'em know there's law for the poor man as well as the rich. Come along, young 'uns, and stop your blubberin', and let them splinters alone!" The poor little things were trying to gather up some of the fragments to which the honey still adhered, but their father was too angry to be kind.

"Was the tree on your own land?" now inquired the young stranger, who had stood by in sympathizing silence during this scene.

"No! but that don't make any difference. The man that found it first, and marked it, had a right to it afore the President of the United States, and that I'll let 'em know, if it costs me my farm. It's on old Keene's land, and I should n't wonder if the old miser had done it himself, — but I'll let him know what's the law in Michigan!"

"Mr. Keene a miser!" exclaimed the young stranger, rather hastily.

"Why, what do *you* know about him?"

"O! nothing! — that is, nothing very particular — but I have heard him well spoken of. What I was going to say was, that I fear you will not find the law able to do anything for you. If the tree was on another person's property — "

"Property! that's just so much as you know about it!" replied Ashburn, angrily. "I tell ye I know the law well enough, and I know the honey was mine — and old Keene shall know it too, if he's the man that stole it."

The stranger politely forbore further reply, and the whole party walked on in sad silence till they reached the village road, when the young stranger left them with a kindly " good night ! "

It was soon after an early breakfast on the morning which succeeded poor Ashburn's disappointment, that Mr. Keene, attended by his lovely orphan niece, Clarissa Bensley, was engaged in his little court-yard, tending with paternal care the brilliant array of autumnal flowers which graced its narrow limits. Beds in size and shape nearly resembling patty-pans, were filled to overflowing with dahlias, china-asters and marigolds, while the walks which surrounded them, daily " swept with a woman's neatness," set off to the best advantage these resplendent children of Flora. A vine-hung porch that opened upon the miniature Paradise was lined with bird-cages of all sizes, and on a yard-square grass-plot stood the tin cage of a squirrel, almost too fat to be lively.

After all was " perform'd to point," — when no dahlia remained unsupported, — no cluster of many-hued asters without its neat hoop, — when no intrusive weed could be discerned, even through Mr. Keene's spectacles, — Clarissa took the opportunity to ask if she might take the pony for a ride.

" To see those poor Ashburns, uncle."

" They 're a lazy, impudent set, Clary."

" But they are all sick, uncle ; almost every one of the family down with ague. Do let me go and carry them something. I hear they are completely destitute of comforts."

" And so they ought to be, my dear," said Mr. Keene, who could not forget what he considered Ashburn's impertinence.

But his habitual kindness prevailed, and he concluded his remonstrance by saddling the pony himself, arranging Clarissa's riding-dress with all the assiduity of a gallant cavalier, and giving into her hand, with her neat silver-mounted whip, a little basket, well-crammed by his wife's kind care with delicacies for the invalids. No wonder that he looked after her with pride as she rode off! There are few prettier girls than the bright-eyed Clarissa.

"How are you this morning, Mrs. Ashburn?" asked the young visitant as she entered the wretched den, her little basket on her arm, her sweet face all flushed, and her eyes more than half suffused with tears.

"Law sakes alive!" was the reply. "I ain't no how. I'm clear tuckered out with these young 'uns. They've had the agur already this morning, and they're as cross as bear-cubs."

"Ma!" screamed one, as if in confirmation of the maternal remark, "I want some tea!"

"Tea! I ha'n't got no tea, and you know that well enough!"

"Well, give me a piece o' sweetcake then, and a pickle."

"The sweetcake was gone long ago, and I ha'n't nothing to make more — so shut your head!" And as Clarissa whispered to the poor pallid child that she would bring him some if he would be a good boy, and not tease his mother, Mrs. Ashburn produced, from a barrel of similar delicacies, a yellow cucumber, something less than a foot long, "pickled" in whiskey and water — and this the child began devouring eagerly.

Miss Bensley now set out upon the table the varied contents of her basket. "This honey," she said, showing some as limpid as water, "was found a day or two ago in uncle's woods — wild honey — isn't it beautiful?"

Mrs. Ashburn fixed her eyes on it without speaking; but her husband, who just then came in, did not command himself so far. "Where did you say you got that honey?" he asked.

"In our woods," repeated Clarissa; "I never saw such quantities; and a good deal of it as clear and beautiful as this."

"I thought as much!" said Ashburn angrily: "and

now, Clary Bensley," he added, "you'll just take that
cursed honey back to your uncle, and tell him to keep it,
and eat it, and I hope it will choke him! and if I live, I'll
make him rue the day he ever touched it."

Miss Bensley gazed on him, lost in astonishment. She
could think of nothing but that he must have gone suddenly mad; and the idea made her instinctively hasten her
steps toward the pony.

"Well! if you won't take it, I'll send it after ye!"
cried Ashburn, who had lashed himself into a rage; and
he hurled the little jar, with all the force of his powerful arm, far down the path by which Clarissa was about to
depart, while his poor wife tried to restrain him with a
piteous "Oh, father! don't! dont!"

Then, recollecting himself a little, — for he is far from
being habitually brutal, — he made an awkward apology to
the frightened girl.

"I ha'n't nothing agin *you*, Miss Bensley; you've
always been kind to me and mine; but that old devil
of an uncle of yours, that can't bear to let a poor man
live, — I'll larn him who he's got to deal with! Tell him
to look out, for he'll have reason!"

He held the pony while Clarissa mounted, as if to atone
for his rudeness to herself; but he ceased not to repeat his
denunciations against Mr. Keene as long as she was within
hearing. As she paced over the logs, Ashburn, his rage
much cooled by this ebullition, stood looking after her.

"I swan!" he exclaimed; "if there ain't that very
feller that went with us to the bee-tree, leading Clary
Bensley's horse over the cross-way!"

Clarissa felt obliged to repeat to her uncle the rude
threats which had so much terrified her; and it needed
but this to confirm Mr. Keene's suspicious dislike of Ashburn, whom he had already learned to regard as one of the
worst specimens of western character that had yet crossed
his path. He had often felt the vexations of his new posi-

206 AMERICAN SHORT STORIES

tion to be almost intolerable, and was disposed to imagine himself the predestined victim of all the ill-will and all the impositions of the neighbourhood. It unfortunately happened, about this particular time, that he had been more than usually visited with disasters which are too common in a new country to be much rega.ded by those who know what they mean. His fences had been thrown down, his corn-field robbed, and even the lodging-place of the peacock forcibly attempted. But from the moment he discovered that Ashburn had a grudge against him, he thought neither of unruly oxen, mischievous boys, nor exasperated neighbours; but concluded that the one unlucky house in the swamp was the ever-welling foundation of all this bitterness. He had not yet been long enough among us to discern how much our "bark is waur than our bite."

It was on a very raw and gusty evening, not long after, that Mr. Keene, with his handkerchief carefully wrapped around his chin, sallied forth after dark, on an expedition to the post-office. He was thinking how vexatious it was — how like everything else in this disorganized, or rather unorganized new country, that the weekly mail should not be obliged to arrive at regular hours, and those early enough to allow of one's getting one's letters before dark. As he proceeded he became aware of the approach of two persons, and though it was too dark to distinguish faces, he heard distinctly the dreaded tones of Silas Ashburn.

"No! I found you were right enough there! I could n't get at him that way; but I'll pay him for it yet!"

He lost the reply of the other party in this iniquitous scheme, in the rushing of the wild wind which hurried him on his course; but he had heard enough! He made out to reach the office, and receiving his paper, and hastening desperately homeward, had scarcely spirits even to read the price-current, (though he did mechanically glance at the corner of the "Trumpet of Commerce,") before he retired to bed in meditative sadness; feeling quite unable to await the striking of nine on the kitchen clock, which, in all ordinary circumstances, " toll'd the hour for retiring."

Mr. Keene's nerves had received a terrible shock on this fated evening, and it is certain that for a man of sober imagination, his dreams were terrific. He saw Ashburn, covered from crown to sole with a buzzing shroud of bees, trampling on his flower-beds, tearing up his honey-suckles root and branch, and letting his canaries and Java sparrows out of their cages ; and, as his eyes recoiled from this horrible scene, they encountered the shambling form of Joe, who, besides aiding and abetting in these enormities, was making awful strides, axe in hand, toward the sanctuary of the pea-fowls.

He awoke with a cry of horror, and found his bed-room full of smoke. Starting up in agonized alarm, he awoke Mrs. Keene, and half-dressed, by the red light which glimmered around them, they rushed together to Clarissa's chamber. It was empty. To find the stairs was the next thought ; but at the very top they met the dreaded bee-finder armed with a prodigious club !

"Oh mercy ! don't murder us ! " shrieked Mrs. Keene, falling on her knees ; while her husband, whose capsicum was completely roused, began pummelling Ashburn as high as he could reach, bestowing on him at the same time, in no very choice terms, his candid opinion as to the propriety of setting people's houses on fire, by way of revenge.

"Why, you 're both as crazy as loons ! " was Mr. Ashburn's polite exclamation, as he held off Mr. Keene at arm's length. " I was comin' up o' purpose to tell you that you needn't be frightened. It 's only the ruff o' the shanty, there, — the kitchen, as you call it."

"And what have you done with Clarissa? " — " Ay ! where 's my niece? " cried the distracted pair.

"Where is she? why, down stairs to be sure, takin' care o' the traps they throw'd out o' the shanty. I was out a 'coon-hunting, and see the light, but I was so far off that they 'd got it pretty well down before I got here. That .

'ere young spark of Clary's worked like a beaver, I tell ye!"

"You need not attempt," solemnly began Mr. Keene, "you need not think to make me believe, that you are not the man that set my house on fire. I know your revengeful temper; I have heard of your threats, and you shall answer for all, sir! before you 're a day older!"

Ashburn seemed struck dumb, between his involuntary respect for Mr. Keene's age and character, and the contemptuous anger with which his accusations filled him. "Well! I swan!" said he after a pause; "but here comes Clary; *she 's* got common sense; ask her how the fire happened."

"It 's all over now, uncle," she exclaimed, almost breathless, "it has not done so *very* much damage."

"Damage!" said Mrs. Keene, dolefully; "we shall never get things clean again while the world stands!"

"And where are my birds?" inquired the old gentleman.

"All safe — quite safe; we moved them into the parlour."

"We! who, pray?"

"Oh! the neighbours came, you know, uncle; and — Mr. Ashburn — "

"Give the devil his due," interposed Ashburn; "you know very well that the whole concern would have gone if it had n't been for that young feller."

"What young fellow? where?"

"Why here," said Silas, pulling forward our young stranger; "this here chap."

"Young man," began Mr. Keene, — but at the moment, up came somebody with a light, and while Clarissa retreated behind Mr. Ashburn, the stranger was recognised by her aunt and uncle as Charles Darwin.

"Charles! what on earth brought you here?"

"Ask Clary," said Ashburn, with grim jocoseness.

Mr. Keene turned mechanically to obey; but Clarissa had disappeared.

"Well! I guess I can tell you something about it, if nobody else won't," said Ashburn; "I'm something of a Yankee, and it's my notion that there was some sparkin' a goin' on in your kitchin, and that somehow or other the young folks managed to set it a-fire."

The old folks looked more puzzled than ever. "*Do* speak, Charles," said Mr. Keene; "what *does* it all mean? Did you set my house on fire?"

"I'm afraid I must have had some hand in it, sir," said Charles, whose self-possession seemed quite to have deserted him.

"You!" exclaimed Mr. Keene; "and I've been laying it to this man!"

"Yes! you know'd I owed you a spite, on account o' that plaguy bee-tree," said Ashburn; "a guilty conscience needs no accuser. But you was much mistaken if you thought I was sich a bloody-minded villain as to burn your gimcrackery for that! If I could have paid you for it, fair and even, I'd ha' done it with all my heart and soul. But I don't set men's houses a-fire when I get mad at 'em."

"But you threatened vengeance," said Mr. Keene.

"So I did, but that was when I expected to get it by law, though; and this here young man knows that, if he'd only speak."

Thus adjured, Charles did speak, and so much to the purpose that it did not take many minutes to convince Mr. Keene that Ashburn's evil-mindedness was bounded by the limits of the law, that precious privilege of the Wolverine. But there was still the mystery of Charles's apparition, and in order to its full unravelment, the blushing Clarissa had to be enticed from her hiding-place, and brought to confession. And then it was made clear that she, with all her innocent looks, was the moving cause of the mighty mischief. She it was who encouraged Charles to believe that her uncle's anger would not last forever; and this had led Charles to venture into the neighbourhood; and it was while consulting together, (on this particular point, of course,) that they managed to set the kitchen curtain on fire.

These things occupied some time in explaining, — but they were at length, by the aid of words and more eloquent blushes, made so clear, that Mr. Keene concluded, not only to new roof the kitchen, but to add a very pretty wing to one side of the house. And at the present time, the steps of Charles Darwin, when he returns from a surveying tour, seek the little gate as naturally as if he had never lived anywhere else. And the sweet face of Clarissa is always there, ready to welcome him, though she still finds plenty of time to keep in order the complicated affairs of both uncle and aunt.

Mr. Keene has done his very best to atone for his injurious estimate of Wolverine honour, by giving constant employment to Ashburn and his sons, and owning himself always the obliged party, without which concession all he could do would avail nothing. And Mrs. Keene and Clarissa have been unwearied in their kind attentions to the family, supplying them with so many comforts that most of them have got rid of the ague, in spite of themselves. The house has assumed so cheerful an appearance that I could scarcely recognise it for the same squalid den it had often made my heart ache to look upon. As I was returning from my last visit there, I encountered Mr. Ashburn, and remarked to him how very comfortable they seemed.

" Yes," he replied ; " I 've had pretty good luck lately ; but I 'm a goin' to pull up stakes and move to Wisconsin. I think I can do better, further West."

FITZ-JAMES O'BRIEN

1828 – 1862

THE facts of O'Brien's life have never been set in order. Even the date of his birth in County Limerick is uncertain. His untimely death was at Cumberland, Virginia, from wounds in the Federal service early in the Civil War. The clearest impression of the man may be had from William Winter's introduction to a collection of his verse and prose, published in Boston, 1881. He seems very like the Thackeray Irishman — generous, impulsive, extravagant with money and words. In the geniality that deserved their warm affection his somewhat Bohemian companions found a touch of genius; but the demands of a spendthrift life hand-to-mouth, and the facility with which these demands could be met, both made against the realisation of this higher promise. That it remained only a promise may be ascribed also to his dying at thirty-four. Youth is evident especially in that his prose is imitative. Poe is suggested almost immediately; and there is often an undertone of Dickens, the Dickens of the Christmas stories. In other aspects, too, O'Brien's writing is the work, not of a craftsman, but of a brilliant amateur. The fancies that he threw upon the periodical press are never quite achieved. Considered as materials, these fancies vary in value all the way from the conceptions of *The Diamond Lens* and *The Wondersmith*, which are not far from pure imagination, to *Tommatoo* and *My Wife's Tempter*, which are mere melodrama. But whatever their potential value, O'Brien's hand was not steady enough to bring it out. The main scene of *The Diamond Lens*, the microscopic vision, is as delicate as it is original, and as vivid as it is delicate; but the preparation for it is fumbling, and the solution unsatisfying. The tale printed below is exceptionally compact in structure and careful in detail. The obvious general resemblance to Poe's tales of physical horror should not obscure certain original merits. The note of realism, for instance, is not merely Poe's verisimilitude; it expresses a differentiation of character more like that of Kipling's similar study, *The End of the Passage*. Prof. Brander Matthews (*Philosophy of the Short-Story*, page 68) points out the similarity in conception of Maupassant's *Le Horla*.

Writing much prose and verse for many magazines now long passed away, and a play or two for Wallack, O'Brien found his steadiest employment with the Harpers between 1853 and 1858, and his most congenial life with the younger journalists and artists of New York.

WHAT WAS IT? A MYSTERY

[From " Harper's Monthly Magazine," March, 1859 ; volume xviii, page 504. The signature is Harry Escott]

IT is, I confess, with considerable diffidence that I approach the strange narrative which I am about to relate.
The events which I purpose detailing are of so extraordinary and unheard-of a character that I am quite prepared
to meet with an unusual amount of incredulity and scorn.
I accept all such beforehand. I have, I trust, the literary
courage to face unbelief. I have, after mature consideration, resolved to narrate, in as simple and straightforward
a manner as I can compass, some facts that passed under
my observation in the month of July last, and which, in
the annals of the mysteries of physical science, are wholly
unparalleled.

I live at No. — Twenty-sixth Street, in this city. The
house is in some respects a curious one. It has enjoyed
for the last two years the reputation of being haunted. It
is a large and stately residence, surrounded by what was
once a garden, but which is now only a green enclosure
used for bleaching clothes. The dry basin of what has been
a fountain, and a few fruit-trees, ragged and unpruned,
indicate that this spot, in past days, was a pleasant, shady
retreat, filled with fruits and flowers and the sweet murmur
of waters.

The house is very spacious. A hall of noble size leads
to a vast spiral staircase winding through its centre, while
the various apartments are of imposing dimensions. It was

built some fifteen or twenty years since by Mr. A——, the well-known New York merchant, who five years ago threw the commercial world into convulsions by a stupendous bank fraud. Mr. A——, as every one knows, escaped to Europe, and died not long after of a broken heart. Almost immediately after the news of his decease reached this country, and was verified, the report spread in Twenty-sixth Street that No. — was haunted. Legal measures had dispossessed the widow of its former owner, and it was inhabited merely by a care-taker and his wife, placed there by the house-agent into whose hands it had passed for purposes of renting or sale. These people declared that they were troubled with unnatural noises. Doors were opened without any visible agency. The remnants of furniture scattered through the various rooms were, during the night, piled one upon the other by unknown hands. Invisible feet passed up and down the stairs in broad daylight, accompanied by the rustle of unseen silk dresses, and the gliding of viewless hands along the massive balusters. The care-taker and his wife declared they would live there no longer. The house-agent laughed, dismissed them, and put others in their place. The noises and supernatural manifestations continued. The neighborhood caught up the story, and the house remained untenanted for three years. Several persons negotiated for it; but somehow, always before the bargain was closed, they heard the unpleasant rumors, and declined to treat any further.

It was in this state of things that my landlady — who at that time kept a boarding-house in Bleecker Street, and who wished to move farther up town — conceived the bold idea of renting No. — Twenty-sixth Street. Happening to have in her house rather a plucky and philosophical set of boarders, she laid her scheme before us, stating candidly everything she had heard respecting the ghostly qualities of the establishment to which she wished to remove us. With the exception of two timid persons, — a sea-captain and a returned Californian, who immediately gave notice that they would leave, — all of Mrs. Moffat's guests declared that they would accompany her in her chivalric incursion into the abode of spirits.

Our removal was effected in the month of May, and we were all charmed with our new residence. The portion of Twenty-sixth Street where our house is situated — between Seventh and Eighth Avenues — is one of the pleasantest localities in New York. The gardens back of the houses, running down nearly to the Hudson, form, in the summer time, a perfect avenue of verdure. The air is pure and invigorating, sweeping, as it does, straight across the river from the Weehawken heights, and even the ragged garden which surrounded the house on two sides, although displaying on washing days rather too much clothes-line, still gave us a piece of green sward to look at, and a cool retreat in the summer evenings, where we smoked our cigars in the dusk, and watched the fire-flies flashing their dark-lanterns in the long grass.

Of course we had no sooner established ourselves at No. — than we began to expect the ghosts. We absolutely awaited their advent with eagerness. Our dinner conversation was supernatural. One of the boarders, who had purchased Mrs. Crowe's "Night Side of Nature" for his own private delectation, was regarded as a public enemy by the entire household for not having bought twenty copies. The man led a life of supreme wretchedness while he was reading this volume. A system of espionage was established, of which he was the victim. If he incautiously laid the book down for an instant and left the room, it was immediately seized and read aloud in secret places to a select few. I found myself a person of immense importance, it having leaked out that I was tolerably well versed in the history of supernaturalism, and had once written a story, entitled "The Pot of Tulips," for *Harper's Monthly*, the foundation of which was a ghost. If a table or a wainscot panel happened to warp when we were assembled in the large drawing-room, there was an instant silence, and every one was prepared for an immediate clanking of chains and a spectral form.

After a month of psychological excitement, it was with the utmost dissatisfaction that we were forced to acknowledge that nothing in the remotest degree approaching the supernatural had manifested itself. Once the black butler asseverated that his candle had been blown out by some invisible agency while he was undressing himself for the night; but as I had more than once discovered this colored gentleman in a condition when one candle must have appeared to him like two, I thought it possible that, by going a step farther in his potations, he might have reversed this phenomenon, and seen no candle at all where he ought to have beheld one.

Things were in this state when an incident took place so awful and inexplicable in its character that my reason fairly reels at the bare memory of the occurrence. It was the tenth of July. After dinner was over I repaired, with my friend Dr. Hammond, to the garden to smoke my evening pipe. Independent of certain mental sympathies which existed between the Doctor and myself, we were linked together by a secret vice. We both smoked opium. We knew each other's secret, and respected it. We enjoyed together that wonderful expansion of thought, that marvellous intensifying of the perceptive faculties, that boundless feeling of existence when we seem to have points of contact with the whole universe, — in short, that unimaginable spiritual bliss, which I would not surrender for a throne, and which I hope you, reader, will never — never taste.

Those hours of opium happiness which the Doctor and I spent together in secret were regulated with a scientific accuracy. We did not blindly smoke the drug of Paradise, and leave our dreams to chance. While smoking, we carefully steered our conversation through the brightest and calmest channels of thought. We talked of the East, and endeavored to recall the magical panorama of its glowing scenery. We criticised the most sensuous poets, those who painted life ruddy with health, brimming with passion, happy in the possession of youth and strength and beauty. If we talked of Shakespeare's "Tempest," we lingered over Ariel, and avoided Caliban. Like the Gebers, we turned our faces to the east, and saw only the sunny side of the world.

This skilful coloring of our train of thought produced in our subsequent visions a corresponding tone. The splendors of Arabian fairy-land dyed our dreams. We paced that narrow strip of grass with the tread and port of kings. The song of the *rana arborea*, while he clung to the bark of the ragged plum-tree, sounded like the strains of divine orchestras. Houses, walls, and streets melted like rain-clouds, and vistas of unimaginable glory stretched away before us. It was a rapturous companionship. We enjoyed the vast delight more perfectly because, even in our most ecstatic moments, we were conscious of each other's presence. Our pleasures, while individual, were still twin, vibrating and moving in musical accord.

On the evening in question, the tenth of July, the Doctor and myself found ourselves in an unusually metaphysical mood. We lit our large meerschaums, filled with fine Turkish tobacco, in the core of which burned a little black nut of opium, that, like the nut in the fairy tale, held within its narrow limits wonders beyond the reach of kings ; we paced to and fro, conversing. A strange perversity dominated the currents of our thought. They would *not* flow through the sun-lit channels into which we strove to divert them. For some unaccountable reason they constantly diverged into dark and lonesome beds, where a continual gloom brooded. It was in vain that, after our old fashion, we flung ourselves on the shores of the East, and talked of its gay bazaars, of the splendors of the time of Haroun, of harems and golden palaces. Black afreets continually arose from the depths of our talk, and expanded, like the one the fisherman released from the copper vessel, until they blotted everything bright from our vision. Insensibly, we yielded to the occult force that swayed us, and indulged in gloomy speculation. We had talked some time upon the proneness of the human mind to mysticism, and the almost universal love of the Terrible, when Hammond suddenly said to me, "What do you consider to be the greatest element of Terror?" The question, I own, puzzled me. That many things were terrible, I knew. Stumbling over a corpse in the dark; beholding, as I once did, a woman floating down a deep and rapid river, with wildly-lifted arms, and awful, upturned face, uttering, as she sank, shrieks that rent one's heart, while we, the spectators, stood frozen at a window which overhung the river at a height of sixty feet, unable to make the slightest effort to save her, but dumbly watching her last supreme agony and her disappearance. A shattered wreck, with no life visible, encountered floating listlessly on the ocean, is a terrible object, for it suggests a huge terror, the proportions of which are vailed. But it now struck me for the first time that there must be one great and ruling embodiment of fear, a King of Terrors to which all others must succumb. What might it be? To what train of circumstances would it owe its existence?

"I confess, Hammond," I replied to my friend, "I never considered the subject before. That there must be one Something more terrible than any other thing, I feel. I cannot attempt, however, even the most vague definition."

"I am somewhat like you, Harry," he answered. "I feel my capacity to experience a terror greater than anything yet conceived by the human mind;—something combining in fearful and unnatural amalgamation hitherto supposed incompatible elements. The calling of the voices in Brockden Brown's novel of 'Wieland' is awful; so is the picture of the Dweller of the Threshold, in Bulwer's 'Zanoni'; but," he added, shaking his head gloomily, "there is something more horrible still than these."

"Look here, Hammond," I rejoined, "let us drop this kind of talk, for Heaven's sake! We shall suffer for it, depend on it."

"I don't know what's the matter with me to-night," he replied, "but my brain is running upon all sorts of weird and awful thoughts. I feel as if I could write a story like Hoffman, to-night, if I were only master of a literary style."

"Well, if we are going to be Hoffmanesque in our talk, I'm off to bed. Opium and nightmares should never be brought together. How sultry it is! Good-night, Hammond."

"Good-night, Harry. Pleasant dreams to you."

"To you, gloomy wretch, afreets, ghouls, and enchanters."

We parted, and each sought his respective chamber. I undressed quickly and got into bed, taking with me, according to my usual custom, a book, over which I generally read myself to sleep. I opened the volume as soon as I had laid my head upon the pillow, and instantly flung it to the other side of the room. It was Goudon's "History of Monsters"—a curious French work, which I had lately imported from Paris, but which, in the state of mind I had then reached, was anything but an agreeable companion. I resolved to go to sleep at once; so, turning down my gas until nothing but a little blue point of light glimmered on the top of the tube, I composed myself to rest.

The room was in total darkness. The atom of gas that still remained lighted did not illuminate a distance of three inches round the burner. I desperately drew my arm across my eyes, as if to shut out even the darkness, and tried to think of nothing. It was in vain. The confounded themes touched on by Hammond in the garden kept obtruding themselves on my brain. I battled against them. I erected ramparts of would-be blankness of intellect to keep them out. They still crowded upon me. While I was lying still as a corpse, hoping that by a perfect physical inaction I should hasten mental repose, an awful incident occurred. A Something dropped, as it seemed, from the ceiling, plumb upon my chest, and the next instant I felt two bony hands encircling my throat, endeavoring to choke me.

I am no coward, and am possessed of considerable physical strength. The suddenness of the attack, instead of stunning me, strung every nerve to its highest tension. My body acted from instinct, before my brain had time to realize the terrors of my position. In an instant I wound two muscular arms around the creature, and squeezed it, with all the strength of despair, against my chest. In a few seconds the bony hands that had fastened on my throat loosened their hold, and I was free to breathe once more. Then commenced a struggle of awful intensity. Immersed in the most profound darkness, totally ignorant of the nature of the Thing by which I was so suddenly attacked, finding my grasp slipping every moment, by reason, it seemed to me, of the entire nakedness of my assailant, bitten with sharp teeth in the shoulder, neck, and chest, having every moment to protect my throat against a pair of sinewy, agile hands, which my utmost efforts could not confine — these were a combination of circumstances to combat which required all the strength and skill and courage that I possessed.

At last, after a silent, deadly, exhausting struggle, I got my assailant under by a series of incredible efforts of strength. Once pinned, with my knee on what I made out to be its chest, I knew that I was victor. I rested for a moment to breathe. I heard the creature beneath me panting in the darkness, and felt the violent throbbing of a heart. It was apparently as exhausted as I was; that was one comfort. At this moment I remembered that I usually placed under my pillow, before going to bed, a large yellow silk pocket-handkerchief, for use during the night. I felt for it instantly; it was there. In a few seconds more I had, after a fashion, pinioned the creature's arms.

I now felt tolerably secure. There was nothing more to be done but to turn on the gas, and, having first seen what my midnight assailant was like, arouse the household. I will confess to being actuated by a certain pride in not giving the alarm before; I wished to make the capture alone and unaided.

Never losing my hold for an instant, I slipped from the bed to the floor, dragging my captive with me. I had but a few steps to make to reach the gas-burner; these I made with the greatest caution, holding the creature in a grip like a vice. At last I got within arm's-length of the tiny speck of blue light which told me where the gas-burner lay. Quick as lightning I released my grasp with one hand and let on the full flood of light. Then I turned to look at my captive.

I cannot even attempt to give any definition of my sensations the instant after I turned on the gas. I suppose I must have shrieked with terror, for in less than a minute afterward my room was crowded with the inmates of the house. I shudder now as I think of that awful moment. *I saw nothing!* Yes; I had one arm firmly clasped round a breathing, panting, corporeal shape, my other hand gripped with all its strength a throat as warm, and apparently fleshly, as my own; and yet, with this living substance in my grasp, with its body pressed against my own, and all in the bright glare of a large jet of gas, I absolutely beheld nothing! Not even an outline, — a vapor!

I do not, even at this hour, realize the situation in which I found myself. I cannot recall the astounding incident thoroughly. Imagination in vain tries to compass the awful paradox.

It breathed. I felt its warm breath upon my cheek. It struggled fiercely. It had hands. They clutched me. Its skin was smooth, like my own. There it lay, pressed close up against me, solid as stone, — and yet utterly invisible!

I wonder that I did not faint or go mad on the instant. Some wonderful instinct must have sustained me; for, absolutely, in place of loosening my hold on the terrible Enigma, I seemed to gain an additional strength in my moment of horror, and tightened my grasp with such wonderful force that I felt the creature shivering with agony.

Just then Hammond entered my room at the head of the household. As soon as he beheld my face — which, I suppose, must have been an awful sight to look at — he hastened forward, crying, " Great heaven, Harry! what has happened?"

" Hammond! Hammond!" I cried, "come here. Oh! this is awful! I have been attacked in bed by something or other, which I have hold of; but I can't see it — I can't see it!"

Hammond, doubtless struck by the unfeigned horror expressed in my countenance, made one or two steps forward with an anxious yet puzzled expression. A very audible titter burst from the remainder of my visitors. This suppressed laughter made me furious. To laugh at a human being in my position! It was the worst species of cruelty. *Now,* I can understand why the appearance of a man struggling violently, as it would seem, with an airy nothing, and calling for assistance against a vision, should have appeared ludicrous. *Then,* so great was my rage against the mocking crowd that had I the power I would have stricken them dead where they stood.

" Hammond! Hammond!" I cried again, despairingly, " for God's sake come to me. I can hold the — the Thing but a short while longer. It is overpowering me. Help me! Help me!"

" Harry," whispered Hammond, approaching me, " you have been smoking too much opium."

" I swear to you, Hammond, that this is no vision," I answered, in the same low tone. " Don't you see how it shakes my whole frame with its struggles? If you don't believe me, convince yourself. Feel it, — touch it."

Hammond advanced and laid his hand in the spot I indicated. A wild cry of horror burst from him. He had felt it!

In a moment he had discovered somewhere in my room a long piece of cord, and was the next instant winding it and knotting it about the body of the unseen being that I clasped in my arms.

"Harry," he said, in a hoarse, agitated voice, for, though he preserved his presence of mind, he was deeply moved, "Harry, it's all safe now. You may let go, old fellow, if you're tired. The Thing can't move."

I was utterly exhausted, and I gladly loosed my hold.

Hammond stood holding the ends of the cord that bound the Invisible, twisted round his hand, while before him, self-supporting as it were, he beheld a rope laced and interlaced, and stretching tightly round a vacant space. I never saw a man look so thoroughly stricken with awe. Nevertheless his face expressed all the courage and determination which I knew him to possess. His lips, although white, were set firmly, and one could perceive at a glance that, although stricken with fear, he was not daunted.

The confusion that ensued among the guests of the house who were witnesses of this extraordinary scene between Hammond and myself — who beheld the pantomime of binding this struggling Something, — who beheld me almost sinking from physical exhaustion when my task of jailer was over — the confusion and terror that took possession of the by-standers, when they saw all this, was beyond description. The weaker ones fled from the apartment. The few who remained clustered near the door, and could not be induced to approach Hammond and his Charge. Still incredulity broke out through their terror. They had not the courage to satisfy themselves, and yet they doubted. It was in vain that I begged of some of the men to come near and convince themselves by touch of the existence in that room of a living being which was invisible. They were incredulous, but did not dare to undeceive themselves. How could a solid, living, breathing body be invisible, they asked. My reply was this. I gave a sign to Hammond, and both of us — conquering

our fearful repugnance to touch the invisible creature —
lifted it from the ground, manacled as it was, and took
it to my bed. Its weight was about that of a boy of
fourteen.

"Now, my friends," I said, as Hammond and myself
held the creature suspended over the bed, "I can give you
self-evident proof that here is a solid, ponderable body
which, nevertheless, you cannot see. Be good enough to
watch the surface of the bed attentively."

I was astonished at my own courage in treating this
strange event so calmly; but I had recovered from my
first terror, and felt a sort of scientific pride in the affair
which dominated every other feeling.

The eyes of the bystanders were immediately fixed on
my bed. At a given signal Hammond and I let the creature fall. There was the dull sound of a heavy body
alighting on a soft mass. The timbers of the bed creaked.
A deep impression marked itself distinctly on the pillow,
and on the bed itself. The crowd who witnessed this gave
a sort of low, universal cry, and rushed from the room.
Hammond and I were left alone with our Mystery.

We remained silent for some time, listening to the low,
irregular breathing of the creature on the bed, and watching the rustle of the bed-clothes as it impotently struggled
to free itself from confinement. Then Hammond spoke.

"Harry, this is awful."

"Ay, awful."

"But not unaccountable."

"Not unaccountable! What do you mean? Such a
thing has never occurred since the birth of the world. I
know not what to think, Hammond. God grant that I am
not mad, and that this is not an insane fantasy!"

"Let us reason a little, Harry. Here is a solid body
which we touch, but which we cannot see. The fact is so
unusual that it strikes us with terror. Is there no parallel,
though, for such a phenomenon? Take a piece of pure
glass. It is tangible and transparent. A certain chemical

coarseness is all that prevents its being so entirely transparent as to be totally invisible. It is not *theoretically impossible*, mind you, to make a glass which shall not reflect a single ray of light — a glass so pure and homogeneous in its atoms that the rays from the sun shall pass through it as they do through the air, refracted but not reflected. We do not see the air, and yet we feel it."

"'That's all very well, Hammond, but these are inanimate substances. Glass does not breathe, air does not breathe. *This* thing has a heart that palpitates, — a will that moves it, — lungs that play, and inspire and respire."

" You forget the strange phenomena of which we have so often heard of late," answered the Doctor, gravely. "At the meetings called ' spirit circles,' invisible hands have been thrust into the hands of those persons round the table — warm, fleshly hands that seemed to pulsate with mortal life."

" What? Do you think, then, that this thing is — "

" I don't know what it is," was the solemn reply; " but please the gods I will, with your assistance, thoroughly investigate it."

We watched together, smoking many pipes, all night long, by the bedside of the unearthly being that tossed and panted until it was apparently wearied out. Then we learned by the low, regular breathing that it slept.

The next morning the house was all astir. The boarders congregated on the landing outside my room, and Hammond and myself were lions. We had to answer a thousand questions as to the state of our extraordinary prisoner, for as yet not one person in the house except ourselves could be induced to set foot in the apartment.

The creature was awake. This was evidenced by the convulsive manner in which the bed-clothes were moved in its efforts to escape. There was something truly terrible in beholding, as it were, those second-hand indications of the terrible writhings and agonized struggles for liberty which themselves were invisible.

Hammond and myself had racked our brains during the long night to discover some means by which we might realize the shape and general appearance of the Enigma. As well as we could make out by passing our hands over the creature's form, its outlines and lineaments were human. There was a mouth; a round, smooth head without hair; a nose, which, however, was little elevated above the cheeks; and its hands and feet felt like those of a boy. At first we thought of placing the being on a smooth surface and tracing its outline with chalk, as shoemakers trace the outline of the foot. This plan was given up as being of no value. Such an outline would give not the slightest idea of its conformation.

A happy thought struck me. We would take a cast of it in plaster of Paris. This would give us the solid figure, and satisfy all our wishes. But how to do it? The movements of the creature would disturb the setting of the plastic covering, and distort the mould. Another thought. Why not give it chloroform? It had respiratory organs — that was evident by its breathing. Once reduced to a state of insensibility, we could do with it what we would. Doctor X—— was sent for; and after the worthy physician had recovered from the first shock of amazement, he proceeded to administer the chloroform. In three minutes afterward we were enabled to remove the fetters from the creature's body, and a well-known modeler of this city was busily engaged in covering the invisible form with the moist clay. In five minutes more we had a mould, and before evening a rough *fac-simile* of the Mystery. It was shaped like a man, — distorted, uncouth, and horrible, but still a man. It was small, not over four feet and some inches in height, and its limbs revealed a muscular development that was unparalleled. Its face surpassed in hideousness anything I had ever seen. Gustave Doré, or Callot, or Tony Johannot, never conceived anything so horrible. There is a face in one of the latter's illustrations to " *Un Voyage où il vous plaira*," which somewhat approaches the countenance of this creature, but does not equal it. It was the physiognomy of what I should have fancied a ghoul to be. It looked as if it was capable of feeding on human flesh.

Having satisfied our curiosity, and bound every one in the house to secrecy, it became a question, what was to be done with our Enigma? It was impossible that we should keep such a horror in our house; it was equally impossible that such an awful being should be let loose upon the world. I confess that I would have gladly voted for the creature's destruction. But who would shoulder the responsibility? Who would undertake the execution of this horrible semblance of a human being? Day after day this question was deliberated gravely. The boarders all left the house. Mrs. Moffat was in despair, and threatened Hammond and myself with all sorts of legal penalties if we did not remove the Horror. Our answer was, " We will go if you like, but we decline taking this creature with us. Remove it yourself if you please. It appeared in your house. On you the responsibility rests." To this there was, of course, no answer. Mrs. Moffat could not obtain for love or money a person who would even approach the Mystery.

The most singular part of the transaction was that we were entirely ignorant of what the creature habitually fed on. Everything in the way of nutriment that we could think of was placed before it, but was never touched. It was awful to stand by, day after day, and see the clothes toss, and hear the hard breathing, and know that it was starving.

Ten, twelve days, a fortnight passed, and it still lived. The pulsations of the heart, however, were daily growing fainter, and had now nearly ceased altogether. It was evident that the creature was dying for want of sustenance. While this terrible life-struggle was going on, I felt miserable. I could not sleep of nights. Horrible as the creature was, it was pitiful to think of the pangs it was suffering.

At last it died. Hammond and I found it cold and stiff one morning in the bed. The heart had ceased to beat, the lungs to inspire. We hastened to bury it in the garden. It was a strange funeral, the dropping of that viewless corpse into the damp hole. The cast of its form I gave to Doctor X——, who keeps it in his museum in Tenth Street.

As I am on the eve of a long journey from which I may not return, I have drawn up this narrative of an event the most singular that has ever come to my knowledge.

NOTE.

[It is rumored that the proprietors of a well-known museum in this city have made arrangements with Dr. X—— to exhibit to the public the singular cast which Mr. Escott deposited with him. So extraordinary a history cannot fail to attract universal attention.]

FRANCIS BRET HARTE

1839 – 1902

BRET HARTE will always be associated with the California of the "forty-niners." Gold digger, teacher, express messenger by turns, he was setting up his own sketches among the compositors of the San Francisco *Golden Era* while still in his 'teens. The sketches brought him into the editorial room, and then to his own chair of the *Weekly Californian*, where he vindicated his title by the clever *Condensed Novels*. A secretaryship in the United States Branch Mint gave him leisure to gain wide popularity in verse. On this he mounted to his height. The year 1868 is cardinal in his life and in the history of American literature; for in that year was founded *The Overland Monthly;* and the young man of the hour was made its editor. Its second number (August, 1868) contained the most widely known, perhaps, of all American short stories, *The Luck of Roaring Camp.* The three years of his editorship include his most popular work, and perhaps his most enduring. He made the whole country laugh and weep by his verse, he established a magazine of solid merit, and he gave new life to the short story.

To this growth his removal to the East in 1871 put a period. Continuing his production pretty steadily on the Atlantic seaboard, in his consulships at Crefeld (1878) and at Glasgow (1880), and finally during seventeen years in London (1885–1902), he hardly advanced in art. That his art survived the transplanting is sufficiently proved by the long list of his books ; but it did not thrive. His constant recurrence to the old themes suggests that he missed the strong western soil.

The familiar tale reprinted here is typical of Bret Harte's field, geographical and artistic. His local color no longer keeps the separate value attached to it alike by many of his admirers and by himself. The California of his stories, sometimes drawn to the life, as in *Johnson's Old Woman*, is often that California, made of stock desperadoes, stage-drivers, and gulches, which is the delight of melodrama. Melodramatic Harte is incorrigibly. *Mrs. Skaggs* is the Dumas adventuress ; and the people of her story can hardly be seen off the boards. *The Iliad of Sandy Bar* shows that cheap shifting from farce humor to false pathos which cat hes the throats of the gallery. Though in fact he had the knowledge of actual contact, he saw California as his master Dickens saw London, through a haze of romance. The stories of both are woven from the suggestions of actual places; but 'n the weaving the actuality has faded.

Rather l r(t Harte's best stories prevail by something not extraneous. . ; l using the primary emotions on a single imaginative situat'on. *Poker Flat* is almost allegory — the gambler, the thief. the plot, the innocents, not so artificially grouped as in Hawthorne's *Seven Vagabonds*, but quite as artfully. It is convincing, not as a transcript of pioneer society, but as a unified conception of unhindered human emotions. The same is true of the famous *Luck of Roaring Camp*, of *Tennessee's Partner*, and of his best work in general. For all its scientific aloofness and worship of fact, is *La maison Tellier* ultimately as human as *The Outcasts of Poker Flat?*

THE OUTCASTS OF POKER FLAT

[*From* "*The Overland Monthly*," *January, 1869; copyright, 1871, by Fields, Osgood & Co.; 1899, by Bret Harte; reprinted here by special arrangement with Messrs. Houghton, Mifflin & Co., authorized publishers of all Bret Harte's works*]

AS Mr. John Oakhurst, gambler, stepped into the main street of Poker Flat on the morning of the twenty-third of November, 1850, he was conscious of a change in its moral atmosphere since the preceding night. Two or three men, conversing earnestly together, ceased as he approached, and exchanged significant glances. There was a Sabbath lull in the air, which, in a settlement unused to Sabbath influences, looked ominous.

Mr. Oakhurst's calm, handsome face betrayed small concern of these indications. Whether he was conscious of any predisposing cause, was another question. "I reckon they're after somebody," he reflected; "likely it's me." He returned to his pocket the handkerchief with which he had been whipping away the red dust of Poker Flat from his neat boots, and quietly discharged his mind of any further conjecture.

In point of fact, Poker Flat was "after somebody." It had lately suffered the loss of several thousand dollars, two valuable horses, and a prominent citizen. It was experiencing a spasm of virtuous reaction, quite as lawless and ungovernable as any of the acts that had provoked it. A secret committee had determined to rid the town of all improper persons. This was done permanently in regard of two men who were then hanging from the boughs of a sycamore in the gulch, and temporarily in the banishment of certain other objectionable characters. I regret to say that some of these were ladies. It is but due to the sex, however, to state that their impropriety was professional, and it was only in such easily established standards of evil that Poker Flat ventured to sit in judgment.

Mr. Oakhurst was right in supposing that he was included in this category. A few of the committee had urged hanging him as a possible example, and a sure method of reimbursing themselves from his pockets of the sums he had won from them. " It's agin justice," said Jim Wheeler, " to let this yer young man from Roaring Camp — an entire stranger — carry away our money." But a crude sentiment of equity residing in the breasts of those who had been fortunate enough to win from Mr. Oakhurst overruled this narrower local prejudice.

Mr. Oakhurst received his sentence with philosophic calmness, none the less coolly that he was aware of the hesitation of his judges. He was too much of a gambler not to accept Fate. With him life was at best an uncertain game, and he recognized the usual percentage in favor of the dealer.

A body of armed men accompanied the deported wickedness of Poker Flat to the outskirts of the settlement. Besides Mr. Oakhurst, who was known to be a coolly desperate man, and for whose intimidation the armed escort was intended, the expatriated party consisted of a young woman familiarly known as "The Duchess"; another, who had gained the infelicitous title of "Mother Shipton"; and "Uncle Billy," a suspected sluice-robber and confirmed drunkard. The cavalcade provoked no comments from the spectators, nor was any word uttered by the escort. Only, when the gulch which marked the uttermost limit of Poker Flat was reached, the leader spoke briefly and to the point. The exiles were forbidden to return at the peril of their lives.

As the escort disappeared, their pent-up feelings found vent in a few hysterical tears from "The Duchess," some bad language from Mother Shipton, and a Parthian volley of expletives from Uncle Billy. The philosophic Oakhurst alone remained silent. He listened calmly to Mother Shipton's desire to cut somebody's heart out, to the repeated statements of "The Duchess" that she would die in the road, and to the alarming oaths that seemed to be bumped out of Uncle Billy as he rode forward. With the easy good-humor characteristic of his class, he insisted upon exchanging his own riding-horse, "Five Spot," for the sorry mule which the Duchess rode. But even this act did not draw the party into any closer sympathy. The young woman readjusted her somewhat draggled plumes with a feeble, faded coquetry; Mother Shipton eyed the possessor of "Five Spot" with malevolence, and Uncle Billy included the whole party in one sweeping anathema.

The road to Sandy Bar — a camp that, not having as yet experienced the regenerating influences of Poker Flat, consequently seemed to offer some invitation to the emigrants — lay over a steep mountain range. It was distant a day's severe journey. In that advanced season, the party soon passed out of the moist, temperate regions of the foot-hills into the dry, cold, bracing air of the Sierras. The trail was narrow and difficult. At noon the Duchess, rolling out of her saddle upon the ground, declared her intention of going no farther, and the party halted.

The spot was singularly wild and impressive. A wooded amphitheatre, surrounded on three sides by precipitous cliffs of naked granite, sloped gently toward the crest of another precipice that overlooked the valley. It was undoubtedly the most suitable spot for a camp, had camping been advisable. But Mr. Oakhurst knew that scarcely half the journey to Sandy Bar was accomplished, and the party were not equipped or provisioned for delay. This fact he

234 AMERICAN SHORT STORIES

pointed out to his companions curtly, with a philosophic commentary on the folly of "throwing up their hand before the game was played out." But they were furnished with liquor, which in this emergency stood them in place of food, fuel, rest, and prescience. In spite of his remonstrances, it was not long before they were more or less under its influence. Uncle Billy passed rapidly from a bellicose state into one of stupor, the Duchess became maudlin, and Mother Shipton snored. Mr. Oakhurst alone remained erect, leaning against a rock, calmly surveying them.

Mr. Oakhurst did not drink. It interfered with a profession which required coolness, impassiveness, and presence of mind, and, in his own language, he "could n't afford it." As he gazed at his recumbent fellow-exiles, the loneliness begotten of his pariah-trade, his habits of life, his very vices, for the first time seriously oppressed him. He bestirred himself in dusting his black clothes, washing his hands and face, and other acts characteristic of his studiously neat habits, and for a moment forgot his annoyance. The thought of deserting his weaker and more pitiable companions never perhaps occurred to him. Yet he could not help feeling the want of that excitement which, singularly enough, was most conducive to that calm equanimity for which he was notorious. He looked at the gloomy walls that rose a ' thousand feet sheer above the circling pines around him; at the sky, ominously clouded; at the valley below, already deepening into shadow. And, doing so, suddenly he heard his own name called.

A horseman slowly ascended the trail. In the fresh, open face of the new-comer Mr. Oakhurst recognized Tom Simson, otherwise known as "The Innocent" of Sandy Bar. He had met him some months before over a "little game," and had, with perfect equanimity, won the entire fortune — amounting to some forty dollars — of that guileless youth. After the game was finished, Mr. Oakhurst drew the youthful speculator behind the door and thus addressed him:

"Tommy, you're a good little man, but you can't gamble worth a cent. Don't try it over again." He then handed him his money back, pushed him gently from the room, and so made a devoted slave of Tom Simson.

There was a remembrance of this in his boyish and enthusiastic greeting of Mr. Oakhurst. He had started, he said, to go to Poker Flat to seek his fortune. "Alone?" No, not exactly alone; in fact — a giggle — he had run away with Piney Woods. Did n't Mr. Oakhurst remember Piney? She that used to wait on the table at the Temperance House? They had been engaged a long time, but old Jake Woods had objected, and so they had run away, and were going to Poker Flat to be married, and here they were. And they were tired out, and how lucky it was they had found a place to camp and company. All this the Innocent delivered rapidly, while Piney — a stout, comely damsel of fifteen — emerged from behind the pine-tree, where she had been blushing unseen, and rode to the side of her lover.

Mr. Oakhurst seldom troubled himself with sentiment, still less with propriety; but he had a vague idea that the situation was not felicitous. He retained, however, his presence of mind sufficiently to kick Uncle Billy, who was about to say something, and Uncle Billy was sober enough to recognize in Mr. Oakhurst's kick a superior power that would not bear trifling. He then endeavored to dissuade Tom Simson from delaying further, but in vain. He even pointed out the fact that there was no provision, nor means of making a camp. But, unluckily, "The Innocent" met this objection by assuring the party that he was provided with an extra mule loaded with provisions, and by the discovery of a rude attempt at a log-house near the trail. "Piney can stay with Mrs. Oakhurst," said the Innocent, pointing to the Duchess, "and I can shift for myself."

Nothing but Mr. Oakhurst's admonishing foot saved Uncle Billy from bursting into a roar of laughter. As it was, he felt compelled to retire up the cañon until he could recover his gravity. There he confided the joke to the tall pine trees, with many slaps of his leg, contortions of his face, and the usual profanity. But when he returned to the party, he found them seated by a fire — for the air had grown strangely chill and the sky overcast — in apparently amicable conversation. Piney was actually talking in an impulsive, girlish fashion to the Duchess, who was listening with an interest and animation she had not shown for many days. The Innocent was holding forth, apparently with equal effect, to Mr. Oakhurst and Mother Shipton, who was actually relaxing into amiability. "Is this yer a d—d picnic?" said Uncle Billy, with inward scorn, as he surveyed the sylvan group, the glancing fire-light, and the tethered animals in the foreground. Suddenly an idea mingled with the alcoholic fumes that disturbed his brain. It was apparently of a jocular nature, for he felt impelled to slap his leg again and cram his fist into his mouth.

As the shadows crept slowly up the mountain, a slight breeze rocked the tops of the pine-trees, and moaned through their long and gloomy aisles. The ruined cabin, patched and covered with pine boughs, was set apart for the ladies. As the lovers parted, they unaffectedly exchanged a kiss, so honest and sincere that it might have been heard above the swaying pines. The frail Duchess and the malevolent Mother Shipton were probably too stunned to remark upon this last evidence of simplicity, and so turned without a word to the hut. The fire was replenished, the men lay down before the door, and in a few minutes were asleep.

Mr. Oakhurst was a light sleeper. Toward morning he awoke benumbed and cold. As he stirred the dying fire, the wind, which was now blowing strongly, brought to his cheek that which caused the blood to leave it, — snow!

He started to his feet with the intention of awakening the sleepers, for there was no time to lose. But turning to where Uncle Billy had been lying, he found him gone. A suspicion leaped to his brain and a curse to his lips. He ran to the spot where the mules had been tethered; they were no longer there. The tracks were already rapidly disappearing in the snow.

The momentary excitement brought Mr. Oakhurst back to the fire with his usual calm. He did not waken the sleepers. The Innocent slumbered peacefully, with a smile on his good-humored, freckled face; the virgin Piney slept beside her frailer sisters as sweetly as though attended by celestial guardians, and Mr. Oakhurst, drawing his blanket over his shoulders, stroked his mustachios and waited for the dawn. It came slowly in a whirling mist of snow-flakes, that dazzled and confused the eye. What could be seen of the landscape appeared magically changed. He looked over the valley, and summed up the present and future in two words, — "Snowed in!"

A careful inventory of the provisions, which, fortunately for the party, had been stored within the hut, and so escaped the felonious fingers of Uncle Billy, disclosed the fact that with care and prudence they might last ten days longer. "That is," said Mr. Oakhurst, *sotto voce* to the Innocent, "if you're willing to board us. If you ain't — and perhaps you'd better not — you can wait till Uncle Billy gets back with provisions." For some occult reason, Mr. Oakhurst could not bring himself to disclose Uncle Billy's rascality, and so offered the hypothesis that he had wandered from the camp and had accidentally stampeded the animals. He dropped a warning to the Duchess and Mother Shipton, who of course knew the facts of their associate's defection. "They'll find out the truth about us *all*, when they find out anything," he added, significantly, "and there's no good frightening them now."

Tom Simson not only put all his worldly store at the disposal of Mr. Oakhurst, but seemed to enjoy the prospect of their enforced seclusion. "We'll have a good camp for a week, and then the snow'll melt, and we'll all go back together." The cheerful gayety of the young man and Mr.

Oakhurst's calm infected the others. The Innocent, with the aid of pine boughs, extemporized a thatch for the roofless cabin, and the Duchess directed Piney in the rearrangement of the interior with a taste and tact that opened the blue eyes of that provincial maiden to their fullest extent. "I reckon now you're used to fine things at Poker Flat," said Piney. The Duchess turned away sharply to conceal something that reddened her cheek through its professional tint, and Mother Shipton requested Piney not to "chatter." But when Mr. Oakhurst returned from a weary search for the trail, he heard the sound of happy laughter echoed from the rocks. He stopped in some alarm, and his thoughts first naturally reverted to the whiskey, which he had prudently *cachéd*. "And yet it don't somehow sound like whiskey," said the gambler. It was not until he caught sight of the blazing fire through the still blinding storm, and the group around it, that he settled to the conviction that it was "square fun."

Whether Mr. Oakhurst had *cachéd* his cards with the whiskey as something debarred the free access of the community, I cannot say. It was certain that, in Mother Shipton's words, he "did n't say cards once" during that evening. Haply the time was beguiled by an accordeon, produced somewhat ostentatiously by Tom Simson, from his pack. Notwithstanding some difficulties attending the manipulation of this instrument, Piney Woods managed to pluck several reluctant melodies from its keys, to an accompaniment by the Innocent on a pair of bone castinets. But the crowning festivity of the evening was reached in a rude camp-meeting hymn, which the lovers, joining hands, sang with great earnestness and vociferation. I fear that a certain defiant tone and Covenanter's swing to its chorus, rather than any devotional quality, caused it speedily to infect the others, who at last joined in the refrain:

"I'm proud to live in the service of the Lord,
And I'm bound to die in His army."

The pines rocked, the storm eddied and whirled above the miserable group, and the flames of their altar leaped heavenward, as if in token of the vow.

At midnight the storm abated, the rolling clouds parted, and the stars glittered keenly above the sleeping camp. Mr. Oakhurst, whose professional habits had enabled him to live on the smallest possible amount of sleep, in dividing the watch with Tom Simson, somehow managed to take upon himself the greater part of that duty. He excused himself to the Innocent, by saying that he had " often been a week without sleep." " Doing what?" asked Tom. " Poker!" replied Oakhurst, sententiously; " when a man gets a streak of luck, — nigger-luck, — he don't get tired. The luck gives in first. Luck," continued the gambler, reflectively, "is a mighty queer thing. All you know about it for certain is that it's bound to change. And it's finding out when it's going to change that makes you. We've had a streak of bad luck since we left Poker Flat — you come along, and slap you get into it, too. If you can hold your cards right along you're all right. For," added the gambler, with cheerful irrelevance,

'I'm proud to live in the service of the Lord,
And I'm bound to die in His army.'"

The third day came, and the sun, looking through the white-curtained valley, saw the outcasts divide their slowly decreasing store of provisions for the morning meal. It was one of the peculiarities of that mountain climate that its rays diffused a kindly warmth over the wintry landscape, as if in regretful commiseration of the past. But it revealed drift on drift of snow piled high around the hut ; a hopeless, uncharted, trackless sea of white lying below the rocky shores to which the castaways still clung. Through the marvellously clear air, the smoke of the pastoral village of Poker Flat rose miles away. Mother Shipton saw it, and from a remote pinnacle of her rocky fastness, hurled in that direction a final malediction. It was her last vituperative attempt, and perhaps for that reason was invested with a certain degree of sublimity. It did her good, she privately informed the Duchess. "Just you go out there and cuss, and see." She then set herself to the task of amusing "the child," as she and the Duchess were pleased to call Piney. Piney was no chicken, but it was a soothing and ingenious theory of the pair thus to account for the fact that she did n't swear and was n't improper.

When night crept up again through the gorges, the reedy notes of the accordeon rose and fell in fitful spasms and long-drawn gasps by the flickering camp-fire. But music failed to fill entirely the aching void left by insufficient food, and a new diversion was proposed by Piney — story-telling. Neither Mr. Oakhurst nor his female companions caring to relate their personal experiences, this plan would have failed, too, but for The Innocent. Some months before he had chanced upon a stray copy of Mr. Pope's ingenious translation of the Iliad. He now proposed to narrate the principal incidents of that poem — having thoroughly mastered the argument and fairly forgotten the words — in the current vernacular of Sandy Bar. And so for the rest of that night the Homeric demigods again walked the earth. Trojan bully and wily Greek wrestled in the winds, and the great pines in the cañon seemed to bow to the wrath of the son of Peleus. Mr. Oakhurst listened with quiet satisfaction. Most especially was he interested in the fate of "Ash-heels," as the Innocent persisted in denominating the "swift-footed Achilles."

So with small food and much of Homer and the accordeon, a week passed over the heads of the outcasts. The sun again forsook them, and again from leaden skies the snow-flakes were sifted over the land. Day by day closer around them drew the snowy circle, until at last they looked from their prison over drifted walls of dazzling white, that towered twenty feet above their heads. It became more and more difficult to replenish their fires, even from the fallen trees beside them, now half-hidden in the drifts. And yet no one complained. The lovers turned from the dreary prospect and looked into each other's eyes, and were happy. Mr. Oakhurst settled himself coolly to the losing game before him. The Duchess, more cheerful than she had been, assumed the care of Piney. Only Mother Shipton — once the strongest of the party — seemed to sicken and fade. At midnight on the tenth day she called Oakhurst to her side. "I'm going," she said, in a voice of querulous weakness, "but don't say anything about it. Don't waken the kids. Take the bundle from under my head and open it." Mr. Oakhurst did so. It contained Mother Shipton's rations for the last week, untouched. "Give 'em to the child," she said, pointing to the sleeping Piney. "You've starved yourself," said the gambler. "That's what they call it," said the woman, querulously, as she lay down again, and, turning her face to the wall, passed quietly away.

The accordeon and the bones were put aside that day, and Homer was forgotten. When the body of Mother Shipton had been committed to the snow, Mr. Oakhurst took The Innocent aside, and showed him a pair of snow-shoes, which he had fashioned from the old pack-saddle. "There's one chance in a hundred to save her yet," he said, pointing to Piney; "but it's there," he added, pointing toward Poker Flat. "If you can reach there in two days she's safe." "And you?" asked Tom Simson. "I'll stay here," was the curt reply.

The lovers parted with a long embrace. "You are not going, too?" said the Duchess, as she saw Mr. Oakhurst apparently waiting to accompany him. "As far as the cañon," he replied. He turned suddenly, and kissed the Duchess, leaving her pallid face aflame, and her trembling limbs rigid with amazement.

Night came, but not Mr. Oakhurst. It brought the storm again and the whirling snow. Then the Duchess, feeding the fire, found that some one had quietly piled beside the hut enough fuel to last a few days longer. The tears rose to her eyes, but she hid them from Piney.

The women slept but little. In the morning, looking into each other's faces, they read their fate. Neither spoke; but Piney, accepting the position of the stronger, drew near and placed her arm around the Duchess's waist. They kept this attitude for the rest of the day. That night the storm reached its greatest fury, and, rending asunder the protecting pines, invaded the very hut.

Toward morning they found themselves unable to feed the fire, which gradually died away. As the embers slowly blackened, the Duchess crept closer to Piney, and broke the silence of many hours: "Piney, can you pray?" "No, dear," said Piney, simply. The Duchess, without knowing exactly why, felt relieved, and, putting her head upon Piney's shoulder, spoke no more. And so reclining, the younger and purer pillowing the head of her soiled sister upon her virgin breast, they fell asleep.

The wind lulled as if it feared to waken them. Feathery drifts of snow, shaken from the long pine boughs, flew like white-winged birds, and settled about them as they slept. The moon through the rifted clouds looked down upon what had been the camp. But all human stain, all trace of earthly travail, was hidden beneath the spotless mantle mercifully flung from above.

They slept all that day and the next, nor did they waken when voices and footsteps broke the silence of the camp. And when pitying fingers brushed the snow from their wan faces, you could scarcely have told from the equal peace that dwelt upon them, which was she that had sinned. Even the Law of Poker Flat recognized this, and turned away, leaving them still locked in each other's arms.

But at the head of the gulch, on one of the largest pine trees, they found the deuce of clubs pinned to the bark with a bowie knife. It bore the following, written in pencil, in a firm hand:

†

BENEATH THIS TREE
LIES THE BODY
OF
JOHN OAKHURST,
WHO STRUCK A STREAK OF BAD LUCK
ON THE 23D OF NOVEMBER, 1850,
AND
HANDED IN HIS CHECKS
ON THE 7TH DECEMBER, 1850.

↓

And pulseless and cold, with a Derringer by his side and a bullet in his heart, though still calm as in life, beneath the snow lay he who was at once the strongest and yet the weakest of the outcasts of Poker Flat.

ALBERT FALVEY WEBSTER

1848 – 1876

READERS of "Appleton's Journal" in the early '70's must have looked forward from week to week to the stories of Albert Webster. For, often as he wrote, he always had a story to tell. It might be merely a romance of incident; it was usually a situation of very human significance; it always showed narrative instinct. With this native sense he was experimenting variously toward his art, while through his investigations of prisons, courts, and medical advice he was developing a serious and definite philosophy of life. But his own life was doomed. The quest of health, very like Stevenson's, may be read in the titles of his descriptive essays during 1875 and 1876: *Spring Days in Aiken, From New York to Aspinwall, The Isthmus and Panama, Up the Mexican Coast, Winter Days in California*, etc. On the steamer from San Francisco to Honolulu he died, and was buried in the Pacific. He was betrothed to Una, eldest daughter of Hawthorne.

Of his many stories perhaps the most striking is *An Operation in Money* ("Appleton's Journal," September 27, 1873, volume x, page 387); the nicest in adjustment, *Miss Eunice's Glove*, printed below. *The Daphne* ("Appleton's Journal," 1873, volume x, page 290) and *A Fool's Moustache* (ibid., 1874, volume xii, page 259) read as if sketched for the stage. How he kept at his work appears pathetically in his leaving behind a tale laid at Santa Barbara and published after his death, *The Owner of "Lara"* (ibid., 1877, new series, volume ii, page 350).

MISS EUNICE'S GLOVE

[*From the " Atlantic Monthly," July, 1873*]

I

FOR a long time blithe and fragile Miss Eunice, demure, correct in deportment, and yet not wholly without enthusiasm, thought that day the unluckiest in her life on which she first took into her hands that unobtrusive yet dramatic book, " Miss Crofutt's Missionary Labors in the English Prisons."

It came to her notice by mere accident, not by favor of proselyting friends ; and such was its singular material, that she at once devoured it with avidity. As its title suggests, it was the history of the ameliorating endeavors of a woman in criminal society, and it contained, perforce, a large amount of tragic and pathetic incident. But this last was so blended and involved with what Miss Eunice would have skipped as commonplace, that she was led to digest the whole volume, — statistics, philosophy, comments, and all. She studied the analysis of the atmosphere of cells, the properties and waste of wheaten flour, the cost of clothing to the general government, the whys and wherefores of crime and evil-doing ; and it was not long before there was generated within her bosom a fine and healthy ardor to emulate this practical and courageous pattern.

She was profoundly moved by the tales of missionary labors proper. She was filled with joy to read that Miss Crofutt and her lieutenants sometimes cracked and broke away the formidable husks which enveloped divine kernels in the hearts of some of the wretches, and she frequently wept at the stories of victories gained over monsters whose defences of silence and stolidity had suddenly fallen into ruin above the slow but persistent sapping of constant kindness. Acute tinglings and chilling thrills would pervade her entire body when she read that on Christmas every wretch seemed to become for that day, at least, a gracious man; that the sight of a few penny tapers, or the possession of a handful of sweet stuff, or a spray of holly, or a hot-house bloom, would appear to convert the worst of them into children. Her heart would swell to learn how they acted during the one poor hour of yearly freedom in the prison-yards; that they swelled their chests; that they ran; that they took long strides; that the singers anxiously tried their voices, now grown husky; that the athletes wrestled only to find their limbs stiff and their arts forgotten; that the gentlest of them lifted their faces to the broad sky and spent the sixty minutes in a dreadful gazing at the clouds.

The pretty student gradually became possessed with a rage. She desired to convert some one, to recover some estray, to reform some wretch.

She regretted that she lived in America, and not in England, where the most perfect rascals were to be found; she was sorry that the gloomy, sin-saturated prisons which were the scenes of Miss Crofutt's labors must always be beyond her ken.

There was no crime in the family or the neighborhood against which she might strive; no one whom she knew was even austere; she had never met a brute; all her rascals were newspaper rascals. For aught she knew, this tranquillity and good-will might go on forever, without affording her an opportunity. She must be denied the smallest contact with these frightful faces and figures, these bars and cages, these deformities of the mind and heart, these curiosities of conscience, shyness, skill, and daring; all these dramas of reclamation, all these scenes of fervent gratitude, thankfulness, and intoxicating liberty, — all or any of these things must never come to be the lot of her eyes; and she gave herself up to the most poignant regret.

But one day she was astonished to discover that all of these delights lay within half an hour's journey of her home; and moreover, that there was approaching an hour which was annually set apart for the indulgence of the inmates of the prison in question. She did not stop to ask herself, as she might well have done, how it was that she had so completely ignored this particular institution, which was one of the largest and best conducted in the country, especially when her desire to visit one was so keen; but she straightway set about preparing for her intended visit in a manner which she fancied Miss Crofutt would have approved, had she been present.

She resolved, in the most radical sense of the word, to be alive. She jotted on some ivory tablets, with a gold pencil, a number of hints to assist her in her observations. For example: "Phrenological development; size of cells; ounces of solid and liquid; tissue-producing food; were mirrors allowed? if so, what was the effect? jimmy and skeleton-key, character of; canary birds: query, would not their admission into every cell animate in the human prisoners a similar buoyancy? to urge upon the turnkeys the use of the Spanish garrote in place of the present distressing gallows; to find the proportion of Orthodox and Unitarian prisoners to those of other persuasions." But besides these and fifty other similar memoranda, the enthusiast cast about her for something practical to do.

She hit upon the capital idea of flowers. She at once ordered from a gardener of taste two hundred bouquets, or rather nosegays, which she intended for distribution among the prisoners she was about to visit, and she called upon her father for the money.

Then she began to prepare her mind. She wished to define the plan from which she was to make her contemplations. She settled that she would be grave and gentle. She would be exquisitely careful not to hold herself too much aloof, and yet not to step beyond the bounds of that sweet reserve that she conceived must have been at once Miss Crofutt's sword and buckler.

Her object was to awaken in the most abandoned criminals a realization that the world, in its most benignant phase, was still open to them ; that society, having obtained a requital for their wickedness, was ready to embrace them again on proof of their repentance.

She determined to select at the outset two or three of the most remarkable monsters, and turn the full head of her persuasions exclusively upon them, instead of sprinkling (as it were) the whole community with her grace. She would arouse at first a very few, and then a few more, and a few more, and so on *ad infinitum*.

It was on a hot July morning that she journeyed on foot over the bridge which led to the prison, and there walked a man behind her carrying the flowers.

Her eyes were cast down, this being the position most significant of her spirit. Her pace was equal, firm, and rapid ; she made herself oblivious of the bustle of the streets, and she repented that her vanity had permitted her to wear white and lavender, these making a combination in her dress which she had been told became her well. She had no right to embellish herself. Was she going to the races, or a match, or a kettle-drum, that she must dandify herself with particular shades of color? She stopped short, blushing. Would Miss Cro———. But there was no help for it now. It was too late to turn back. She proceeded, feeling that the odds were against her.

She approached her destination in such a way that the prison came into view suddenly. She paused with a feeling of terror. The enormous gray building rose far above a lofty white wall of stone, and a sense of its prodigious strength and awful gloom overwhelmed her. On the top of the wall, holding by an iron railing, there stood a man with a rifle trailing behind him. He was looking down into the yard inside. His attitude of watchfulness, his weapon, the unseen thing that was being thus fiercely guarded, provoked in her such a revulsion that she came to a standstill.

What in the name of mercy had she come here for? She began to tremble. The man with the flowers came up to her and halted. From the prison there came at this instant the loud clang of a bell, and succeeding this a prolonged and resonant murmur which seemed to increase. Miss Eunice looked hastily around her. There were several people who must have heard the same sounds that reached her ears, but they were not alarmed. In fact, one or two of them seemed to be going to the prison direct. The courage of our philanthropist began to revive. A woman in a brick house opposite suddenly pulled up a window-curtain and fixed an amused and inquisitive look upon her.

This would have sent her into a thrice-heated furnace. "Come, if you please," she commanded the man, and she marched upon the jail.

She entered at first a series of neat offices in a wing of the structure, and then she came to a small door made of black bars of iron. A man stood on the farther side of this, with a bunch of large keys. When he saw Miss Eunice he unlocked and opened the door, and she passed through.

She found that she had entered a vast, cool, and lofty cage, one hundred feet in diameter; it had an iron floor, and there were several people strolling about here and there. Through several grated apertures the sunlight streamed with strong effect, and a soft breeze swept around the cavernous apartment.

Without the cage, before her and on either hand, were three more wings of the building, and in these were the prisoners' corridors.

At the moment she entered, the men were leaving their cells, and mounting the stone stairs in regular order, on their way to the chapel above. The noisy files went up and down and to the right and to the left, shuffling and scraping and making a great tumult. The men were dressed in blue, and were seen indistinctly through the lofty gratings. From above and below and all around her there came the metallic snapping of bolts and the rattle of moving bars; and so significant was everything of savage repression and impending violence, that Miss Eunice was compelled to say faintly to herself, " I am afraid it will take a little time to get used to all tnis."

She rested upon one of the seats in the rotunda while the chapel services were being conducted, and she thus had an opportunity to regain a portion of her lost heart. She felt wonderfully dwarfed and belittled, and her plan of recovering souls had, in some way or other, lost much of its feasibility. A glance at her bright flowers revived her a little, as did also a surprising, long-drawn roar from over her head, to the tune of "America." The prisoners were singing.

Miss Eunice was not alone in her intended work, for there were several other ladies, also with supplies of flowers, who with her awaited until the prisoners should descend into the yard and be let loose before presenting them with what they had brought. Their common purpose made them acquainted, and by the aid of chat and sympathy they fortified each other.

Half an hour later the five hundred men descended from the chapel to the yard, rushing out upon its bare broad surface as you have seen a burst of water suddenly irrigate a road-bed. A hoarse and tremendous shout at once filled the air, and echoed against the walls like the threat of a volcano. Some of the wretches waltzed and spun around like dervishes, some threw somersaults, some folded their arms gravely and marched up and down, some fraternized, some walked away pondering, some took off their tall caps and sat down in the shade, some looked towards the rotunda with expectation, and there were those who looked towards it with contempt.

There led from the rotunda to the yard a flight of steps. Miss Eunice descended these steps with a quaking heart, and a turnkey shouted to the prisoners over her head that she and others had flowers for them.

ALBERT FALVEY WEBSTER 253

No sooner had the words left his lips, than the men rushed up pell-mell.

This was a crucial moment.

There thronged upon Miss Eunice an army of men who were being punished for all the crimes in the calendar. Each individual here had been caged because he was either a highwayman, or a forger, or a burglar, or a ruffian, or a thief, or a murderer. The unclean and frightful tide bore down upon our terrified missionary, shrieking and whooping. Every prisoner thrust out his hand over the head of the one in front of him, and the foremost plucked at her dress.

She had need of courage. A sense of danger and contamination impelled her to fly, but a gleam of reason in the midst of her distraction enabled her to stand her ground. She forced herself to smile, though she knew her face had grown pale.

She placed a bunch of flowers into an immense hand which projected from a coarse blue sleeve in front of her; the owner of the hand was pushed away so quickly by those who came after him that Miss Eunice failed to see his face. Her tortured ear caught a rough "'Thank y', miss!'" The spirit of Miss Crofutt revived in a flash, and her disciple thereafter possessed no lack of nerve.

She plied the crowd with flowers as long as they lasted, and a jaunty self-possession enabled her finally to gaze without flinching at the mass of depraved and wicked faces with which she was surrounded. Instead of retaining her position upon the steps, she gradually descended into the yard, as did several other visitors. She began to feel at home; she found her tongue, and her color came back again. She felt a warm pride in noticing with what care and respect the prisoners treated her gifts; they carried them about with great tenderness, and some compared them with those of their friends.

Presently she began to recall her plans. It occurred to her to select her two or three villains. For one, she imme-

254 AMERICAN SHORT STORIES

diately pitched upon a lean-faced wretch in front of her.
He seemed to be old, for his back was bent and he leaned
upon a cane. His features were large, and they bore an
expression of profound gloom. His head was sunk upon
his breast, his lofty conical cap was pulled over his ears,
and his shapeless uniform seemed to weigh him down, so
infirm was he.

Miss Eunice spoke to him. He did not hear; she
spoke again. He glanced at her like a flash, but without
moving; this was at once followed by a scrutinizing look.
He raised his head, and then he turned toward her gravely.

The solemnity of his demeanor nearly threw Miss Eunice
off her balance, but she mastered herself by beginning to
talk rapidly. The prisoner leaned over a little to hear
better. Another came up, and two or three turned around
to look. She bethought herself of an incident related in
Miss Crofutt's book, and she essayed its recital. It concerned a lawyer who was once pleading in a French criminal
court in behalf of a man whose crime had been committed
under the influence of dire want. In his plea he described
the case of another whom he knew who had been punished
with a just but short imprisonment instead of a long one,
which the judge had been at liberty to impose, but from
which he humanely refrained. Miss Eunice happily remembered the words of the lawyer: "That man suffered
like the wrong-doer that he was. He knew his punishment
was just. Therefore there lived perpetually in his breast an
impulse toward a better life which was not suppressed and
stifled by the five years he passed within the walls of the
jail. He came forth and began to labor. He toiled hard.
He struggled against averted faces and cold words, and he
began to rise. He secreted nothing, faltered at nothing,
and never stumbled. He succeeded; men took off their
hats to him once more; he became wealthy, honorable,
God-fearing. I, gentlemen, am that man, that criminal."
As she quoted this last declaration, Miss Eunice erected
herself with burning eyes and touched herself proudly upon

the breast. A flush crept into her cheeks, and her nostrils dilated, and she grew tall.

She came back to earth again, and found herself surrounded with the prisoners. She was a little startled.

"Ah, that was good!" ejaculated the old man upon whom she had fixed her eyes. Miss Eunice felt an inexpressible sense of delight.

Murmurs of approbation came from all of her listeners, especially from one on her right hand. She looked around at him pleasantly.

But the smile faded from her lips on beholding him. He was extremely tall and very powerful. He overshadowed her. His face was large, ugly, and forbidding; his gray hair and beard were cropped close, his eyebrows met at the bridge of his nose and overhung his large eyes like a screen. His lips were very wide, and, being turned downwards at the corners, they gave him a dolorous expression. His lower jaw was square and protruding, and a pair of prodigious white ears projected from beneath his sugarloaf cap. He seemed to take his cue from the old man, for he repeated his sentiment.

"Yes," said he, with a voice which broke alternately into a roar and a whisper, "that was a good story."

"Y-yes," faltered Miss Eunice, "and it has the merit of being t-rue."

He replied with a nod, and looked absently over her head while he rubbed the nap upon his chin with his hand. Miss Eunice discovered that his knee touched the skirt of her dress, and she was about to move in order to destroy this contact, when she remembered that Miss Crofutt would probably have cherished the accident as a promoter of a valuable personal influence, so she allowed it to remain. The lean-faced man was not to be mentioned in the same breath with this one, therefore she adopted the superior villain out of hand.

She began to approach him. She asked him where he lived, meaning to discover whence he had come. He replied in the same mixture of roar and whisper, "Six undered un one, North Wing."

Miss Eunice grew scarlet. Presently she recovered sufficiently to pursue some inquiries respecting the rules and customs of the prison. She did not feel that she was interesting her friend, yet it seemed clear that he did not wish to go away. His answers were curt, yet he swept his cap off his head, implying by the act a certain reverence, which Miss Eunice's vanity permitted her to exult at. Therefore she became more loquacious than ever. Some men came up to speak with the prisoner, but he shook them off, and remained in an attitude of strict attention, with his chin on his hand, looking now at the sky, now at the ground, and now at Miss Eunice.

In handling the flowers her gloves had been stained, and she now held them in her fingers, nervously twisting them as she talked. In the course of time she grew short of subjects, and, as her listener suggested nothing, several lapses occurred; in one of them she absently spread her gloves out in her palms, meanwhile wondering how the English girl acted under similar circumstances.

Suddenly a large hand slowly interposed itself between her eyes and her gloves, and then withdrew, taking one of the soiled trifles with it.

She was surprised, but the surprise was pleasurable. She said nothing at first. The prisoner gravely spread his prize out upon his own palm, and after looking at it carefully, he rolled it up into a tight ball and thrust it deep in an inner pocket.

This act made the philanthropist aware that she had made progress. She rose insensibly to the elevation of patron, and she made promises to come frequently and visit her ward and to look in upon him when he was at work; while saying this she withdrew a little from the shade his huge figure had supplied her with.

He thrust his hands into his pockets, but he hastily took them out again. Still he said nothing and hung his head.

It was while she was in the mood of a conqueror that Miss Eunice went away. She felt a touch of repugnance at stepping from before his eyes a free woman, therefore she took pains to go when she thought he was not looking.

She pointed him out to a turnkey, who told her he was expiating the sins of assault and burglarious entry. Outwardly Miss Eunice looked grieved, but within she exulted that he was so emphatically a rascal.

When she emerged from the cool, shadowy, and frowning prison into the gay sunlight, she experienced a sense of bewilderment. The significance of a lock and a bar seemed greater on quitting them than it had when she had perceived them first. The drama of imprisonment and punishment oppressed her spirit with tenfold gloom now that she gazed upon the brilliancy and freedom of the outer world. That she and everybody around her were permitted to walk here and there at will, without question and limit, generated within her an indefinite feeling of gratitude; and the noise, the colors, the creaking wagons, the myriad voices, the splendid variety and change of all things excited a profound but at the same time a mournful satisfaction.

Midway in her return journey she was shrieked at from a carriage, which at once approached the sidewalk. Within it were four gay maidens bound to the Navy-Yard, from whence they were to sail, with a large party of people of nice assortment, in an experimental steamer, which was to be made to go with kerosene lamps, in some way. They seized upon her hands and cajoled her. Would n't she go? They were to sail down among the islands (provided the oil made the wheels and things go round), they were to lunch at Fort Warren, dine at Fort Independence, and dance at Fort Winthrop. Come, please go. Oh, do! The Germanians were to furnish the music.

Miss Eunice sighed, but shook her head. She had not yet got the air of the prison out of her lungs, nor the figure of her robber out of her eyes, nor the sense of horror and repulsion out of her sympathies.

At another time she would have gone to the ends of the earth with such a happy crew, but now she only shook her head again and was resolute. No one could wring a reason from her, and the wondering quartet drove away.

II

BEFORE the day went, Miss Eunice awoke to the disagreeable fact that her plans had become shrunken and contracted, that a certain something had curdled her spontaneity, and that her ardor had flown out at some crevice and had left her with the dry husk of an intent.

She exerted herself to glow a little, but she failed. She talked well at the tea-table, but she did not tell about the glove. This matter plagued her. She ran over in her mind the various doings of Miss Crofutt, and she could not conceal from herself that that lady had never given a glove to one of her wretches; no, nor had she ever permitted the smallest approach to familiarity.

Miss Eunice wept a little. She was on the eve of despairing.

In the silence of the night the idea presented itself to her with a disagreeable baldness. There was a thief over yonder that possessed a confidence with her.

They had found it necessary to shut this man up in iron and stone, and to guard him with a rifle with a large leaden ball in it.

This villain was a convict. That was a terrible word, one that made her blood chill.

She, the admired of hundreds and the beloved of a family, had done a secret and shameful thing of which she dared not tell. In these solemn hours the madness of her act appalled her.

She asked herself what might not the fellow do with the glove? Surely he would exhibit it among his brutal companions, and perhaps allow it to pass to and fro among them. They would laugh and joke with him, and he would laugh and joke in return, and no doubt he would kiss it to their great delight. Again, he might go to her friends, and, by working upon their fears and by threatening an exposure of her, extort large sums of money from them. Again, might he not harass her by constantly appearing to her at all times and all places and making all sorts of claims and demands? Again, might he not, with terrible ingenuity, use it in connection with some false key or some jack-in-the-box, or some dark-lantern, or something, in order to effect his escape; or might he not tell the story times without count to some wretched curiosity-hunters who would advertise her folly all over the country, to her perpetual misery?

She became harnessed to this train of thought. She could not escape from it. She reversed the relation that she had hoped to hold toward such a man, and she stood in his shadow, and not he in hers.

In consequence of these ever-present fears and sensations, there was one day, not very far in the future, that she came to have an intolerable dread of. This day was the one on which the sentence of the man was to expire. She felt that he would surely search for her; and that he would find her there could be no manner of doubt, for, in her surplus of confidence, she had told him her full name, inasmuch as he had told her his.

When she contemplated this new source of terror, her peace of mind fled directly. So did her plans for philanthropic labor. Not a shred remained. The anxiety began to tell upon her, and she took to peering out of a certain shaded window that commanded the square in front of her house. It was not long before she remembered that for good behavior certain days were deducted from the convicts' terms of imprisonment. Therefore, her ruffian might be released at a moment not anticipated by her. He might, in fact, be discharged on any day. He might be on his way towards her even now.

She was not very far from right, for suddenly the man did appear.

He one day turned the corner, as she was looking out at the window fearing that she should see him, and came in a diagonal direction across the hot, flagged square.

Miss Eunice's pulse leaped into the hundreds. She glued her eyes upon him. There was no mistake. There was the red face, the evil eyes, the large mouth, the gray hair, and the massive frame.

What should she do? Should she hide? Should she raise the sash and shriek to the police? Should she arm herself with a knife? or — what? In the name of mercy, what? She glared into the street. He came on steadily, and she lost him, for he passed beneath her. In a moment she heard the jangle of the bell. She was petrified. She heard his heavy step below. He had gone into the little reception room beside the door. He crossed to a sofa opposite the mantel. She then heard him get up and go to a window, then he walked about, and then sat down; probably upon a red leather seat beside the window.

Meanwhile the servant was coming to announce him. From some impulse, which was a strange and sudden one, she eluded the maid, and rushed headlong upon her danger. She never remembered her descent of the stairs. She awoke to cool contemplation of matters only to find herself entering the room.

Had she made a mistake, after all? It was a question that was asked and answered in a flash. This man was pretty erect and self-assured, but she discerned in an instant that there was needed but the blue woollen jacket and the tall cap to make him the wretch of a month before.

He said nothing. Neither did she. He stood up and occupied himself by twisting a button upon his waistcoat. She, fearing a threat or a demand, stood bridling to receive it. She looked at him from top to toe with parted lips.

He glanced at her. She stepped back. He put the rim of his cap in his mouth and bit it once or twice, and then looked out at the window. Still neither spoke. A voice at this instant seemed impossible.

He glanced again like a flash. She shrank, and put her hands upon the bolt. Presently he began to stir. He put out one foot, and gradually moved forward. He made another step. He was going away. He had almost reached the door, when Miss Eunice articulated, in a confused whisper, " My — my glove; I wish you would give me my glove."

He stopped, fixed his eyes upon her, and after passing his fingers up and down upon the outside of his coat, said, with deliberation, in a husky voice, " No, mum. I'm goin' fur to keep it as long as I live, if it takes two thousand years."

" Keep it ! " she stammered.

" Keep it," he replied.

He gave her an untranslatable look. It neither frightened her nor permitted her to demand the glove more emphatically. She felt her cheeks and temples and her hands grow cold, and midway in the process of fainting she saw him disappear. He vanquished quietly. Deliberation and respect characterized his movements, and there was not so much as a jar of the outer door.

Poor philanthropist !

This incident nearly sent her to a sick-bed. She fully expected that her secret would appear in the newspapers in full, and she lived in dread of the onslaught of an angry and outraged society.

The more she reflected upon what her possibilities had been and how she had misused them, the iller and the more distressed she got. She grew thin and spare of flesh. Her friends became frightened. They began to dose her and to coddle her. She looked at them with eyes full of supreme melancholy, and she frequently wept upon their shoulders.

In spite of her precautions, however, a thunderbolt slipped in.

One day her father read at the table an item that met his eye. He repeated it aloud, on account of the peculiar statement in the last line : —

"Detained on suspicion. — A rough-looking fellow, who gave the name of Gorman, was arrested on the high-road to Tuxbridge Springs for suspected complicity in some recent robberies in the neighborhood. He was fortunately able to give a pretty clear account of his late whereabouts, and he was permitted to depart with a caution from the justice. Nothing was found upon him but a few coppers and an old kid glove wrapped in a bit of paper."

Miss Eunice's soup spilled. This was too much, and she fainted this time in right good earnest ; and she straightway became an invalid of the settled type. They put her to bed. The doctor told her plainly that he knew she had a secret, but she looked at him so imploringly that he refrained from telling his fancies ; but he ordered an immediate change of air. It was settled at once that she should go to the "Springs" — to Tuxbridge Springs. The doctor knew there were young people there, also plenty of dancing. So she journeyed thither with her pa and her ma and with pillows and servants.

They were shown to their rooms, and strong porters followed with the luggage. One of them had her huge trunk upon his shoulder. He put it carefully upon the floor, and by so doing he disclosed the ex-prisoner to Miss Eunice and Miss Eunice to himself. He was astonished, but he remained silent. But she must needs be frightened and fall into another fit of trembling. After an awkward moment he went away, while she called to her father and begged piteously to be taken away from Tuxbridge Springs instantly. There was no appeal. She hated, *hated*, HATED Tuxbridge Springs, and she should die if she were forced to remain. She rained tears. She would give no reason, but she could not stay. No, millions on millions could not persuade her ; go she must. There was no alternative. The party quitted the place within the hour, bag and baggage. Miss Eunice's father was perplexed and angry, and her mother would have been angry also if she had dared.

They went to other springs and stayed a month, but the patient's fright increased each day, and so did her fever. She was full of distractions. In her dreams everybody laughed at her as the one who had flirted with a convict. She would ever be pursued with the tale of her foolishness and stupidity. Should she ever recover her self-respect and confidence?

She had become radically selfish. She forgot the old ideas of noble-heartedness and self-denial, and her temper had become weak and childish. She did not meet her puzzle 'face to face, but she ran away from it with her hands over her ears. Miss Crofutt stared at her, and therefore she threw Miss Crofutt's book into the fire.

After two days of unceasing debate, she called her parents, and with the greatest agitation told them *all*.

It so happened, in this case, that events, to use a railroad phrase, made connection.

No sooner had Miss Eunice told her story than the man came again. This time he was accompanied by a woman.

" Only get my glove away from him," sobbed the unhappy one, "that is all I ask ! " This was a fine admission ! It was thought proper to bring an officer, and so a strong one was sent for.

Meanwhile the couple had been admitted to the parlor. Miss Eunice's father stationed the officer at one door, while he, with a pistol, stood at the other. Then Miss Eunice went into the apartment. She was wasted, weak, and nervous. The two villains got up as she came in, and bowed. She began to tremble as usual, and laid hold upon the mantelpiece. " How much do you want?." she gasped.

The man gave the woman a push with his forefinger. She stepped forward quickly with her crest up. Her eyes turned, and she fixed a vixenish look upon Miss Eunice. She suddenly shot her hand out from beneath her shawl and extended it at full length. Across it lay Miss Eunice's glove, very much soiled.

"Was that thing ever yours?" demanded the woman, shrilly.

"Y-yes," said Miss Eunice, faintly.

The woman seemed (if the apt woid is to be excused) staggered. She withdrew her hand, and looked the glove over. The man shook his head, and began to laugh behind his hat.

"And did you ever give it to him?" pursued the woman, pointing over her shoulder with her thumb.

Miss Eunice nodded.

"Of your own free will?"

After a moment of silence she ejaculated, in a whisper, "Yes."

"Now wait," said the man, coming to the front; "'nough has been said by you." He then addressed himself to Miss Eunice with the remains of his laugh still illuminating his face.

"This is my wife's sister, and she's one of the jealous kind. I love my wife" (here he became grave), "and I never showed her any kind of slight that I know of. I've always been fair to her, and she's always been fair to me. Plain sailin' so far; I never kep' anything from her — but this." He reached out and took the glove from the woman, and spread it out upon his own palm, as Miss Eunice had seen him do once before. He looked at it thoughtfully. "I wouldn't tell her about this; no, never. She was never very particular to ask me; that's where her trust in me came in. She knowed I was above doing any-thing out of the way — that is — I mean — " He stam-mered and blushed, and then rushed on volubly. "But her sister here thought I paid too much attention to it; she thought I looked at it too much, and kep' it secret. So she nagged and nagged, and kept the pitch boilin' until I had to let it out: I told 'em" (Miss Eunice shivered). "'No,' says she, my wife's sister, 'that won't do, Gorman.

That 's chaff, and I 'm too old a bird.' Ther'fore I fetched her straight to you, so she could put the question direct."

He stopped a moment as if in doubt how to go on. Miss Eunice began to open her eyes, and she released the mantel. The man resumed with something like impressiveness :

" When you last held that," said he, slowly, balancing the glove in his hand, " I was a wicked man with bad intentions through and through. When I first held it I became an honest man, with good intentions."

A burning blush of shame covered Miss Eunice's face and neck.

" An' as I kep' it my intentions went on improvin' and improvin', till I made up my mind to behave myself in future, forever. Do you understand? — forever. No backslidin', no hitchin', no slippin'-up. I take occasion to say, miss, that I was beset time and again; that the instant I set my foot outside them prison-gates, over there, my old chums got round me ; but I shook my head. ' No,' says I, ' I won't go back on the glove.' "

Miss Eunice hung her head. The two had exchanged places, she thought; she was the criminal and he the judge.

" An' what is more," continued he, with the same weight in his tone, " I not only kep' sight of the glove, but I kep' sight of the generous sperrit that gave it. I did n't let *that* go. I never forgot what you meant. I knowed — I knowed," repeated he, lifting his forefinger, — " I knowed a time would come when there would n't be any enthoosiasm, any ' hurrah,' and then perhaps you 'd be sorry you was so kind to me; an' the time did come."

Miss Eunice buried her face in her hands and wept aloud.

" But did I quit the glove? No, mum. I held on to it. It was what I fought by. I was n't going to give it up, because it was asked for. All the police-officers in the city could n't have took it from me. I put it deep into my pocket and I walked out. It was differcult, miss. But I come through. The glove did it. It helped me stand out against temptation when it was strong. If I looked at it, I remembered that once there was a pure heart that pitied me. It cheered me up. After a while I kinder got out of the mud. Then I got work. The glove again. Then a girl that knowed me before I took to bad ways married me, and no questions asked. Then I just took the glove into a dark corner and blessed it."

Miss Eunice was belittled.

A noise was heard in the hall-way. Miss Eunice's father and the policeman were going away.

The awkwardness of the succeeding silence was relieved by the moving of the man and the woman. They had done their errand, and were going.

Said Miss Eunice, with the faint idea of making a practical apology to her visitor, "I shall go to the prison once a week after this, I think."

"Then may God bless ye, miss," said the man. He came back with tears in his eyes and took her proffered hand for an instant. Then he and his wife's sister went away.

Miss Eunice's remaining spark of charity at once crackled and burst into a flame. There is sure to be a little something that is bad in everybody's philanthropy when it is first put to use; it requires to be filed down like a faulty casting before it will run without danger to anybody. Samaritanism that goes off with half a charge is sure to do great mischief somewhere; but Miss Eunice's, now properly corrected, henceforth shot off at the proper end, and inevitably hit the mark. She purchased a new Crofutt.

BAYARD TAYLOR

1825 – 1878

BAYARD TAYLOR, in the '60's and '70's, was among the best known of our men of letters. Typical American in enterprise and resource, he gave most of his life to foreign lands and letters. *Views Afoot* (1846), which has sent across the Atlantic hundreds of young Americans like him in large ambition and small purse, was the first of a series extending through his life. For a really Viking spirit of travel urged him over the habitable globe, from Africa to Iceland, from California to Japan. The store of observations first made newspaper correspondence. His profession was journalism. Some of the material was subsequently cast in lectures; most of it appeared finally in books. Thus his trip across the world (1851–1853) to join Perry furnished, first, copy for the New York "Tribune," then many popular lectures, and finally *The Lands of the Saracen* (1854) and *A Visit to India, China and Japan* (1855). His wide knowledge of foreign societies and his intimate acquaintance with Germany brought him naturally into public life as minister to Berlin (1877–1878).

Admirable journalist, Taylor was not content with journalism. In 1863 at Gotha, where he had found a wife in 1857, he was deep in the study of Goethe. From 1868–1870, after intervening travels, he gave himself to the translation of "Faust." Lecturing then at Cornell as Professor of German Literature, he went back to Germany to pursue Goethe still further at Weimar. So his knowledge of Scandinavia was of the literature as well as of the land.

His great ambition, and doubtless his measure of success, was poetry. From his youthful ventures in Philadelphia almost to the day of his death he published verse; and the recognition of the public appears in the choice of him to read the Harvard Φ B K poem in 1850 and the National Ode at the Centennial

Exposition of 1876. Since his death this part of his work has been so far slighted that there is some need of recalling his consistently high aim and the technical mastery evinced by performances so widely different as the delicious parodies of *The Echo Club* and the noble rendering of " Faust." No criticism of Taylor as a poet should obscure the fact that his " Faust " takes rank with the few great verse translations.

Taylor's versatility achieved also a lesser, but still a considerable, success in novels and tales. The interest aroused by the lively opening of *Who Was She?* is sustained with no little art. Perhaps the import would be more poignant if it were less dangerously near to abstract proposition ; but it is very human.

WHO WAS SHE?

[*From the "Atlantic Monthly," September, 1874*]

COME, now, there may as well be an end of this!
Every time I meet your eyes squarely, I detect the
question just slipping out of them. If you had spoken it,
or even boldly looked it; if you had shown in your motions
the least sign of a fussy or fidgety concern on my account;
if this were not the evening of my birthday, and you the
only friend who remembered it; if confession were not
good for the soul, though harder than sin to some people,
of whom I am one, — well, if all reasons were not at this
instant converged into a focus, and burning me rather violently, in that region where the seat of emotion is supposed
to lie, I should keep my trouble to myself.

Yes, I have fifty times had it on my mind to tell you the
whole story. But who can be certain that his best friend
will not smile — or, what is worse, cherish a kind of charitable pity ever afterwards — when the external forms of a
very serious kind of passion seem trivial, fantastic, foolish?
And the worst of all is that the heroic part which I imagined
I was playing proves to have been almost the reverse. The
only comfort which I can find in my humiliation is that I
am capable of feeling it. There isn't a bit of a paradox in
this, as you will see; but I only mention it, now, to prepare
you for, maybe, a little morbid sensitiveness of my moral
nerves.

The documents are all in this portfolio, under my elbow.
I had just read them again completely through, when you
were announced. You may examine them as you like, afterwards: for the present, fill your glass, take another Cabaña,

and keep silent until my "ghastly tale" has reached its most lamentable conclusion.

The beginning of it was at Wampsocket Springs, three years ago last summer. I suppose most unmarried men who have reached, or passed, the age of thirty — and I was then thirty-three — experience a milder return of their adolescent warmth, a kind of fainter second spring, since the first has not fulfilled its promise. Of course, I was n't clearly conscious of this at the time : who is? But I had had my youthful passion and my tragic disappointment, as you know : I had looked far enough into what Thackeray used to call the cryptic mysteries, to save me from the Scylla of dissipation, and yet preserved enough of natural nature to keep me out of the Pharisaic Charybdis. My devotion to my legal studies had already brought me a mild distinction ; the paternal legacy was a good nest-egg for the incubation of wealth, — in short, I was a fair, respectable "party," desirable to the humbler mammas, and not to be despised by the haughty exclusives.

The fashionable hotel at the Springs holds three hundred, and it was packed. I had meant to lounge there for a fortnight and then finish my holidays at Long Branch ; but eighty, at least, out of the three hundred, were young and moved lightly in muslin. With my years and experience I felt so safe, that to walk, talk, or dance with them became simply a luxury, such as I had never — at least so freely — possessed before. My name and standing, known to some families, were agreeably exaggerated to the others, and I enjoyed that supreme satisfaction which a man always feels when he discovers, or imagines, that he is popular in society. There is a kind of premonitory apology implied in my saying this, I am aware. You must remember that I am culprit, and culprit's counsel, at the same time.

You have never been at Wampsocket? Well, the hills sweep around in a crescent, on the northern side, and four or five radiating glens, descending from them, unite just above the village. The central one, leading to a water-fall (called "Minne-hehe" by the irreverent young people, because there is so little of it), is the fashionable drive and promenade; but the second ravine on the left, steep, crooked, and cumbered with bowlders which have tumbled from somewhere and lodged in the most extraordinary groupings, became my favorite walk of a morning. There was a footpath in it, well-trodden at first, but gradually fading out as it became more like a ladder than a path, and I soon discovered that no other city feet than mine were likely to scale a certain rough slope which seemed the end of the ravine. With the aid of the tough laurel-stems I climbed to the top, passed through a cleft as narrow as a doorway, and presently found myself in a little upper dell, as wild and sweet and strange as one of the pictures that haunts us on the brink of sleep.

There was a pond — no, rather a bowl — of water in the centre; hardly twenty yards across, yet the sky in it was so pure and far down that the circle of rocks and summer foliage inclosing it seemed like a little planetary ring, floating off alone through space. I can't explain the charm of the spot, nor the selfishness which instantly suggested that I should keep the discovery to myself. Ten years earlier, I should have looked around for some fair spirit to be my "minister," but now —

One forenoon — I think it was the third or fourth time I had visited the place — I was startled to find the dint of a heel in the earth, half-way up the slope. There had been rain during the night and the earth was still moist and soft. It was the mark of a woman's boot, only to be distinguished from that of a walking-stick by its semicircular form. A little higher, I found the outline of a foot, not so small as to awake an ecstasy, but with a suggestion of lightness, elasticity, and grace. If hands were thrust through holes in a board-fence, and nothing of the attached bodies seen, I can easily imagine that some would attract and others repel us : with footprints the impression is weaker, of course, but we cannot escape it. I am not sure whether I wanted to find the unknown wearer of the boot within my precious personal solitude : I was afraid I should see her, while passing through the rocky crevice, and yet was disappointed when I found no one.

But on the flat, warm rock overhanging the tarn — my special throne — lay some withering wild-flowers, and a book ! I looked up and down, right and left : there was not the slightest sign of another human life than mine. Then I lay down for a quarter of an hour, and listened : there were only the noises of bird and squirrel, as before. At last, I took up the book, the flat breadth of which suggested only sketches. There were, indeed, some tolerable studies of rocks and trees on the first pages ; a few not very striking caricatures, which seemed to have been commenced as portraits, but recalled no faces I knew ; then a number of fragmentary notes, written in pencil. I found no name, from first to last ; only, under the sketches, a monogram so complicated and laborious that the initials could hardly be discovered unless one already knew them.

The writing was a woman's, but it had surely taken its character from certain features of her own : it was clear, firm, individual. It had nothing of that air of general debility which usually marks the manuscript of young ladies, yet its firmness was far removed from the stiff, conventional slope which all Englishwomen seem to acquire in youth and retain through life. I don't see how any man in my situation could have helped reading a few lines — if only for the sake of restoring lost property. But I was drawn on, and on, and finished by reading all : thence, since no further harm could be done, I re-read, pondering over certain passages until they stayed with me. Here they are, as I set them down, that evening, on the back of a legal blank.

"It makes a great deal of difference whether we wear social forms as bracelets or handcuffs."

"Can we not still be wholly our independent selves, even while doing, in the main, as others do? I know two who are so ; but they are married."

"The men who admire these bold, dashing young girls treat them like weaker copies of themselves. And yet they boast of what they call 'experience!'"

"I wonder if any one felt the exquisite beauty of the noon as I did, to-day? A faint appreciation of sunsets and storms is taught us in youth, and kept alive by novels and flirtations; but the broad, imperial splendor of this summer noon!—and myself standing alone in it,—yes, utterly alone!"

"The men I seek *must* exist: where are they? How make an acquaintance, when one obsequiously bows himself away, as I advance? The fault is surely not all on my side."

There was much more, intimate enough to inspire me with a keen interest in the writer, yet not sufficiently so to make my perusal a painful indiscretion. I yielded to the impulse of the moment, took out my pencil, and wrote a dozen lines on one of the blank pages. They ran something in this wise:—

"IGNOTUS IGNOTÆ!—You have bestowed without intending it, and I have taken without your knowledge. Do not regret the accident which has enriched another. This concealed idyl of the hills was mine, as I supposed, but I acknowledge your equal right to it. Shall we share the possession, or will you banish me?"

There was a frank advance, tempered by a proper caution, I fancied, in the words I wrote. It was evident that she was unmarried, but outside of that certainty there lay a vast range of possibilities, some of them alarming enough. However, if any nearer acquaintance should arise out of the incident, the next step must be taken by her. Was I one of the men she sought? I almost imagined so—certainly hoped so.

I laid the book on the rock, as I had found it, bestowed another keen scrutiny on the lonely landscape, and then descended the ravine. That evening, I went early to the ladies' parlor, chatted more than usual with the various damsels whom I knew, and watched with a new interest those whom I knew not. My mind, involuntarily, had already created a picture of the unknown. She might be twenty-five, I thought: a reflective habit of mind would hardly be developed before that age. Tall and stately, of course; distinctly proud in her bearing, and somewhat reserved in her manners. Why she should have large dark eyes, with long dark lashes, I could not tell; but so I seemed to see her. Quite forgetting that I was (or had meant to be) *Ignotus*, I found myself staring rather significantly at one or the other of the young ladies, in whom I discovered some slight general resemblance to the imaginary character. My fancies, I must confess, played strange pranks with me. They had been kept in a coop so many years, that now, when I suddenly turned them loose, their rickety attempts at flight quite bewildered me.

No! there was no use in expecting a sudden discovery. I went to the glen betimes, next morning: the book was gone, and so were the faded flowers, but some of the latter were scattered over the top of another rock, a few yards from mine. Ha! this means that I am not to withdraw, I said to myself: she makes room for me! But how to surprise her? — for by this time I was fully resolved to make her acquaintance, even though she might turn out to be forty, scraggy and sandy-haired.

I knew no other way so likely as that of visiting the glen at all times of the day. I even went so far as to write a line of greeting, with a regret that our visits had not yet coincided, and laid it under a stone on the top of *her* rock. The note disappeared, but there was no answer in its place. Then I suddenly remembered her fondness for the noon hours, at which time she was "utterly alone." The hotel *table d'hôte* was at one o'clock: her family, doubtless, dined later, in their own rooms. Why, this gave me, at least, her place in society! The question of age, to be sure, remained unsettled; but all else was safe.

The next day I took a late and large breakfast, and sacrificed my dinner. Before noon the guests had all straggled back to the hotel from glen and grove and lane, so bright and hot was the sunshine. Indeed, I could hardly have supported the reverberation of heat from the sides of the ravine, but for a fixed belief that I should be successful. While crossing the narrow meadow upon which it opened, I caught a glimpse of something white among the thickets higher up. A moment later, it had vanished, and I quickened my pace, feeling the beginning of an absurd nervous excitement in my limbs. At the next turn, there it was again! but only for another moment. I paused, exulting, and wiped my drenched forehead. "She cannot escape me!" I murmured between the deep draughts of cooler air I inhaled in the shadow of a rock.

A few hundred steps more brought me to the foot of the steep ascent, where I had counted on overtaking her. I was too late for that, but the dry, baked soil had surely been crumbled and dislodged, here and there, by a rapid foot. I followed, in reckless haste, snatching at the laurel-branches right and left, and paying little heed to my footing. About one third of the way up I slipped, fell, caught a bush which snapped at the root, slid, whirled over, and before I fairly knew what had happened, I was lying doubled up at the bottom of the slope.

I rose, made two steps forward, and then sat down with a groan of pain; my left ankle was badly sprained, in addition to various minor scratches and bruises. There was a revulsion of feeling, of course, — instant, complete, and hideous. I fairly hated the Unknown. "Fool that I was!" I exclaimed, in the theatrical manner, dashing the palm of my hand softly against my brow: "lured to this by the fair traitress! But, no! — not fair: she shows the artfulness of faded, desperate spinsterhood; she is all compact of enamel, 'liquid bloom of youth' and hair-dye!"

There was a fierce comfort in this thought, but it could n't help me out of the scrape. I dared not sit still, lest a sunstroke should be added, and there was no resource but to hop or crawl down the rugged path, in the hope of finding a forked sapling from which I could extemporize a crutch. With endless pain and trouble I reached a thicket, and was feebly working on a branch with my pen-knife, when the sound of a heavy footstep surprised me.

A brown harvest-hand, in straw hat and shirt-sleeves, presently appeared. He grinned when he saw me, and the thick snub of his nose would have seemed like a sneer at any other time.

"Are you the gentleman that got hurt?" he asked. "Is it pretty tolerable bad?"

"Who said I was hurt?" I cried, in astonishment.

"One of your town-women from the hotel — I reckon she was. I was binding oats, in the field over the ridge; but I have n't lost no time in comin' here."

While I was stupidly staring at this announcement, he whipped out a big clasp knife, and in a few minutes fashioned me a practicable crutch. Then, taking me by the other arm, he set me in motion towards the village.

Grateful as I was for the man's help, he aggravated me by his ignorance. When I asked if he knew the lady, he answered: "It's more 'n likely *you* know her better." But where did she come from? Down from the hill, he guessed, but it might ha' been up the road. How did she look? was she old or young? what was the color of her eyes? of her hair? There, now, I was too much for him. When a woman kept one o' them speckled veils over her face, turned her head away, and held her parasol between, how were you to know her from Adam? I declare to you, I could n't arrive at one positive particular. Even when he affirmed that she was tall, he added, the next instant: "Now I come to think on it, she stepped mighty quick; so I guess she must ha' been short."

By the time we reached the hotel, I was in a state of fever; opiates and lotions had their will of me for the rest of the day. I was glad to escape the worry of questions, and the conventional sympathy expressed in inflections of the voice which are meant to soothe, and only exasperate. The next morning, as I lay upon my sofa, restful, patient, and properly cheerful, the waiter entered with a bouquet of wild flowers.

"Who sent them?" I asked.

"I found them outside your door, sir. Maybe there's a card; yes, here's a bit o' paper."

I opened the twisted slip he handed me, and read: "From your dell — and mine." I took the flowers; among them were two or three rare and beautiful varieties, which I had only found in that one spot. Fool, again! I noiselessly kissed, while pretending to smell them, had them placed on a stand within reach, and fell into a state of quiet and agreeable contemplation.

Tell me, yourself, whether any male human being is ever too old for sentiment, provided that it strikes him at the right time and in the right way! What did that bunch of wild flowers betoken? Knowledge, first; then, sympathy; and finally, encouragement, at least. Of course she had seen my accident, from above; of course she had sent the harvest laborer to aid me home. It was quite natural she should imagine some special, romantic interest in the lonely dell, on my part, and the gift took additional value from her conjecture.

Four days afterwards, there was a hop in the large dining-room of the hotel. Early in the morning, a fresh bouquet had been left at my door. I was tired of my enforced idleness, eager to discover the fair unknown, (she was again fair, to my fancy!) and I determined to go down, believing that a cane and a crimson velvet slipper on the left foot would provoke a glance of sympathy from certain eyes, and thus enable me to detect them.

The fact was, the sympathy was much too general and effusive. Everybody, it seemed, came to me with kindly greetings; seats were vacated at my approach, even fat Mrs. Huxter insisting on my taking her warm place, at the head of the room.   But Bob Leroy, — you know him, — as gallant a gentleman as ever lived, put me down at the right point, and kept me there.   He only meant to divert me, yet gave me the only place where I could quietly inspect all the younger ladies, as dance or supper brought them near.

One of the dances was an old-fashioned cotillon, and one of the figures, the " coquette," brought every one, in turn, before me.   I received a pleasant word or two from those whom I knew, and a long, kind, silent glance from Miss May Danvers.   Where had been my eyes?   She was tall, stately, twenty-five, had large dark eyes, and long dark lashes !   Again the changes of the dance brought her near me ; I threw (or strove to throw) unutterable meanings into my eyes, and cast them upon hers.   She seemed startled, looked suddenly away, looked back to me, and — blushed. ⸢I knew her for what is called "a nice girl" — that is, tolerably frank, gently feminine, and not dangerously intelligent.   Was it possible that I had overlooked so much character and intellect?

As the cotillon closed, she was again in my neighborhood, and her partner led her in my direction.   I was rising painfully from my chair, when Bob Leroy pushed me down again, whisked another seat from somewhere, planted it at my side, and there she was !

She knew who was her neighbor, I plainly saw ; but instead of turning towards me, she began to fan herself in a nervous way and to fidget with the buttons of her gloves. I grew impatient.

" Miss Danvers ! " I said, at last.

" Oh ! " was all her answer, as she looked at me for a moment.

" Where are your thoughts? " I asked.

Then she turned, with wide, astonished eyes, coloring softly up to the roots of her hair.   My heart gave a sudden leap.

" How can you tell, if I cannot? " she asked.

" May I guess? "

She made a slight inclination of the head, saying nothing. I was then quite sure.

"The second ravine, to the left of the main drive?"

This time she actually started ; her color became deeper, and a leaf of the ivory fan snapped between her fingers.

"Let there be no more a secret!" I exclaimed. "Your flowers have brought me your messages ; I knew I should find you " —

Full of certainty, I was speaking in a low, impassioned voice. She cut me short by rising from her seat; I felt that she was both angry and alarmed. Fisher, of Philadelphia, jostling right and left in his haste, made his way towards her. She fairly snatched his arm, clung to it with a warmth I had never seen expressed in a ball-room, and began to whisper in his ear. It was not five minutes before he came to me, alone, with a very stern face, bent down, and said : —

"If you have discovered our secret, you will keep silent. You are certainly a gentleman."

I bowed, coldly and savagely. There was a draft from the open window; my ankle became suddenly weary and painful, and I went to bed. Can you believe that I did n't guess, immediately, what it all meant? In a vague way, I fancied that I had been premature in my attempt to drop our mutual incognito, and that Fisher, a rival lover, was jealous of me. This was rather flattering than otherwise ; but when I limped down to the ladies' parlor, the next day, no Miss Danvers was to be seen. I did not venture to ask for her; it might seem importunate, and a woman of so much hidden capacity was evidently not to be wooed in the ordinary way.

So another night passed by ; and then, with the morning, came a letter which made me feel, at the same instant, like a fool and a hero. It had been dropped in the Wampsocket post-office, was legibly addressed to me and delivered with some other letters which had arrived by the night mail. Here it is ; listen !

" NOTO IGNOTA ! — Haste is not a gift of the gods, and you have been impatient, with the usual result. I was almost prepared for this, and thus am not wholly disappointed. In a day or two more you will discover your mistake, which, so far as I can learn, has done no particular harm. If you wish to find *me*, there is only one way to seek me; should I tell you what it is, I should run the risk of losing you, —that is, I should preclude the manifestation of a certain quality which I hope to find in the man who may — or, rather, must — be my friend. This sounds enigmatical, yet you have read enough of my nature, as written in those random notes in my sketch-book, to guess, at least, how much I require. Only this let me add: mere guessing is useless.

" Being unknown, I can write freely. If you find me, I shall be justified ; if not, I shall hardly need to blush, even to myself, over a futile experiment.

" It is possible for me to learn enough of your life, henceforth, to direct my relation towards you. This may be the end ; if so, I shall know it soon. I shall also know whether you continue to seek me. Trusting in your honor as a man, I must ask you to trust in mine, as a woman."

I *did* discover my mistake, as the Unknown promised. There had been a secret betrothal between Fisher and Miss Danvers ; and singularly enough, the momentous question and answer had been given in the very ravine leading to my upper dell ! The two meant to keep the matter to themselves, but therein, it seems, I thwarted them ; there was a little opposition on the part of their respective families, but all was amicably settled before I left Wampsocket.

The letter made a very deep impression upon me. What was the one way to find her? What could it be but the triumph that follows ambitious toil, — the manifestation of all my best qualities, as a man? Be she old or young, plain or beautiful, I reflected, hers is surely a nature worth knowing, and its candid intelligence conceals no hazards for me. I have sought her rashly, blundered, betrayed that I set her lower, in my thoughts, than her actual self: let me now adopt the opposite course, seek her openly no longer, go back to my tasks, and, following my own aims vigorously and cheerfully, restore that respect which she seemed to be on the point of losing. For, consciously or not, she had communicated to me a doubt, implied in the very expression of her own strength and pride. She had meant to address me as an equal, yet, despite herself, took a stand a little above that which she accorded to me.

I came back to New York earlier than usual, worked steadily at my profession and with increasing success, and began to accept opportunities (which I had previously declined) of making myself personally known to the great, impressible, fickle, tyrannical public. One or two of my speeches in the hall of the Cooper Institute, on various occasions — as you may perhaps remember — gave me a good headway with the party, and were the chief cause of my nomination for the State office which I still hold. (There, on the table, lies a resignation, written to-day, but not yet signed. We'll talk of it, afterwards.) Several months passed by, and no further letter reached me. I gave up much of my time to society, moved familiarly in more than one province of the kingdom here, and vastly extended my acquaintance, especially among the women; but not one of them betrayed the mysterious something or other — really I can't explain precisely what it was! — which I was looking for. In fact, the more I endeavored quietly to study the sex, the more confused I became.

At last, I was subjected to the usual onslaught from the strong-minded. A small but formidable committee entered my office one morning and demanded a categorical declaration of my principles. What my views on the subject were, I knew very well; they were clear and decided; and yet, I hesitated to declare them! It wasn't a temptation of Saint Anthony — that is, turned the other way — and the belligerent attitude of the dames did not alarm me in the least; but *she!* What was *her* position? How could I best please her? It flashed upon my mind, while Mrs. ——

was making her formal speech, that I had taken no step for months without a vague, secret reference to *her*. So, I strove to be courteous, friendly, and agreeably noncommittal; begged for further documents, and promised to reply by letter, in a few days.

I was hardly surprised to find the well-known hand on the envelope of a letter, shortly afterwards. I held it for a minute in my palm, with an absurd hope that I might sympathetically feel its character, before breaking the seal. Then I read it with a great sense of relief.

" I have never assumed to guide a man, except towards the full exercise of his powers. It is not opinion in action, but opinion in a state of idleness or indifference, which repels me. I am deeply glad that you have gained so much since you left the country. If, in shaping your course, you have thought of me, I will frankly say that, *to that extent*, you have drawn nearer. Am I mistaken in conjecturing that you wish to know my relation to the movement concerning which you were recently interrogated ? In this, as in other instances which may come, I must beg you to consider me only as a spectator. The more my own views may seem likely to sway your action, the less I shall be inclined to declare them. If you find this cold or unwomanly, remember that it is not easy ! "

Yes ! I felt that I had certainly drawn much nearer to her. And from this time on, her imaginary face and form became other than they were. She was twenty-eight — three years older; a very little above the middle height, but not tall ; serene, rather than stately, in her movements ; with a calm, almost grave face, relieved by the sweetness of the full, firm lips ; and finally eyes of pure, limpid gray, such as we fancy belonged to the Venus of Milo. I found her, thus, much more attractive than with the dark eyes and lashes, — but she did not make her appearance in the circles which I frequented.

Another year slipped away. As an official personage, my importance increased, but I was careful not to exaggerate it to myself. Many have wondered (perhaps you among the rest) at my success, seeing that I possess no remarkable abilities. If I have any secret, it is simply this — doing faithfully, with all my might, whatever I undertake. Nine tenths of our politicians become inflated and careless, after the first few years, and are easily forgotten when they once lose place. I am a little surprised, now, that I had so much patience with the Unknown. I was too important, at least, to be played with ; too mature to be subjected to a longer test; too earnest, as I had proved, to be doubted, or thrown aside without a further explanation.

Growing tired, at last, of silent waiting, I bethought me of advertising. A carefully-written " Personal," in which *Ignotus* informed *Ignota* of the necessity of his communicating with her, appeared simultaneously in the Tribune, Herald, World, and Times. I renewed the advertisement as the time expired without an answer, and I think it was about the end of the third week before one came, through the post, as before.

Ah, yes! I had forgotten. See! my advertisement is pasted on the note, as a heading or motto for the manuscript lines. I don't know why the printed slip should give me a particular feeling of humiliation as I look at it, but such is the fact. What she wrote is all I need read to you : —

" I could not, at first, be certain that this was meant for me. If I were to explain to you why I have not written for so long a time, I might give you one of the few clews which I insist on keeping in my own hands. In your public capacity, you have been (so far as a woman may judge) upright, independent, wholly manly: in your relations with other men I learn nothing of you that is not honorable : towards women you are kind, chivalrous, no doubt, overflowing with the *usual* social refinements, but — Here, again, I run hard upon the absolute necessity of silence. The way to me, if you care to traverse it, is so simple, so very simple ! Yet, after what I have written, I cannot even wave my hand in the direction of it, without certain self-contempt. When I feel free to tell you, we shall draw apart and remain unknown forever.

"You desire to write? I do not prohibit it. I have heretofore made no arrangement for hearing from you, in turn, because I could not discover that any advantage would accrue from it. But it seems only fair, I confess, and you dare not think me capricious. So, three days hence, at six o'clock in the evening, a trusty messenger of mine will call at your door. If you have anything to give her for me, the act of giving it must be the sign of a compact on your part, that you will allow her to leave immediately, unquestioned and unfollowed."

You look puzzled, I see: you don't catch the real drift of her words? Well, — that's a melancholy encouragement. Neither did I, at the time: it was plain that I had disappointed her in some way, and my intercourse with, or manner towards, women, had something to do with it. In vain I ran over as much of my later social life as I could recall. There had been no special attention, nothing to mislead a susceptible heart; on the other side, certainly no rudeness, no want of "chivalrous" (she used the word!) respect and attention. What, in the name of all the gods, was the matter?

In spite of all my efforts to grow clearer, I was obliged to write my letter in a rather muddled state of mind. I had *so* much to say! sixteen folio pages, I was sure, would only suffice for an introduction to the case; yet, when the creamy vellum lay before me and the moist pen drew my fingers towards it, I sat stock dumb for half an hour. I wrote, finally, in a half-desperate mood, without regard to coherency or logic. Here's a rough draft of a part of the letter, and a single passage from it will be enough : —

"I can conceive of no simpler way to you than the knowledge of your name and address. I have drawn airy images of you, but they do not become incarnate, and I am not sure that I should recognize you in the brief moment of passing. Your nature is not of those which are instantly legible. As an abstract power, it has wrought in my life and it continually moves my heart with desires which are unsatisfactory because so vague and ignorant. Let me offer you, personally, my gratitude, my earnest friendship: you would laugh if I were *now* to offer more."

Stay! here is another fragment, more reckless in tone : —

" I want to find the woman whom I can love — who can love me. But this is a masquerade where the features are hidden, the voice disguised, even the hands grotesquely gloved. Come! I will venture more than I ever thought was possible to me. You shall know my deepest nature as I myself seem to know it. Then, give me the commonest chance of learning yours, through an intercourse which shall leave both free, should we not feel the closing of the inevitable bond! "

After I had written that, the pages filled rapidly. When the appointed hour arrived, a bulky epistle, in a strong linen envelope, sealed with five wax seals, was waiting on my table. Precisely at six there was an announcement: the door opened, and a little outside, in the shadow, I saw an old woman, in a threadbare dress of rusty black.

"Come in! " I said.

"The letter! " answered a husky voice. She stretched out a bony hand, without moving a step.

" It is for a lady — very important business," said I, taking up the letter; " are you sure that there is no mistake? "

She drew her hand under the shawl, turned without a word, and moved towards the hall door.

"Stop! " I cried : " I beg a thousand pardons! Take it — take it ! You are the right messenger! "

She clutched it, and was instantly gone.

Several days passed, and I gradually became so nervous and uneasy that I was on the point of inserting another " Personal " in the daily papers, when the answer arrived. It was brief and mysterious ; you shall hear the whole of it.

" I thank you. Your letter is a sacred confidence which I pray you never to regret. You nature is sound and good. You ask no more than is reasonable, and I have no real right to refuse. In the one respect which I have hinted, _I_ may have been unskillful or too narrowly cautious : I must have the certainty of this. Therefore, as a generous favor, give me six months more! At the end of that time I will write to you again. Have patience with these brief lines: another word might be a word too much."

You notice the change in her tone? The letter gave me the strongest impression of a new, warm, almost anxious interest on her part. My fancies, as first at Wampsocket, began to play all sorts of singular pranks: sometimes she was rich and of an old family, sometimes moderately poor and obscure, but always the same calm, reposeful face and clear gray eyes. I ceased looking for her in society, quite sure that I should not find her, and nursed a wild expectation of suddenly meeting her, face to face, in the most unlikely places and under startling circumstances. However, the end of it all was patience, — patience for six months.

There's not much more to tell; but this last letter is hard for me to read. It came punctually, to a day. I knew it would, and at the last I began to dread the time, as if a heavy note were falling due, and I had no funds to meet it. My head was in a whirl when I broke the seal. The fact in it stared at me blankly, at once, but it was a long time before the words and sentences became intelligible.

"The stipulated time has come, and our hidden romance is at an end. Had I taken this resolution a year ago, it would have saved me many vain hopes, and you, perhaps, a little uncertainty. Forgive me, first, if you can, and then hear the explanation!

"You wished for a personal interview: *you have had, not one, but many.* We have met, in society, talked face to face, discussed the weather, the opera, toilettes, Queechy, Aurora Floyd, Long Branch and Newport, and exchanged a weary amount of fashionable gossip; and you never guessed that I was governed by any deeper interest! I have purposely uttered ridiculous platitudes, and you were as smilingly courteous as if you enjoyed them: I have let fall remarks whose hollowness and selfishness could not have escaped you, and have waited in vain for a word of sharp, honest, manly reproof. Your manner to me was unexceptionable, as it was to all other women: but there lies the source of my disappointment, of — yes, — of my sorrow!

"You appreciate, I cannot doubt, the qualities in woman which men value in one another, — culture, independence of thought, a high and earnest apprehension of life; but you know not how to seek them. It is not true that a mature and unperverted woman is flattered by receiving only the general obsequiousness which most men give to the whole sex. In the man who contradicts and strives with her, she discovers a truer interest, a nobler respect. The empty-headed, spindle-shanked youths who dance admirably, understand something of billiards, much less of horses, and still less of navigation, soon grow inexpressibly wearisome to us; but the men who adopt their social courtesy, never seeking to arouse, uplift, instruct us, are a bitter disappointment.

"What would have been the end, had you really found me? Certainly a sincere, satisfying friendship. No mysterious magnetic force has drawn you to me or held you near me, nor has my experiment inspired me with an interest which cannot be given up without a personal pang. I am grieved, for the sake of all men and all women. Yet, understand me! I mean no slightest reproach. I esteem and honor you for what you are. Farewell!"

There! Nothing could be kinder in tone, nothing more humiliating in substance. I was sore and offended for a few days; but I soon began to see, and ever more and more clearly, that she was wholly right. I was sure, also, that any further attempt to correspond with her would be vain. It all comes of taking society just as we find it, and supposing that conventional courtesy is the only safe ground on which men and women can meet.

The fact is — there's no use in hiding it from myself (and I see, by your face, that the letter cuts into your own conscience) — she is a free, courageous, independent character, and — I am not.

But who *was* she?

HENRY CUYLER BUNNER

1855 – 1896

FROM early manhood until his death H. C. Bunner was the editor of " Puck." Those who appreciated the flavor of *Airs from Arcady* and *Rowen*, and who knew of " Puck " only that it was our most popular comic weekly, felt here an incongruity. If they had followed the editorial page, they would have found dignity no less than pungency, and might have comprehended the man as more than a maker of delicate verses and more than a humorist. In the ordinary sense he was hardly a humorist. Humor was large in him, but all suffused with fancy. Loving New York as Charles Lamb loved London, he was even more like Lamb in that his quip habitually carried a sentiment springing from human sympathy. This ultimate quality reconciled the others of a singularly original composition.

His fiction shows all these traits, and also a nice sense of form. He was a student of Boccaccio; he experimented with various adaptations, as in *The Third Figure of the Cotillion* with the method of Irving; and, though his preference was for freer and more spontaneous structure, he was keenly aware, as in the story below, of the value of the unities.

THE LOVE–LETTERS OF SMITH

[*From "Short Sixes," copyright, 1890, by Keppler and Schwarz-mann; reprinted here by their special permission*]

WHEN the little seamstress had climbed to her room in the story over the top story of the great brick tenement house in which she lived, she was quite tired out. If you do not understand what a story over a top story is, you must remember that there are no limits to human greed, and hardly any to the height of tenement houses. When the man who owned that seven-story tenement found that he could rent another floor, he found no difficulty in persuading the guardians of our building laws to let him clap another story on the roof, like a cabin on the deck of a ship; and in the southeasterly of the four apartments on this floor the little seamstress lived. You could just see the top of her window from the street — the huge cornice that had capped the original front, and that served as her window-sill now, quite hid all the lower part of the story on top of the top-story.

The little seamstress was scarcely thirty years old, but she was such an old-fashioned little body in so many of her looks and ways that I had almost spelled her sempstress, after the fashion of our grandmothers. She had been a comely body, too; and would have been still, if she had not been thin and pale and anxious-eyed.

She was tired out to-night because she had been working hard all day for a lady who lived far up in the " New Wards " beyond Harlem River, and after the long journey home, she had to climb seven flights of tenement-house stairs. She was too tired, both in body and in mind, to cook the two little chops she had brought home. She would save them for breakfast, she thought. So she made herself a cup of tea on the miniature stove, and ate a slice of dry bread with it. It was too much trouble to make toast.

But after dinner she watered her flowers. She was never too tired for that : and the six pots of geraniums that caught the south sun on the top of the cornice did their best to repay her. Then she sat down in her rocking-chair by the window and looked out. Her eyry was high above all the other buildings, and she could look across some low roofs opposite, and see the further end of Tompkins Square, with its sparse Spring green showing faintly through the dusk. The eternal roar of the city floated up to her and vaguely troubled her. She was a country girl, and although she had lived for ten years in New York, she had never grown used to that ceaseless murmur. To-night she felt the languor of the new season as well as the heaviness of physical exhaustion. She was almost too tired to go to bed.

She thought of the hard day done and the hard day to be begun after the night spent on the hard little bed. She thought of the peaceful days in the country, when she taught school in the Massachusetts village where she was born. She thought of a hundred small slights that she had to bear from people better fed than bred. She thought of the sweet green fields that she rarely saw nowadays. She thought of the long journey forth and back that must begin and end her morrow's work, and she wondered if her employer would think to offer to pay her fare. Then she pulled herself together. She must think of more agreeable things, or she could not sleep. And as the only agreeable things she had to think about were her flowers, she looked at the garden on top of the cornice.

A peculiar gritting noise made her look down, and she saw a cylindrical object that glittered in the twilight, advancing in an irregular and uncertain manner toward her flower-pots. Looking closer, she saw that it was a pewter beer-mug, which somebody in the next apartment was pushing with a two-

foot rule. On top of the beer-mug was a piece of paper,
and on this paper was written, in a sprawling, half-formed
hand :

> *porter*
> *pleas excuse the libberty And*
> *drink it*

The seamstress started up in terror, and shut the window.
She remembered that there was a man in the next apartment. She had seen him on the stairs, on Sundays. He
seemed a grave, decent person ; but — he must be drunk.
She sat down on her bed, all a-tremble. Then she reasoned
with herself. The man was drunk, that was all. He probably would not annoy her further. And if he did, she had
only to retreat to Mrs. Mulvaney's apartment in the rear,
and Mr. Mulvaney, who was a highly respectable man and
worked in a boiler-shop, would protect her. So, being a
poor woman who had already had occasion to excuse — and
refuse — two or three "libberties" of like sort, she made
up her mind to go to bed like a reasonable seamstress, and
she did. She was rewarded, for when her light was out, she
could see in the moonlight that the two-foot rule appeared
again, with one joint bent back, hitched itself into the mug-
handle, and withdrew the mug.

The next day was a hard one for the little seamstress, and
she hardly thought of the affair of the night before until the
same hour had come around again, and she sat once more
by her window. Then she smiled at the remembrance.
"Poor fellow," she said in her charitable heart, "I 've no
doubt he 's *awfully* ashamed of it now. Perhaps he was
never tipsy before. Perhaps he did n't know there was a
lone woman in here to be frightened."

Just then she heard a gritting sound. She looked down.
The pewter pot was in front of her, and the two-foot rule
was slowly retiring. On the pot was a piece of paper, and
on the paper was :

> *porter*
> *good for the helth*
> *it makes meet*

This time the little seamstress shut her window with a bang of indignation. The color rose to her pale cheeks. She thought that she would go down to see the janitor at once. Then she remembered the seven flights of stairs; and she resolved to see the janitor in the morning. Then she went to bed and saw the mug drawn back just as it had been drawn back the night before.

The morning came, but, somehow, the seamstress did not care to complain to the janitor. She hated to make trouble — and the janitor might think — and — and — well, if the wretch did it again she would speak to him herself, and that would settle it.

And so, on the next night, which was a Thursday, the little seamstress sat down by her window, resolved to settle the matter. And she had not sat there long, rocking in the creaking little rocking-chair which she had brought with her from her old home, when the pewter pot hove in sight, with a piece of paper on the top.

This time the legend read :

> *Perhaps you are afrade i will*
> *adress you*
> *i am not that kind*

The seamstress did not quite know whether to laugh or to cry. But she felt that the time had come for speech. She leaned out of her window and addressed the twilight heaven.

" Mr. — Mr. — sir — I — will you *please* put your head out of the window so that I can speak to you?"

The silence of the other room was undisturbed. The seamstress drew back, blushing. But before she could nerve herself for another attack, a piece of paper appeared on the end of the two-foot rule.

> *when i Say a thing i*
> *mene it*
> *i have Sed i would not*
> *Adress you and i*
> *Will not*

What was the little seamstress to do? She stood by the window and thought hard about it. Should she complain to the janitor? But the creature was perfectly respectful. No doubt he meant to be kind. He certainly was kind, to waste these pots of porter on her. She remembered the last time — and the first — that she had drunk porter. It was at home, when she was a young girl, after she had had the diphtheria. She remembered how good it was, and how it had given her back her strength. And without one thought of what she was doing, she lifted the pot of porter and took one little reminiscent sip — two little reminiscent sips — and became aware of her utter fall and defeat. She blushed now as she had never blushed before, put the pot down, closed the window, and fled to her bed like a deer to the woods.

And when the porter arrived the next night, bearing the simple appeal :

Dont be afrade of it
drink it all

the little seamstress arose and grasped the pot firmly by the handle, and poured its contents over the earth around her largest geranium. She poured the contents out to the last drop, and then she dropped the pot, and ran back and sat on her bed and cried, with her face hid in her hands.

" Now," she said to herself, " you 've done it ! And you 're just as nasty and hard-hearted and suspicious and mean as — as pusley ! "

And she wept to think of her hardness of heart. " He will never give me a chance to say I am sorry," she thought. And, really, she might have spoken kindly to the poor man, and told him that she was much obliged to him, but that he really must n't ask her to drink porter with him.

" But it 's all over and done now," she said to herself as she sat at her window on Saturday night. And then she looked at the cornice, and saw the faithful little pewter pot traveling slowly toward her.

She was conquered. This act of Christian forbearance was too much for her kindly spirit. She read the inscription on the paper:

porter is good for Flours
but better for Fokes

and she lifted the pot to her lips, which were not half so red as her cheeks, and took a good, hearty, grateful draught.

She sipped in thoughtful silence after this first plunge, and presently she was surprised to find the bottom of the pot in full view.

On the table at her side a few pearl buttons were screwed up in a bit of white paper. She untwisted the paper and smoothed it out, and wrote in a tremulous hand — she *could* write a very neat hand —

Thanks.

This she laid on the top of the pot, and in a moment the bent two-foot rule appeared and drew the mail-carriage home. Then she sat still, enjoying the warm glow of the porter, which seemed to have permeated her entire being with a heat that was not at all like the unpleasant and oppressive heat of the atmosphere, an atmosphere heavy with the Spring damp. A gritting on the tin aroused her. A piece of paper lay under her eyes.

fine groing weather
            Smith
it said.

Now it is unlikely that in the whole round and range of conversational commonplaces there was one other greeting that could have induced the seamstress to continue the exchange of communications. But this simple and homely phrase touched her country heart. What did "*groing weather*" matter to the toilers in this waste of brick and mortar? This stranger must be, like herself, a country-bred soul, longing for the new green and the upturned brown mould of the country fields. She took up the paper, and wrote under the first message:

Fine

But that seemed curt; *for* she added: *"for"* what? She did not know. At last in desperation she put down *potatos.* The piece of paper was withdrawn and came back with an addition:

Too mist for potatos.

And when the little seamstress had read this, and grasped the fact that *m-i-s-t* represented the writer's pronunciation of "moist," she laughed softly to herself. A man whose mind, at such a time, was seriously bent upon potatos, was not a man to be feared. She found a half-sheet of note-paper, and wrote:

I lived in a small village before I came to New York, but I am afraid I do not know much about farming. Are you a farmer?

The answer came:

have ben most Every thing
farmed a Spel in Maine
Smith

As she read this, the seamstress heard a church clock strike nine.

"Bless me, is it so late?" she cried, and she hurriedly penciled *Good Night,* thrust the paper out, and closed the window. But a few minutes later, passing by, she saw yet another bit of paper on the cornice, fluttering in the evening breeze. It said only *good nite,* and after a moment's hesitation, the little seamstress took it in and gave it shelter.

. . . .

After this, they were the best of friends. Every evening the pot appeared, and while the seamstress drank from it at her window, Mr. Smith drank from its twin at his; and notes were exchanged as rapidly as Mr. Smith's early education permitted. They told each other their histories, and Mr. Smith's was one of travel and variety, which he seemed to consider quite a matter of course. He had followed the sea, he had farmed, he had been a logger and a hunter in the Maine woods. Now he was foreman of an East River lumber yard, and he was prospering. In a year or two he would have enough laid by to go home to Bucksport and buy a share in a ship-building business. All this dribbled out in the course of a jerky but variegated correspondence, in which autobiographic details were mixed with reflections, moral and philosophical.

A few samples will give an idea of Mr. Smith's style :

> *i was one trip to van demens*
> *land*

To which the seamstress replied :

> *It must have been very interesting.*

But Mr. Smith disposed of this subject very briefly :

> *it wornt*

Further he vouchsafed :

> *i seen a chinese cook in*
> *hong kong could cook flap jacks*
> *like your Mother*
>
> *a mishnery that sells Rum*
> *is the menest of Gods crechers*
>
> *a bulfite is not what it is*
> *cract up to Be*
>
> *the dagos are wussen the*
> *brutes*
>
> *i am 6 1¾*
> *but my Father was 6 foot 4*

The seamstress had taught school one Winter, and she could not refrain from making an attempt to reform Mr.

Smith's orthography. One evening, in answer to this communication:

> *i killd a Bare in Maine 600*
> *lbs waight*

she wrote:

> *Is n't it generally spelled Bear?*

but she gave up the attempt when he responded:

> *a bare is a mene animle any*
> *way you spel him*

The Spring wore on, and the Summer came, and still the evening drink and the evening correspondence brightened the close of each day for the little seamstress. And the draught of porter put her to sleep each night, giving her a calmer rest than she had ever known during her stay in the noisy city; and it began, moreover, to make a little *"meet"* for her. And then the thought that she was going to have an hour of pleasant companionship somehow gave her courage to cook and eat her little dinner, however tired she was. The seamstress's cheeks began to blossom with the June roses.

And all this time Mr. Smith kept his vow of silence unbroken, though the seamstress sometimes tempted him with little ejaculations and exclamations to which he might have responded. He was silent and invisible. Only the smoke of his pipe, and the clink of his mug as he set it down on the cornice, told her that a living, material Smith was her correspondent. They never met on the stairs, for their hours of coming and going did not coincide. Once or twice they passed each other in the street — but Mr. Smith looked straight ahead of him, about a foot over her head. The little seamstress thought he was a very fine-looking man, with his six feet one and three-quarters and his thick brown beard. Most people would have called him plain.

Once she spoke to him. She was coming home one Summer evening, and a gang of corner-loafers stopped her and demanded money to buy beer, as is their custom.

Before she had time to be frightened, Mr. Smith appeared — whence, she knew not — scattered the gang like chaff, and, collaring two of the human hyenas, kicked them, with deliberate, ponderous, alternate kicks, until they writhed in ineffable agony. When he let them crawl away, she turned to him and thanked him warmly, looking very pretty now, with the color in her cheeks. But Mr. Smith answered no word. He stared over her head, grew red in the face, fidgeted nervously, but held his peace until his eyes fell on a rotund Teuton, passing by.

"Say, Dutchy!" he roared.

The German stood aghast.

"I ain't got nothing to write with!" thundered Mr. Smith, looking him in the eye. And then the man of his word passed on his way.

And so the Summer went on, and the two correspondents chatted silently from window to window, hid from sight of all the world below by the friendly cornice. And they looked out over the roof, and saw the green of Tompkins Square grow darker and dustier as the months went on.

Mr. Smith was given to Sunday trips into the suburbs, and he never came back without a bunch of daisies or black-eyed Susans or, later, asters or golden-rod for the little seamstress. Sometimes, with a sagacity rare in his sex, he brought her a whole plant, with fresh loam for potting.

He gave her also a reel in a bottle, which, he wrote, he had "*maid*" himself, and some coral, and a dried flying-fish, that was somewhat fearful to look upon, with its sword-like fins and its hollow eyes. At first, she could not go to sleep with that flying-fish hanging on the wall.

But he surprised the little seamstress very much one cool September evening, when he shoved this letter along the cornice :

Respected and Honored Madam :

Having long and vainly sought an opportunity to convey to you the expression of my sentiments, I now avail myself of the privilege of epistolary communication to acquaint you with the fact that the Emotions, which you have raised in my breast, are those which should point to Connubial Love and Affection rather than to simple Friendship. In short, Madam, I have the Honor to approach you with a Proposal, the acceptance of which will fill me with ecstatic Gratitude, and enable me to extend to you those Protecting Cares, which the Matrimonial Bond makes at once the Duty and the Privilege of him, who would, at no distant date, lead to the Hymeneal Altar one whose charms and virtues should suffice to kindle its Flames, without extraneous Aid

I remain, Dear Madam,
Your Humble Servant and
Ardent Adorer, I. Smith

The little seamstress gazed at this letter a long time. Perhaps she was wondering in what Ready Letter-Writer of the last century Mr. Smith had found his form. Perhaps she was amazed at the results of his first attempt at punctuation. Perhaps she was thinking of something else, for there were tears in her eyes and a smile on her small mouth.

But it must have been a long time, and Mr. Smith must have grown nervous, for presently another communication came along the line where the top of the cornice was worn smooth. It read:

If not understood will you
mary me

The little seamstress seized a piece of paper and wrote:

If I say Yes, will you speak to me?

Then she rose and passed it out to him, leaning out of the window, and their faces met.

HAROLD FREDERIC

1856 – 1898

HAROLD FREDERIC was bred and schooled, at college and at journalism, in Central New York. His fictions were almost all written in London during the later years of his correspondence with the " New York Times." The most popular of these, *The Damnation of Theron Ware*, shows him stronger in the novel. His own fondness for his short stories is due in part, doubtless, to their being closer to his native soil ; but the one reprinted below shows also a distinct appreciation of the form.

THE EVE OF THE FOURTH

IT was well on toward evening before this Third of July
all at once made itself gloriously different from other
days in my mind.

There was a very long afternoon, I remember, hot and
overcast, with continual threats of rain, which never came
to anything. The other boys were too excited about the
morrow to care for present play. They sat instead along
the edge of the broad platform-stoop in front of Delos
Ingersoll's grocery-store, their brown feet swinging at vary-
ing heights above the sidewalk, and bragged about the
manner in which they contemplated celebrating the anniversary of their Independence. Most of the elder lads
were very independent indeed ; they were already secure
in the parental permission to stay up all night, so that the
Fourth might be ushered in with its full quota of ceremonial. The smaller urchins pretended that they also had
this permission, or were sure of getting it. Little Denny
Cregan attracted admiring attention by vowing that he
should remain out, even if his father chased him with a
policeman all around the ward, and he had to go and live
in a cave in the gulf until he was grown up.

My inferiority to these companions of mine depressed
me. They were allowed to go without shoes and stockings ; they wore loose and comfortable old clothes, and
were under no responsibility to keep them dry or clean or
whole ; they had their pockets literally bulging now with

all sorts of portentous engines of noise and racket — huge
brown " double-enders," bound with waxed cord ; long, slim,
vicious-looking " nigger-chasers ; " big " Union torpedoes,"
covered with clay, which made a report like a horse-pistol,
and were invaluable for frightening farmers' horses ; and so
on through an extended catalogue of recondite and sinister
explosives upon which I looked with awe, as their owners
from time to time exhibited them with the proud simplicity
of those accustomed to greatness. Several of these boys
also possessed toy cannons, which would be brought forth
at twilight. They spoke firmly of ramming them to the
muzzle with grass, to produce a greater noise — even if it
burst them and killed everybody.

By comparison, my lot was one of abasement. I was a
solitary child, and a victim to conventions. A blue neck-
tie was daily pinned under my Byron collar, and there were
gilt buttons on my zouave jacket. When we were away in
the pasture playground near the gulf, and I ventured to
take off my foot-gear, every dry old thistle-point in the
whole territory seemed to arrange itself to be stepped upon
by my whitened and tender soles. I could not swim ; so,
while my lithe, bold comrades dived out of sight under the
deep water, and darted about chasing one another far beyond their depth, I paddled ignobly around the " baby-
hole " close to the bank, in the warm and muddy shallows.

Especially apparent was my state of humiliation on this
July afternoon. I had no " double-enders," nor might hope
for any. The mere thought of a private cannon seemed
monstrous and unnatural to me. By some unknown process of reasoning my mother had years before reached the
theory that a good boy ought to have two ten-cent packs of
small fire-crackers on the Fourth of July. Four or five succeeding anniversaries had hardened this theory into an
orthodox tenet of faith, with all its observances rigidly fixed.
The fire-crackers were bought for me overnight, and placed
on the hall table. Beside them lay a long rod of punk.
When I hastened down and out in the morning, with these

ceremonial implements in my hands, the hired girl would give me, in an old kettle, some embers from the wood-fire in the summer kitchen. Thus furnished, I went into the front yard, and in solemn solitude fired off these crackers one by one. Those which, by reason of having lost their tails, were only fit for "fizzes," I saved till after breakfast. With the exhaustion of these, I fell reluctantly back upon the public for entertainment. I could see the soldiers, hear the band and the oration, and in the evening, if it did n't rain, enjoy the fireworks; but my own contribution to the patriotic noise was always over before the breakfast dishes had been washed.

My mother scorned the little paper torpedoes as flippant and wasteful things. You merely threw one of them, and it went off, she said, and there you were. I don't know that I ever grasped this objection in its entirety, but it impressed my whole childhood with its unanswerableness. Years and years afterward, when my own children asked for torpedoes, I found myself unconsciously advising against them on quite the maternal lines. Nor was it easy to budge the good lady from her position on the great two-packs issue. I seem to recall having successfully undermined it once or twice, but two was the rule. When I called her attention to the fact that our neighbor, Tom Hemingway, thought nothing of exploding a whole pack at a time inside their wash-boiler, she was not dazzled, but only replied: "Wilful waste makes woful want."

Of course the idea of the Hemingways ever knowing what want meant was absurd. They lived a dozen doors or so from us, in a big white house with stately white columns rising from veranda to gable across the whole front, and a large garden, flowers and shrubs in front, fruit-trees and vegetables behind. Squire Hemingway was the most important man in our part of the town. I know now that he was never anything more than United States Commissioner of Deeds, but in those days, when he walked down the street with his gold-headed cane, his blanket-shawl folded

over his arm, and his severe, dignified, close-shaven face
held well up in the air, I seemed to behold a companion of
Presidents.

This great man had two sons. The elder of them, De
Witt Hemingway, was a man grown, and was at the front.
I had seen him march away, over a year before, with a
bright drawn sword, at the side of his company. The other
son, Tom, was my senior by only a twelvemonth. He was
by nature proud, but often consented to consort with me
when the selection of other available associates was at low
ebb.

It was to this Tom that I listened with most envious
eagerness, in front of the grocery-store, on the afternoon
of which I speak. He did not sit on the stoop with the
others — no one expected quite that degree of condescen-
sion — but leaned nonchalantly against a post, whittling
out a new ramrod for his cannon. He said that this year
he was not going to have any ordinary fire-crackers at all;
they, he added with a meaning glance at me, were only fit
for girls. He might do a little in "double-enders," but
his real point would be in "ringers" — an incredible giant
variety of cracker, Turkey-red like the other, but in size
almost a rolling-pin. Some of these he would fire off singly,
between volleys from his cannon. But a good many he
intended to explode, in bunches say of six, inside the tin
wash-boiler, brought out into the middle of the road for
that purpose. It would doubtless blow the old thing sky-
high, but that did n't matter. They could get a new one.

Even as he spoke, the big bell in the tower of the town-
hall burst forth in a loud clangor of swift-repeated strokes.
It was half a mile away, but the moist air brought the
urgent, clamorous sounds to our ears as if the belfry had
stood close above us. We sprang off the stoop and stood
poised, waiting to hear the number of the ward struck, and
ready to scamper off on the instant if the fire was anywhere
in our part of the town. But the excited peal went on and
on, without a pause. It became obvious that this meant

something besides a fire. Perhaps some of us wondered vaguely what that something might be, but as a body our interest had lapsed. Billy Norris, who was the son of poor parents, but could whip even Tom Hemingway, said he had been told that the German boys on the other side of the gulf were coming over to "rush" us on the following day, and that we ought all to collect nails to fire at them from our cannon. This we pledged ourselves to do — the bell keeping up its throbbing tumult ceaselessly.

Suddenly we saw the familiar figure of Johnson running up the street toward us. What his first name was I never knew. To every one, little or big, he was just Johnson. He and his family had moved into our town after the war began ; I fancy they moved away again before it ended. I do not even know what he did for a living. But he seemed always drunk, always turbulently good-natured, and always shouting out the news at the top of his lungs. I cannot pretend to guess how he found out everything as he did, or why, having found it out, he straightway rushed homeward, scattering the intelligence as he ran. Most probably Johnson was moulded by Nature as a town-crier, but was born by accident some generations after the race of bellmen had disappeared. Our neighborhood did not like him ; our mothers did not know Mrs. Johnson, and we boys behaved with snobbish roughness to his children. He seemed not to mind this at all, but came up unwearyingly to shout out the tidings of the day for our benefit.

"Vicksburg 's fell ! Vicksburg 's fell ! " was what we heard him yelling as he approached.

Delos Ingersoll and his hired boy ran out of the grocery. Doors opened along the street and heads were thrust inquiringly out.

"Vicksburg 's fell ! " he kept hoarsely proclaiming, his arms waving in the air, as he staggered along at a dog-trot past us, and went into the saloon next to the grocery.

I cannot say how definite an idea these tidings conveyed

to our boyish minds. I have a notion that at the time I assumed that Vicksburg had something to do with Gettysburg, where I knew, from the talk of my elders, that an awful fight had been proceeding since the middle of the week. Doubtless this confusion was aided by the fact that an hour or so later, on that same wonderful day, the wire brought us word that this terrible battle on Pennsylvanian soil had at last taken the form of a Union victory. It is difficult now to see how we could have known both these things on the Third of July — that is to say, before the people actually concerned seemed to have been sure of them. Perhaps it was only inspired guesswork, but I know that my town went wild over the news, and that the clouds overhead cleared away as if by magic.

The sun did well to spread that summer sky at eventide with all the pageantry of color the spectrum knows. It would have been preposterous that such a day should slink off in dull, Quaker drabs. Men were shouting in the streets now. The old cannon left over from the Mexican war had been dragged out on to the rickety covered river-bridge, and was frightening the fishes, and shaking the dry, worm-eaten rafters, as fast as the swab and rammer could work. Our town bandsmen were playing as they had never played before, down in the square in front of the post-office. The management of the Universe could not hurl enough wild fireworks into the exultant sunset to fit our mood.

The very air was filled with the scent of triumph — the spirit of conquest. It seemed only natural that I should march off to my mother and quite collectedly tell her that I desired to stay out all night with the other boys. I had never dreamed of daring to prefer such a request in other years. Now I was scarcely conscious of surprise when she gave her permission, adding with a smile that I would be glad enough to come in and go to bed before half the night was over.

I steeled my heart after supper with the proud resolve that if the night turned out to be as protracted as one of those Lapland winter nights we read about in the geography, I still would not surrender.

The boys outside were not so excited over the tidings of my unlooked-for victory as I had expected them to be. They received the news, in fact, with a rather mortifying stoicism. Tom Hemingway, however, took enough interest in the affair to suggest that, instead of spending my twenty cents in paltry fire-crackers, I might go down town and buy another can of powder for his cannon. By doing so, he pointed out, I would be a part-proprietor, as it were, of the night's performance, and would be entitled to occasionally touch the cannon off. This generosity affected me, and I hastened down the long hill-street to show myself worthy of it, repeating the instruction of " Kentucky Bear-Hunter-coarse-grain " over and over again to myself as I went.

Half-way on my journey I overtook a person whom, even in the gathering twilight, I recognized as Miss Stratford, the school-teacher. She also was walking down the hill and rapidly. It did not need the sight of a letter in her hand to tell me that she was going to the post-office. In those cruel war-days everybody went to the post-office. I myself went regularly to get our mail, and to exchange shin-plasters for one-cent stamps with which to buy yeast and other commodities that called for minute fractional currency.

Although I was very fond of Miss Stratford — I still recall her gentle eyes, and pretty, rounded, dark face, in its frame of long, black curls, with tender liking — I now coldly resolved to hurry past, pretending not to know her. It was a mean thing to do ; Miss Stratford had always been good to me, shining in that respect in brilliant contrast to my other teachers, whom I hated bitterly. Still, the " Kentucky Bear-Hunter-coarse-grain " was too important a matter to wait upon any mere female friendships, and I quickened my pace into a trot, hoping to scurry by unrecognized.

" Oh, Andrew ! is that you ? " I heard her call out as I

ran past. For the instant I thought of rushing on, quite as if I had not heard. Then I stopped and walked beside her.

"I am going to stay up all night: mother says I may; and I am going to fire off Tom Hemingway's big cannon every fourth time, straight through till breakfast time," I announced to her loftily.

"Dear me! I ought to be proud to be seen walking with such an important citizen," she answered, with kindly playfulness. She added more gravely, after a moment's pause: "Then Tom is out playing with the other boys, is he?"

"Why, of course!" I responded. "He always lets us stand around when he fires off his cannon. He's got some 'ringers' this year too."

I heard Miss Stratford murmur an impulsive "Thank God!" under her breath.

Full as the day had been of surprises, I could not help wondering that the fact of Tom's ringers should stir up such profound emotions in the teacher's breast. Since the subject so interested her, I went on with a long catalogue of Tom's other pyrotechnic possessions, and from that to an account of his almost supernatural collection of postage-stamps. In a few minutes more I am sure I should have revealed to her the great secret of my life, which was my determination, in case I came to assume the victorious rôle and rank of Napoleon, to immediately make Tom a Marshal of the Empire.

But we had reached the post-office square. I had never before seen it so full of people.

Even to my boyish eyes the tragic line of division which cleft this crowd in twain was apparent. On one side, over by the Seminary, the youngsters had lighted a bonfire, and were running about it — some of the bolder ones jumping through it in frolicsome recklessness. Close by stood the band, now valiantly thumping out "John Brown's Body" upon the noisy night air. It was quite dark by this time, but the musicians knew the tune by heart. So did the throng about them, and sang it with lusty fervor. The doors of the saloon toward the corner of the square were flung wide open. Two black streams of men kept in motion under the radiance of the big reflector-lamp over these doors — one going in, one coming out. They slapped one another on the back as they passed, with exultant screams and shouts. Every once in a while, when movement was for the instant blocked, some voice lifted above the others would begin "Hip-hip-hip-hip — " and then would come a roar that fairly drowned the music.

On the post-office side of the square there was no bonfire. No one raised a cheer. A densely packed mass of men and women stood in front of the big square stone building, with its closed doors, and curtained windows upon which, from time to time, the shadow of some passing clerk, bare-headed and hurried, would be momentarily thrown. They waited in silence for the night mail to be sorted. If they spoke to one another, it was in whispers — as if they had been standing with uncovered heads at a funeral service in a graveyard. The dim light reflected over from the bonfire, or down from the shaded windows of the post-office, showed solemn, hard-lined, anxious faces. Their lips scarcely moved when they muttered little low-toned remarks to their neighbors. They spoke from the side of the mouth, and only on one subject.

"He went all through Fredericksburg without a scratch—"

"He looks so much like me — General Palmer told my brother he'd have known his hide in a tan-yard —"

"He's been gone — let 's see — it was a year some time last April—"

"He was counting on a furlough the first of this month. I suppose nobody got one as things turned out —"

"He said, 'No; it ain't my style. I 'll fight as much as you like, but I won't be nigger-waiter for no man, captain or no captain '—"

Thus I heard the scattered murmurs among the grown-up heads above me, as we pushed into the outskirts of the throng, and stood there, waiting for the rest. There was no sentence without a " he " in it. A stranger might have fancied that they were all talking of c.ie man. I knew better. They were the fathers and mothers, the sisters, brothers, wives of the men whose regiments had been in that horrible three days' fight at Gettysburg. Each was thinking and speaking of his own, and took it for granted the others would understand. For that matter, they all did understand. The town knew the name and family of every one of the twelve-score sons she had in this battle.

It is not very clear to me now why people all went to the post-office to wait for the evening papers that came in from the nearest big city. Nowadays they would be brought in bulk and sold on the street before the mail-bags had reached the post-office. Apparently that had not yet been thought of in our slow old town.

The band across the square had started up afresh with " Annie Lisle " — the sweet old refrain of " Wave willows, murmur waters," comes back to me now after a quarter-century of forgetfulness — when all at once there was a sharp forward movement of the crowd. The doors had been thrown open, and the hallway was on the instant filled with a swarming multitude. The band had stopped as suddenly as it began, and no more cheering was heard. We could see whole troops of dark forms scudding toward us from the other side of the square.

" Run in for me — that 's a good boy — ask for Dr. Stratford's mail," the teacher whispered, bending over me.

It seemed an age before I finally got back to her, with the paper in its postmarked wrapper buttoned up inside my jacket. I had never been in so fierce and determined a crowd before, and I emerged from it at last, confused in wits and panting for breath. I was still looking about through the gloom in a foolish way for Miss Stratford, when I felt her hand laid sharply on my shoulder.

"Well — where is it? — did nothing come?" she asked, her voice trembling with eagerness, and the eyes which I had thought so soft and dove-like flashing down upon me as if she were Miss Pritchard, and I had been caught chewing gum in school.

I drew the paper out from under my roundabout, and gave it to her. She grasped it, and thrust a finger under the cover to tear it off. Then she hesitated for a moment, and looked about her. "Come where there is some light," she said, and started up the street. Although she seemed to have spoken more to herself than to me, I followed her in silence, close to her side.

For a long way the sidewalk in front of every lighted store-window was thronged with a group of people clustered tight about some one who had a paper, and was reading from it aloud. Beside broken snatches of this monologue, we caught, now groans of sorrow and horror, now exclamations of proud approval, and even the beginnings of cheers, broken in upon by a general "'Sh-h!" as we hurried past outside the curb.

It was under a lamp in the little park nearly half-way up the hill that Miss Stratford stopped, and spread the paper open. I see her still, white-faced, under the flickering gas-light, her black curls making a strange dark bar between the pale-straw hat and the white of her shoulder shawl and muslin dress, her hands trembling as they held up the extended sheet. She scanned the columns swiftly, skimmingly for a time, as I could see by the way she moved her round chin up and down. Then she came to a part which called for closer reading. The paper shook perceptibly now, as she bent her eyes upon it. Then all at once it fell from her hands, and without a sound she walked away.

I picked the paper up and followed her along the gravelled path. It was like pursuing a ghost, so weirdly white did her summer attire now look to my frightened eyes, with such a swift and deathly silence did she move. The path upon which we were described a circle touching the four sides of the square. She did not quit it when the intersection with our street was reached, but followed straight round again toward the point where we had entered the park. This, too, in turn, she passed, gliding noiselessly forward under the black arches of the overhanging elms. The suggestion that she did not know she was going round and round in a ring startled my brain. I would have run up to her now if I had dared.

Suddenly she turned, and saw that I was behind her. She sank slowly into one of the garden-seats, by the path, and held out for a moment a hesitating hand toward me. I went up at this and looked into her face. Shadowed as it was, the change I saw there chilled my blood. It was like the face of some one I had never seen before, with fixed, wide-open, staring eyes which seemed to look beyond me through the darkness, upon some terrible sight no other could see.

"Go — run and tell — Tom — to go home ! His brother — his brother has been killed," she said to me, choking over the words as if they hurt her throat, and still with the same strange dry-eyed, far-away gaze covering yet not seeing me.

I held out the paper for her to take, but she made no sign, and I gingerly laid it on the seat beside her. I hung about for a minute or two longer, imagining that she might have something else to say — but no word came. Then, with a feebly inopportune " Well, good-by," I started off alone up the hill.

It was a distinct relief to find that my companions were congregated at the lower end of the common, instead of their accustomed haunt farther up near my home, for the walk had been a lonely one, and I was deeply depressed by what had happened. Tom, it seems, had been called away some quarter of an hour before. All the boys knew of the calamity which had befallen the Hemingways. We talked about it, from time to time, as we loaded and fired the cannon which Tom had obligingly turned over to my friends. It had been out of deference to the feelings of the stricken household that they had betaken themselves and their racket off to the remote corner of the common. The solemnity of the occasion silenced criticism upon my conduct in forgetting to buy the powder. "There would be enough as long as it lasted," Billy Norris said, with philosophic decision. We speculated upon the likelihood of De Witt Hemingway's being given a military funeral. These mournful pageants had by this time become such familiar things to us that the prospect of one more had no element of excitement in it, save as it involved a gloomy sort of distinction for Tom. He would ride in the first mourning-carriage with his parents, and this would associate us, as we walked along ahead of the band, with the most intimate aspects of the demonstration. We regretted now that the soldier company which we had so long projected remained still unorganized. Had it been otherwise we would probably have been awarded the right of the line in the procession. Some one suggested that it was not too late — and we promptly bound ourselves to meet after breakfast next day to organize and begin drilling. If we worked at this night and day, and our parents instantaneously provided us with uniforms and guns, we should be in time. It was also arranged that we should be called the De Witt C. Hemingway Fire Zouaves, and that Billy Norris should be side captain. The chief command would, of course, be reserved for Tom. We would specially salute him as he rode past in the closed carriage, and then fall in behind, forming his honorary escort.

None of us had known the dead officer closely, owing to his advanced age. He was seven or eight years older than even Tom. But the more elderly among our group had seen him play base-ball in the academy nine, and our neighborhood was still alive with legends of his early audacity and skill in collecting barrels and dry-goods boxes at night for election bonfires. It was remembered that once he carried away a whole front-stoop from the house of a little German tailor on one of the back streets. As we stood around the heated cannon, in the great black

solitude of the common, our fancies pictured this redoubt-
able young man once more among us — not in his blue
uniform, with crimson sash and sword laid by his side, and
the gauntlets drawn over his lifeless hands, but as a taller
and glorified Tom, in a roundabout jacket and copper-
toed boots, giving the law on this his playground. The
very cannon at our feet had once been his. The night
air became peopled with ghosts of his contemporaries —
handsome boys who had grown up before us, and had
gone away to lay down their lives in far-off Virginia or
Tennessee.

These heroic shades brought drowsiness in their train.
We lapsed into long silences, punctuated by yawns, when
it was not our turn to ram and touch off the cannon.
Finally some of us stretched ourselves out on the grass,
in the warm darkness, to wait comfortably for this turn to
come.

What did come instead was daybreak — finding Billy
Norris and myself alone constant to our all-night vow. We
sat up and shivered as we rubbed our eyes. The morning
air had a chilling freshness that went to my bones — and
these, moreover, were filled with those novel aches and
stiffnesses which beds were invented to prevent. We stood
up, stretching out our arms, and gaping at the pearl-and-
rose beginnings of the sunrise in the eastern sky. The
other boys had all gone home, and taken the cannon with
them. Only scraps of torn paper and tiny patches of
burnt grass marked the site of our celebration.

My first weak impulse was to march home without delay,
and get into bed as quickly as might be. But Billy Norris
looked so finely resolute and resourceful that I hesitated
to suggest this, and said nothing, leaving the initiative to
him. One could see, by the most casual glance, that he
was superior to mere considerations of unseasonableness
in hours. I remembered now that he was one of that
remarkable body of boys, the paper-carriers, who rose
when all others were asleep in their warm nests, and

trudged about long before breakfast distributing the *Clarion* among the well-to-do households. This fact had given him his position in our neighborhood as quite the next in leadership to Tom Hemingway.

He presently outlined his plans to me, after having tried the centre of light on the horizon, where soon the sun would be, by an old brass compass he had in his pocket — a process which enabled him, he said, to tell pretty well what time it was. The paper would n't be out for nearly two hours yet — and if it were not for the fact of a great battle, there would have been no paper at all on this glorious anniversary — but he thought we would go down-town and see what was going on around about the newspaper office. Forthwith we started. He cheered my faint spirits by assuring me that I would soon cease to be sleepy, and would, in fact, feel better than usual. I dragged my feet along at his side, waiting for this revival to come, and meantime furtively yawning against my sleeve.

Billy seemed to have dreamed a good deal, during our nap on the common, about the De Witt C. Hemingway Fire Zouaves. At least he had now in his head a marvellously elaborated system of organization, which he unfolded as we went along. I felt that I had never before realized his greatness, his born genius for command. His scheme halted nowhere. He allotted offices with discriminating firmness; he treated the question of uniforms and guns as a trivial detail which would settle itself; he spoke with calm confidence of our offering our services to the Republic in the autumn; his clear vision saw even the materials for a fife-and-drum corps among the German boys in the back streets. It was true that I appeared personally to play a meagre part in these great projects; the most that was said about me was that I might make a fair third-corporal. But Fate had thrown in my way such a wonderful chance of becoming intimate with Billy that I made sure I should swiftly advance in rank — the more so as I discerned in the background of his thoughts, as it were, a grim determination to make short work of Tom Hemingway's aristocratic pretensions, once the funeral was over.

We were forced to make a detour of the park on our way down, because Billy observed some half-dozen Irish boys at play with a cannon inside, whom he knew to be hostile. If there had been only four, he said, he would have gone in and routed them. He could whip any two of them, he added, with one hand tied behind his back. I listened with admiration. Billy was not tall, but he possessed great thickness of chest and length of arm. His skin was so dark that we canvassed the theory from time to time of his having Indian blood. He did not discourage this, and he admitted himself that he was double-jointed.

The streets of the business part of the town, into which we now made our way, were quite deserted. We went around into the yard behind the printing-office, where the carrier-boys were wont to wait for the press to get to work ; and Billy displayed some impatience at discovering that here too there was no one. It was now broad daylight, but through the windows of the composing-room we could see some of the printers still setting type by kerosene lamps.

We seated ourselves at the end of the yard on a big, flat, smooth-faced stone, and Billy produced from his pocket a number of "em" quads, so he called them, with which the carriers had learned from the printers' boys to play a very beautiful game. You shook the pieces of metal in your hands and threw them on the stone ; your score depended upon the number of nicked sides that were turned uppermost. We played this game in the interest of good-fellowship for a little. Then Billy told me that the carriers always played it for pennies, and that it was unmanly for us to do otherwise. He had no pennies at that precise moment, but would pay at the end of the week what he had lost ; in the meantime there was my twenty cents to go on with. After this Billy threw so many nicks uppermost that my courage gave way, and I made an attempt to stop the game ; but a single remark from him as to the military destiny which he was reserving for me, if I only displayed true soldierly nerve and grit, sufficed to quiet me once more, and the play went on. I had now only five cents left.

Suddenly a shadow interposed itself between the sunlight and the stone. I looked up, to behold a small boy with bare arms and a blackened apron standing over me, watching our game. There was a great deal of ink on his face and hands, and a hardened, not to say rakish expression in his eye.

"Why don't you 'jeff' with somebody of your own size?" he demanded of Billy after having looked me over critically.

He was not nearly so big as Billy, and I expected to see the latter instantly rise and crush him, but Billy only laughed and said we were playing for fun ; he was going to give me all my money back. I was rejoiced to hear this, but still felt surprised at the propitiatory manner Billy adopted toward this diminutive inky boy. It was not the demeanor befitting a side-captain — and what made it worse was that the strange boy loftily declined to be cajoled by it. He sniffed when Billy told him about the military company we were forming ; he coldly shook his head, with a curt "Nixie !" when invited to join it ; and he laughed aloud at hearing the name our organization was to bear.

"He ain't dead at all — that De Witt Hemingway," he said, with jeering contempt.

"Hain't he though !" exclaimed Billy. "The news come last night. Tom had to go home — his mother sent for him — on account of it !"

"I 'll bet you a quarter he ain't dead," responded the practical inky boy. "Money up, though !"

"I 've only got fifteen cents. I 'll bet you that, though," rejoined Billy, producing my torn and dishevelled shinplasters.

"All right ! Wait here !" said the boy, running off to

the building and disappearing through the door. There was barely time for me to learn from my companion that this printer's apprentice was called " the devil," and could not only whistle between his teeth and crack his fingers, but chew tobacco, when he reappeared, with a long narrow strip of paper in his hand. This he held out for us to see, indicating with an ebon forefinger the special paragraph we were to read. Billy looked at it sharply, for several moments in silence. Then he said to me : " What does it say there? I must 'a' got some powder in my eyes last night."

I read this paragraph aloud, not without an unworthy feeling that the inky boy would now respect me deeply :

" CORRECTION. Lieutenant De Witt C. Hemingway, of Company A, —th New York, reported in earlier despatches among the killed, is uninjured. The officer killed is Lieutenant Carl Heinninge, Company F, same regiment."

Billy's face visibly lengthened as I read this out, and he felt us both looking at him. He made a pretence of examining the slip of paper again, but in a half-hearted way. Then he ruefully handed over the fifteen cents and, rising from the stone, shook himself.

"Them Dutchmen never was no good!" was what he said.

The inky boy had put the money in the pocket under his apron, and grinned now with as much enjoyment as dignity would permit him to show. He did not seem to mind any longer the original source of his winnings, and it was apparent that I could not with decency recall it to him. Some odd impulse prompted me, however, to ask him if I might have the paper he had in his hand. He was magnanimous enough to present me with the proof-sheet on the spot. Then with another grin he turned and left us.

Billy stood sullenly kicking with his bare toes into a sand-heap by the stone. He would not answer me when I spoke to him. It flashed across my perceptive faculties that he was not such a great man, after all, as I had imagined. In another instant or two it had become quite clear to me that I had no admiration for him whatever. Without a word I turned on my heel and walked determinedly out of the yard and into the street, homeward bent.

All at once I quickened my pace; something had occurred to me. The purpose thus conceived grew so swiftly that soon I found myself running. Up the hill I sped, and straight through the park. If the Irish boys shouted after me I knew it not, but dashed on heedless of all else save the one idea. I only halted, breathless and panting, when I stood on Dr. Stratford's doorstep, and heard the night-bell inside jangling shrilly in response to my excited pull.

As I waited, I pictured to myself the old doctor as he would presently come down, half-dressed and pulling on his coat as he advanced. He would ask, eagerly, "Who is sick? Where am I to go?" and I would calmly reply that he unduly alarmed himself, and that I had a message for his daughter. He would, of course, ask me what it was, and I, politely but firmly, would decline to explain to any one but the lady in person. Just what might ensue was not clear — but I beheld myself throughout commanding the situation, at once benevolent, polished, and inexorable.

The door opened with unlooked-for promptness, while my self-complacent vision still hung in midair. Instead of the bald and spectacled old doctor, there confronted me a white-faced, solemn-eyed lady in a black dress, whom I did not seem to know. I stared at her, tongue-tied, till she said, in a low, grave voice, "Well, Andrew, what is it?"

Then of course I saw that it was Miss Stratford, my teacher, the person whom I had come to see. Some vague sense of what the sleepless night had meant in this house came to me as I gazed confusedly at her mourning, and heard the echo of her sad tones in my ears.

"Is some one ill?" she asked again.

"No; some one — some one is very well!" I managed

to reply, lifting my eyes again to her wan face. The spectacle of its drawn lines and pallor all at once assailed my wearied and overtaxed nerves with crushing weight. I felt myself beginning to whimper, and rushing tears scalded my eyes. Something inside my breast seemed to be dragging me down through the stoop.

I have now only the recollection of Miss Stratford's kneeling by my side, with a supporting arm around me, and of her thus unrolling and reading the proof-paper I had in my hand. We were in the hall now, instead of on the stoop, and there was a long silence. Then she put her head on my shoulder and wept. I could hear and feel her sobs as if they were my own.

"I — I did n't think you'd cry — that you'd be so sorry," I heard myself saying, at last, in despondent self-defence.

Miss Stratford lifted her head and, still kneeling as she was, put a finger under my chin to make me look her in her face. Lo! the eyes were laughing through their tears; the whole countenance was radiant once more with the light of happy youth and with that other glory which youth knows only once.

"Why, Andrew, boy," she said, trembling, smiling, sobbing, beaming all at once, "did n't you know that people cry for very joy sometimes?"

And as I shook my head she bent down and kissed me.

BIBLIOGRAPHICAL NOTE

[Since any list approaching a complete bibliography would be unduly long, these suggestions are merely for the convenience of those who, without special research, wish to read further and compare. They remain after rejection of many essays that seem hardly to advance the discussion.]

Cairns, William B., *On the Development of American Literature from 1815 to 1833*, with especial reference to periodicals; Bulletin of the University of Wisconsin, Philology and Literature Series, volume i, no. ı, pages 1–87.

Canby, Henry Seidel, *The Short Story;* Yale Studies in English, xii (revised as introduction to *The Book of the Short Story*, edited by Alexander Jessup and Henry Seidel Canby).

Chassang, A., *Histoire du Roman . . . dans l'Antiquité Grecque et Latine;* Paris (2d ed.), 1862.

Gilbert, E., *Le Roman en France pendant le xix⁰ Siècle;* Paris (2d ed.), 1896.

Hart, Walter Morris, *The Evolution of the Short Story;* address delivered before the Alumni Association of Haverford College, June 12, 1901.

Matthews, Brander, *The Philosophy of the Short Story;* New York, 1901. (This, the standard essay on the subject, is now published separately, with notes and a few striking references.)

Moland et d'Héricault, *Nouvelles Françoises en Prose du xiiiᵐᵉ Siècle;* Paris, 1856 (l'Empereur Constant, Amis et Amile, le Roi Flore et la Belle Jehane, la Comtesse de Ponthieu, Aucassin et Nicolette; introduction, notes).

Morris, William, *Old French Romances done into English by William Morris*, with introduction by Joseph Jacobs; London, 1896 (translation of the same tales as in the preceding, except Aucassin and Nicolette).

Peck, Harry Thurston, *Trimalchio's Dinner* by Petronius Arbiter, translated from the original Latin, with an introduction and bibliographical appendix; New York, 1898. (The introduction discusses prose fiction in Greece and Rome.)

Perry, Bliss, *A Study of Prose Fiction;* Boston, 1902.

INDEX

[Titles of books and periodicals are in quotation marks; titles of separate stories, in italics]

ADDISON, a model for Irving, 6
Aldrich, Thomas Bailey, 34
Alice Doane's Appeal (Hawthorne), 13
Allegory, 10, 14, 23, 230
Ambitious Guest, The (Hawthorne), 14
American literature, brevity of, 1; wherein American, 1–4, 8, 35; American life in, 3–6, 11, 12
"American Monthly Magazine, The," 113
Amis and Amile, 25
Anecdote, 10, 24, 26, 27, 29
Annuals, American, 2, 4, 5, 9–12, 18
Antonius Diogenes, 24
"Appleton's Journal," 245
Apuleius, 30
Aristides of Miletus, 24
Aristotle, "Poetics," 13, 19, 20
Arsène Guillot (Mérimée), 31
Artificiality in short story, 20, 32
"Ass, The," of Lucian, 24
"Atlantic Monthly, The," 247
"Atlantic Souvenir, The," 2, 4, 5, 11
Aucassin and Nicolette, 25, 27, 31
Austin, William, 1, 10, 12, 59–95; biographical and critical sketch, 59; *Joseph Natterstrom*, 1, 10; *Peter Rugg*, 10, 12, 60–95

BACON, Delia, 11
Balzac, Honoré de, 32–33; *El verdugo, Les proscrits, La messe de l'athée, Z. Marcas*, 32; form in, 32–33
Bandello, 29

Beckwith, Hiram W., 97
Bee-Tree, The (Kirkland), 195–210
Beers, Henry A., 2, 177
Ben Hadar (Paulding), 10
Berenice (Poe), 2, 3, 16, 18, 21, 22, 33
Blackwell, Robert, 97
Boccaccio, "The Decameron," 26–28, 30
"Boston Book, The," 61
Brunetière, Ferdinand, 26
Buckthorne and His Friends (Irving), 8
Bunner, Henry Cuyler, 289–301; biographical and critical note, 289; *The Third Figure of the Cotillion*, 289; *The Love Letters of Smith*, 291–301
Burton's "Gentleman's Magazine," 154

CABLE, George W., 5, 34; *Posson Jone*, 34
Cairns, William B., 2, 6, 325
Canby, Henry Seidel, 325
Carmen (Mérimée), 31
Catholic, The, 4
"Cena Trimalchionis," of Petronius, 24
"Cent nouvelles nouvelles, Les," 28, 30
Character, development of, 13, 26, 27
Chassang, A., 325
Chaucer, 25, 28; *The Man of Law, The Pardoner, Troilus and Criseyde*, 25
Chivalric Sailor, The (Sedgwick), 11

Clemens, Samuel L. (Mark Twain), 4, 34; *The Jumping Frog*, 34
Climax (*see* Culmination)
Colomba (Mérimée), 31
Combe à l'homme mort, La (Nodier), 29, 30
Compression of time, in short story, 8, 11, 12, 13, 19, 20, 27, 28, 33 (*see* Unity)
"Condensed Novels " (Harte), 229
Consistency of form, 9, 23, 26–28, 31, 32, 33 (*see* Unity)
Conte and *nouvelle*, 30, 31, 33
"Contes de la Reine de Navarre " (*see* " Heptameron ")
Cooper, James Fenimore, 1, 5
Cornelius Sisenna, 24
Culmination, in short story, 7, 8, 10, 20–22, 26–28, 31, 32, 33

DAMNATION of Theron Ware, The (Frederic), 303
Dana, Richard Henry, *Paul Felton*, 11
Daphne, The (Webster), 245
Daphnis and Chloe, 24–25
" Dashes at Life with a Free Pencil " (Willis), 178
Daudet, Alphonse, 30, 34
David Swan (Hawthorne), 14
" Decameron, The," 26–28
De Quincey, Thomas, 30
Descriptive sketches, 9, 12, 14, 31, 99, 113, 193
Dialogue and monologue, 19, 27
Diamond Lens, The (O'Brien), 211
Dickens, Charles, influence of, on Bret Harte, 230; on O'Brien, 211
Dio Chrysostom, 25
Directness of movement, 18, 19, 20, 26, 27
Documentary interest, in fiction, 3, 30
Dominant, use of a single detail as, 16, 21, 22
Drama, influence of, on novel and short story, 26, 34
Dumas, Alexandre, influence of, on Bret Harte, 230

EDGEWORTH, Maria, 26
Emigrant's Daughter, The, 5
End of the Passage, The (Kipling), 212

Enlèvement de la redoute, Le (Mérimée), 31
Esmeralda, The (Wallace), 11
Essay tendency in tales, 6, 7, 10, 14, 15, 18, 32
Ethan Brand (Hawthorne), 13
Eve of the Fourth, The (Frederic), 305–324
Exposition in tales (*see* Essay tendency)

FALL of the House of Usher, The (Poe), 18, 154–176
Fancy's Show Box (Hawthorne), 14
Filleule du Seigneur, La (Nodier), 30
Flaubert, Gustave, 30
Flint, Timothy, 5
Florus, King, and the Fair Jehane, 25
Fool's Moustache, A (Webster), 245
" Forest Life " (Kirkland), 193
France, Anatole, 29
Frederic, Harold, 303–324 ; biographical and critical note, 303 ; " In the Sixties," 303 ; *The Eve of the Fourth*, 305–324 ; *The Damnation of Theron Ware*, 303
Fromentin, Eugène, 3
Frontier, tales of the, 5, 10, 12, 97–127, 193–210, 229–243

GAUTIER, Théophile, 30, 33 ; *Le nid de rossignols, La mort amoureuse*, 33 ; preferred *nouvelle* to *conte*, diffuseness, influence of Sterne, tendency to mere description, likeness to Poe, 33
Genlis, Mme. de, moral tales of, 10
" Gentleman's Magazine and American Monthly Review," Burton's, 154
German Student, The (Irving), 8
Gift-books (*see* Annuals)
Gilbert, E., 29, 325
Gilman, Mrs., 5
" Golden Era, The," 229
Goldsmith, influence on Irving, 6
Gradation, 20–23, 32 (*see* Sequence)
Great Good Place, The (James), 34
Great Stone Face, The (Hawthorne), 14

INDEX

HALE, Mrs., 5
Hall, James, 5, 9, 11, 12, 97–112;
biographical and critical note, 97;
"The Illinois Intelligencer," "The
Illinois Magazine," "The Western
Monthly Magazine," "Letters from
the West," "Sketches of the
West," "Notes on the Western
States," "The Wilderness and the
War Path," 97; "The Western
Souvenir," 5, 97; The Indian
Hater, Pete Featherton, 5; The
Village Musician, 9; The French
Village, 5, 9, 12, 99–112
Harmonisation, 16, 23
"Harper's Monthly Magazine," 212,
213
Hart, Walter Morris, 325
Harte, Francis Bret, 4, 229–243;
biographical and critical note, 229;
"Condensed Novels," 229; The
Luck of Roaring Camp, 229, 230;
Johnson's Old Woman, Mrs.
Skaggs's Husbands, The Iliad of
Sandy Bar, Tennessee's Partner,
230; The Outcasts of Poker Flat,
231–243; influence of Dickens, 230;
of Dumas, 230; tendency to melodrama, 230; local truth, 229; symbolism, 230
Hawthorne, Nathaniel, 2, 5, 9, 10, 12–
15, 16, 18, 23, 30, 31, 32, 59, 129–
142, 230; bent not toward short
story, 12–15, 31; allegory, symbolism, 14, 23, 230; vocabulary, 16;
tendency toward description, 14;
toward essay, 14, 15, 18, 30; expository introductions, 18; unity
compared with Poe's, 23; likeness
to Nodier, 30; "Twice-Told Tales,"
131; The Gentle Boy, 12; The
Wives of the Dead, 12, 13; Roger
Malvin's Burial, Alice Doane's
Appeal, Ethan Brand, 13; The
Scarlet Letter, 13, 14; Sunday at
Home, Sights from a Steeple,
Main Street, The Village Uncle,
The Ambitious Guest, Fancy's
Show Box, David Swan, The Snow
Image, The Great Stone Face, 14;
The Marble Faun, 15; The White

Old Maid, 13, 131–142; The Seven
Vagabonds, 230
"Heptameron, The," of the Queen
of Navarre, 29
Hermit of the Prairies, The, 5
"Hermite de la Chaussée d'Antin,
Le," 6
Higginson, Thomas Wentworth, 59
Historical tales, 4, 5, 9, 10, 11
Hoax-story, 10, 34
Horla, Le (Maupassant), 212

ILIAD of Sandy Bar, The (Harte),
230
"Illinois Intelligencer, The," 97
"Illinois Magazine, The," 97
"In the Sixties" (Frederic), 305
Indian Hater, The (Hall), 5
Inlet of Peach Blossoms, The (Willis),
179–191
Inroad of the Nabajo, The (Pike)
115–127
Intensity, in short story, 12, 22, 32,
34
Introductions to tales, 7, 10, 17, 18,
19, 31, 99, 195
Irving, Washington, 1, 4, 5, 6–9, 18,
29, 37–58, 143, 289; looseness of
form, 7, 8; characterisation, 7;
unity of tone, 7; influence of, 8, 9,
143, 289; introductions, 18; "The
Sketch Book," 7; "Tales of a
Traveller," 8, 143; The Wife,
The Widow and Her Son, The
Pride of the Village, The Spectre
Bridegroom, 7; Buckthorne and
His Friends, The German Stu-
dent, 8; Philip of Pokanoket, 9;
Rip Van Winkle, 7, 8, 37–58

JACOBS, Joseph, 25
James, Henry, 34
Jean François-les-bas-bleus (Nodier),
30
Johnson's Old Woman (Harte),
230
Joseph Natterstrom (Austin), 1, 10
Jouy, M. de, 6
Jumping Frog, The (Mark Twain),
34

KEEPSAKES (*see* Annuals)
Kennedy, John Pendleton, 5, 9; "Swallow Barn," 9
Kinetic narrative, and static, 22
King Pest (Poe), 18, 22
Kipling, Rudyard, 34, 212; *The End of the Passage*, 212
Kirkland, Mrs., 5, 6, 193-210; biographical and critical note, 193; "A New Home — Who'll Follow," "Forest Life," "Western Clearings," 193; *The Bee-Tree*, 195-210
Kirkland, William, 193

LANDOR, Walter Savage, 30
"Letters from Arkansas" (Pike), 113
"Letters from the West" (Hall), 97
Lidivine (Nodier), 30
Ligeia (Poe), 16, 18
"Literati" (Poe), 193
Local color, 3-6, 9, 11, 12, 34, 97, 113, 193, 229, 303
Longfellow, Henry Wadsworth, 143-151; biographical and critical note, 143; "Outre-Mer," 143; *The Notary of Périgueux*, 145-151
Longus, 24, 25
Love Letters of Smith, The (Bunner), 291-301
Lucian, 24
Luck of Roaring Camp, The (Harte), 229, 230

MAGAZINES, American, 2-5, 9, 34 (and see separate titles)
Main Street (Hawthorne), 14
Maison Tellier, La (Maupassant), 230
Man of Law, The (Chaucer), 25
Marble Faun, The (Hawthorne), 15
Margaret of Angoulême, Queen of Navarre, the "Heptameron" of, 29
Marjorie Daw (Aldrich), 34
Mary Dyre (Sedgwick), 11
Matron of Ephesus, The (Petronius), 24
Matthews, Brander, 8, 11, 22, 31, 212, 325; edition of Irving's "Tales of a Traveller," 8; "The Philosophy of the Short-Story," 11, 22, 31, 212, 325
Maupassant, Guy de, 30, 34, 212, 230; *La maison Tellier*, 230; *Le Horla*, 212
Mediæval tales. 23-29, 31
Melodrama, tendency toward, in earlier American tales, 4, 5, 11; in O'Brien, 211; in Bret Harte, 230
Mérimée, Prosper, 30-34; narrative conciseness, 31; preferred *nouvelle* to *conte*, 31, 34; and Poe, 32; *Carmen, Colomba, Arsène Guillot, L'enlévement de la redoute, Tamango, La vision de Charles XI, Le vase étrusque*, 31; *La Vénus d'Ille*, 31, 32
Messe de l'athée, La (Balzac), 32
Methodist's Story, The, 4
Metzengerstein (Poe), 16, 18, 22
Milesian tales, 24
"Mirror, The New York," 177, 178
Miss Eunice's Glove (Webster), 247-266
Mitchell, Donald G., 1
Mitford, Mary Russell, 193
Moland and d'Héricault, 325
Monologue, Poe's, 19
Moral tales, 4, 9, 10, 14, 30; allegory in, 10, 14; of Mme. de Genlis, 10; of Nodier, 10, 30; oriental setting for, 10
Morella (Poe), 16, 17, 18, 21, 22
Morris, William, 25, 326
Morte Amoureuse, La (Gautier), 33
Mrs. Skaggs's Husbands (Harte), 230
Musset, Alfred de, 33
My Wife's Tempter (O'Brien), 211

NARANTSAUK, 4
Nationality in literature, 3-6, 11, 12
"New England Galaxy, The," 61
"New England Magazine, The," 2, 131
"New Home, A, — Who'll Follow" (Kirkland), 193
"New York Mirror, The," 177, 178
Nid de rossignols, Le (Gautier) 33
Nodier, Charles, 10, 29, 30, 31; preferred *nouvelle* to *conte*, 30, 31; similarity to Hawthorne, 30; *Les*

quatre talismans, 10; *La combe à l'homme mort*, 29, 30; *Smarra*, *Jean François-les-bas-bleus, Lidivine, La filleule du Seigneur*, 30
" Notes on the Western States" (Hall), 97
Nouvelle, and *conte*, 30, 31, 33; and *roman*, 31
Novel and short story, 8, 12, 13, 15, 21, 25, 26
Novelette, 31
Novella, 27, 30

O'BRIEN, Fitz-James, 211–228; biographical and critical note, 211; *The Diamond Lens, The Wondersmith, Tommatoo, My Wife's Tempter*, 211; *What Was It?*, 213–228
Operation in Money, An (Webster), 245
Oriental tales, 10, 25
Outcasts of Poker Flat, The (Harte), 231–243
" Outre-Mer " (Longfellow), 143
"Overland Monthly, The," 229, 231
Owner of "Lara," The (Webster), 245

PARDONER, The (Chaucer), 25
Pastoral romance, 25
Paul Felton (Dana), 11
Paulding, James K., *Ben Hadar*, 10
Peck, Harry Thurston, 326
" Pencillings by the Way " (Willis), 177
Periodicals (*see* Annuals, Magazines)
Perry, Bliss, 326
Pete Featherton (Hall), 5
Peter Rugg, the Missing Man (Austin), 10, 12, 60–95
Petronius, "Cena Trimalchionis," "Satyricon," 24
Philip of Pokanoket (Irving), 9
Picaresque story, 24
Pike, Albert, 12, 113–127; biographical and critical note, 113; " Prose Sketches and Poems," 12, 115; "Letters from Arkansas," 113; "Hymns to the Gods," 113; *The Inroad of the Nabajo*, 115–127

Plot (*see* Compression, Culmination Novel, Short story, Time-lapse, Unity)
Plots, simple or complex, 12, 13
Poe, Edgar Allan, 3, 4, 9, 12, 15–23, 32, 33, 153–176, 193, 211; genius for form, 9, 16; preoccupation with structure, 16; review of Hawthorne, 14, 22; characters, 16; detective stories, 16, 20; harmonisation, 16, 23; refrain, 16, 17, 21; vocabulary, 16, 17; cadence, 16; suppression of introductions, 18, 19; simplification for directness, 19; setting, 19; habit of monologue, 19; gradation, 20–23; artificiality, 20, 32; grotesque, 22; kinetic narrative, and static, 22; conception of unity, 22, 23; application of Schlegel, 22; review of Mrs. Sigourney, 22; symbolism, 23; and Hawthorne, 18, 20, 23; and Mérimée, 32; and Gautier, 33; and O'Brien, 211; " Literati," 193; *Berenice*, 2, 3, 16, 18, 21, 22, 33; *Metzengerstein*, 16, 18, 22; *Morella*, 16, 17, 18, 21, 22; *Ligeia*, 16, 18; *King Pest*, 18, 22; *The Tell-Tale Heart*, 18; *The Fall of the House of Usher*, 18, 154–176
" Poetics," of Aristotle, 13, 19, 20
" Portfolio, The," 97
Posson Jone (Cable), 34
Poushkin, 34
Premonition, 21, 31
Pride of the Village, The (Irving), 7
Proscrits, Les (Balzac), 32
" Prose Sketches and Poems " (Pike), 12, 114
" Puck," 289

QUATRE talismans, Les (Nodier), 10

REMINISCENCE of Federalism, A (Sedgwick), 11
Richepin, 34
Rip Van Winkle (Irving), 7, 8, 37–58
Roger Malvin's Burial (Hawthorne), 13
Romances, short, 4, 10, 11, 25, 27; American, 4, 11; summary or scen-

ario, 10, 25; pastoral, 25; mediæ-val, 25-28, 29
Romanticism, 4, 7, 8, 11

"SATYRICON" (Petronius), 24
  Scarlet Letter, The (Haw-thorne), 13, 14
Scenario, or summary romance, 10, 13, 24, 26, 27
Schlegel, Poe's application of, 22
Scott, Sir Walter, influence of, 11, 37
Sedgwick, Charlotte M., A Reminis-cence of Federalism, Mary Dyre, The Chivalric Sailor, 11
Sequence of incidents, 7, 8, 9, 10, 16, 20-23 (see Gradation)
Setting, 16 (see Local color)
Seven Vagabonds, The (Hawthorne), 230
"Short Sixes" (Bunner), 291
Short story, in antiquity, 24, 25; in middle age, 25-29; in France, 29-35; in America, 1-23, 34, 35; in Eng-land, 33, 34; in other countries, 34; popularity of, 3, 34; distinct from tale and novel, 2, 6, 7, 8, 11, 12, 13, 21, 23-27, 29-31; unity of, 7, 8, 11-13, 15-23; intensity of, 12, 13, 32 (see Unity)
"Short-Story, The Philosophy of the" (Matthews), 11, 12, 31, 212, 325
Sights from a Steeple (Hawthorne), 14
Simple plots and complex, 13-15, 25, 26
Simplification of narrative mechanism, 7, 8, 11, 12, 13, 17-20, 23 (see Unity)
Singleness, 13, 15, 19, 31 (see Unity)
Situation, a single, in short story, 12, 26, 27, 28, 31
"Sketch Book, The" (Irving), 7, 8, 37
"Sketches of the West" (Hall), 97
Smarra (Nodier), 30
Snow Image, The (Hawthorne), 14
"Southern Literary Messenger, The," 2, 33
"Spectator, The," 6, 7, 9; influence on Irving, 6, 7; on the British

novel, 6; in France; 6, on J. P. Kennedy, 9; in Virginia, 9
Spectre Bridegroom, The (Irving), 7
Static narrative, and kinetic, 22
Sterne, Lawrence, influence on Gautier, 33
Stevenson, Robert Louis, 34
Stockton, Frank R., The Wreck of the Thomas Hyke, 34
Sunday at Home (Hawthorne), 14
Suspense, 10, 16, 20
"Swallow Barn" (Kennedy), 9
Symbolism, 10, 14, 23, 230

TALE, a constant literary form, 25, 26; distinct from short story (which see); anecdote, 10, 24, 26, 29; summary or fragmentary, 13, 15, 23, 24, 27; moral, 4, 9, 10, 14, 30; historical, 4, 5, 9, 10, 11; yarn, 10, 34; oriental, 10, 25
Tales, ancient, 23-25; Milesian, 24; mediæval, 25-29, 31; modern French, 30; American, before 1835, 1-12
"Tales of a Traveller" (Irving), 8, 143
Tamango (Mérimée), 31
Taylor, Bayard, 267-287; biographi-cal and critical note, 267; Who Was She? 269-287
Tell-Tale Heart, The (Poe), 18
Tennessee's Partner (Harte), 230
Theocritus, the fifteenth idyl of, 25
Thoreau, Henry David, 1
Time-lapse, management of, 8, 11, 12, 13, 19-21, 27-29, 31, 32
"Token, The," 2, 5
Tommatoo (O'Brien), 211
Totality of interest, Poe's principle of, 22
Troilus and Criseyde (Chaucer), 25

UNITIES, the classical, 19, 20, 34, 289
Unity, in short story, of purpose, 8, 16-23; of tone, 7, 16-19, 22, 23; of form, 7, 8, 10, 12, 13, 16-19, 22, 23, 25-29, 31-33, 59, 113, 143, 177, 193, 211, 230, 289; of time, 8, 11, 12, 13, 19-21, 27-29, 31, 32; of place,

12, 13, 19, 27, 29, 32; by suppression, 19, 32; and artificiality, 20, 32

VASE étrusque, Le (Mérimée), 31
Vénus d'Ille, La (Mérimée), 31
Verdugo, El (Balzac), 32
Village Uncle, The (Hawthorne), 14
Vision de Charles XI, La (Mérimée), 31
Voltaire, 10

WALLACE, Godfrey, *The Esmeralda*, 11
Webster, Albert Falvey, 245–266; biographical and critical note, 245; *An Operation in Money, The Daphne, A Fool's Moustache, The Owner of Lara*, 245; *Miss Eunice's Glove*, 247–266
"Weekly Californian, The," (Harte), 229
"Western Clearings" (Kirkland), 193; 195
"Western Monthly Magazine, The" (Hall), 97
"Western Monthly Review, The," 5

"Western Souvenir, The " (Hall), 5, 97, 99
What Was It? (O'Brien), 213–228
White Old Maid, The (Hawthorne), 13, 131–142
Whitman, Walt, 3
Who Was She? (Taylor), 269–287
Widow and Her Son, The (Irving), 7
Wife, The (Irving), 7
"Wilderness and the War Path, The" (Hall), 97
Wilkins, Mary E., 11
Willis, Nathaniel Parker, 177–191, 193; biographical and critical note, 177; "Pencillings by the Way," "Dashes at Life with a Free Pencil," 177; *The Inlet of Peach Blossoms*, 179–191
Wives of the Dead, The (Hawthorne), 12, 13
Wondersmith, The (O'Brien), 211
Wreck of the Thomas Hyke, The (Stockton), 34

YARN, 10, 34

Z. MARCAS (Balzac), 32

Fic
BAL

Printed in the United States
139597LV00002B/157/P

9 781409 779292